P9-EKS-211

"Jos[...] he muttered huskily. And was lost.

There was between them a moment like the sudden flash of heat lightning, taut, highly charged, filled with the adrenaline that still surged frenziedly through them at their torturous ride, at their having come so close to death, so narrowly escaped it. They were young and alive; life was sweet, and they clung to it, clung to each other as, without warning, Durango's eyes darkened with passion, and growling low in his throat, he swept Josselyn into his arms, his hands twisting roughly in her unbound hair, his mouth closing, hard and hungry, over hers.

━━━━━━━━━━

"Ms. Brandewyne's sweetest, most loving novel to date. . . . With love and sensitivity, Rebecca Brandewyne pens an emotionally moving tribute to America's *Heartland*, Kansas. A stunning and awesome romance that will be read and reread and belongs on every western romance reader's shelf."

—*Romantic Times* on *Heartland*

*　　*　　*

"The sexual tension is high, the pioneer life in Kansas is lovingly detailed . . . the humor shines through."

—*Rendezvous* on *Heartland*

Also by Rebecca Brandewyne

Across a Starlit Sea
And Gold Was Ours
Desire in Disguise
Forever My Love
Heartland
Love, Cherish Me
No Gentle Love
The Outlaw Hearts
Rose of Rapture
Upon a Moon-Dark Moor

Published by
Warner Books

Rebecca Brandewyne
RAINBOW'S END

WARNER BOOKS

A Time Warner Company

WARNER BOOKS EDITION

Cover illustration by Elaine Duillo
Cover design by Jacki Merri Meyer
Hand lettering by Carl Dellacroce

Warner Books, Inc.
666 Fifth Avenue
New York, N.Y. 10103

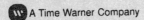 A Time Warner Company

Printed in the United States of America

First Printing: November, 1991

10 9 8 7 6 5 4 3 2 1

For Grandma and Granddaddy,
Who always made me feel so special.
In loving memory.

The Players

Contents

Rainbow's End

It was the South Platte River in Eighteen Fifty-eight
That lured men up the Rocky Mountain road.
"There's gold in them there hills," they cried,
And came afoot, on mules, and by the wagonload.
"Pikes Peak or Bust!" their painted signs did vow,
Though half soon read: "Busted, by God."
Still, there were four bold men who persevered
To stake their claim on the alpine sod.

They were opportunists Houghton and O'Rourke, by name,
And De Navarre, a gambling desperado,
Gresham, a bowler-hatted, silver-tongued dude. . . .
All sought a fortune in the New Eldorado.
Into their midst came first Lady Luck, and then greed,
For gold has a way of turning good men wrong,
And as the years passed, one of the four grew determined
That to him alone all they owned would belong.

An explosion shook the earth, and an angel appeared,
Freed from the realm of her heavenly cage,
Hair aflame as a sunset, eyes green as an aspen,
Her gilded chariot a dusty overland stage.
Of the world, she knew little; of life, even less,
Though she feared not what they held in store.
For justice was her province, vengeance her domain,
And all this, she would have—and more.

For there was something more precious than a mother lode
Beyond the main shaft dug deep into the ground,
In the tunnels that led to the rich veins of ore
With which the Rocky Mountain land did abound.
So it happened that when she had traversed the last winze
And rounded the last turned house's bend,
At the heart of the mine, she struck a prospector's dream
And found the true gold at the Rainbow's End.

PROLOGUE

The Explosion

The Rocky Mountains, Colorado, 1877

It was like the spine of the world, the man thought, awed, as he stared up at the great, daunting mountain range that towered over him and effectively bisected the vast expanse of land that stretched away endlessly on either side from the foothills below. The realization that mere men such as he had not only dared to pit themselves against these perilous crags, but had conquered them never ceased to amaze him. That, tonight, he intended to snap this mammoth backbone in two seemed egotistical in the extreme, the goal of a madman. Yet his mind was sound; his scheme, although many would have labeled it crazy, had been carefully and thoroughly thought through, down to the last detail. Now, all that remained was its enactment.

His eyes narrowing, the man hoisted more securely over his shoulder the burlap bag full of dynamite, blasting caps, and fuses retrieved from where he had hidden it early that morning, amid a cluster of boulders. Then he trudged on furtively up the snowy slope of the mountain where he and his three partners had staked their claim more than a decade ago. When it had been just the four of them working the placer mine, they had been friends, their camaraderie born of mutual eagerness and determination to wrest whatever they could from this wild, magnificent land, and of their heady excitement when—with nothing more than their pans, picks, and shovels, at first, and then with crude "Long Tom" rockers and sluices—they had struck gold. Those had been the easy years, the good years. For gradually, as the initial "blossom rock" had played out and they had started the laborious process of hard-rock mining, things had changed—and not for the better. Greed had reared its ugly head among them, making them mistrustful of one another.

Gold did that to men.

Among them, wordlessly, war had been declared; and tonight, the man hunched against the wind and the flurrying snow was about to deliver a punishing, deliberately crippling blow to the enemy. He had laid his plans well, he reassured himself again. Now, he would carry them out and see what fruit the seeds he planted bore. With the rime and loose stones that covered the ground crunching sharply beneath his sturdy leather boots, he resolutely continued his clandestine trek along the narrow dirt trail up the mountainside to the Rainbow's End, the gold mine that belonged to him and his three partners.

The track was steep and rough in more than a few places, and the going was made even more hazardous than usual by the slick patches of ice that encrusted the rocky earth, the deep snowdrifts that the bitter wind whipping and whining through the mountains had blown across the path. The thin alpine atmosphere combined with the wind and the climb took the man's breath away. He paused for a moment, gasping for air through his frost-coated woolen muffler, his breath forming white clouds of mist in the darkness where only the hazy silver glimmer of the stars illuminated the black night sky. Lowering his heavy sack to the ground, he rubbed his hands—numb despite his thick, fur-lined leather gloves—briskly to restore their circulation, then slapped the sides of his arms vigorously. Then, once more hefting his burden upon his shoulder, he slogged on.

Bundled up against the cold of a Rocky Mountain winter, lumbering up the incline, he might have been mistaken for a bear. But still, the man took care to conceal himself, skulking in the shadows of the sparse trees, boulders, ridges, and outcrops that strewed the acclivity. He was unlikely to be spotted on such an inhospitable night; but a handful of men lived and worked at the gold mine, and he wasn't taking any chances on being observed and identified. Visible now, nestled in a hollow of land, were the silhouettes of the crude, ramshackle wooden buildings that composed the Rainbow's End—the tall shaft house and pump house, the small barn where the two burros were stabled, the toolshed, the modest bunkhouse and cookhouse, and the squalid outhouse. Although all appeared quiet, shut down for the night, there was always the possibility that one of the men inside the bunkhouse might be a restless sleeper or would need to use the privy.

Like all miners, the men who worked the Rainbow's End were a tough, shrewd lot, relying upon their instincts and their wits for survival, for mining was a hard, moiling, dangerous job. One single slip might cost a man his life or bring death to his fellows. Men lacking in gumption and grit didn't last long in the mines; and a man who did possess these necessary attributes, wakened by an alien sound or spying a foreign shape in the darkness, would be more apt than most to investigate and to rouse the rest in the bunkhouse, if necessary.

But this, too, the man lurking in the thin stand of trees just beyond the gold mine had prepared for. He had arranged earlier that afternoon to have a keg of whiskey delivered from the Mother Lode saloon to the Rainbow's End—"to take the edge off the chilly night" was how he had phrased the message that had accompanied the liquor. By now, he hoped, those in the bunkhouse had drunk themselves into an oblivious stupor guaranteed to result in pounding heads and roiling stomachs in the morning. For a brief moment, he grinned at the thought. Then, recalling his mission, he sobered, slipping through the snow and the shadows to where a tunnel for disgorging ore had been blasted out from within the mountainside. This would be his means of entering the gold mine, since he could not, alone, operate the windlass in the shaft house.

The timber-framed entrance to the drift was barred by a stout wooden door that was chained and padlocked, a precaution against thieves and other unauthorized intruders. But undeterred, the man set down his burlap bag and went to work. Using the small hacksaw he had tucked inside his heavy coat, he managed in minutes to cut through one of the chain's thick, icy iron links, stiff and brittle from the cold. With a dull, ringing clatter that was lost amid the keening of the wind, both chain and padlock fell to the ground. Slowly, the man began to swing open the door on its creaking hinges, only to have it caught by the wind and ripped without warning from his half-frozen fingers. The sheer force of the sudden gust howling around the mountainside flung the door open wide, slamming it flat against the timber frame so its far, lower corner gouged into the solid earth of the slope. Stuck fast, the door groaned and trembled in the wind. The man spat a curse, glancing about anxiously, as though expecting to see a horde of miners, all armed with hammers and picks, rushing toward him from the bunkhouse. But except for the shrieking wind and the swirling snow, the night was still. Satisfied that his machinations had gone unheard, that his presence at the Rainbow's End remained as yet undetected, he lugged his sack into the tunnel. Then, with difficulty, he yanked the lodged door free, hauling it shut behind him as he stepped into the gold mine.

Once inside, the man stood stock still for an instant, accustoming his eyes to the absolute blackness within. His head cocked, he listened intently for any unusual sound that would warn him that he was not alone; for there had been murder done here, he thought—though he had as yet no proof of the deed—and he was not about to become the next victim. But to his grim satisfaction, he heard only the muted soughing of the wind through the secondary shafts, the drifts, crosscuts, and turned houses, and the raises, winzes, and stopes; the moaning and straining of the massive post-and-cap timbers that shored up the tunnels; the faint clank of the windlass cable and its primitive ore bucket in the main shaft, and the hollow echo of the steadily dripping water that was ever present in the gold mine. Certain, then, that all was as it should be, he bent, fumbling in the darkness for the Davy lamp he had prudently left here upon the floor earlier in the day. His hands had warmed a little now that he was no longer subject to the full fury of the wintry elements outside, and when he found the lantern, he was able, after only a few tries, to strike a match and light the wick.

The tunnel that stretched before him sprang into shadowy relief. Retrieving his burlap bag, he lifted the lamp and held it high to illuminate his path, then started down the serpentine passage, following the railed track upon which the ore cars, the "giraffes"—the incline cars—and the timber trucks ran. He knew every inch of the Rainbow's End and had no problem making his way to the sites he had chosen after much deliberation. At each of these locations, he meticulously placed sticks of dynamite in select niches in the rock walls, leaving the charges' long fuses, called rattails, dangling. Despite the dangers involved in handling the dynamite, his hands were steady and sure as he worked, for he was no novice at blasting. Of all the men at the gold mine, only two of his partners could have done the job as well—a fact that the man was counting on to ensure the success of his scheme.

At last, when the charges were carefully positioned, he cut with his knife a shorter fuse, a "spitter," and lighted it with a match. Then, beginning at the point farthest from the tunnel through which he had gained access to the gold mine and through which he would also exit it, the man broke into a run, using the spitter to ignite the rattails as he went. With split-second timing born of long experience, he set the final rattail afire just as the sparking spitter grew short enough to singe his gloved fingers. Dropping the sputtering fuse, he raced on, his breath coming in hard rasps, his heart pounding, the lantern he held before him swinging crazily.

He was halfway through the passage when the first of the dynamite blew, shattering the hush of the wintry night—and the Rainbow's End. Prepared for the explosion, the man, though rocked on his feet, was quickly able to recover. Despite his labored breathing and the shock of the vibrations to his body, he rushed on, knowing how swiftly and fatally shafts and tunnels alike would collapse behind him, effectively sealing off—but not destroying—the gold mine. He was headed down the mountainside, a dark silhouette melting into the even darker shadows of the few trees, when the sleeping miners, jarred awake abruptly by the resounding blasts and the violent quaking of the earth, rushed from the bunkhouse to see what was amiss. Spying the smoke and debris belching from the shaft house and the main tunnel, the men began shouting and swearing. Half of them were still tugging their breeches and boots up over their long flannel underwear and heavy woolen socks. One of the miners lost his balance and staggered about comically for a moment before toppling off the wooden porch of the bunkhouse into a snowdrift.

Watching from the trees, the dynamiter recognized that it

was Old Sourdough thrashing about in the snow, trying to regain his footing. The saboteur grinned; then, turning, he hurried on down the acclivity, his grin twisting into a wolfish smile as he thought of his three partners' reactions when they learned of this latest disaster.

Book One

A Dusty Overland Stage

Chapter One

Boston, Massachusetts, 1877

The city of Boston was ringed by hills, from mere mounds
on the north to the larger Blue Hills on the south, though of
the Trimountain that had used to rise from the Common, only
Beacon Hill, now greatly diminished, remained. Much of it
and all of its two sister peaks had been carted away during
the current century to fill in coves, mud flats, and salt marshes.
Now, the Shawmut Peninsula, upon which Boston had been
founded and which had once been almost completely encircled by water, was scarcely discernible from the mainland.

Like the peninsula upon which it stood, the small, poor
Ursuline convent, ringed not by hills, but by high red brick
walls modestly veiled by tall, ancient elms, seemed to blend

into its surroundings. Nestled amid a close crowd of buildings, it rose at the fringe of the city's North End, an area whose inhabitants at the middle of the century had been almost exclusively Irish, but who, in recent years, had moved away as Jewish immigrants moved in. Too poor to follow the Irish emigration, the convent remained, quiet and unobtrusive, its devout Sisters rarely venturing beyond its walls, diligently applying themselves now to the upbringing and education of the girls entrusted to their care.

Most of these came from good Irish Catholic families of modest means, though some were orphans, or practically so. It was into this last category that the young woman kneeling in the convent's chapel fell. She had come to the Sisters when she was seven years old, her mother having recently died of some lingering illness, and her father unable to work and look after her at the same time. So, though parting from his only child had nearly broken his heart, he had left her with the Sisters and set off to make his way in the world. His daughter had been with them now for the past twelve years.

More than a decade of instruction at the Ursuline convent would have been enough to turn most girls into proper ladies of virtue and gentility; and as she gazed down the aisle of the chapel to where the slender, veiled figure knelt in the foremost pew, head bowed, hands folded just so, fingers wrapped about a plain rosary, the Reverend Mother Maire knew she could not have asked for an outwardly more decorous, more dedicated disciple than Josselyn O'Rourke. From the unkempt, scared, mutinous ugly duckling she had been when she had arrived at the convent, Josselyn had matured into a swan of beauty, of courage, and of grace. But still, as she studied the young woman kneeling in apparently devout prayer, the Reverend Mother was neither gratified nor deceived by the pious picture Josselyn presented. The young woman's saintly appearance was, the abbess knew only too well, a carefully cultivated pose that all too often succeeded in fooling eyes less discerning than her own. The Sisters thought Josselyn an angel. The Reverend Mother Maire frequently thought otherwise. Indeed, after more than a decade, she had come to believe that as He had for the soul of Job, God had wagered with the devil for possession of her own soul and to test her faith to its utmost had sent her Josselyn O'Rourke.

Twelve highly structured years at the convent and all the Reverend Mother's admonitions had bridled but failed to tame the young woman's wild spirit. The inner strength that kept her upright on the kneeling board, her back straight as a ramrod, her shoulders squared, stemmed not from her deep, abiding faith and convictions, but from her stubborn, willful nature. Like as not, she was reciting limericks rather than prayers as she counted off the decades of her rosary, the abbess conjectured ruefully. But when she thought of the recent, horrifying scandal at the convent, in which Josselyn had played such a sad part, the Reverend Mother Maire knew she was being too hard on the young woman. After all, Josselyn had been unnaturally—and therefore unhealthily, in the Reverend Mother's opinion—subdued ever since the terrible affair. She had actually insisted that she would never leave the convent, that she wished to take her final vows and become a nun. Though the abbess, aware the decision had been made under extreme emotional duress, had tried to discourage Josselyn from her sudden, rash resolve, the young woman had stood firm, quietly, fiercely, frighteningly defiant in the face of all opposition; and at last, reluctantly, the Reverend Mother Maire had given her permission for Josselyn to enter the convent permanently.

Despite her doubts about the depth of Josselyn's vocation, the Reverend Mother was disturbed by the thought of the young woman's being so cruelly and abruptly dragged forth into the world—as she surely would be by the tragic news that had reached the convent not an hour ago. Dear, merciful God, why this now, coming so hard on the heels of the other? the abbess had questioned silently as she had read the letter addressed to her.

For so long, Josselyn had been cocooned within the convent. Like a caterpillar, she had been nurtured and had grown, aware but largely ignorant of the life that teemed outside— until so very recently, when she had been deeply hurt by its harsh realities. Now, despite her present longing to hide from the world, the time had come when she must emerge from her secure, sheltered environment. The Reverend Mother Maire was worried about her charge, for she knew that although, with all her heart, Josselyn had lately, earnestly, tried to act the moth, she was, in truth, a butterfly.

In Josselyn O'Rourke burned a sensuality of which she herself must now be painfully cognizant. Through the years, despite the Reverend Mother's strictures, this earthiness had always been there—in the eager light of the young woman's sloe green eyes when, thinking herself alone, unobserved, she stood staring longingly through the wrought-iron gates of the convent at the city of Boston that lay beyond; in the unhesitant plunging of her bare hands into the loam of the convent's garden, where she tended the flowers and herbs, the fruits and vegetables that were the mainstay of the convent's infirmary and kitchen; in the joyous uplifting of her piquant face to the warm summer sun streaming through the branches of the fruit trees that dotted the convent's small orchard; and in the graceful sway of her lissome body beneath the layers of her novice's habit. Josselyn's passions ran deep; the recent scandal was proof enough of that. Although the affair had not resulted in the explosion the Reverend Mother Maire had long feared, Josselyn's determination to clamp the lid down on her emotions instead was not a good thing.

Neither the scandal nor its aftermath boded well for the young woman's future as a nun. A novice about to take her final vows should know her own mind thoroughly and be at peace with it, wholeheartedly certain of her calling, of her vocation. This, the abbess thought with despair, could certainly not be said of Josselyn. Though her faith was not in question, that God intended her to serve Him as a bride of Christ was.

Glancing down again at the two letters she held in her hand, one envelope as yet unopened, the Reverend Mother Maire sighed deeply. The heartrending news she must impart was bound to shake Josselyn ruthlessly from her restrained state and to uproot her from the convent in which she now so doggedly sought a solace she would not find here. The Reverend Mother thought regretfully that Josselyn needed more comfort than her faith alone gave her. How strange it was that a few heavily crossed pages should have the power to accomplish what she herself had not been able to, the abbess reflected, seeing the irony in that. But then, God, all-seeing, all knowing, had always worked in mysterious ways; surely, this, then, was a sign from Him, however afflictive, that Josselyn was not meant to serve Him as a nun, that He needed her elsewhere. Ardently, the Reverend Mother Maire hoped that it was so. She did not want, because of her own inner fears and conflicts, to counsel the young woman wrongly. Although Josselyn had often proved a severe trial to her, the Reverend Mother had always had a secret fondness for her and now deeply pitied her, too.

At last, praying silently for guidance as to how best to handle her distressing task, the abbess started slowly down the aisle of the chapel to where Josselyn knelt in the foremost pew, unaware of how her own passionate prayers were about to be answered.

Josselyn had been in the chapel for well over an hour, contemplating her future and earnestly beseeching God for some sign that would indicate the path in life she should take. If she were honest with herself, she must admit that God had not "called" her to do His work. In fact, He had been very silent on the subject, leading her to believe that He disapproved of her decision to take her final vows. She had fallen so short of the goodness to which a nun aspired and, indeed, would have fallen from grace entirely if not for Rosie Maguire. Just the thought of what had happened to Rosie—and had nearly happened to her own self—was enough to make Josselyn shudder violently and thank God that she, at least, had been spared.

It had all begun so innocently, a simple meeting with a stranger at the gates of the convent, lost and asking his way. Josselyn had been attracted to him right from the start. Men were such a rarity in her life, and Antoine Fouché was so young, handsome, and appealing, standing there so forlornly, unsure of where he was or how far he was from his destination. Quite naturally, after she had given him directions, they had fallen into conversation, during which time she had learned he was an immigrant from France and had only recently arrived in Boston. Having no other family, he was to have joined his uncle in the city. But after Antoine had set sail from France to America, his uncle had been killed in a tragic carriage accident. Antoine had docked in Boston's harbor, only to find his uncle dead and he himself practically penniless. Knowing no one else in the city and lacking the money to return to France, he had set about immediately in search of work, but so far, he had been unsuccessful in finding employment. En route to apply for a job when he had lost his way, he had feared that the position would be gone by the time he finally got there.

Deeply touched by his tragic story and captivated by his tousled black hair and soulful black eyes that had contrasted so poetically with his pale skin and sensual mouth—Josselyn had pressed on him a handful of coins. She knew where the keys to the convent's alms chest were kept, and although she had felt guilty about doing so without permission, she had taken the money to lend to him. Her faith in him was affirmed when a few days later Antoine had reappeared at the convent's gates to repay her. He had got the job after all. Thanking her profusely, he had taken her hand, and that touch had been the beginning of their clandestine romance. Josselyn had recklessly slipped away time and again from the convent to meet him secretly, so the Sisters would not see them together and prevent her from meeting him again. What would have been the end of the affair, if not for Rosie, Josselyn now shivered to think.

After some weeks of stolen long walks and even longer kisses and caresses, Antoine had at last persuaded her to run away with him. He could not live without her; they must be married at once, he had declared fervently. Josselyn, young and in love for the first time in her life, had not thought to ask either Antoine or herself why he did not simply propose that they inform the Reverend Mother Maire of their intent to wed and appeal to her not only for her understanding and forgiveness of their improper conduct, but for her blessing. Now, of course, Josselyn knew to her horror that it was because Antoine had been the basest of liars, that he had never meant to marry her, only cold-bloodedly to seduce her and then sell her to a brothel. His true work had been as a procurer of nubile flesh; and this particular whorehouse had, some months before, acquired a high-paying customer with a depraved fetish for chaste convent girls and who was kept blithely ignorant of the fact that it was Antoine who first divested them of their virtue. Had not poor Rosie Maguire, herself a victim of Antoine's rape and treachery, managed somehow to escape from the bordello and return to the convent to pour out the entire grisly tale to the Reverend Mother Maire, Josselyn would have become his next victim. The very day she was to elope with him, he had been arrested for his heinous crimes. That night, Josselyn, unaware of Antoine's real self and fate, had been discovered sneaking out of her room, baggage in hand, a note propped up on her chest of drawers, explaining that she had run away to wed her lover.

The truth about Antoine Fouché had destroyed Josselyn's faith in her own goodness. Now, whenever she remembered how she had kissed him so feverishly and—in her newly wakened passion, her newfound love—permitted him to take other liberties with her, she felt sick inside—not just because she had let him touch her, but because she had actually enjoyed it. Even now, sometimes late at night, under the covers of her bed, she would brush her hands across her breasts, as Antoine had done, and the wonderful feelings he had stirred in her would once more leap excitingly to life. Oh, she was wanton and wicked! she thought—unlike poor Rosie, who, never wanting to be touched by any man again, had, upon her lucky getaway to the convent, set about at once to take her final vows. Rosie had been shy and sweet, dreaming of rose-shaded romance; the physical reality of a man's forcing himself on her had damaged her irreparably. Though Josselyn was naturally glad to have escaped a like fate, sometimes even now she could not seem to help wondering what she had missed—not that she wanted to be raped, of course, which, observing what it had done to Rosie, she thought must be an absolutely hideous experience. But, oh, yes! However sinful it was, she *did* wish she had discovered where all those delicious kisses and caresses of Antoine's would eventually have led had he truly loved her!

Made dreadfully ashamed, however—beneath the Reverend Mother's severe, disapproving gaze—of her wayward behavior, deeply mortified by what a gullible fool she had proved herself to be, Josselyn had presently announced her own intention to become a nun. Determinedly quelling her memories of those exquisite sensations Antoine had evoked in her, she persevered at her studies and hid her inner uncertainties about entering the convent permanently. She knew, even so, that the abbess suspected her of harboring them. The Reverend Mother Maire's insight was uncanny; there was little that evaded her notice.

Yet if she did not take her final vows, Josselyn did not now know what would become of her. Unlike most of the other young women at the convent, she had no family to return to, no young man—now—waiting in the wings. Her mother was dead, and she had not seen her father in several long years, ever since he had left Boston for Colorado more than a decade ago, a sign that had read "Pikes Peak or Bust" bravely tacked to the side of the battered old trunk that had contained all he had owned in the world.

Da had finally settled in Mountain City, which had eventually been engulfed by Central City, so-called because it sat at the heart of the mining district, Gregory Gulch, between the towns of Black Hawk and Nevadaville. At first, Central City had been little more than a rough mining camp, a collection of tents, lean-tos, and other crude shelters hastily erected all along the famous gulch, where John Gregory had, in 1859, discovered the gold that had brought the initial influx of would-be prospectors to the territory—a drove of more than a thousand men in just the first two weeks alone following his strike. It had hardly been a fit place then in which to rear a young girl; and so Josselyn had remained at the convent. But in later years, despite his having staked a claim to a gold mine in the Rocky Mountains, where Central City lay, it seemed somehow that Da was always short of cash, with never enough money to send for her.

Her father wrote that he was sure the Rainbow's End, as he had christened the gold mine, possessed several rich veins of ore and possibly even a mother lode, all as yet untapped, which would eventually yield a fortune. But the difficulties involved in hard-rock mining—the extraction of the unprocessed ore from deep beneath the earth's surface—were numerous, Josselyn had gathered from his letters; and so, even now, he had little to show for all his years of effort. Most of the "blossom rock" yield resulting from the early placer mining had been spent on her upkeep at the convent, she knew. Da was not one to accept charity for himself or his daughter so long as he had a strong, broad back and two good hands.

This past year, too, there had been trouble at the gold mine, he had reported, "accidents" that he suspected were, in reality, acts of sabotage by one of his three partners. One of these men, Da felt, had grown greedy over the years, no longer content with just a quarter of the moderate profits from the Rainbow's End and intent on causing so much costly damage to the gold mine and so many delays in the actual mining process that the rest of the partners would be only too happy to sell him their shares. Then, a few months ago, one partner, Forbes Houghton, had been killed in one of the so-called accidents at the Rainbow's End. Though he lacked proof, her father believed that Forbes had really been murdered. Da suspected that one of his other two partners— Durango de Navarre or Wylie Gresham—might be the saboteur and the killer; and the matter had been further complicated by the fact that Forbes had left a will, bequeathing his shares in the gold mine to his wife, Victoria, possibly giving her a motive for wishing him dead, as well. This was why, Da had explained, he continued to delay Josselyn's joining him in Central City. He hoped to work things out before her arrival so he could devote himself to getting to know his daughter, to making up for all the lost time between them. She, however, had sensed there was more to it than that.

Reading between the lines of his letters, she had, sadly, come to believe that her father did not truly want her to leave the convent, that he had, in fact, grown accustomed to life without her, and that an adult daughter would prove a complication he did not want or need, however much he loved her. He had, once or twice, mentioned squiring a woman friend to this affair or that; and Josselyn, feeling a sharp twinge of jealousy, had thought that the woman, Nell Tierney, appeared to be looking after Da quite well. Upon learning that Mrs. Tierney was an actress, Josselyn had hotly decided that the woman was a designing hussy who had got her clutches into Da and would not welcome his daughter, in fact, might actively resent her presence in Central City. She might even be working at turning Da against her! Hurt by the supposition that Da might prefer Mrs. Tierney over her, Josselyn had secretly begun to wonder what she would do in the future, how she would support herself, if she did not join her father in Colorado.

Her father had several times called Central City a rough,

hard place and had hinted strongly that she, gently reared and educated, might find her hopes and expectations of life doomed to disappointment there. But still, before Antoine had come into them, there had been many times when Josselyn had found her ordered days at the convent far too tame for her liking, when she had yearned for excitement and challenge, anything to break the routine of her peaceful but unexceptional existence. She had often gazed through the wrought-iron gates of the convent at the city of Boston beyond, avidly drinking in the sights that had met her eyes— the street vendors hawking their wares, the passing horses and carriages, the endless variety of townspeople—and fervidly wished herself among them, amid the hustle and bustle that was life; and she had thought that if Boston appealed, how much more would Central City, not so old and established, but young and brash, still finding its way—as she had been, and still was.

In the past, Josselyn had always felt as though she were only marking time at the convent until the day when Da would send for her. But as his letters had made this appear more and more unlikely, she had finally miserably but resolutely compelled herself to tuck away her dreams of being reunited with him, feeling somehow as though he were gone, as Mam was gone. Josselyn felt alone in the world, her parents' love for her only a distant memory, and that of the Sisters what they bestowed upon every girl at the convent—kind but, in the end, detached. Empty years of being a governess or a companion, for in truth, she was suited to little else, stretched before her, long and lonely; but what other viable avenue of escape from the convent had she? There was none; she must resign herself simply to existing. Thus, when Antoine had walked into her world, she had been only too willing to elope with him, thinking only, eagerly, that she was not to be cheated of a special love, of a real *life* of her own, after all.

Now, Josselyn shrank from leaving the convent, apprehensive that only a nun's habit would keep her safe—not only from the predatory males who stalked the hard roads of life, but from the sinful wantonness within her own self. Still, perversely, the moment she had informed the abbess that she wanted to take her final vows, Josselyn had for some inexplicable reason wished the words unspoken; but her pride, her stubbornness, and, most of all, her fear had prevented her from saying so. Now, she had remained silent for so long and had taken up so many hours of the Sisters' time with her training that despite the Reverend Mother Maire's persistent probing, she felt she must honor her decision. She had written to Da to tell him of her intention to remain at the convent permanently, although she had not told him her reasons. So far, she had received no reply to her letter. Her father's lack of response had been yet another disappointment; Josselyn had secretly hoped he would write back at once, insisting she travel to Central City posthaste to join him. But he had not.

Da's silence seemed proof that he approved of her plan to become a nun and was pleased by it—and she wanted more than anything in the world to make her father happy and proud of her. It was the Reverend Mother, with her benign but penetrating eyes, who had, in the end, quietly but stoutly declared that Josselyn must examine her mind and her heart more deeply before irrevocably committing herself to taking such a monumental step in her life. This was why she had come to the chapel today, to search her soul and to ask God to show her the way.

Now, as she heard behind her the measured footsteps and the whisper of voluminous robes that could only belong to the abbess, Josselyn hastily finished her prayers and, after crossing herself, rose from the kneeling board of the pew, her hands tightening involuntarily upon her rosary as she caught sight of the Reverend Mother Maire's grave, pitying face.

Something has happened, Josselyn thought, an icy foreboding suddenly trickling down her spine. The matter must be serious, else the Reverend Mother Maire would never have disturbed her at prayer. As she spied the letters in the Reverend Mother's hand, Josselyn's slanted green eyes widened with apprehension. Her face whitened, and one hand fluttered involuntarily to her throat. She gripped the beads of her rosary so hard that they dug into her perspiring palms, but she did not feel the pain, only the pangs of anxiety. *Something terrible has happened.*

"Reverend Mother?" she asked, afraid, as all her father's suspicions about his partners and the sabotage and murder at the gold mine rose abruptly to mind. "What's wrong? It's Da, isn't it? *Isn't it?* Something's happened to Da, an accident—"

"Sit down, child!" the abbess instructed quietly but sharply to quell Josselyn's rising hysteria. "Sit down and listen to me. Yes, there's been an accident . . . at the Rainbow's End, a horrible explosion. I had hoped to break this tragic news to you more gently, but— Josselyn, I'm sorry, so very sorry, but I'm afraid your father was . . . killed—"

"No! No! It can't be true! It just *can't* be! There must be some mistake—" Josselyn cried as her knees slowly buckled beneath her and she sank down upon the pew.

"You don't know how much I heartily wish there were, child," the Reverend Mother Maire said, "for your sake. But sadly, these letters"—she lifted the hand that held them—"make it clear there can be little doubt that your father is dead."

For a moment, Josselyn felt numb, as though she had been struck a violent, physical blow. Then, gradually, the reality of what she had been told gripped her, and she began softly to weep. Despite all her recent plans to stay at the convent permanently, she had still hoped that her father would send for her. Now, that would never be possible. Da was dead, and she would never see him again.

"How—how did it happen, Reverend Mother?"

"Josselyn, I know how very difficult this must be for you. Are you sure you want to hear all this right now? Wouldn't you rather go to your room and lie down, to be alone for a while with your sorrow? I can ask Sister Ailis to bring you some hot tea if you like. The details of your father's death can wait—''

"No." Josselyn shook her head vehemently as she groped in the pocket of her habit for a handkerchief. "No. I want to know . . . I *need* to know what happened. . . .''

"Very well, then.'' The Reverend Mother sighed heavily as she slowly removed one of the letters from its open envelope, unfolded it, and put on her wire-rimmed spectacles. "According to Mr. Killian, your father's attorney"—and here, she began to read—'' 'a person or persons unknown entered the Rainbow's End sometime after its closing for the evening and, at approximately midnight, set off several charges of dynamite whose blasts resulted in the collapse of various strategic drifts and winzes in the gold mine, sealing all stopes currently undergoing quarrying. Unfortunately, for reasons that can only be guessed at, Mr. O'Rourke was apparently inside the Rainbow's End at the time. It is possible his presence was unknown to the intruder. However, given that sabotage was clearly at work, it is perhaps more than likely that he stumbled on the perpetrator in the act of the crime and that there was a struggle, which ended in Mr. O'Rourke's being badly injured or even killed. In any event, Mr. O'Rourke has not been seen since the explosion, and since his hat was discovered amid the debris in the gold mine, I regret to inform you that he must be presumed dead and buried beneath the rubble, although his body has yet to be recovered. It is, however, expected to be located as excavation and reconstruction of the Rainbow's End progress. . . .' '' Here, the abbess ceased to read. Removing her glasses, she handed the letter to Josselyn, along with the second, unopened envelope, which bore Josselyn's name across the front. "It was Mr. Killian's wish that I, rather than he, break this news to you, child," the Reverend Mother Maire explained. "He felt that it would be kinder coming from me than your learning of it from a total stranger.''

Her head bowed, Josselyn blinked back her tears and dabbed with her plain white cotton handkerchief at the corners of her eyes as Mr. Killian's unfamiliar handwriting wavered before her blurred vision. There was little more in his letter to the Reverend Mother, other than his apology for laying upon her the difficult task of being the bearer of such bad tidings, and his condolences. Now, her hands trembling, Josselyn slowly opened the second envelope and began to read Mr. Killian's letter to her. She learned that her father had left a will, naming her as his heiress.

"It seems," Josselyn told the abbess, "that Da has bequeathed me his shares in the—in the Rainbow's End." She sniffled as she continued to read aloud bits and pieces from the letter. "Mr. Killian wants me to—to come to Central City to—to settle the estate, as there are apparently some—some conditions, which he does not explain, that must be satisfied before the shares can be transferred to me. The enclosed funds are for my—for my traveling expenses. I'm to wire my reply— Oh, Reverend Mother"—she glanced up, her tearful countenance pale and puzzled—"I—I don't understand what he means. To what 'conditions' could he be referring that would necessitate my journeying to Central City? And—and how can I possibly leave the convent now, when I am shortly to become a nun?"

"That must be the least of your worries right now, child," the Reverend Mother Maire asserted firmly. "I know what a blow your father's death is to you, and I believe that under the circumstances, it will be best if you postpone the taking of your final vows for the time being. As to the other, I suspect that Mr. Killian is referring to various legal formalities, for which your presence must be necessary. I very much doubt that he would have insisted on your making such a long trip otherwise; and that being the case, I think you must indeed go to Central City, Josselyn."

"Oh, Reverend Mother, I feel so torn! I *do* want to go, if only to discover who is responsible for—for Da's . . . death.

But I want to stay here, too, for somehow, I feel that if I leave the convent, I shall never return to it, that my life will be irrevocably changed."

The Reverend Mother smiled gently.

"Perhaps it will be, child. But you must not fear that; you must not fear *life*. It is for living, and God calls us each as He wills. There are many ways of serving Him, Josselyn. Becoming a nun is not the only one, nor is it necessarily the right one for you. I believe that if you are honest with yourself, you will admit that you have many times doubted your decision, perhaps even rebelled against it inwardly—though I think that because you are a woman of principle, you have striven to honor your commitment and have not spoken of the conflict that is in your heart. Is that not so?"

"Y-yes, Reverend Mother," Josselyn confessed, both reluctant and relieved to have the truth out at last, "it is so. I don't want to disappoint you and the Sisters; really, I don't! It's just that since Antoi—well . . . lately, I've—I've felt so mixed up inside—and now this horrible accident at the gold mine . . . Da dead. I still can't believe it—"

"You need time, child . . . time to mourn, time to heal, time to know yourself, the world, and life better," the abbess declared. "God works in mysterious ways, both giving and taking away; and while His reasons for this are not always clear to us, we can find comfort in the fact that they are known to Him and that He never gives us a burden too heavy to bear. Perhaps this dreadful day and this unexpected journey are His way of answering your prayers for guidance about your future. It may be that you will never come back to the convent, Josselyn. But know that wherever you may go, whatever you may decide, you have our blessing and that our door will always be open to you."

"Thank you, Reverend Mother." Josselyn's voice was tremulous as tears once more welled in her eyes. "Thank you for being so very wise and kind."

Chapter Two

Central City, Colorado, 1877

The trip had been long and tiring to one unaccustomed to travel. Yet perversely, Josselyn was as on edge as a tightrope walker, sick with grief, fear, and yet excitement, as well, unable to rest. She had come halfway across the country, and now, her destination was close, nestled in the heart of the Rocky Mountains that just moments ago had risen up suddenly, cutting a startling oblique into the sky. Reflecting the brilliant rays of the spring sun, sparkling like diamonds and amethysts, sapphires and emeralds, the towering peaks swelled above the rich, sprawling land, like a woman's bejeweled bosom above a gold-lace bodice—majestic, breathtaking, a challenge few men could resist. By the thousands, they had come to plunder this pristine paradise that was as near to heaven as some of them could ever expect to get. How many of them had died along the way, she wondered. Too many, she thought, judging from the discarded mining tools and the tombstones she had spied alongside the railroad tracks during her journey—although some of the wooden grave markers had obviously been falsely erected, inscribed, as they had been, by the words "Here lies the body of D. C. Oakes, killed for aiding the Pikes Peak hoax." But Da's death was real; he had been killed—not for aiding a hoax, but because he had stood between a grasping partner and the Rainbow's End. Da was dead. The thought struck at her heart; resolutely, she forced it away, not wanting, even now, to face the truth. Somehow, deep down inside, she knew she would not really believe that her father was gone until she saw his grave. Until then, against all odds, she would cling to her stubborn hope that Mr. Killian had made some ghastly mistake and that Da was still alive.

The Colorado Central Railroad train, which Josselyn had boarded in Golden, bore steadily westward and upward toward James Peak in the distance, clattering roughly but rhythmically over the narrow-gauge tracks that wound through the steep Clear Creek Canyon, its once-clear, flowing stream now turned a dull greenish grey from "tailings," the sandy waste generated by the concentration mills that were an integral part of the hard-rock mining process. Eventually, huffing and puffing from its long, hard climb, the train chugged its way into the small Black Hawk depot that was the end of the line.

As the train slowed to a screeching halt, Josselyn leaned forward to press her face against one window of the passenger car, against all logic, searching the platform outside for a red-haired, red-bearded giant of a man, which, in the perspective of her childhood, was how she remembered her father. Breathing was difficult for her in the high altitude and grew even harder as a painful lump rose in her throat. Da was nowhere in sight—as, surely, he would have been if he were still alive. Desperately, she kept on looking for a long minute, just to make sure. But all she could see through the blur of her sudden tears were the close-set brick buildings of the town, streaked with coal dust from the stamp and concentration mills, the smelters, and the refineries for which Black Hawk, known as the mill city of the Rockies, was famous.

Half the ore mined in Gilpin County was treated here, Josselyn recollected from Da's many letters over the years. Hearing the loud, incessant clanging and crashing of powerful machinery and of the crushing stamps, she could well believe it. The noise was excruciating. Wincing and blinking back her tears, she turned away from the window and began to gather her belongings. Then, after a last glance about to make certain she was not leaving anything behind, she exited the train, still hoping that somehow, Da would miraculously appear.

She hoped in vain. No one was there to meet her. Only a grizzled old bum sitting with his back against one wall of the depot, half asleep or drunk, paid her any heed. From beneath the brim of his battered felt hat, he peered at her; and after a moment, Josselyn turned her back to him, made slightly uneasy by his close scrutiny. She had not forgotten what had happened to Rosie, what had so nearly happened to her own self; and so, although it was broad daylight and the town teemed with both people and activity, she remained wary of being accosted. As a precaution against this, she edged nearer to the conductor to wait while her leather-bound trunk was unloaded from the train, reasoning that the Colorado Central Railroad had a responsibility to protect its passengers. Nervously, she gripped both her reticule and the large, plain wooden cross that hung from a simple thong about her neck, glad of the novice's habit she continued to wear, as though it were a suit of armor to shield her from the dangers of the world.

Now that Josselyn had disembarked from the train, the cacophony of Black Hawk was even more deafening, and the noxious smell made her reach into her bag for a handkerchief and press it to her nostrils in an attempt to filter out the worst of the polluted air. Everywhere she looked, spirelike smoke-stacks belched soot and smoke skyward, so it seemed that endless black clouds drifted over the town, raining cinders. She would be glad to arrive at Mrs. Harrietta Munroe's boarding-house on Roworth Street, where Mr. Killian had arranged a room for her, and to wash away the grime that must be covering her.

When her trunk had been heaved down beside her on the platform, she hired an innocuous-looking young man standing out front of the Gilpin Hotel across the street from the Central Colorado Railroad depot to carry her luggage over to the Wells Fargo Express station, whence she would travel by Studebaker coach the mile-long road through Gregory Gulch up to Central City. She purchased her ticket, and presently, the stage, caked and dusty with dried mud from the spring rains, was loaded and under way.

As the driver whipped forward the team of six bay horses, Josselyn could not repress the tiny thrill that shot through her when she gazed out the window of the jouncing coach at her surroundings. Never had she seen such a hodgepodge of buildings and bustle. The towns of Gold Dust Village—nicknamed "Little Chinatown" because of the Chinese immigrants who worked the placer mines there—Black Hawk, Mountain City, Central City, Dogtown, and Nevadaville were as tightly woven together as the scraps of fabric in a crazy quilt, a haphazard pattern of edifices stacked one on top of another in the confined gulches that riddled the "richest square mile on earth," as the mineral-abundant area had come to be known. All the hillsides had been stripped bare of trees, and a maze of mines, mills, smelters, stables, saloons, shops, hotels, and houses had sprung up wherever there was space. The narrow, winding side streets had no semblance of order, and the structures, some of them on stilts, perched at peculiar angles, as though, at any moment, they might actually come tumbling down the slopes. The front porches of the houses crammed together on the hillsides appeared to sit upon the roofs of their neighbors below—a circumstance, Josselyn would soon learn, that frequently caused many a tobacco-chewing citizen to complain that he dared not open his front door to spit, for fear of hitting another man's chimney and dousing the fire inside. Some of the buildings were hideous; others, like the so-called Lace House, which she noticed as the stage struggled up the steep road to Central City, were beautiful. Here and there were touches of Gothic revival in the Victorian architecture, particularly in the finer residences that dotted the inclines, especially the houses along the avenue known as The Casey. This was a road built in 1863, for a cost of $2,000, by an illiterate Irishman, Pat Casey, who had struck it rich in the early years and who had needed a shortcut from his mine in Nevadaville to his mill in Chase Gulch—just one example of the extravagances that the discovery of gold in Gregory Gulch had made possible.

The heart of the business district was at the junction of Lawrence, Eureka, and Main Streets. The three formed an odd, sharp angle because Main Street came uphill at a queer slant from where Nevada and Spring Gulches met below. At this bizarre intersection stood Elias Goldman's Dry Goods Store and Saloon—commonly referred to as "Goldman's Corner." It was shaped like a wedge, while across from it, the First National Bank sat on a corner that was much wider than a right angle. Packed together like sardines in a tin can, some with costly cast-iron storefronts, were bank and newspaper office, soda fountain and pharmacy, mercantile and grocery, clothier and barbershop.

Almost all of the businesses were solidly constructed of brick and stone. This was because the original wooden edifices, with their false, two-story fronts, had burned down in two disastrous fires in 1873 and 1874. During the first blaze, Da had written, J. O. Raynolds's Hazard Powder Co. had narrowly escaped exploding only because Mrs. Raynolds, despite the flames singeing her skirts, had torn up all her sheets, soaked them in buckets of water, and then used them to keep all the building's wooden doors and window frames wet. The second blaze had started in Dostal Alley, when the paper decorations of the Chinese immigrants who inhabited the poor "Chinatown" had caught flame from joss sticks and incense during a celebration. Those responsible for the tragic accident, Da had reported, had nearly been lynched by a righteously angry mob of townspeople. But luckily, the Chinese held accountable had been smuggled out of Central City in time to avoid being hanged.

Now that she was actually seeing for the first time many of the things her father had described to her in his letters, Josselyn felt his absence even more keenly. As the stage, reaching its destination in Central City, lumbered to a halt before the Wells Fargo Express station, she could not help searching for him again. With a small sigh of disappointment, she slowly stepped down from the coach.

"Miss O'Rourke?" A dapper, grey-haired gentleman spoke, approaching her.

"Yes . . . ?" Josselyn's tone was cautious, faintly inquiring.

"I'm Patrick Killian, your father's lawyer," the man announced, his speech tinged with a brogue. Respectfully, he swept off his hat, executing a slight bow. " 'Tis a pleasure to meet you, ma'am, though I deeply regret that it must be under such sad circumstances. Please allow me to offer my condolences on your father's untimely death. Red O'Rourke was a fine man and a good friend."

"Thank you, Mr. Killian," Josselyn replied quietly, grateful for his kind words and politely extending her hand. "Da's—Da's dying has been such a blow to me that even now, I still can't believe he's really gone. I confess I kept hoping all the way from Boston that somehow there'd been some horrible mistake and that he would be waiting for me at the depot. But he wasn't. . . ."

"No, ma'am." Killian shook his head, his handshake conveying both warmth and sympathy. "Sure and don't I know how you feel? For I've missed him sorely myself. We spent many a long winter's eve together, battling over a chessboard— Ah, 'twas a sorry day indeed when he died. But, there. He's gone, ma'am, and no mistake, for though, due to the slowness of the excavation and reconstruction of the gold mine, his body has yet to be found, he's not been seen hide nor hair of since the explosion at the Rainbow's End that unhappy night. Red poured his sweat and blood into that gold mine. He wouldn't have just walked away from it or disappeared without so much as a word to anyone. And what with his hat's being unearthed from the debris . . . well, ma'am, I'm afraid there can be little doubt that he's dead and buried beneath a mountain of rock.''

"I—I know," Josselyn admitted, biting her lip at the recognition. "But still, it's so hard, somehow, to give up hope. . . ."

"Aye, well, the wound left by the loss of a loved one takes time to heal, Miss O'Rourke." Killian, sharing her sorrow, was silent for a moment. Then he continued briskly. "Well, I trust you had a good journey. You must be tired after such a long trip, and wanting to get settled in, I'm thinking. So, if you're ready, I'll drive you up to the boardinghouse. My buggy's over there." He indicated a nearby vehicle, drawn by a single horse. "Is that your trunk?" he asked, pointing at the sole piece of baggage that now remained out front of the Wells Fargo Express station.

Josselyn nodded, and hefting the trunk onto one shoulder, Killian ushered her toward his waiting buggy. It was just noon, the hour when the miners changed shifts. Now, from all the surrounding hills, she saw groups of men, getting off work, beginning to make their way down to the towns that sprawled along the gulches. The miners were covered with grime from their day's labor; most were ill-clothed, a ragtag lot, though all wore stout boots. Josselyn heard the clink of the men's tin dinner pails, a harmonious counterpoint, somehow, to the miners' voices, raised in song. As the haunting notes of the melody they sang drifted on the wind to the vehicle rumbling toward Roworth Street, Killian noticed Josselyn's interest in the men.

"They're a motley crew, the miners," he told her. "Irishmen and Cousin Jacks, mostly."

"Cousin Jacks?" she queried, curious.

"That's what we call the Cornishmen hereabouts," Killian explained. He pointed out several businesses that lined the streets. "See all that fine brickwork and stonework on those buildings? Cousin Jacks did most of it. 'Tis a skill they learned in the Old Country and brought to America, in addition to their knowledge of mining. They don't dig gold, but tin and china clay in Cornwall; still, the basic principles are the same. You won't hardly find a mine for miles around that doesn't have at least one Cousin Jack at work in it, and probably more. The Cornish are a clannish bunch, and they look after their own. A Cornishman gets ahead here in America, and at a mine owner's request, he sends for his relatives back home, for there're jobs here for all skilled miners. That's how they came to be nicknamed Cousin Jacks. The women are known as Cousin Jennies. But there are plenty of Irish here, too, as well as a smattering of Slavs—'Bohunks,' we call them, and mean no disrespect, for they're hard workers, big, strong fellows, most of them, good at heavy labor. We've also some Germans, French, Mexicans, Chinese, even a few native Indians. This region of Colorado is a real melting pot."

"It certainly appears to be," Josselyn agreed as she studied the miners descending from the hills whose sites and names, like those of the gulches, she would gradually come to recognize and know in the passing days—hills such as Negro, Winnebago, Gunnell, Casto, Bates, Silver, Nevada, Floyd, Central, Mammoth, Quartz, Bobtail, Gregory, Signal, Justice, Guy, and Dory.

They were, she would discover, literally riddled with hundreds of mines, many with names as fanciful as the Rainbow's End—among them the Hunky Dory Mine, the Lost Dollar Mine, the Shamrock Mine, and the Queen Bee Mine. Some were already played out and abandoned. But the wealth of others, like that of the Rainbow's End, had scarcely been tapped yet. Their claimants often lacked the funds to hire the men and to purchase the machinery vital to the hard-rock mining process. Most of the prospectors who had come to Colorado to strike it rich were doomed to disappointment. But still, they all dreamed of finding a mother lode. Many of the men who went into the hills never returned. Stricken with gold fever, they kept on searching for that vein of prosperity—and died of starvation, disease, winterkill, and mining accidents instead, leaving widows and orphans to go on as best they could without a man in a man's world. Josselyn had come to the "richest square mile on earth," but as she gazed about from Killian's buggy, she was not blind to the poverty the area contained, as well.

Here, as in the slums of Boston, painted prostitutes plied their trade, and hungry urchins begged on street corners. It was cruelly ironic, she reflected, that in the midst of so much wealth, there should be want. In that moment, she suddenly recalled the Reverend Mother Maire's words to her about there being many ways of serving God; and at the thought, without her consciously even realizing it, like those she had used to plant in the convent garden, a tiny seed was planted in her fertile mind.

By the time they drew up before the boardinghouse, Josselyn and Killian were on a first-name basis and she felt she had made at least one friend in town. She was grateful that he had met her at the Wells Fargo Express station and had arranged suitable and inexpensive living accommodations for her, for she wasn't at all sure she could have managed on her own.

Killian pulled his horse to a stop and carefully set the brake on the buggy. After assisting Josselyn down from the vehicle, he again hoisted her trunk onto one shoulder. Then he pushed open the gate of the short white picket fence that enclosed the small yard of the modest, two-story cottage that sat back from the street, its flower beds a riot of colorful spring blossoms. Preceding him up the path, Josselyn stepped onto the wooden front porch of the white clapboard building that despite its otherwise neat appearance was, like everything else in Central City, streaked with soot. Despite her grief, her heart pounded with excitement at the thought that for the time being, anyway, this would be her new home. Killian rapped on the door, and it was opened by a tiny, plump older woman with a warm, welcoming smile, apple cheeks, and eyes that, behind wire-rimmed spectacles, twinkled merrily.

"Why, it's Mr. Killian! And you must be Miss O'Rourke!" the woman cried, slightly out of breath from having hurried down the hallway to the door. "I'm Mrs. Harrietta Munroe, but everybody calls me plain old Miss Hattie. Come in, come in. We've been expecting you. Zeb!" she called, turning to glance toward the back of the boardinghouse. "Zeb! Now, where is that boy? Oh, there you are," she said as a slender young man with an unruly shock of blond hair appeared from what Josselyn guessed by its swinging door must be the kitchen. "This here's Zebulon, my grandson," she declared proudly, beaming. "Zeb, this is Miss Josselyn O'Rourke, our new boarder, come all the way from Boston."

"How do, ma'am." The young man tugged at his forelock shyly and ducked his head.

"Zeb, you take Miss O'Rourke's trunk on upstairs to her room," Hattie instructed. "We'll be along in a minute, just as soon as I find out if Mr. Killian is planning on staying to dinner. Well, sir?" She looked expectantly at the attorney.

"Well, now, Miss Hattie," he began, "that's right kind of you, but with a desk stacked high with paperwork waiting back at the office—"

"It's mulligan stew, Mr. Killian," Hattie announced slyly, as though she knew that the lawyer would be unable to refuse such a savory offering, "and fresh bread I took from the oven just before you and Miss O'Rourke arrived."

"Sure and you're a shameless baggage, Miss Hattie," Killian bantered, grinning. "It ought to be against the law, I'm thinking, how you tempt a man. My, oh, my. Mulligan stew. Well, and doesn't a man work better with a full stomach, after all?"

"So my late husband was always fond of saying," Hattie

claimed. "You go on into the dining room, Mr. Killian. Miss O'Rourke and I will join you shortly." Turning to Josselyn, she directed, "Follow me now, and I'll show you to your room."

Josselyn's bedroom was on the second floor, tucked away beneath the eaves of the cottage. It was small but charmingly decorated, with touches she guessed were Miss Hattie's handiwork. The mansion bed was covered with a bright patchwork quilt; the washstand boasted two hand towels that had been beautifully embroidered, and cheerful braided rag rugs were scattered across the floor. A Queen Anne chair, a chest of drawers for her clothing, and a nightstand that housed the chamber pot completed the simple furnishings. To Josselyn, accustomed to a plain, Spartan room at the convent, which she had shared with a number of different girls over the years, the cozy room she now surveyed and the fact that it was to be hers alone seemed the height of luxury.

Despite herself, her spirits lifted a little. She could be happy here, she thought, in this room, in Central City, if only her father were alive. . . .

That Da's last will and testament was to be read tomorrow she learned from Killian as she and Miss Hattie joined him, Zeb, and the other boarders downstairs in the dining room to consume the excellent meal that Miss Hattie had prepared. Josselyn was to be in the attorney's office at two o'clock the following afternoon, at which time she would not only meet Da's partners in the Rainbow's End, but they would all be apprised of the contents of her father's will.

She was curious about the "conditions" to which Killian had referred in the letter she had received in Boston. But to her puzzlement, he adroitly deflected her questions about these, insisting that everything would be best discussed when all concerned were present. Although she instinctively liked Killian and knew that her father had trusted him implicitly, Josselyn received the distinct and vaguely troubling impression that the lawyer was being deliberately evasive. Surely, the matter involved little more than a few legal formalities, the signing of some papers, as the Reverend Mother Maire had seemed to think. Why, then, should Killian balk at answering her questions, Josselyn wondered.

That night, as she unpacked her trunk and put away her garments and the rest of her few belongings, she found herself again pondering Killian's equivocal behavior, and thinking, also, about Durango de Navarre, Wylie Gresham, and the now-deceased Forbes Houghton, her father's original three partners in the gold mine. From Da's letters over the years, she knew something of the history of all three men.

Had Forbes Houghton still been alive, Josselyn would have suspected him of being the culprit responsible for blowing up the Rainbow's End and killing Da; for from what her father had reported, Forbes had been little better than an obnoxious drunk, loud, crude, and domineering, accustomed to riding roughshod over anybody who had stood in his way. But Forbes was dead; and so, in her mind, Josselyn had already concluded that of Da's remaining partners, the more likely candidate for committing sabotage and murder was De Navarre.

He was the illegitimate son of a white man and a Mexican woman, and his father was rumored to have been an outlaw forced to flee south of the border to escape from a posse. Perhaps there was some truth to the tale, for although De Navarre never confirmed it, he apparently never denied it, either. Some even swore he had ridden with his father for a time and so was himself a desperado—although if his name and description had ever appeared on a wanted poster, no one had ever proved brave enough to collect the reward. According to Da, De Navarre had a gun hand like greased lightning, which he did not hesitate to use should the circumstances warrant, and a temperament reminiscent of a timber wolf. Before coming to what had then been the Colorado Territory, he had—or so he claimed—earned his living as a bounty hunter and a gambler, which latter profession he still practiced, owning, in addition to his shares in the Rainbow's

End, a local saloon, the Mother Lode. All this had led Josselyn to believe that De Navarre was at best a rogue who walked both sides of the law as he pleased, and at worst a criminal who ought to be locked up in a jail cell. She had never understood how her father had come to be mixed up with such a notorious man, to trust him enough to take him on as a partner.

Then she recalled how she had been duped by Antoine Fouché, and she thought dully that it was easy to be fooled by someone bent on concealing his true character. After that, she felt guilty and slightly ashamed for prejudging De Navarre, and so harshly. She determined to try to keep an open mind, something that was especially difficult when she remembered what she knew of Da's partner Wylie Gresham.

"A southern gentleman," her father had pronounced him, of an old, moneyed family who had, in the War Between the States, lost most of what they had possessed, including their stately Mississippi plantation, Magnolia Hall. The fashionable clothes and elegant manners he still maintained had in past years often caused Gresham to be mistaken for a dude —although, Da had noted, Gresham's expertise with the two-shot derringer he always carried made certain that few people ever called him that to his face a second time. Though he had arrived virtually penniless in the Colorado Territory, his enterprise and acumen had served him well. Originally peddling goods in a tent, he had built a thriving mercantile business, and now owned, in addition to his shares in the gold mine, both a store on Lawrence Street and a shipping company on Main Street. Like Henry M. Teller, Central City's most prominent resident, Gresham was both active and respected in the community. He hardly, Josselyn thought, fit the profile of a man who would creep up a mountainside in the middle of the night to cripple the operation of the Rainbow's End and murder her father.

Still she must be on her guard against both men, she decided. She had been sternly reminded by the Reverend Mother

Maire that vengeance was God's province, but Josselyn was nevertheless determined to ferret out Da's killer and to see that the culprit was brought to justice. She had loved her father; she owed it to him to expose his murderer—and the O'Rourkes had always paid their debts.

Chapter Three

Patrick Killian had left with Josselyn a hand-drawn map of Central City, with directions to his office, which he had pointed out to her yesterday, en route to Miss Hattie's boardinghouse. Unlike Boston, Central City was not large, so despite its convoluted streets, Josselyn had no difficulty, after dinner the following afternoon, in making her way to Eureka Street, where the lawyer's office was located.

What a beautiful spring day, she thought as she walked along, eagerly taking in the sights at close hand.

By now, the sun had broken through the clinging mist that had cloaked the mountains earlier that morning, though gently floating cloud wisps still enshrouded the highest of the snow-capped peaks. In the distance, the trees thickened from the sparse stands below the pinnacles of the crags to forests of feathery ponderosa pines, tall blue spruce, and white-barked aspen that seemed to tumble down the mountainsides, where alpine flowers bloomed in a profusion of color amid lush green and silver grasses. The crisp, clean mountain air was invigorating, although, as yet unaccustomed to its thinness, Josselyn was left slightly breathless as she strolled along the steep and twisting boardwalks. Gasping a little for air, she paused briefly outside Killian's office to collect herself. Then, after a moment, she opened the door and went in.

Obviously expecting her, the attorney's secretary, Miss Earnshaw, greeted her congenially. But as they exchanged polite amenities, Josselyn could not help but notice the anxious glances the young woman surreptitiously cast at the closed door of Killian's office or fail to hear the sound of heated voices that emanated from within.

"The others have already arrived," Miss Earnshaw informed her a trifle apologetically, by way of explaining the disturbance. "I'm afraid they're . . . er . . . somewhat impatient to begin, so if you'll follow me, please, I'll just show you inside."

Killian's office was very small, very crowded, and it seemed to be on fire. Startled, Josselyn drew up short—suddenly, unexpectedly, panicked as, at her entrance, the room fell abruptly silent and, through the cloud of acrid smoke that hung in the air, five unfriendly pairs of eyes riveted on her. Involuntarily, she shrank back against the door, only to discover that the secretary, after announcing her and departing, had pulled it shut, sealing off the only avenue of escape. For an awful minute, Josselyn felt like a butterfly pinned to a board, being peered at through a huge magnifying glass by eyes that were ominously large and terrifyingly distorted. She fumbled behind her for the closed door's brass knob, even as, dimly, she wondered why no one else seemed anxious to escape from the fumes. Then, feeling like a fool, she realized that the lawyer and the other two men in the room were puffing away at cigars and appeared to be enjoying the pungent smoke.

"Ah, Josselyn, there you are," Killian, standing behind

his massive oak desk, observed a shade too heartily in an effort to dispel the unmistakable tension that permeated the office, "and right on time, too. I take it, then, that you had no problem in finding your way here. Come in and let me introduce you to everyone. These two gentlemen are . . . er . . . that is to say . . . they *were* Red's partners in the Rainbow's End, Wylie Gresham and Durango de Navarre, and the ladies are Mrs. Victoria Stanhope Houghton, also a partner, through her late husband, Forbes, and Mrs. Nell Tierney, a . . . er . . . close friend of Red's. Gentlemen, ladies, this is Red's daughter, Miss Josselyn O'Rourke."

While Killian had been speaking, the two men had risen from their chairs; and now, Josselyn saw that her initial perception of the attorney's office was due not so much to its modest size as to the fact that Gresham and De Navarre dominated it so powerfully, causing all about them to pale in comparison. It was as though the room could not hold them, as though its high ceiling were too low, its walls too close, too confining for them. Josselyn herself, though neither a small nor a frail woman, felt uncomfortably dwarfed by the two men, both of them tall and dark, with glistening black hair and broad-shouldered bodies hard with muscles, bodies so patently virile that she felt instinctively threatened by their potent masculinity. And their prime. She had not known that Gresham and De Navarre were so young. Since they were Da's partners, she had always assumed they were his contemporaries. Instead, both must be at least twenty years younger than her father, nearer her own age, in fact.

Da's partners in the gold mine. *Her* partners now, Josselyn comprehended suddenly, stricken anew with panic at the idea of her having to deal with two such men—especially when one of them was undoubtedly a saboteur and a murderer. She must have been mad to believe that she would prove a match for them. That she would be able to unmask the one who had killed her father and, in all likelihood, Forbes Houghton, now seemed next to impossible. There was something about both Gresham and De Navarre that made her think of wild, willful animals—they were neither soft nor slack, but shrewd and savage, accustomed to demanding, and getting, what they wanted. Maybe they were in on the malignant plot together, she conjectured, and would therefore prove doubly dangerous.

One, or perhaps even both, of these men wanted the Rainbow's End badly enough to have committed sabotage and at least one, possibly even two, murders for it. One—or both —of the two men was perhaps even now thinking how simple it would be to acquire her father's shares in the gold mine from her, a green girl fresh from an Ursuline convent back East. Impossibly, one—or both—of them was perhaps even now smiling secretly with satisfaction, certain that the crimes would remain unsolved, unpunished, because Red O'Rourke's daughter was nothing more than a timid young novice—quickly, easily, sent packing.

At the galling realization, Josselyn's chin came up defiantly. Her green eyes flashed as she squared her shoulders determinedly. She would *not* be a stupid, trusting fool again! She would *not* permit all that Da had worked so hard to obtain to be wrested without a fight from her. She would *not* be driven back to Boston from Central City before she had accomplished what she had come to do. Instead, she would show both Gresham and De Navarre that Red O'Rourke's daughter, though she wore a novice's habit, was made of the same stern stuff as her father.

"I'm pleased to make your acquaintance, gentlemen," she said, and forced herself to advance across the floor, to extend her hand to the nearest man. "Da has told me so much about you both that I feel as though I know you already."

"Then I'm afraid you have us at a distinct disadvantage, Miss O'Rourke," Gresham declared as he shook her hand warmly, "for unfortunately, although Red could boast with the best of men, he was . . . well . . . quite frankly, a bit taciturn when it came to his private life. He spoke of you only rarely—although always with the utmost devotion, I assure you. My prayers and sympathies are with you in your hour of grief, Miss O'Rourke.''

"Thank you, Mr. Gresham," Josselyn replied, thinking that, surely—unless he were a consummate actor, which she doubted—he could not sound so sincere if he were the man responsible for her father's death. Or could he? Antoine had certainly sounded absolutely sincere when he had whispered his impassioned words of love to her.

She had to admit she did not as yet know Gresham well enough to know if he shared Antoine's cleverness at dissembling. Covertly, from beneath her demurely downcast lashes, she peeked up at him, in her veiled eyes now a glint of hardness and calculation they had not held since her childhood, when Da had deposited her small, unwilling figure at the gates of the convent.

Gresham was a handsome man, stylishly attired in a grey broadcloth suit and a grey-and-black paisley waistcoat, from which hung a sterling-silver watch chain adorned with a single fob and seal. At the throat of the frothy white jabot that spilled down his crisp white cambric shirt, he wore a black cravat pierced by a pearl tiepin. On the desk behind him lay a black bowler hat, a pair of grey leather gloves, and a malacca walking stick, all of which Josselyn correctly assumed must belong to him, since they seemed naturally to complete his fine ensemble.

His cool grey eyes gleamed with intelligence as they assessed her. Beneath his black handlebar mustache, the imperious curve of his lips and the resolute thrust of his jaw gave evidence of his proud and purposeful nature. She suspected he possessed that backbone of steel that is inbred rather than acquired, and her wits sharpened by her recent unhappy experience, she felt intuitively that those who crossed him seldom came off the best in the encounter. His manners, though tinged with hauteur, were refined, and he set Josselyn at her ease with his thoughtful words. Entranced by his southern accent, his slow, slurring voice, like warm molasses melting in her ears, she was charmed by his prepossessing mien, his dashing air of gallantry. That he might prove both a saboteur and a killer simply could not, she thought, be true.

Unfortunately, the same could not be said, however, of De Navarre, a ruffian if she had ever seen one, Josselyn decided stoutly as she turned reluctantly toward him. She wished fervently that she need not offer him her hand. She felt certain that his own was dirty in more ways than one—with grime and dynamite powder from the Rainbow's End, and with the blood of her father and Forbes Houghton, too. But she compelled herself to perform the courtesy, not expecting at all the sudden, violent, inexplicable quiver that shot through her as De Navarre's fingers closed firmly around hers, a tremor such as she had once felt when she had accidentally, in the convent garden, struck her hoe hard against the trunk of a tree. It was all she could do to prevent herself from rudely wrenching her hand away, the sheer strength and animal magnetism the man exuded were so overpowering, so frightening to her, who had so cruelly experienced the perfidy of such a man.

Beneath the black brows that swooped like a raven's wings across his broad forehead, his black eyes were half shuttered by thick, spiky black lashes that made it impossible for Josselyn to guess his thoughts. But still, she sensed his amusement at her consternation, glimpsed the sardonic half smile that fleetingly twisted his sensual mouth as he deliberately tightened his hand around hers before releasing it.

"My condolences, also, on your loss, Miss O'Rourke." De Navarre's low, silky, Spanish-accented voice sent a shiver up her spine; for she felt that he mocked her, that this was but his opening move in the game he would play to rid himself of her, as he had rid himself of her father and Forbes Houghton. "Red's death was both unfortunate and untimely."

Josselyn was not appeased by his polite words, for she felt that inwardly, De Navarre was laughing at her. Truly, the man was as much a scoundrel as Antoine had been, she thought, shuddering. Worse, even—for Antoine had at least possessed Gresham's elegant manners. De Navarre had not even bothered to remove his black, flat-brimmed sombrero, but had only tipped it slightly in her direction. The scuffed black leather boots he wore, with their silver Mexican spurs—"cartwheels," she would learn they were called— were surely more at home in a saloon than an office or a parlor. Had he taken any care with his appearance, he might have been deemed handsome in a coarse, common way, she supposed. But as it was, he looked as though he had not bathed or shaved in days, and he smelled distinctly not only of cheroot smoke, but of liquor. Indeed, a bottle of some clear liquid she could only assume to be alcohol sat on the floor, by one leg of his chair, and it seemed plain that he had been drinking from it before her arrival. His black silk shirt with its silver-rimmed black studs was open at the throat, flagrantly revealing smooth bronze skin and a mat of fine black hair. A black bandanna was carelessly knotted about his neck. Slung low at his hips was a black leather gun belt, whose holster bore a dangerous-looking revolver. Black breeches hugged his corded legs.

He was scarcely, Josselyn reflected bitterly, in mourning for her father, so she could only suppose that De Navarre preferred the somber color. She admitted to herself that it did suit his devilish appearance—and nature, she added mentally as, now, from beneath the hat that half shadowed his dark, unshaven face, his glittering black eyes raked her boldly— as no man ought to have looked at a lady—and that wicked half smile once more curved his lips. Surely, that smile was the triumphant smirk of a man who believed she would prove no hindrance whatsoever to his plans, a man who believed that he had got away with murder.

She despised him on sight. In her mind, she had already tried and convicted him for her father's killing. Now, all that remained was to see De Navarre hanged, as he so assuredly deserved! And this, she *would* do, Josselyn vowed silently to herself, no matter what it took to get the deed done.

Her simmering annoyance was not improved by her being

forced next to greet Victoria Stanhope Houghton, Forbes's young but sophisticated-looking widow, and Nell Tierney, the actress who had, Josselyn felt certain, been something more to Da than just the "close friend" that Killian had described.

For the first time in her life, as she shook Victoria's slender, coolly proferred hand, Josselyn was consumed by terrible envy. Like parched earth soaking up rain, her eyes drank in every detail of Victoria's dramatic black silk mourning ensemble, from its plumed and somehow enchantingly rakish hat set atop her smartly coiffed brunet head, to the high-necked, ruffle-collared gown with cameo brooch at the throat and bodice drawn back at the waist to emphasize her sleek, feline figure, to the fashionable black parasol, reticule, and leather button shoes that completed the outfit. Although she knew that vanity was a sin, Josselyn wished ardently at that moment that she were clothed in a manner to rival the widow rather than in her own plain novice's habit, which did little, she knew, to enhance her good looks.

"How do you do, Miss O'Rourke," Victoria said, her sparkling brown eyes and her pouting scarlet mouth tinged with faint traces of amusement and contempt as her gaze flicked over Josselyn shrewdly.

Why, she's laughing at me, too! Josselyn thought hotly— and instantly decided that De Navarre and the widow were bedded down together in more ways than one. *They did it! They must have murdered her husband and my father! No doubt, Wylie Gresham and I shall be next! I must befriend him right away, else I shall have no ally at all in this grisly struggle to seize control of the gold mine!*

She had no time to reflect further upon this, however; for startling her from her reverie, Nell Tierney grabbed Josselyn's hand warmly with both of her own and pumped it enthusiastically.

"My dear child! Oh, my dear, dear child! 'Tis so good to meet you!" Nell declared. Then she sighed deeply, smiled tremulously, and dabbed with her handkerchief at the corners of her eyes. "Red's daughter. Faith, if you aren't the spitting image of your father! 'Tis so happy I am to make your acquaintance at last, colleen, though I *do* so hate that it must be under the unhappy circumstance of Red's death. I want you to know that your father meant the world to me. My life just hasn't been the same since his dying. Oh, I do so hope we're going to be good friends, Josselyn—I may call you that, mayn't I? And of course, you must call me Nell. Having you here in Central City will be a little like having a part of Red back again; and it does so help to share one's grief, or so I've always thought. You will be coming to see me, then, won't you? I warn you: I won't take no for an answer."

Since the last thing Josselyn wished to do was to spend time with the woman who, she was certain, had connived so effectively to prevent her from joining Da in Central City, she murmured a polite, noncommittal response, though she seethed inside at what she perceived as Nell's hypocrisy. Nell was, Josselyn was grudgingly compelled to admit, an attractive older woman. The pale highlights in her dark, honey-gold hair, however, owed something to more than just nature, and her face, to Josselyn's shock, was expertly, albeit lightly, painted; but of course, Nell was an actress, which adequately accounted for the crocodile tears she managed convincingly to conjure. The woman certainly had nerve, Josselyn thought, her stomach churning with unfamiliar emotions, as well as from the cigar smoke that still filled the office. She felt as though she were going to faint or, worse, to throw up; and she was relieved when Killian indicated they should all be seated.

Taking the only unoccupied chair, she sank down upon it gratefully, coughing delicately into the handkerchief she pressed to her face in an effort to filter out the worst of the smoke she was being forced to inhale. Seeing her discomfort, Killian and Gresham, who had courteously stubbed out their cheroots at her arrival, glared censuringly at De Navarre, who had rudely failed to extinguish his. After a moment, he observed that everyone in the room was staring at him expectantly and abruptly leaned forward to crush his cigar out in a nearby brass ashtray.

"My apologies, Miss O'Rourke," De Navarre muttered, grinning at her in a way that made Josselyn think he was not in the least bit sorry. Then, much to her disgust, he nonchalantly rocked back in his chair, tipped his hat down low over his eyes, propped his long, muscular legs up on Killian's desk, roweling the woodwork with his spurs, and, taking a generous swig from the bottle beside him on the floor, demanded, "Well, Patrick, let's get on with it, shall we? I've got a saloon to run, and I don't have all day to waste hanging around here, twiddling my thumbs."

"Durango"—the attorney spoke through gritted teeth as he peered over his wire-rimmed spectacles at De Navarre—"kindly remove your boots and your spurs from the top of my desk . . . at once! This is a legal proceeding, *not* a burlesque, and I'll be thanking you to show the proper respect!" To Josselyn's surprise, though plainly unabashed, De Navarre nevertheless complied. Killian frowned at him a long, hard minute. Then, rustling through some papers on his desk, the lawyer gruffly cleared his throat and continued.

"Now. As you are all aware, we are gathered here today for the reading of the last will and testament of Seamus—better known to us as 'Red'—O'Rourke. Let me state first, for the record, that this is indeed Red's last will and testament, to which I can and will swear, as I drafted it myself just a few days before he died. Further, it was duly witnessed by my associate, Liam Calhoun, and my secretary, Margaret Earnshaw, so there can be no doubt that it will stand up in a court of law. I tell you this because Red's will is . . . er . . . somewhat irregular, and I don't want any of you making the mistake of thinking you can successfully contest it, because you can't. 'Tis solid as the Rocky Mountains, and no judge worthy of the title will be saying otherwise."

"Well, now that you've given us fair warning, Patrick, will you get on with the reading of the damned thing!" De

Navarre ordered impatiently. "I swear! I can't for the life of me figure why you're so dead set on keeping us all in the dark. Red's been buried under a mountain of rock long enough for us to know there's no chance of his walking out of the Rainbow's End alive; and still, despite that, you've kept me and Wylie and Victoria cooling our heels for weeks, refusing even to hint at the contents of Red's will, while we've waited for Miss O'Rourke to arrive. Well, now, she's here; and I, for one, am tired of all this shilly-shallying around. Red didn't own much more than his shares in the Rainbow's End and a few personal odds and ends; and since you needed Miss O'Rourke present for the reading of his will, it seems obvious he didn't leave 'em to a children's home!"

"No, he did not," Killian agreed tersely. "Very well, then. I will proceed." Clearing his throat again, he slowly unfolded the document he held in his hand and began to read. " 'I, Seamus "Red" O'Rourke, being of sound mind and body, do hereby declare this to be my last will and testament. To my only daughter, Josselyn Aingeal O'Rourke, I bequeath all my worldly possessions, save for my book of Shakespearean plays, which I bequeath to Mrs. Nell Tierney, for reasons that are well known to her. Further, to my aforesaid daughter, Josselyn, I bequeath all my shares in the gold mine known as the Rainbow's End, which shares have been duly registered in my name, provided, however, that she shall not, at the time of my death, be a nun. If she should not be a nun, such shares shall be hers absolutely, to retain, invest, convey, sell, or otherwise dispose of as she may desire and sees fit, upon the following condition: that within one year from the date of my death, she shall marry either one of my two bachelor partners in the Rainbow's End, Durango de Navarre or Wylie Gresham—' " Here, Killian was abruptly compelled to break off the reading as there erupted in his office the vehement outburst he had feared and expected all afternoon.

"Well, well, well." De Navarre's tone was deadly. "Damn me to hell if Red didn't get the last laugh, after all.

No wonder you were so loath to proceed with the reading, Patrick. You're lucky I don't shoot you for drawing up a will like that! In fact, I still might!''

No one present made the mistake of assuming that this was an idle threat. However, before Killian could respond, Gresham spoke heatedly.

''Why, it's—it's preposterous!'' he sputtered, indignant. ''The very idea! No offense, Miss O'Rourke,'' he added hastily, observing Josselyn's ashen face. ''But, my God! Do you mean to sit there and tell me, Patrick, that one of us is to wed a *nun*?''

''What do you mean, 'one of us,' Wylie?'' De Navarre gibed maliciously before taking another liberal gulp from his bottle, then wiping his mouth off on his sleeve. ''You ain't a Catholic!''

As the full import of this—and all its attendant implications—sank in, Gresham was rendered speechless with impotent ire, while Josselyn, inhaling sharply, turned even whiter; for despite her shock, she correctly deduced that while Gresham was not of her faith, De Navarre was. Seeing her distress, De Navarre grinned at her insolently, though his smile did not quite reach his narrowed eyes, which now appraised her cringing figure slowly, deliberately, making her feel as though she were a slave upon a block and he a prospective buyer.

''I assume,'' he went on ruthlessly, ''that since Patrick introduced you as 'Miss' rather than 'Sister' O'Rourke, you *are* free to marry.''

Josselyn was so stricken that she couldn't manage even to shake her head, much less choke out an answer. She felt numb, aghast. No wonder Killian, despite his friendliness, had been so evasive yesterday about the conditions she must satisfy to inherit her father's shares in the Rainbow's End! This was a nightmare, she thought, a dreadful nightmare, one from which she prayed fervently that she would soon awaken. Surely, Da could not have done this to her. Surely, he could not!

As though from far away, she heard Killian confirm that she had not yet taken her final vows. Blindly, she saw De Navarre's lips tighten derisively at the news before he once more upended his bottle and took another long swallow.

With morbid fascination, Josselyn stared at him. Dumbly, she thought that quite apart from the fact that she believed him to be her father's killer, he was as slovenly a man as she had ever seen and that, worse, he cursed, he smoked, and he drank. He was probably more than a little drunk at this very instant, she surmised, as an explanation for his contemptible, ill-mannered behavior. The notion that her father—that *anyone*—could seriously expect her to wed such a man appalled her. Yet Da must have known that Gresham wasn't a Catholic and that she would never even consider marrying outside of her faith. As incredible as it seemed, then, Da had surely intended her to choose De Navarre. Grasping this, Josselyn was irresistibly drawn to gaze again at the man who continued, from beneath the brim of his sombrero, to survey her lewdly, as though, in his mind, he were stripping her stark naked. His eyes locked on hers and, to her fright and fury, he once more grinned at her scornfully above the rim of his bottle. She shivered as, unbidden, a picture of him as her husband, free to do as he pleased with her, *to* her, rose to terrify her.

Sweet Mary, mother of Jesus! Josselyn thought, one hand going involuntarily to her throat at the idea of her being totally in De Navarre's power, helpless against him, utterly at his mercy.

Her father must have been out of his mind to think she would willingly wed such a man. Though she knew he had loved her, had wanted the best for her, still, she could not begin to fathom Da's reason for inserting such a hideous stipulation in his will, much less bring herself even to contemplate fulfilling his last wish.

"Patrick," Victoria asked, a curiously sharp note underlying her quiet tone, "what happens if Miss O'Rourke *doesn't* marry either Durango or Wylie?"

"Yes, I think we would all be highly interested in learning

that,'' Gresham insisted grimly, his grey eyes like steel as, briefly, they locked with Victoria's brown ones.

''Very well. As you wish. If you are all ready, then, I shall go on with the reading.'' Killian mopped his damp brow, then removed his glasses and polished their lenses. Replacing the spectacles on his nose, he turned back to the will, re-reading the lines that had caused the stir. '' '. . . that within one year from the date of my death, she'—meaning Josselyn—'shall marry either one of my two bachelor partners in the Rainbow's End, Durango de Navarre or Wylie Gresham, thereby securing both a husband and her future. However, if she should, at the time of my death, be a nun, or if she should, for any reason during the year herein stipulated, find herself unable to fulfill the condition herein set forth, then all my shares in the gold mine known as the Rainbow's End shall pass irrevocably to Mrs. Nell Tierney, to be hers absolutely, to retain, invest, convey, sell, or otherwise dispose of as she may desire and sees fit, upon the following condition: that she shall use the revenue from same to establish her own theater, in order that her career may continue to flourish and that, upon her retirement, she will not lack for means of financial support. On this date, I have affixed my signature hereto.' That's it,'' Killian ended.

''Yeah, well, Red knew how to be short, sweet, and to the point when he wanted,'' De Navarre remarked sourly. ''Now, let's be sure we've all got this straight, Patrick. Basically, what Red's will says is this: that if Miss O'Rourke here doesn't wed either me or Wylie within the year, then Nell's gonna be building herself one hell of an opera house. Is that it?''

''In a nutshell,'' the attorney articulated, casting an anxious, sympathetic glance at Josselyn, who continued to sit still as a statue, mute with shock, frozen with horror.

She felt oddly removed from her surroundings, as though she were somehow viewing Killian's office from a great distance, as though all of this were happening to somebody else instead of her. Her mouth tasted unnaturally dry; with dif-

ficulty, she swallowed. Her palms perspired profusely. Her
heart pounded at an alarming rate, and her head throbbed.
She couldn't seem to get her breath—panicked, she realized
she was actually desperate for air—and the stench of stale
smoke from the cigars the three men had smoked earlier was
nauseating her, besides. Drops of sweat beading her brow
and upper lip, she swayed on the edge of her seat, knowing
that she was either about to swoon or to vomit.

"¡Sangre de Cristo!" De Navarre growled, lunging without warning from his chair, startling everyone.

Three short steps brought him to Josselyn's side. She
opened her mouth to scream as, abruptly, he towered over
her, as she felt his muscular arms—like iron bands—tighten
around her. But what emanated from her throat was no more
than a soft moan, for he had seized her handkerchief and was
now pressing it over her face, muffling her cries of terror.
Before her dazed eyes, Killian's office reeled sickeningly as
De Navarre forcibly swept her up and carried her from the
room, his spurs jingling as he strode swiftly across the plank
floor. Dimly, she was aware of De Navarre's strength, of his
hard, masculine body, and of being held fast in his embrace,
intimately crushed against his chest. She could smell the male
scent of him, tinged with traces of saddle soap and leather,
smoke and liquor. She could feel the stubble on his face
grazing the top of her veiled head as he clasped her to him,
ignoring her whimpers and her futile, pitiful attempts to free
herself.

With one hand, he wrenched open the office door and
kicked it aside, startling Miss Earnshaw as he moved rapidly
through the main room to fling wide the front door.

Once outside, De Navarre unceremoniously dumped Josselyn facedown over the wooden hitching rail out front,
roughly pushing her head down between her knees.

"Breathe, damn it!" he snapped. "Breathe!"

Gratefully, she gulped air, her chest expanding as though
it would burst as the cool spring breeze wafting down from
the mountains rushed in to fill her lungs. Frantically, again

and again, like a person drowning, she inhaled deeply the welcome fresh air, feeling as though she would never get enough of it. But finally, much to her relief, her dizziness and queasiness passed, and her composure began slowly to return.

"Better?" De Navarre asked as, shakily, she righted herself.

"Y-y-yes, much, th-th-thank you," Josselyn stammered, her cheeks staining bright crimson with embarrassment as she recalled his hands upon her body, lifting her, enfolding her against him. Of its own volition, her pulse quickened at the remembrance. How strong De Navarre was, she thought uncomfortably. How vital! He had borne her as easily as though she weighed no more than a feather. His body had been warm as a gaslight. Her own tingled peculiarly, as though from an electric current, at the memory. Horrified by this terrible, unreal afternoon and the disturbing images and emotions that suddenly threatened to overwhelm her, she bit her lip and tears stung her eyes. She did not know which was worse: Da's awful will, the fact that De Navarre had laid his hands on her, or the fact that if he had not, she would surely have passed out on Killian's office floor. Feeling as though she had been wrung through a wringer, Josselyn wanted nothing more than to return to Miss Hattie's boardinghouse and lie down.

By this time, the others had gathered on the boardwalk. Now, they crowded about her, solicitously inquiring as to her health.

"She's all right. She was just suddenly overcome for a moment, a combination of the smoke and the shock, I suspect," De Navarre explained. "It was simply too much for her."

"Well, I suppose we have you and Red to thank for that, Patrick," Gresham reproached Killian, his lip curling. "Red for dreaming up that outrageous will and you for drawing it up! It is patently clear that neither of you considered Miss O'Rourke's feelings in the matter. Any gentleman would have known that it was bound to prove devastating to one of her sheltered upbringing and maidenly sensibilities; and I therefore find myself compelled to say that I don't believe that either of you acted with Miss O'Rourke's best interests at heart. Despite your warning, Patrick, I feel that it is only fair to inform you that I fully intend to apprise Judge Ascot of the contents of Red's will and to ask the judge's opinion of this entire underhanded affair.''

''Suit yourself, Wylie,'' Killian rejoined shortly, ''but I'm telling you right now that regardless of what you may think to the contrary, there was nothing 'underhanded' about the matter. 'Twas all done proper and legal, and if I know the judge, he'll not be advising you otherwise.''

''Yes, well, we'll just see about that!'' Gresham's mouth tightened with ill-concealed anger. Then, turning to Josselyn and forcing a smile to his lips, he said, ''My buggy's just down the street, at the livery stable, Miss O'Rourke. I'd be happy to drive you back to Miss Hattie's boardinghouse.''

''And will ye then be goin' down the hill ta Pine Street, Wylie,'' De Navarre drawled wickedly in a highly exaggerated brogue, while Victoria caught her breath with a hiss, ''ta see Faather Flanagan about larnin' the catechism?''

''You know, Durango, one of these days, I'm going to permanently shut your insulting mouth,'' Gresham vowed through clenched teeth, shooting him a dark glance that would have made a lesser man quail.

De Navarre, however, only grinned.

''When they ice skate in hell, Wylie,'' he retorted softly, unperturbed, as he leaned against the hitching post, his thumbs arrogantly hooked in his gun belt. ''When they ice skate in hell.''

For a taut moment, the two men glared at each other, Gresham visibly restraining his rage, De Navarre openly goading—Victoria watching as though hypnotized, a strange, hard light in her eyes, her nostrils flared. But fortunately, Gresham was not to be baited. Pointedly turning his back on De Navarre, he addressed Josselyn again instead.

"Come, Miss O'Rourke." He took her politely but firmly by the arm. "Durango has never been fit company for a lady, I fear, and today is no exception, it appears. We'll just step inside to collect my hat, gloves, and cane; and then we'll fetch my buggy. I know that you must be most upset by Red's shocking will and desirous of reflecting upon it in privacy. Victoria, my dear"—he turned to Forbes's disdainful widow—"under the circumstances, I'm sure that either Patrick or Nell will be good enough to drive you home."

Victoria seemed about to protest this dismissal. Then, abruptly, she closed her mouth and nodded.

"As you wish," she replied stiffly, only Durango noting that her hands tightened angrily on the parasol she carried.

"I'll take you, Victoria," Killian offered courteously at once. "Wait here. I'll get my buggy and join you momentarily." Then he headed toward the livery stable.

Josselyn could not help but appreciate Gresham's gentlemanly conduct, his sensitive consideration of her feelings, his understanding of her inner turmoil—in sharp contrast to De Navarre's manhandling and mockery of her. Despite the terms of her father's will and De Navarre's being a Catholic, she told herself that Da could not possibly have intended her to marry De Navarre; and for the first time, she wondered uneasily if De Navarre had somehow coerced Da into setting forth the condition she must meet in order to inherit her father's shares in the gold mine.

Just as Gresham had started to escort Josselyn toward the livery stable, an old bum, shuffling down the street, slowly approached the small group assembled in front of Killian's office. A scraggly, stooped, shabbily dressed man, the tramp had a bloody bandage wrapped around his head and his left eye, and he was limping badly, relying heavily on a crutch to make his way along the boardwalk. Clearly, he had been in some sort of an accident, no doubt in one of the hundreds of mines that dotted the hillsides. For a disconcerting instant, Josselyn thought he looked oddly familiar. Then she recognized that this was because he vaguely resembled the drunken derelict loitering yesterday at the Central Colorado Railroad depot in Black Hawk, when she had disembarked from the train. A would-be miner turned piker. There must be hundreds of such men in the region, she realized, saddened, as her eyes fastened pityingly on those of the infirm vagrant.

"Can you spare a dime for a poor fellow down on his luck, Sister?" the man queried in a low, gravelly voice, tentatively stretching a quivering hand out toward her.

"Away! Away!" Gresham struck out with his walking stick at the bum. "Be off with you, beggar! No, Miss O'Rourke"—he stayed her hand as she began to reach into the reticule tied securely to the cestus at her waist—"don't give him one red cent. He will only waste it on rotgut whiskey—no doubt in Durango's saloon!"

"Unfortunately, Wylie's right, Josselyn," Nell agreed, scowling and shaking her head, while Victoria, withdrawing a lacy white handkerchief from her reticule and pressing it to her nose, sniffed audibly. " 'Tis sad but true that half these beggars don't really even have anything wrong with them. Faith, I'd bet my bottom dollar that that fellow's bandage and crutch are nothing more than stage props! I'm an actress, so I should know. For shame!" she cried to the tramp, abruptly grabbing hold of his arm and hustling him away, thereby exposing that he was fully capable, despite his crutch, of spry movement. "For shame! The very idea! Trying so deceitfully to take advantage of a nun's charity! 'Tis a disgrace, you are, and no mistake!"

"Hey! Old-timer!" De Navarre called, a sudden, curious, intent expression on his face as he stared hard at the vagrant. "Here's two bits." He tossed him a quarter, which the man, despite his seeming blindness in one eye, caught deftly. "Go buy yourself a square meal."

"Thank you kindly, sir." The bum smiled and nodded, revealing blackened teeth. Then he looked again at Josselyn, touching his greasy forelock. "Good day to you, Sister," he said before Nell determinedly hauled him off, lecturing him severely as they went.

Gresham, grumbling under his breath about indigent prospectors, turned once more to Josselyn, debonairly proffering his arm.

"Shall we go, Miss O'Rourke?"

"What?" she asked absently, lost in reverie, a small frown knitting her brow as she gazed at the street corner where Nell and the tramp had eventually disappeared. "What? Oh, oh, yes, Mr. Gresham. Of course."

They were halfway down the boardwalk when Josselyn, puzzled as she continued to ponder De Navarre's surprising and wholly unexpected altruism, glanced back over her shoulder at him. He was still standing alongside Victoria, by the hitching rail in front of Killian's office, watching them as they made their way toward the livery stable. Spying Josselyn studying him thoughtfully, De Navarre deliberately pulled a cigar from his pocket, struck a match on the sole of his boot, and lighted the cheroot. He dragged on it deeply for a moment. Then, with a grin, he shouted, "Hey, Wylie! Don't do anything I'd do!" Josselyn blushed—and a muscle twitched alarmingly in Gresham's set jaw.

"A spiteful but entirely idle threat, that—intended only to rile Wylie," Victoria observed astringently to De Navarre as Josselyn and Gresham vanished from view. "For you know that you would no more touch a nun than—than—"

"Than I'd touch *you*?" De Navarre supplied bluntly, his eyes hard as they pierced her in a way that made her long violently to strike him with her parasol. He laughed softly, jeeringly. "My dear, you can be certain of the latter—although I wouldn't be too sure, if I were you, about the former," he lied maliciously. "After all, there is a gold mine at stake—a gold mine that may prove extremely profitable, if Red's speculations were correct—and now that he's dead and you and Wylie have got so very . . . chummy since Forbes died, well, I've got to look out for my own interests. I would strongly suggest that you do the same—though I fully expect that you will, since you always have. I don't know what ever possessed Red to leave such a damnable will;

but from the look of things today, it seems clear that Wylie may prefer a naive nun to a scheming strumpet. You'd best sheathe your sharp talons and tongue, Victoria, lest you find yourself on my side of the tracks, after all.''

"Poor darling, how could you possibly think I would *ever* stoop so low?" she shot back; however, her nerves jerked at hearing voiced aloud her own secret dread. Although lovers, she and Wylie were uneasy allies, all of the partners certain now since Red's death that the so-called accidents at the Rainbow's End had not really been accidents at all, but the work of one of their own number who had also surely murdered both Forbes and Red.

"My dear, *you* would hardly be the one doing the stooping," De Navarre taunted derisively, both his words and his sarcastic smile like a slap in her face. "But don't worry. As you are only too well aware, even I have *some* scruples."

"Don't flatter yourself, Durango!" she retorted, tossing her head and laughing scornfully, although her cheeks were high with color at his insults. "I'd sooner bed down with a snake than with you—you greaser-pig!''

"Come, come, Victoria. That tired old refrain again?" He spoke lightly, mockingly, but his smoldering eyes gave the lie to his words. "Surely, even a woman of your limited talents can do better. What a pity you are such a bad liar. It must be deeply frustrating for you. No, save your breath, for there's no use in your trying to deny what we have both known since that night on The Casey, when you crept from Forbes's bed to try to slip into mine. My poor dear. It has always eaten at you, has it not? The fact that you might actually enjoy wallowing in the mud with a swinish half-Mexican bastard like me. And you *would* enjoy it, too, I promise you." His eyes roamed over her lazily, lewdly, and his arrogant smirk made her hands itch to claw it from his face. "However, as I have before, I really am afraid I must refuse you the pleasure of indulging yourself, since—unlike Wylie—I have always believed in honor even among thieves and my taste has never run to faithless tarts and artful gold diggers. Frankly, I don't know how Wylie dares to close his eyes at night in your bed. If he has a lick of sense—and certainly, I've never thought he lacked his fair share—he sleeps with one eye open, lest he find your knife at his throat . . . or elsewhere. Perhaps that is why he departed with the nun this afternoon—in search of a good night's relaxation, in more ways than one, hmh?''

"How I hope you live to rue the day you made an enemy out of me, Durango,'' Victoria announced in a voice that dripped acid. Then she smiled with false sweetness. "But at the rate the partners in the Rainbow's End are dropping dead, I very much fear I shall be cheated of my revenge on you. Perhaps, as Forbes and Red did, you and Wylie, too, should see Patrick about drawing up wills.''

"Naming you as our heiress, of course, since we are both of us without other relations? No, thanks, Victoria. Unlike Forbes and Red, we are both of us young, and neither of us is planning on pushing up daisies anytime soon. Besides''— De Navarre's eyes narrowed intently—"what makes you so damned sure that, unlike the rest of us, you're immune to suffering a so-called accident at the mine?''

"Are you accusing me . . . or threatening me?''

"Pick a slipper, my dear—preferably the one that fits.''

"Sorry, you're just not my idea of a handsome prince. But perhaps the nun, who, one presumes, is wholly ignorant of men, will proffer her foot—for as Judas was tempted by silver, so a nun may be tempted by gold, I imagine, if not by your dubious appeal. Perhaps you had better run after her and Wylie. I know him so well—he is so like me, you see —that I do not think he will scruple to play both ends against the middle; and then where will you be, when, thanks to his skillful mastery of us women, he is firmly in charge of the Rainbow's End? Why, under his thumb, I do believe—where I freely confess I should so dearly love to see you squirming, Durango, that I think I may not find it so very hard, after all, to share him. She has a nun's scruples, for heaven's sake. There is a certain amusing irony in that, don't you agree?

That, no matter what, she shall not have a prayer of truly taking him from me. For Wylie has certain . . . sinful appetites, shall we say? And, alas, I fear that our would-be nun will prove but a pitiful morsel he shall gobble up in one big bite. Poor Red's daughter, child of the convent.'' With feigned sorrow, Victoria shook her head. Then she sighed heavily with pretended reproval. "*Tsk, tsk*, Durango. How unfortunate you must find it at this moment that you are not a marrying man. How ever will *you* dare to close your eyes at night—knowing yourself not only a Catholic, but the nearest thing to a son Red ever hoped to have?''

Such was the murderous wrath that suddenly flared in De Navarre's eyes at that that, frightened, knowing she had pushed him too far, Victoria took a hasty step back, savagely positioning her parasol like a weapon between them, as though it would hold him at bay. But quick as a pouncing mountain lion, he snatched it from her, brutally snapping it in half over his knee; and afterward, she thought he would have throttled her in the next instant had not Killian pulled up just then in his buggy to drive her home. Fiercely, De Navarre shoved the broken halves of the parasol into her hands.

"Next time, Victoria, I swear that it'll be your goddamned neck!'' he snarled before abruptly pivoting on his booted heel and striding off, on his face such a forbidding look that passersby shied from his path.

Shivering, she watched him go, wondering not for the first time if it was he who had murdered Forbes, and even Red; for truly, Durango was, she thought, capable of almost anything, caring for no one and nothing but his own proud neck, and his violent black Latin rages were such that when one was upon him, even Red had seldom dared to stand in his way.

Chapter Four

Nell Tierney was beside herself as she gazed with a mixture of love, amusement, and ire at the man standing before her washbowl, grimacing at himself in the mirror as he vigorously scrubbed the boot blacking from his otherwise perfect white teeth. Draped over a nearby chair was a bandage that had, with the judicious application of catsup, been made to appear bloody. Propped up in a corner was a crutch that had been cast aside the moment Nell and the man had reached her small but cheerful cottage on Spring Street.

"Truly, I have never felt so deeply ashamed in my life!" Nell cried suddenly as, like a caged tigress, she paced the bedroom floor, agitatedly pulling and twisting one dark, honey-gold curl that had come loose from its pins. "To think I actually agreed to be a party to this dreadful deception . . . oh! I shall never forget the look on that poor colleen's face this afternoon . . . as though she had been hit with a hammer over the head— Red O'Rourke! How could you? Your own daughter, for heaven's sake! Reared in a convent and no more than a lamb flung to those two wolves . . . oh! May God have mercy on my soul, for Father Flanagan surely will not!''

"Whist, Nellie!'' Red O'Rourke—very much alive and well, contrary to popular belief—exclaimed with alarm. "Ye've not been blathering to the good Faather, have ye, then?''

"No, of course not.'' She sniffed indignantly, shooting him a wounded glance. "For I'd not betray you—and you know it, you red-haired devil. But faith, if I'd known beforehand what you intended, known about that accursed will that—Lord only knows how—you somehow bamboozled Patrick into drawing up . . . well . . . I'd have withheld my consent to become a part of this mad scheme of yours—and that's the God's honest truth of it, Red! 'Twas bad enough when I—when I just had to pretend to Josselyn that you were dead. But I tell you, when I saw her today, it fair broke my heart! 'Twas all I could do to keep from blurting out the truth then and there. And then when Patrick read the terms of that terrible will . . . I just wanted to die! I know that Josselyn thought I was no better than a designing hussy who'd got you in my wicked clutches and who now meant to wind up with your shares in the Rainbow's End, as well, so I could build myself a theater . . . oh! You *know* how much I've always longed for a daughter, how much I was looking forward to having Josselyn become a part of our lives, Red, and now, thanks to *you*, she'll probably never forgive me— And worse, Durango and Wylie between them will surely eat her alive, and you can be certain that vulture Victoria will be there to pick the bones, too—''

"Now, now, Nellie, me darling girl,'' he wheedled with all his dazzling charm, which was considerable, "there's no need for ye to be in such a dither. I'll put matters aright between ye and Jossie, once this is all over, I swear. And reared in a convent or nay, 'tis first and foremost an O'Rourke she is, and in the end, she'll not be forgetting it; of that, ye may be sure! Ye'll see. Once she gets her feet firmly planted on this rich Colorado soil, she'll be giving those partners of mine a run for their money, and then we'll be flushing the fox out of the thicket—or my name isn't Seamus O'Rourke!''

"Oh, Red, you saw her—''

"Saw her?" he echoed, astonished. "Why, of course I did, Nellie. Ye don't think I've been trigging meself out in these damned uncomfortable disguises for naught, do ye?'' He shook his head, frowning, at the very idea. Then his green eyes softened, and he smiled gently. "Ah, she's a pretty colleen, isn't she, Nellie? The spitting image of her dear, departed mam, Bluinse, may the saints be praised. I tell ye, my heart fair turned over in me breast when I spied her stepping down from the train. Me daughter. After all these years, me daughter. 'Twas purt' near busting me buttons with pride, I was. Why, 'twas all I could do to keep me mouth shut so I wouldn't be spoiling the jig, for I was wanting with every last bone in my body to claim her as me own flesh and blood then and there, to tell her that her old da had not forgotten her, but had met her at the depot, just as he'd always promised.''

"She loves you, Red," Nell said quietly. "She's grieving her poor heart out, thinking you're dead. Oh, Red! This is all wrong! Why did you never send for her all these years?''

He was silent for such a long time—busying himself with combing his dyed, unkempt hair and beard, and straightening his tattered clothes—that at first, Nell thought he did not mean to answer. Then, finally, sighing heavily and laying down the comb, he turned from the washstand, shaking his head sadly as he spoke.

"At the time, I thought I had plenty of good reasons, Nellie. But now, I'm thinking that maybe they weren't so good, after all, that maybe I did wrong, that I wasted all those years Jossie and I might have had together. Ah, I don't know. Life was so hard here, at first, in those early years, so crude and rough—the whole of these hills and gulches, as far as the eye could see, nothing but tents on claims, crawling with men gone crazy for gold and the whores who had come like buzzards for the pickings. I couldn't have brought Jossie here, then, so small, so lost after Bluinse died; I couldn't have looked after her proper, trying, as I was, just to keep me own head above water.

"And then as the years passed . . . well, I never told ye this before, Nellie, but I . . . I began to grow afraid. As God is my witness, I began to grow afraid that me own daughter wouldn't be able to love me or to be proud of me anymore. Whist! Maybe 'twas just plain foolishness on my part—I don't know. But . . . I hadn't seen her since I'd left her at the convent gates all those years before, and her just a seven-year-old lass at the time. Maybe she'd forgotten her old da over the years, or remembered him as being better than he truly was . . . is. I could tell as much from her letters. Ah, Nellie! Jossie's letters . . . written in such an elegant, genteel hand, they were, telling me all about her life at the convent and the things she was learning—not just religion, but history and composition, foreign languages and art—things of which I knew so little, ye see. And as the years passed, I came to realize more and more what a well-bred, educated lass she must have come to be, and I got to thinking what a poor, common working man I was, knowing little more than how to put in an honest, hard day's labor with me own two God-given hands; and in my heart, I grew afraid that . . . that Jossie, being so fine and ladylike, would be . . . well . . . ashamed of her old da.

"Ah, Nellie, me love, ye know what I am!" he burst out suddenly. "I can hold me poteen well as the next man, and me own in a brawl with the best of 'em—and 'tis proud of both I am, make no mistake. But I'm a rough diamond, and that's the God's honest truth of it. I've a tongue given more to spouting blarney and curses than refined conversation, and I've no more book learning than to sign me own name, to write a bad letter, and to figure whether a man's cheating me. I like me cigars and me whiskey, and a little flutter at the card table now and again, and I've an eye for a pretty lass, too." He smiled ruefully, laying his hand tenderly against Nell's cheek. "So tell me, then, what else could Jossie, with all her convent upbringing, think of her old da when she saw him, save that he was a rogue and a sinner— and me knowing that she was right on both counts and that I'd be the last man on God's green earth to deny it?"

"Oh, Red." Nell's heart ached for him as she covered his hand with hers. "Did you never tell Josselyn of your fears? Did you never ask her if after all her years in a convent, she could still love and be proud of her old da, sins and all?"

"Nay, Nellie, for wasn't I already knowing the answer? —or so I thought at the time! And even if she'd said yes, it wouldn't have mattered; for by then, she'd become a woman grown, and I knew that if she looked anything at all like Bluinse—who was God's own sweet angel come down from heaven to earth—every goddamned, hot-blooded buck in the territory would be after her; for sure and wasn't it with me fists that I won Bluinse for meself over every accursed miither's coxcomb in five Irish counties?"

"Well, if all that was why you never brought Josselyn out here to Central City, then I'm sorry to say, Red, that I think you did her an injustice," Nell declared firmly. "You should have given her the chance to know you better and to judge for herself whether you were a father she could not only love, but be proud of. You should have given her the chance to learn about men—under your watchful eye and mine—and not kept the poor colleen shut up in a convent, especially once you decided to draw up that awful will! Oh! How *could* you do such a thing to her, Red, your own daughter, innocent as a babe in the woods—"

"Aye, well, not so innocent as all that, Nellie—for Jossie was not so safe in the convent as I thought!" Red scowled darkly at the notion. " 'Tis knowing that I am now since I got the Reverend Mother Maire's letter all those weeks back! Bloody hell! The minx!"

"Who? The Reverend Mother?" Nell cried, scandalized.

"Good Lord, nay, Nellie! Me daughter, that's who! All those years I thought to shield her from rascals like meself, and there she was, sneaking out of the convent to carry on a romance with some jackanapes of a Frenchman! 'Tis lucky she was not to have been seduced by the blackguard! So much for all me worrying that she'd be too much of a lady to love this wild, hazardous Colorado land, that damned, crude, hard-rock mine I christened the Rainbow's End, and her rough old da and his motley pack of partners. Now, I know that for all that she might be softer and sweeter, Jossie's still an acorn that didn't fall too far from the oak. She's got her old da's good, strong, earthy Irish blood in her, and I thank God for it—even if it *did* nearly lead her down a primrose path!—for Bluinse was so delicate and frail. Though a body might be able to quote chapter and verse from every blasted book ever written, 'tis strength and determination and plain common sense that count most in this world. Jossie is now the wiser for her folly, I'll wager, and she'll not be giving her heart so easily a second time around."

"Or so foolishly, with her old da doing the choosing for her?" Nell inquired tartly. Then, anguished, she blurted, "Oh, Red! How can you say that when you know good and well that either Durango or Wylie may be a saboteur and possibly even a murderer? Good God! They may even be in cahoots *together*!"

"Nay, in all truth, Nellie, I don't know for certain any such thing—about either of them. I've only me suspicions to go on, after all, though I feel in me bones that what I believe is right. It was just too much of a coincidence, to me own way of thinking, how all those damned, queer accidents began after I mentioned to Durango, Wylie, and Forbes all three that I felt we were getting close to a mother lode— And then with Forbes's falling down the shaft into the sump . . . Well, God knows, he drank far too much and couldn't hold his liquor. But still, there's always the chance that some-body just happened to give him a shove in. Even Victoria is strong enough to have done that, and she and Wylie have always been thicker than thieves. 'Tis my belief she's always had a roving eye, even when Forbes was alive; for she was forty years younger than he was, after all. But then, there's no fool like an old fool, and Forbes always was too god-damned mule-headed to listen to anybody.''

"But—but if you're right about the accidents, about Forbes, then *why* did you have Patrick draw up that hideous will?'' Nell queried, biting her lip anxiously. '' 'Tis bound to place Josselyn in danger—''

"The devil ye say, Nellie!'' Red's voice throbbed with emotion. "Do ye honestly think that for the sake of a few gold nuggets, I'd be sending me own daughter into peril? Bite yer tongue, lass! 'Tis like a guardian angel I'll be watching over her. Neither Durango nor Wylie shall be touching a hair on her beautiful red head, or he shall be answering to me for it, by God! I reckon I'm not so old yet that I can't mop up the floor with either one of those two young Corinthians.'' He was silent for a moment. Then he continued.

"Faith, Nellie! After Jossie's last letter, I was desperate! She was going to become a nun—a *nun*, for Christ's sake! Knowing—for all her education—so little of the world, so little of *life*! And how could she, when she'd never had the chance to learn, when because of my own foolish fears, I had discouraged her from joining me in Colorado? I had to make it up to her somehow, don't ye see? The will forced her to come to Central City; the year I stipulated she have to make up her mind will compel her to stay. Once she gets her bearings and sees what the world and life have to offer, she'll not go back to the convent. She's no true vocation, or she would not have been slipping off to meet that accursed French knave!—and ye'll not be telling me otherwise, Nellie, for ye're as Catholic as I, and ye know better. 'Twas doubtless due only to her having some girlish notion of suffering a broken heart at that bastard's hands that made her get it into her head to take her final vows in the first place—else why was I not hearing of it until her last letter, and her giving me no good reason for it, either, not knowing that the Reverend

Mother Maire had already written me the truth? Eh? Answer me that, then, Nellie!''

"Well, perhaps you are right," she agreed finally. "But even so, I cannot like how you have further knotted this already-tangled skein of yours. What if Josselyn actually winds up *marrying* Durango or Wylie, for God's sake?"

"Why, before that happens, the banns'll have to be published, and then 'tis rising from the grave I'll be, Nellie, me love, and learning whether 'tis me daughter or me shares in the Rainbow's End that the rascal is wanting so badly. Ye see, me darling girl, the wording of the will was but a ruse to lure whoever is the cheat at the card table into tipping his—or even her—hand; for I've raised the stakes now, don't ye see?—made Jossie a wild card in the deck, one who can cause the balance of power to shift in any number of ways, depending upon who's what and which way the wind blows. But don't ye fret about me daughter, Nellie. Naught will happen to her. Jossie's me own flesh and blood, after all, and I love her. I'd never do anything I thought would harm her; ye know that. She'll be safer here than she was in the convent; for at least, 'tis knowing those two scamps, Durango and Wylie, I am, and able to deal with their like. Sure and I'm as canny an Irishman as what ever sailed from the old sod. Don't ye see? Under the terms of my will, Jossie's worth nothing as far as the gold mine goes unless she stays alive to be wedded and bedded—which will mean posting the banns, as I've already reminded ye, so 'tis not as though she shall be dragged away without any warning, Nellie, me love, and coerced into marriage. Neither Durango nor Wylie will be so foolish as to compromise Jossie, not knowing her and whether she might return to the convent or set the law on him afterward rather than wed him. So any tying of the knot will need to be done legally; and even if Durango or Wylie were somehow to succeed in marrying her, well, why would a man be killing his own beautiful wife, when her shares in the Rainbow's End had already become his on their wedding day?

"Besides, mark my words: She'll not be making up her mind anytime soon about marrying either Durango or Wylie, because she's already been burned once. Right now, she's doubtless like a pet bird who's suddenly discovered that the cage door's been left wide open. She'll be needing to spread her wings and to give them a try; and all the while, I'll wager, she'll be leading Durango and Wylie both a merry chase, with each of them trying to best the other—and both of them, to say nothing of Victoria, fit to be tied! Ah, Nellie, 'twill be a sight for sore eyes!'' Red laughed uproariously at the prospect. Then, after a moment, sobering, he went on.

"And if the right man of the two *does* happen to take Jossie's fancy, why, then, that's not such a bad thing, is it? A headstrong filly needs an even stronger rider in the saddle, and if there's weakness in either Durango or Wylie, ye may be sure 'tis not that sort! At least, she'll not be wasting her life in a convent—and glad I'll be of it, in truth, though 'tis as God-fearing as any Irishman I am, with nothing but the utmost respect for the good Sisters of the Church.''

"Well, at the very least, it is certainly a novel way of procuring Josselyn a husband, I'll say that, Red.'' Despite his reassurances, Nell's face remained troubled. "I know how hard this must be for you, my dearest darling. I know that you looked upon Durango and even Wylie as the sons you never had. To think that one, or even both, of them has turned against you, has stooped to sabotage and maybe even to murder— Well, 'tis just too hard, too painful to imagine!'' She paused, shaking her head at the thought of how good men sometimes went so bad. Then she continued.

"I don't know which one you suspect the most, which one you feel in your heart is innocent, which one you would wish, if the situation were different, that Josselyn would choose. But I'm sorry to say that if you hoped she and Wylie would make a match of it, you forgot to consider one small but important detail: Wylie's not a Catholic, and for that reason alone, even if she falls in love with him, Josselyn won't marry him. However, if you thought that Durango's faith would deal him a winning hand, I must warn you that I would not bank on that, either, he having long ago fallen from grace. . . .''

"Aye, well, with me daughter being worth her weight in gold—in more ways than one, thanks to me will—if they're even half the men I think they are, they'll both be hying themselves down the hill to Pine Street soon enough, Wylie to see Faather Flanagan about being instructed in the catechism, and Durango to rejoin the fold," Red uttered dryly. Then he asked briskly, "So, tell me: *Was* it Wylie, then, that Jossie looked on most kindly in Patrick's office this afternoon? Or Durango?" Grinning as he saw Nell's lashes sweep down to veil her golden eyes, he tipped her face up to his and brushed her mouth with his own. "Ah, Nellie," he sighed, " 'tis knowing ye too well I am for ye to cozen me with a lie, and ye know it. Confess. *'Twas* Wylie who won her favor, was it not?"

"I can't deny it," she admitted reluctantly, knowing that Durango had always been Red's favorite of the two, "but, good heavens, Red, if you'd seen how Durango acted today, even you would have been appalled. His behavior would have tried the patience of a saint! Frankly, I'm surprised he and Wylie didn't come to blows!"

"Mad enough to spit nails about my will was Durango, then? And Wylie with a bee in his bowler hat, as well?" Red's green eyes danced with malicious mirth at the notion.

"Yes to both questions."

"Splendid! Why, we may see them each at the other's throat even sooner than I'd hoped, and then we'll be learning what's what! Now, ye're certain, Nellie, that neither Durango nor Wylie—nor Victoria, for that matter—has any inkling that 'twas I who blasted the Rainbow's End and sealed off the stopes so the mother lode—if 'tis there, as I feel in me bones that it is—will be safe until we can discover the truth of this entire sorry affair?"

"Not so far as any of them have let on," she reported, "and why should they? As far as they know, you're buried under a heap of rubble, an unfortunate victim of an unknown saboteur's handiwork.''

"Aye, well, what they all know and what they let on are two different matters entirely, for they're a pack of young wolves on the prowl, and Durango, even more than Wylie, is nobody's fool. He tossed me that quarter so he could look me over sharp today, when I flaunted meself right under their noses to see if any of them would prove clever enough to sniff out the scent! Still, we'll assume for the moment that ye're right.'' Red rubbed his hands together with gleeful anticipation. "That means that trigged out in me disguises, I'll be free to move about, spying upon them all, just as we originally planned. Ah, today, we gave an old, dead log a swift, hard kick, Nellie, me love! Now, we've naught to do but to sit back and wait—to see what comes crawling out from the rot! So, let us think of some pleasant way to pass the time while we're waiting. What do ye say, me darling girl? Be a good lass and give me a kiss, then, hmh? Everything will turn out all right in the end, I promise.''

"I hope so, Red. Truly, I do,'' she replied with heartfelt sincerity. Then, sighing forlornly, she said, "But still, I can't help remembering what Robert Burns wrote in 'To a Mouse.' ''

"And what was that, Nellie, me love?''

"That 'the best laid schemes o' mice and men / Gang aft a-gley.' ''

Chapter Five

For the next several days following that dreadful afternoon in Killian's office, Josselyn kept to the boardinghouse on Roworth Street, so apprehensive about what might next unexpectedly befall her that she was afraid to leave its pleasantly secure confines. She whiled away the hours by becoming better acquainted with Miss Hattie, Zeb, and the other boarders; gazing out her window at the bustling streets below, trying to get her bearings, now and then catching an occasional, unsettling glimpse of either Wylie Gresham or Durango de Navarre; thinking hard about Da's disturbing will and her own future, whether she was intended by God as a nun or a wife; reading her Bible and praying, and writing at length to the Reverend Mother Maire, explaining all that had happened and begging for her advice. In the end, however, it was this last that finally forced Josselyn to venture from

Miss Hattie's cottage, at least as far as the corner of Eureka and Pine Streets, where the post office was located; for without a stamp, she could not mail the letter.

As she was coming out of the post office, she literally bumped into Wylie Gresham. Fumbling to put her change away in her reticule, which she had untied from the cestus at her waist, Josselyn did not see him entering the building, and she crashed into him, losing hold of her bag and spilling its contents and coins all over the floor.

"Oh, no!" she cried, dropping to her hands and knees as she scrambled frantically to retrieve the money, knowing how carefully she must hoard it, lest she become destitute; for Killian had warned her that until the Rainbow's End was once more operable—which might be months from now—she could expect little, if any, income from the gold mine.

"I'm terribly sorry, ma'am," Gresham said as he knelt gallantly to assist her. "It was my fault entirely— Why, Miss O'Rourke. What a pleasant surprise." He swept off his bowler hat, looking so incongruous kneeling there, with his derby pressed against his chest, that despite herself, she could not help but smile, unexpectedly delighted to see him again and thinking he was not just her best, but her only choice as a friend and an ally in the battle for the Rainbow's End, though she had not yet made up her mind just what to do in the matter.

"Oh, Mr. Gresham—"

"Wylie, please, ma'am," he insisted, his grey eyes twinkling. "Mr. Gresham sounds so formal. Besides, all my friends call me Wylie, and I do so hope we are going to be friends, despite that distinctly awkward will your father saw fit to leave. Doubtless, it was his idea of a joke on us all," he observed, his lighthearted tone taking any sting from his words. "Red did so enjoy a good laugh."

"Yes, yes, he did," Josselyn agreed, her heart aching at the remembrance. "His letters were always full of jokes and descriptions of funny things: people he knew and incidents that happened here in Central City. . . ." Her voice trailed away, choked with tears.

"You miss him very much, don't you?" Wylie's voice was kind as he pretended not to notice how her eyes suddenly brimmed over and how she groped in the pocket of her habit for her handkerchief.

"Yes, I-I do . . . that is, I miss his letters. I hadn't actually seen Da since I entered the convent and he left for Colorado. I kept hoping to—to join him here someday, in Central City. But somehow, it just never seemed to—to work out, and now, it's . . . too late—" She broke off abruptly, turning her head away until she could master her emotions, while Wylie remained respectfully silent.

Then, after a moment, glancing around at the floor, he spoke again, briskly.

"Well, I think we've found just about everything." He handed her her reticule and helped her to her feet. "No other harm done, I hope?" he inquired as she brushed herself off.

"No, none." Josselyn shook her head as she firmly retied the bag to the cestus at her waist.

"You know, Miss O'Rourke—"

"Josselyn. Please. It seems only fair if I'm to call you Wylie, and, well, until I met Mr. Killian—Patrick—nobody called me Miss O'Rourke. To tell you the truth, it sounds so strange that I—that I hardly recognize when someone is addressing me."

"All right, then . . . Josselyn." Wylie smiled at her engagingly as he shoved the envelopes he held in his hand into the nearby mail slot and escorted her outside, walking her down Eureka Street, finally drawing to a halt just across from his mercantile. "What I was about to say is this: I know from painful experience just how difficult losing a loved one can be. Perhaps you know that I lost my whole family during the War Between the States?"

"Yes, Da mentioned that in one of his letters to me."

"Yes, well, I was . . . only seventeen at the time, so, as

you can imagine, it was a . . . very hard blow to me. At any rate, what I'm trying to say is this: Sometimes, it helps to share your grief with another person. So, if ever you find you'd like to talk to someone about Red, I'd be honored to listen and happy to tell you anything I can about him.''

"Why, that's so kind of you, Wylie," Josselyn declared, touched, "and there *is* a great deal I'd like to know about— about Da . . . how he lived, where he went, what he liked to do— He spoke so little, really, about himself in his letters.''

"I know that it won't be the same as if I were your father, but I'd be pleased to show you Central City and the surrounding towns, as Red knew them, Josselyn, and to answer all your questions about him. Would tomorrow be too soon? How would noon suit you? I'll pick you up at Miss Hattie's boardinghouse. We can have lunch at John Best's soda fountain in the pharmacy and become better acquainted. Then I'll drive you on a guided tour of the region.''

"Why, that—that sounds wonderful, Wylie." She blushed shyly with pleasure, her gaze modestly downcast, her heart beating fast. "I'll—I'll look forward to seeing you then.''

"As shall I you.''

Feeling even more flustered as his eyes regarded her warmly, Josselyn hurried away, as giddy and nervous as a schoolgirl at the realization that Wylie Gresham was actually going to call on her, to take her out in his buggy. Surely, it was a sin, she thought, uncomfortably reminded of Antoine, for her to be feeling as she did at this moment—and so soon after Da's death, too! Still, her feet seemed to have wings as she fairly flew down Eureka Street.

Lost in reverie, she was unaware of the grizzled prospector who, some distance behind her, unobtrusively dogged her footsteps or of the tall, dark man who had just glimpsed her and Wylie's passing figures from the door of the Mother Lode saloon, along what was commonly referred to as "Gamblers Row," and who had sauntered down to the corner to spy on them. But both Red O'Rourke and Durango de Navarre were keenly conscious of the young woman in the novice's habit, now parting from Wylie.

As he studied his daughter, Red had all he could do to keep from laughing out loud, for he had just witnessed Wylie's opening move at the post office—not at all the chance meeting Josselyn had believed that it was. In fact, too shrewd and smooth to attempt to approach her directly, correctly deducing that she would only rebuff him, Wylie had, for the past several days, been glued to the front windows of his mercantile, opera glasses in hand as he'd searched the streets of Central City for some sign of her. Upon observing Josselyn heading toward the post office, he had hurriedly grabbed a stack of mail off his store counter, then had stridden from the mercantile, just in time to intercept her neatly as she was exiting from the post office.

Poor Jossie, Red thought now, shaking his head and sighing. Despite all his hopes that she had learned something from her encounter with that unscrupulous Frenchman, it now seemed that perhaps Nell was right. His daughter might well be a babe in the woods, too innocent and trusting even to suspect that her stumbling into Wylie at the post office had been cleverly contrived. Good thing, Red mused, that he was watching out for her as she spread her wings and attempted to fly.

From the doorframe in which he had temporarily taken refuge, lest his daughter see him, he continued to observe her as she made her way down the street. His eyes narrowed slightly with speculation when he caught sight of Durango swaggering up to the corner just beyond the Mother Lode, his own gaze riveted on Josselyn's slender form.

Even more than Wylie, Durango made Red nervous, for while the crafty logic of Wylie's mind was easy for Red to follow, that of Durango's was not. Wylie was sharp; no denying that. But Wylie was also inclined to believe himself smarter than everyone else, so he was prone not to see the forest for the trees. Durango was, Red had always believed, even more intelligent and cunning—and more dangerous, too, because he was so unpredictable. He played his cards as close to his chest as a man was able, never underestimated his opponent, and, when necessary, ran an exceedingly cool bluff.

With frequently maddening amusement, he would bear Wylie's ridicule but would shoot another man over the very same insults—and not always in a particularly gentlemanly fashion. Red recalled one incident in the early years, when he, Forbes, Durango, and Wylie had surprised a smart-mouthed, would-be claim jumper at their gold mine. Incensed, Forbes and Wylie had been all for hanging the man. But before this act could be carried out, Durango had simply grabbed the nearest shotgun, sprayed the claim jumper's hind end full of buckshot, and booted him off the Rainbow's End. Even now, Red still grinned when he remembered how the man had rolled head over heels down the mountainside, howling indignantly at every bump and burr along the way. He had landed in the gulch at the bottom, scrambled to his feet, and hobbled off fast as he was able, clutching his painful posterior.

"Just as I suspected," Durango had drawled insolently as they had all watched the claim jumper skedaddle. "For all his big talk, the man had no gumption at all. No sense in us wasting an expensive piece of good rope on him."

A man couldn't hardly argue with reasoning like that, Red had thought wryly at the time.

So, now, despite all the reassurances to the contrary he had given Nell, Red was forced to admit to himself that he was not quite so certain about how his scheme would turn out. For if Josselyn were the wild card in the deck he had shuffled and dealt, he felt that Durango was surely the cheat, fully capable of holding an ace or two up his sleeve.

Following that afternoon in Killian's office, Durango had returned to the Mother Lode, and there, he had steadfastly remained ever since, drinking, gambling, and whoring as though nothing out of the ordinary had occurred—although he *had* flung himself with a strange vengeance into his usual activities, like a man trying to forget all his cares. Unlike Wylie, Durango had apparently spent no time at all looking out of his saloon's front windows, in search of Josselyn. That he had been outside of the Mother Lode when she and Wylie had paused on the corner was pure chance; Durango had been throwing an inebriated miner off the saloon's premises.

Still, Red had been pleased to note that after seeing Josselyn and Wylie, Durango had not returned to the Mother Lode, but, in fact, had started up the street toward the corner, where he now lingered, contemplating her retreating figure.

It was, Durango realized, the first time he had seen her since that afternoon in Killian's office. Idly, he wondered where she had been keeping herself. Then he reflected uncharitably that she had no doubt been in a chapel—praying for God to deliver her from the predicament in which her father's preposterous will had landed her.

What on earth could Red possibly have been thinking of, Durango wondered, leaving behind such an absurd document? Only two answers occurred to him: first, that Red had sincerely believed that his daughter would be wasted as a nun and had set about in this unorthodox fashion to acquire her a husband; or second, that Red had deliberately intended to set his three partners, Durango and Wylie, particularly, at one another's throats, a falling out among thieves, as it were. Red had been wild as any man Durango had ever known. But still, there had always been a method, however convoluted, to his madness; so if the second theory held true, then he was definitely up to something—which meant, in all likelihood, that he was not dead, as everyone believed. And *that* notion, Durango mused, opened up all sorts of interesting possibilities. For if that *were* the case, it could only mean Red was the saboteur, perhaps even had killed Forbes, and must somehow hope to get his hands on the whole of the Rainbow's End. Durango found it difficult to believe all this of Red. Still, doubt plagued him. Gold had a way of turning good men wrong, and Red had been certain they were on the verge of hitting a mother lode at the Rainbow's End. It was

entirely possible he had set the explosions that had sealed off
the stopes in the gold mine and staged his own death so he
could continue behind the scenes whatever dirty work he had
planned. If so, Miss Josselyn O'Rourke was either hand in
glove with her father and the best actress Durango had ever
seen, on stage or off, or she was an unwitting tool in whatever
underhanded plot Red had dreamed up.

Either way, it would certainly behoove him, Durango decided, his black eyes narrowing, to become much better acquainted with her. For all he knew, she no more had been
reared in a convent than he; they, all of them, even Patrick,
had only Red's word and hers for it, after all. In reality, Miss
Josselyn O'Rourke might just as easily have spent the past
years in a Boston opera house—or even a bordello! Durango
thought derisively. He could have sworn her performance in
Killian's office had been genuine; but now, he began to wonder if it hadn't been just a shade too incredible to be believed.
Those thick black lashes with which she had demurely shuttered her eyes had also served quite effectively to hide whatever thoughts had been chasing through her mind at the
reading of the will—just as her veil and her habit had totally
concealed every part of her but her face. He did not, Durango
realized suddenly, even know the color of Josselyn's hair. If
she were to venture abroad in street clothes, it was possible
he wouldn't even recognize her. Why, she could actually be
spying on him, Wylie, and Victoria—and none of them would
be the wiser!

That idea made Durango recall abruptly the beggar who
had approached Josselyn outside of Killian's office that day
of the reading of the will. There had been something distinctly
odd about that whole episode—even at the time, Durango
had thought so—especially when Nell had almost forcibly
hauled the tramp away. Durango had flipped the bum a
quarter, just to get a better look at him. Something about the
man had nagged at him. Now, as Durango slowly replayed
the incident in his mind, he was struck by a notion so ex-
traordinary that if not for everything else, he would instantly

have dismissed it as too ludicrous to be believed. Under the circumstances, however, he felt that his idea definitely bore closer scrutiny; and this could only be accomplished by his ingratiating himself with Josselyn, who might, in truth, be no nun at all, but a deceitful witch. If Red proved to be alive and his daughter his confederate, Durango would certainly give her enough rope and time to hang herself.

But what if she were innocent, Red alive but she herself his ignorant dupe, or he truly dead and she at the mercy of his execrable will? Ah, therein lay the worm at the core of the apple, the Ouroborus that had turned and gnawed inside him ever since Victoria's incendiary words to him that day outside of Killian's office. Again and again, it had fed on itself, coming full cycle, only to spawn viciously anew. Even aside from Red's shares in the Rainbow's End, if Josselyn were indeed a nun, how could he, Durango, permit her to fall victim to Wylie, particularly after what Victoria had said? Red's daughter, the nun, in Wylie's clutches, in Wylie's *bed*, for Christ's sake!—the same bed he shared with Victoria. A complete waste of time to think that Wylie would be faithful to Victoria; fidelity did not number among his own virtues, any more than it did hers. Yet what could Durango do? He was damned if he did, damned if he did not! If he asked Josselyn to marry him, if he cautioned her against Wylie, she would surely believe that it was only because he, Durango, was after her inheritance, and she would not only refuse his proposal, but disregard his warning; and if she did not, if she accepted him as her husband and Red were still alive and she his accomplice, then he, Durango, would surely be next in line to suffer a fatal accident at the gold mine. His own shares in the Rainbow's End would go to Josselyn, thus effectively giving Red a one-half interest against the quarter shares Wylie and Victoria held—for was blood not thicker than water?

Regardless—however the deck was stacked—the cards had been shuffled and dealt, and the stakes had been set for what certainly promised to be one hell of a game, Durango reflected grimly. Then he sourly decided that since it appeared from the look of things that Wylie had just anted up, he himself had better toss his own chips into the pot if he wished to sit down at the table to play the opening hand. With that both treacherous and seductive thought in mind, he strode purposefully down Eureka Street, after Josselyn.

Chapter Six

"Why don't you go inside—and try it on for size?" Durango's voice was low in Josselyn's ear, startling her as she stood on the boardwalk, staring through a dress-shop window at what was surely the most gorgeous gown she had ever seen in her life.

"Mr. de Navarre!" One hand fluttered nervously to her throat, as though she feared he were an animal who would rip out her jugular vein. "What a fright you gave me for a moment. I—I didn't see you approach."

"All my friends—and even my enemies—call me Durango, Sister," he drawled, his black eyes gleaming speculatively as he surveyed her, a half smile curving his lips, "and no, you didn't notice me. In fact, you were so engrossed in examining that dress that for a while there, I thought that maybe your feet had put down roots in the boardwalk! But still, it was not my intent to alarm you, and for that, I do apologize.''

He turned to inspect the outfit that had caught her attention, observing with a practiced eye that it was an excellent copy of what had doubtless been a Worth original. Of green silk shot through with fine gold threads, it had huge, beautifully ruffled and puffed, off-the-shoulder sleeves drawn up with ornate bows twined by French knots at their centers, and a wide, scalloped border of delicate, bud-and-vine-patterned lace dipping down to a daring, heart-shaped décolletage whose point ended somewhere below the breastbone; in exquisite contrast, the rest of the gown was severely tailored, a tightly fitted basque and waist sweeping down to a narrow, bell-shaped skirt. There were green lace gauntlet gloves, a reticule, and morocco slippers to match. For a moment, he tried to picture a nun wearing such a recherché ensemble, could not, and gave it up. But then he remembered Red's description of his deceased wife and distant cousin, Bluinse. A ''red-haired, green-eyed, white Celtic witch,'' Red had called her; and suddenly, stealing into Durango's mind, there rose a like image of Josselyn, clothed in the green frock, her red hair—of course, it must be red; what else?—a mass of artfully arrayed, tumbling curls, her slanted green eyes—yes, they *were* green, green as the silk of the dress—smoldering and mysterious, her smooth white shoulders and full, upthrusting breasts rising from that sinfully delicious bodice, like foam from the sea. He inhaled sharply.

As Judas was tempted by silver, so a nun may be tempted by gold . . . Victoria's scornful words echoed in his ears, mocking him.

''It looks to be a perfect fit. Why don't you go inside—and try it on for size,'' he suggested again to Josselyn, wanting abruptly to know what lay beneath her veil, her habit.

''No, I . . . I can't.'' She shook her head regretfully. ''I'm a nun . . . almost. It—it wasn't meant for someone like me, and even if it were, I'm afraid the price would prove too dear.''

In more ways than one, perhaps, Durango thought, but did not speak the words aloud. Instead, he asked casually, "Am I to assume from all that that you have decided to relinquish your claim to your inheritance and return to your convent in Boston, then?"

At that, a confused but wary look came into her eyes, putting him suddenly on his own guard, his body inwardly tensing. Maybe she was a lost lamb, but her instincts were all in the right place, those eyes telling him that she scented a wolf—or was she one herself, in sheep's clothing? He glanced again at the gown in the window. Had she, in a moment of curiosity, stopped to yearn, to dream, to envision herself as other than what she was—or had she paused to remind herself of the sort of expensive folderols she would be buying once she and her father had got hold of the Rainbow's End, unearthed the mother lode Red had been sure lay at the gold mine's heart?

"No, I—I haven't yet made up my mind about going back to Boston, to the convent," she answered, her lashes sweeping down to conceal her thoughts from Durango, her cheeks staining with color, like scarlet roses against her lily-white skin soft and delicate-looking as petals. Her rosebud mouth parted, its lush lower lip seeming to tremble, a flower attracting the sting of his beelining gaze. He had not really paid close attention to her before, Red's will having hit him like a ton of ore, knocking him senseless, maddening him. But he looked at her now, and despite her habit, what roiled in his brain was not chaste. "Such a step as this . . . changing the course of my life . . . I dare not take it lightly," she said.

No, tread carefully, very carefully, sweet angel-witch, for I have not yet made up my mind about you, either. A mouth like that doesn't belong on a nun, kissing a rosary instead of a man. If I'd had a daughter like you, I'd have kept her shut up in a convent, too. Red, you devil!—waiting all these years to spring her on me and Wylie . . . and then leaving us to wonder if she is a prize or a snare. Worth her weight in gold, regardless . . . the gold at the Rainbow's End. . . .

"You have a year," Durango noted.

"Yes"—breathlessly.

The way he was staring at her made Josselyn feel distinctly uneasy. Antoine had looked at her like that, twin flames flickering in his dark eyes. She had not felt so threatened by Wylie. Wylie, she thought, was a gentleman; if he possessed base desires, he at least troubled to hide them. Durango made no such effort, had no compunctions about his. From the insolent rake of his eyes to the provocative thrust of his stance, he was blatantly all male, virile, sexual, a brute, a beast, a panther stalking her, batting her between his paws, licking his chops anticipatorily. She shivered with a mixture of fright and perverse excitement at the notion, not enjoying the prey-like feeling he aroused in her, but helplessly thrilled by the adrenaline that rushed through her body. A man who had not scrupled to shove Forbes Houghton down a rocky shaft or to blast her father away was not about to permit a green girl, a naive nun, to stand between him and a gold mine. Yet somehow, she must, Josselyn thought; she owed it to Da.

Taking her final vows would have to wait—at least, for a while; the convent would still be there, in Boston, a year from now, if that was how long it took to expose this black-guard. And perhaps, in the end, she would marry Wylie, after all, and never go back; for in truth, she knew in her heart that she had no real vocation, and she could not bear the thought of Nell Tierney's building a theater with Da's shares in the Rainbow's End, as the conniving actress must surely hope to do. Still, it was deeply comforting to know that the convent was there, waiting, a refuge if Josselyn ever needed it. Meanwhile, her habit alone would have to suffice for protection. Reluctantly, she compelled herself to turn away from the entrancing gown in the dress-shop window, the costume that, from its defiant décolletage to its gauntlet gloves, issued a bold invitation.

"I must go now." Somehow, the untruth rolled smoothly off her tongue—a sin to tell a lie. Guilt at the knowledge caused her face to flush, her eyes to lower, betraying her.

For the first time in years, her days were without structure; she was completely free to do as she pleased—and yet wholly at loose ends, bewildered and lost without the dulcet ringing of the convent angelus to guide her. Without order, there must inevitably be chaos; had not the Reverend Mother Maire told her so time and again? Like an abyss, that chaos seemed to yawn before her, dark and perilous; one false step and she would fall, would tumble into its fathomless, churning depths. There had been safety in dull routine; she knew that now, when it lay a thousand miles beyond her reach. "Good afternoon, Mr. de Navarre," Josselyn stated, in a voice cool as Victoria Stanhope Houghton's, though, despite herself, a tremulous note underlay her tone.

Remembering the shy smile she had bestowed upon Wylie, Durango wanted abruptly to seize her and slap some sense into her, to growl at her that whether she was a saint or a sinner, she would be better off casting her lot in with him than with Wylie, beneath whose deceptively fine manner and fashionable attire lurked a man cold as ice, fickle, and jaded. A nun might prove a new twist, but the novelty would soon wear off; a trollop would hold his interest not at all, for why exchange one for another? Still, his hands clenched by his sides, Durango told himself angrily that it was not his responsibility to look after Red's daughter, that Red had had no damned business making her a stake in this game and should have known better. If not for Red's bequest to her, Durango himself would not have given her more than a passing glance. He liked his bachelor life, but it piqued him that she would prefer Wylie. Despite himself, Durango had hoped she was better than that.

He wondered if he should tell Wylie he half suspected that Red was actually still alive. Then, at last, shrugging, Durango pragmatically decided against it. Wylie would only think he was lying, trying to cut him out of the running with Josselyn and thereby do him out of Red's shares. Besides, Wylie was a big boy; he could look out for himself. If his trifling with Red's daughter brought Red crawling out from under some rock to kill him, well, that would be one fewer partner to worry about in the gold mine, one fewer partner with whom to divvy up the spoils. Life was hard; a man who was smart took what he could get, however he could get it—and Durango had never been stupid.

"Good afternoon, Sister." Like a lightly wielded whip, his voice flicked her, a goad driving her toward something she instinctively feared—and worried that might in the end prove inescapable as fate.

Josselyn shuddered at the thought. It took every ounce of willpower she possessed to turn her back on Durango, to walk rather than to run away from him, sensing, as though it were a tangible thing creeping up from behind to grab her about the throat, how he stood there, staring after her until long after she had disappeared from his sight.

She ought not, Josselyn reprimanded herself sternly, be enjoying Wylie's company so. So long as she continued to cling to her habit, to hold herself out as destined to become a bride of Christ—not of any man—she should behave accordingly, she thought guiltily. But still, it was difficult to remember that in Wylie's presence. He was so handsome and debonair that she found it hard not to be attracted to him. Indeed, with each passing day, it seemed more and more that feelings Antoine had first stirred to life were now burgeoning inside her, yearnings too long suppressed. They were wild urges she believed were wanton and thus wicked; they were treasured dreams she had only so lately, and painfully, concluded she must tuck away forever but that now, the hope chest of her heart once more unlocked and opened, she dared to lift out and shake loose and examine lovingly, longingly. A home of her own. A husband. Children. All of the things a nun renounced to devote herself to the serving of God and the doing of His will and His work. When such things had looked bleakly far beyond Josselyn's grasp, so cruelly snatched away from her and trampled upon by Antoine, the sacrifice had not appeared so great. But now that they seemed tantalizingly within her reach, Josselyn knew how much she wanted them. But the price was Da's shares in the Rainbow's End. Was it too high? In some corner of her mind, she had begun to think not.

For the past several weeks, Wylie had called for her at the boardinghouse nearly every other day. They had breakfasted at Miss Hattie's. They had lunched at Englishman John Best's soda fountain in the pharmacy. They had dined at the Teller House, one of the most elegant hotels between Chicago and San Francisco, despite the fact that before its grand opening in 1872, its site, Central City, had boasted only one hotel that had even offered mattresses; the rest of the town's hotels had had nothing but "hay beds." World renowned, the Teller House was the hub of all business and social activity in the region: Central City's high society, Colorado's elite, the nation's prominent men and women . . . hardly a day passed that the hotel's register did not exhibit the signatures of personages from all over the world. Even President Ulysses S. Grant had twice stayed there, once walking across thousands of dollars' worth of solid-silver ingots that, in his honor, had been laid from the stagecoach to the hotel steps, gold's being considered too common in the area to do him justice. Wylie had told Josselyn about it—among other things, the most flattering of which had been that she was more beautiful in her novice's habit ornamented by only her plain wooden cross than all of the Worth-frocked, jewel-bedecked ladies in the lobby. How that compliment had warmed her heart, even as she had gazed yearningly at those gowns and gems, and wistfully imagined herself in them.

In his stylish buggy drawn by a pair of sleek, matched greys, Wylie had shown Josselyn Central City, pointing out one building after another, as well as where the new Central City depot would be located, and Tom Pollock's old livery stable site, where the first opera house in all of Colorado was shortly to be erected, a rich complement to the Teller House.

Wylie had also taken her down to Black Hawk and up to Nevadaville. During their tours, he had proved, to Josselyn's delight, both an informative and entertaining raconteur, educating her about the history of the gold-mining towns, amusing her with anecdotes about the early years, when he, Durango, Forbes, and her father had groveled in the muck for the gold that would drag them out of the mire.

"There's an interesting residence," he had remarked during one of their outings, pointing to a Gothic cottage just off Country Road, "Sheriff Billy Cozen's house. You know, there's an old story about how one night, before Gilpin County had a jail, the sheriff took two prisoners home with him, so they wouldn't escape, and chained 'em to his bedpost for safekeeping—although his wife was sick in bed at the time!"

"Oh, Wylie," Josselyn had said, smiling, "you're joking!"

"Not at all," he had insisted. Then, looking at her in a way that had made her heart beat fast and her eyes glance down shyly at her hands folded sedately in her lap, he had continued. "In fact, another legend has it that it was actually the sheriff's wedding night." He had paused for a meaningful moment. Then, persuaded by the confusion on her face that he was making progress in the right direction, Wylie had clucked to the horses and driven on.

There was one place, however, that he had adamantly refused, however politely and pleasantly, to take her—the Rainbow's End. Like many gold mines, it was a crude, dangerous site, he had declared, worked by a crew of rough, hard men, and no fit place for a lady. Josselyn had understood, but still, she remained extremely disappointed. She very much wanted to see the Rainbow's End, the gold mine that had, in more ways than one, taken her father from her. If she were to discover the identity of Da's murderer, it was important that she learn all she could about the Rainbow's End and everyone connected with it. After all, in reality, she had nothing more to go on than Da's suspicions that one of his partners was a saboteur and a killer. Her father might have been mistaken in his beliefs. It was possible that someone else at the gold mine was the real culprit—although Josselyn still clung tenaciously to her conviction that Durango de Navarre, doubtless aided by Victoria Stanhope Houghton, was to blame; for if ever there were a sinner, it was he. How could Da ever even have suspected a fine, decent, upstanding gentleman such as Wylie of being the malefactor!

Central City was not a large town. She and Wylie had, on two occasions, run into Durango, once at the Teller House, where he had come swaggering out of the Elevator Bar, a cigar in his mouth, a bottle in one hand, and a ravishing woman on each arm; and again at the livery stable, where he had been putting away his high-spirited black stallion, which, Wylie had informed Josselyn dryly, bore the unholy Spanish name of *Diablo*—Devil.

"Perhaps not quite so appropriate a handle as Barnum and Bailey, Wylie," Durango had drawled mockingly, grinning at Wylie's prized greys. "But then, I ain't a circus barker, either." He had sneered, deliberately ridiculing Wylie's selling of wares, making it sound as though he duped his customers. "I'm just one hell of a good gambler—especially when it comes to Mexican Sweat; or has it been so long since we've played that game, Wylie, that you've forgotten just how good I am? In that case, perhaps you're overdue a reminder, and since you appear to be so goddamned hell-bent on raising me, I reckon I'm just gonna be forced to up my bet so I can see my cards—and the rest of yours, too!"

Josselyn had not understood these veiled gibes, although she had guessed the gist when, after that day, Durango himself had started calling on her, refusing so determinedly to be fobbed off that she had not known how to dissuade him from coming. Despite her own ambivalent emotions about seeing him, she was aware she must allow herself to get to know him better; for how was she to unmask the man she believed was Da's murderer if she balked at having anything to do with him? She would serve her own ends far better by trying to lull Durango into a false sense of complacency, she had finally decided, in the hope that he would sooner or later make some misstep that would prove his undoing. But still, every time he showed up at Miss Hattie's boardinghouse, it was all that Josselyn could do to grit her teeth and compel herself to suffer his attentions. He was no gentleman; that much was clear.

His courtship—if such it was—was markedly different from Wylie's, for Durango's behavior frequently exceeded the bounds of propriety, being both insolent and provoking. He seldom spared Josselyn's sensibilities, but spoke to her most improperly, taking maddening satisfaction in her blushes, mocking amusement in her anger. He held her hand far longer than was necessary in assisting her in and out of his buggy, and frequently outraged her by surveying her in a brazen, thoroughly reprehensible way. Indeed, although she knew that only by marrying her could he acquire her father's shares in the Rainbow's End, Durango seemed, to her great puzzlement, perversely not to care about winning her favor, to be, in fact, decidedly bent on losing it. More than once, Josselyn gave him an indignant set-down; but instead of putting an end to his misbehavior, her remarks challenged him, and he continued to try to destroy her composure.

Intensifying her deep frustration was the fact that despite all the time she spent with both Durango and Wylie, she felt no closer now to exposing Da's killer than she had been upon her arrival in Central City nearly three months ago. Now, Josselyn thought again that if she were going to unearth anything at all about the saboteur and murderer, she must make it her business to learn all she could about the Rainbow's End and the process of mining gold. Her taking an interest in the actual gold mine itself she hoped would unsettle the culprit responsible for blowing it up; and since Wylie would not escort her there, she had reluctantly resolved that she must beard the mountain lion—Durango—in his den and insist that he accompany her. She did not like to turn to him; the thought of venturing alone up into the hills with him riddled her with anxiety. But whom else could she ask to take her? The odds of Victoria's consenting to do so were remote; she had rarely set foot on the Rainbow's End even when Forbes was alive and had, significantly, not done so at all since his death. Further, the widow knew next to nothing about hard-rock mining and so would be useless as either a guide or an informant. No, there was no alternative to Durango. He might be insulting and infuriating, but he wasn't dumb; and since he wasn't a gentleman, either, he would not scruple to squire Josselyn up to the gold mine that Wylie had labeled ''no fit place for a lady.''

So, at last, one cool but otherwise fine spring afternoon, her mind made up, her courage screwed up, she determinedly set forth from the boardinghouse toward Gamblers Row and the Mother Lode, in search of Durango. She would not wait for one of his unscheduled visits, but would approach him this very afternoon about taking her up to the Rainbow's End, she vowed, lest she lose her nerve utterly. She reached the saloon, fully prepared to march boldly inside. But as the sound of the revelry within—shouts, laughter, and the lively but jarring notes that issued from a badly tuned and played piano—wafted past the swinging, louvered doors, she hesitated outside on the muddy boardwalk. She simply could *not* bring herself to step foot in such a wicked place! She almost returned to the boardinghouse. But at last, compromising, she persuaded a passing miner to go inside and ask Durango to come out.

After that, such a seemingly interminable length of time passed that Josselyn finally concluded that Durango had rudely decided to ignore her request. But just as she was turning to depart, he appeared at the saloon doors, the inevitable glowing-tipped cheroot in his mouth and the liquor bottle in his hand.

''Sorry for the delay, Sister,'' he greeted her impudently, his black eyes raking her lazily, his lips curving with amusement at her ruffled feathers, ''but even you could hardly expect me to throw in a winning hand now, could you? Well,

well, well. You're calling on me for a change. This *is* a surprise. To what do I owe this wholly unexpected pleasure?''

Much to Josselyn's shock, before she could reply, he suddenly let out a startling and an extremely foul oath, pitched both his cigar and his bottle on the saloon floor, and burst without warning from the Mother Lode's doors, leaving them banging violently behind him as, spurs jingling, he took off running down the boardwalk, heedlessly bumping passersby right and left. Her mouth agape, Josselyn stared after him, dumbfounded as he abruptly grabbed the collar of a small Mexican boy, and snatched him up off the ground and shook him roughly.

"Oh! How dare you, you despicable villain!" Josselyn cried in protest as she hurried to the scene. "What do you think you are doing? Put that poor child down at once, do you hear?''

" 'Poor child,' my foot!" Durango snorted, glaring at her. "He's a goddamned thief, Sister, and if you weren't such a gullible, self-righteous fool, you'd see he cut your reticule clean off your waist!''

Josselyn glanced down to where her bag normally hung from the cestus at her waist and saw only the reticule's dangling strings, neatly sliced through by a sharp knife. Her bag itself was clutched in the Mexican boy's hands, indisputable proof that he had stolen it. Speechless with disbelief and dismay, she gazed at the thin, dirty, ill-clothed youngster. He scowled at her furiously through his tears and started once more to struggle futilely to escape from Durango's iron grasp.

"Lemme go! Lemme go, damn you!" the child yelped, uttering a string of curses that left Josselyn's stunned ears ringing. "Help! Help!''

"*¡Silencio!*" Durango snarled, giving the rebellious but frightened boy another hard shake and jerking Josselyn's bag from his small, clenched fists. "You are in a great deal of trouble, *muchacho*, and if you don't behave yourself, I may be tempted to summon the sheriff and turn you over to the law for your crime.''

"Oh, no, Durango!" Josselyn cried, distraught. "He's only a child! I'm certain that he didn't mean any harm, that it was only a very bad prank. Surely, his parents or Father Flanagan can devise an appropriate punishment."

At that, Durango began to speak rapidly in Spanish to the boy, giving him another shake now and then when the youngster mutinously refused to respond. This went on for several long minutes. Then, for Josselyn's sake, Durango translated the gist of the coversation.

"His name is Cisco. He either does not know or has long since forgotten his surname. His parents are dead, and he does not remember them. He thinks that his father was killed in a mining accident and that his mother died of some lingering complaint. He is seven years old and has lived on the streets since he was four. He has survived by eating garbage and begging for and stealing whatever food, garments, and money he could. He is sorry he took your bag, but he was hungry. He last ate two days ago, some scraps of rotten meat and stale bread he found in the trash in Dostal Alley."

"But . . . that's horrible!" Josselyn responded.

"Unfortunately, it is a common story in the mining district, Josselyn," Durango declared grimly. "Not all are so lucky as to have a convent upbringing like yours, sheltered from harsh realities. Life is hard, and the world is a cruel place— as you would doubtless have learned had this young but artful scamp succeeded in making off with your reticule, in which, I can only assume from the woebegone expression on your face and the clinking weight of your purse, you have most unwisely chosen to carry every cent you possess," he observed, hefting her bag once or twice before returning it to her.

"That is surely not your concern, Durango," she replied stiffly as she gripped her reticule tightly in her hands.

"It is my concern when because of your stupidity, I might, for Red's sake, wind up being forced to support you!" he retorted, annoyed.

"Oh! How dare you presume even to *think* that I—that I would accept money from you, like a—like a—"

"Kept woman?" he supplied, devilishly quirking one black brow and grinning unpleasantly. "Climb down off your pulpit, Sister! This is the real world, and if you were to find yourself penniless tomorrow, you'd have only three choices: to return to your convent in Boston and take your final vows, in which case you'd need money to get back there; to subsist on the charity of either me or Wylie, because you for damned sure wouldn't get any out of Victoria; or to wed either me or Wylie—and since I ain't a marrying man and since, for all that Wylie's been squiring you up and down these hills and gulches for the past several weeks, I ain't yet heard any wedding bells ringing, I'd venture to guess that, like it or not, you'd have to swallow your pride and accept a handout, salving your conscience as best you could."

"Why, I'd live on the streets before I'd do that!"

"Don't behave even more foolishly than you already have, Sister," Durango sneered, his glinting eyes roaming in the way she hated over her habited figure. "There's only one way women survive on the streets—and frankly, I doubt seriously that you have what it takes!"

His vulgar remark was like a slap in Josselyn's face. She whitened as though he had hit her. Her nostrils flared, and an incredible anger welled inside her, so powerful that she half raised her weighty reticule to strike him and wipe the smirk from his lips. Then she caught sight of Cisco's scared, tearful face and was abruptly recalled to her senses.

"You are no gentleman, Durango." She spoke the words quietly, coldly, visibly summoning her dignity, shaming him until he crossly reminded himself of his suspicions that she was probably no nun at all, but a better actress than Nell Tierney and hand in glove with Red to seize control of the Rainbow's End. "And you are making a scene in public, in front of the boy," she said. "If you will excuse us and point me in the right direction, I will see he is properly placed in an orphanage, where he belongs."

"There aren't any," Durango rejoined curtly.

"I—I beg your pardon," Josselyn stammered, believing she surely could not have heard him right.

"Orphanages. Children's homes. Whatever you want to call 'em. There aren't any."

"Not—not one?" she inquired faintly, aghast.

"Not one," he echoed flatly.

"But that's—that's terrible . . . unconscionable. . . ."

"It's a fact of life, Sister."

"Oh, I do wish you would stop calling me that! You only do it to vex me, for you know I am not a nun yet, Durango."

"Yes, and just think," he said with feigned innocence, his eyes suddenly shuttered so she could not read his thoughts, "if you become one, all of Red's shares in the Rainbow's End will go toward the building of a theater for Nell Tierney—instead of something more worthwhile . . . like, say, an orphanage."

"I see that you are not content with just sticking a knife into someone, Durango," Josselyn noted, discomfited. "No, you must twist the blade, as well. But then, I expected no less from you. However, since it appears there is no refuge for the boy—and not likely to be anytime soon," she added meaningfully, "then I must take it upon myself to see he is adequately cared for."

"A noble, if misguided, gesture, Sister," Durango pronounced. "What can a . . . supremely chaste woman like yourself possibly know about children—about boys, in particular?"

"There were children at the convent—"

"Miscreants like Cisco here? I sincerely doubt that, Sister. He is both clever and cunning—he could not have survived on the streets as long as he has otherwise—and I don't think life in a convent has prepared you to cope with the likes of him. Why, he cut your reticule from your waist, and you didn't even know it! I'll wager that within five minutes of my turning him over to you, he'd once more have your purse pinched in his grubby, greedy little fists and have given you the slip, just as neat as you please, besides!"

"No, he wouldn't!" she replied, indignant.

"*Sí,* I would!" Cisco interrupted boastfully, having by now grasped that he was not to be handed over to the authorities and having, as a result, dried his tears and recovered some of his aplomb. "And next time, you wouldn't catch me, either, so there!" Then he rudely stuck his tongue out at her.

"Hey! Mind your manners, *muchacho.*" Durango gave the youngster yet another shake. "Or I swear I'll turn you over my knee and give you a hiding you won't soon forget."

"But, *señor,*" the child protested, "she is only a woman, a nun—and a foolish one at that! You said so yourself—"

"Never mind what I said!" Durango snapped, reddening at the boy's all-too-accurate accusation. "If you know what's good for you, you'll keep a civil tongue in your head, or else. You're much too young to have such a smart mouth, and if I were in your shoes right now, I'd be showing some respect. It's still not too late for me to haul you down to the calaboose, you know."

Duly chastened, Cisco fell silent and stopped struggling against Durango's steely hold.

Josselyn sighed as she gazed at the youngster's stubborn, set face. She did not know what to do. Reluctantly, she was forced to admit to herself that he would indeed prove too much for her to manage, for it was plain that he was not in the least frightened by her, as he was by Durango. The boy knew nothing but deprivation and hardship, which had made him shrewd and tough. He needed a stronger hand than hers to compel him in the right direction, someone kind but firm. . . .

"Wylie!" she declared suddenly, her countenance brightening. "Wylie can take him in."

Upon hearing this, Durango stood openmouthed for a moment, so astonished that he was rendered speechless. Then, much to Josselyn's annoyance, he fell up against the wall of the nearest building, laughing so hard that he nearly lost his grip on Cisco, who, seizing on this unexpected reprieve, started again to squirm about vigorously in an effort to escape, at the same time brazenly trying to snatch Josselyn's reticule from her hands. Fortunately, Durango foiled both attempts, though his chuckles did not subside.

"Wylie . . . take . . . him . . . in!" he choked out at last between his howls of merriment, wiping his streaming eyes. "Wylie saddle himself with a larcenous orphan brat! That, I'd like to see!"

"Very well, then." Josselyn sniffed loftily to show him just exactly what she thought of his amusement—to say nothing of his all-too-apparent low opinion of Wylie. "You may escort us over to the mercantile. At once, if you please."

To her surprise, this suggestion was no sooner received than it was acted upon. Durango took her arm and, marching her along, firmly propelled the recalcitrant Cisco before them. The bell on the door of Wylie's store clanged loudly as they entered, and a clerk, spying Durango, scurried forward to assist them.

"Tell Wylie that Durango and the good Sister are here," Durango instructed, "with a present for him."

"Yes, sir, Mr. de Navarre," the clerk answered respectfully. "Right away, sir."

He disappeared toward the back of the mercantile, and presently, Wylie appeared, the corners of his mouth turned down sourly. When he glimpsed Josselyn, he smiled immediately—although his good humor vanished again when he caught sight of Durango and the reedy, ragged boy at her side.

"Josselyn, this would be a delightful surprise if it were not for the dubious company you have with you," Wylie greeted her, taking her hand in his and kissing it. The light, loverlike gesture was not lost on Durango, whose sardonic grin faltered for an instant, then steadied—though his eyes remained hard. Releasing Josselyn, Wylie glanced sharply, challengingly, at his partner before turning back to her. "I simply cannot believe that you encouraged Durango's presence, so I can only assume he has been imposing his unwelcome self on you. If so, just say the word, and I'll send him on about his business—''

"No, no, it's nothing like that—'' Josselyn began.

"Then I'm afraid I don't quite understand.'' Wylie's voice distinctly chilled, and his grey eyes frosted over, hurting and upsetting her a little, for she had come to value both his friendship and his approval. "Quigg said that you had a—a present for me— But surely, he was mistaken . . . ?''

"No, indeed, he was not!'' She laid her hand imploringly upon his arm. "Oh, Wylie! I do so need your help, and once you understand why, I'm sure you won't hesitate to do the right thing.'' Then, in a rush, glossing over why she had been standing out in front of the Mother Lode saloon to begin with, she explained what had happened, ending breathlessly, "So, you see, Cisco desperately needs a home and a father, and I thought—I thought . . . that is—''

"Josselyn, you can't possibly mean for *me* to take the boy in!'' Wylie exclaimed with distaste. "A filthy street urchin who would doubtless rob me blind at every opportunity! Look around you. This is a mercantile, for heaven's sake—not a home for wayward foundlings. Do you know what it costs me to have these goods shipped up here to the Rocky Mountains? Why, that little thief would have a heyday picking my store clean and would undoubtedly wind up ruining me. I'm a businessman, a bachelor—not a boy's benefactor. No, I'm sorry, Josselyn, much as I'd like to assist you, truly, I must refuse. It won't do. It just won't do. Surely, you can see that?''

"No, I can't, Wylie,'' she replied forlornly. "I thought that you, of all people, would understand—''

"I do, Josselyn. Believe me, I do,'' he asserted more gently, "and if it were anything else, I'd be more than happy to oblige you. But I work long, hard hours; I live in four rooms above the mercantile, and I eat all my meals out. I don't even have a spare bed. Honestly, Josselyn, what sort of a home do you think I could provide for the boy?'' When she didn't respond, he rounded angrily on Durango. "You put her up to this, Durango—I know it!—trying to cast me in a bad light. I suppose that now that you think you've shown Josselyn my 'true colors,' you'll play the hero and offer to take the misbegotten whelp in yourself!"

"He's not a proper person to have charge of the boy," Josselyn replied, her disappointment in Wylie plain.

"Maybe not, Josselyn," Durango drawled, his contemptuous smile slowly widening and twisting his lips unpleasantly. "But then, I ain't a cold-hearted bastard like Wylie here, either." He gazed down at Cisco. "Come along, son," he ordered kindly. "The air in here stinks to high heaven. I wonder if Wylie's customers know he's selling 'em rotten merchandise?"

"Why, you—" Wylie burst out.

"Huh-uh. Temper, temper, Wylie," Durango jeered. "You wouldn't want the good Sister here to get the wrong idea about you, now, would you? That might prove costly if you want to stay in this game!"

"Don't pay him any mind, Josselyn." Wylie spoke through gritted teeth. "You can see what he's doing, can't you? This is all just a ruse on his part to win your favor and turn you against me. He'd like nothing better than to get his greedy hands on Red's shares in the Rainbow's End, so he can try to force me and Victoria out—just as he forced out the others—and have it all. Are you planning to kill me, too, Durango, and make it look like an accident—the same way you murdered Forbes and Red?"

Josselyn gasped, the blood draining from her face as she heard her own secret suspicions about Durango voiced aloud, each terrible, taunting word echoing monstrously in the sudden, lethal silence that had fallen.

"By God, if you were armed with more than that toy pistol of yours, Wylie, I'd shoot you where you stand for that!" Durango's voice was so deadly that it sent chills up Josselyn's spine, prickling the fine hairs on her nape. "I'm warning you: If you ever dare to repeat that accusation, you'd best be wearing a gun belt—because I won't walk away a second time, not even for the sake of the early years.''

Then, pulling Cisco along behind him, Durango exited the mercantile, pausing only once, at the door, to look back, his eyes flicking disdainfully over Josselyn's trembling figure.

''A word of advice, Sister: If I were you, I'd put my money in the bank—where it belongs,'' he told her tersely.

Then the door closed behind him, its bell tolling like a death knell in the grim hush that now enshrouded the store.

Chapter Seven

"Did he kill my father, Wylie?" Josselyn asked tremulously in the heavy silence that lay upon the mercantile. "Did he? Answer me, Wylie! *Did Durango murder my father?*"

"I believe so, yes," he said quietly, his grey eyes shadowed with some indefinable emotion. Then, his voice rising, he called, "Wait, Josselyn, wait!"

But it was too late. In a whirl of skirts, her veil flying, she was gone, running blindly out the door and into the street. There, a heavily loaded wagon drew up short. A team of horses whinnied shrilly and reared, their hooves narrowly missing knocking her to the ground and trampling her. A terrified driver shouted and cursed her for a crazy woman. She did not see. She did not hear. She was too intent on reaching Durango's tall, dark figure, striding swiftly toward Gamblers Row and the Mother Lode, Cisco in tow.

"Durango! Durango!" she cried, feeling as though her lungs would burst in the high altitude as she raced down the street. "Durango!"

At last, just as he was about to enter the saloon, he heard her and, turning, spied her rushing toward him. He glowered at her darkly. Nevertheless, he paused on the boardwalk and waited until she reached him—out of breath, panting for air, and a painful stitch in her side.

"Is it . . . true? Did you . . . do it?" Josselyn gasped out, her eyes searching his own desperately for the truth. "Did you . . . murder . . . my father?"

"Would you believe me if I said no?"

"I don't know," she admitted honestly, for in that moment when he faced her—openly, seemingly with nothing to hide—she was suddenly no longer so certain of her suspicions.

"Then what's the point in my denying it?" Durango demanded harshly, a muscle throbbing in his set jaw.

"I don't know."

"Then why did you follow me?" His voice was sharp. His glittering black eyes were narrowed, focused intently, speculatively, on her pale face.

"I don't know," she repeated yet a third time.

"Sister, you don't know much—and that's a fact." He paused for a long minute, studying her. Then, turning toward the saloon doors, he yelled, "Ho-Sing! Get out here on the double!" At Durango's shout, there presently appeared, smiling and bowing, a Chinese, a long black queue hanging down his back, an apron tied around his waist, a cleaver in one hand. "Ho-Sing, this is Cisco." Durango introduced the Mexican boy, whose hand he still held tightly. "I want you to take him inside, give him a bath, find him some clean clothes to wear, and feed him a hot meal. Then lock him up in the storeroom until I get back. I warn you: He will fight you every step of the way. He will try to escape. It is your responsibility to see that he does not succeed. If he does, I shall personally slice off your pigtail."

Despite this dire threat, the Chinese continued to smile, but it was obvious he took his boss's orders seriously.

Glancing with a martial glint in his eye at Cisco, Ho-Sing took over.

"You not cause Ho-Sing to lose queue, small dirty boy. You take bath. You put on crothes. You eat. You stay in storeloom. Come arong." He stretched out one hand and grabbed Cisco tightly by the ear. When the boy protested, the Chinese shook him. "Hush! Stop lacket at once! Missies upstairs, tlying to sleep. You not give Ho-Sing trouble, small, dirty boy, or I chop you into rittle pieces and cook you in stewpot!" he threatened, brandishing his cleaver wildly. "Not much meat on bones, but I bet you tasty, anyway. Hmmh, hmh. Make good Chinese dinner." Ho-Sing pretended to smack his lips at the prospect.

Cisco was struck by terror at this announcement, but try as he might, he could not wriggle free. He shrieked and swore shrilly in English and Spanish at both Josselyn and Durango until, with the flat of the cleaver, the Chinese rapped the child smartly on the head and determinedly dragged him into the saloon, all the while rebuking him severely in a combination of pidgin English and fluent Chinese that was nearly as incomprehensible as the boy's own linguistic hodgepodge.

"Are you really going to keep Cisco?" Josselyn inquired as she turned back to Durango, curious and, despite herself, unable to repress her smile at the comical scene.

"Well, the Mother Lode may not be the best place in the world for Cisco, but I reckon it's better than no place at all," he declared dryly. "At least, he'll have a roof over his head and three square meals a day—and if he tries any of his tricks on me, he'll definitely live to regret it, because I'm not about to be outwitted by a mere child!"

Josselyn found she could not argue with his logic. Even a saloon, she reluctantly supposed, was to be considered a haven when the alternative was a cold, sooty corner in some dark, deserted alley. She could not approve of Cisco's being exposed to such sinful temptations as liquor, gambling, and the "missies upstairs." Seeing no other choice at the present, however, she at last decided that she would make no objection to the arrangement, at least until on Sunday, after the Mass at St. Patrick's church, when she could speak to Father Flanagan about the matter. It was evident that although their work was certainly cut out for them, neither Durango nor Ho Sing would allow Cisco to escape or would have too many problems handling him. Still, she was surprised by Durango's bothering to take the boy in. It was, she reflected, a kindness she would not have expected of him, and it was certainly far more than Wylie had done for the child. She wondered if Durango might have ulterior motives for providing a home for Cisco, but oddly, she remained unconvinced that any deep, dark purpose lay behind Durango's behavior.

"I guess I should thank you for taking the boy in," she said.

"Yeah, well, don't think I'm not gonna exact a price for it." Durango's mouth turned down cynically at the corners. "In return for my good deed of putting a roof over your hapless waif's head, I'm afraid I'm gonna have to insist on walking you over to the bank, where you can open an account and deposit your money. I confess that while I doubt that the Mother Lode will be totally disrupted by the presence of one small boy, the thought of your falling victim to yet another miscreant and foisting him off onto me is, quite frankly, more than I can bear."

Taking her arm, he ushered her across the street to the First National Bank, where they transacted her business, then departed, Josselyn leaving with a much lighter reticule and mind, now that she knew that her funds were safely stored in the bank's secure metal vault. She should, she belatedly realized, have put her money there immediately upon her arrival in Central City. But the thought had not even occurred to her; she had never before needed to make use of a bank. At the convent, she had kept the small sums of cash Da had periodically sent her tucked away in a little chest in her room. She hadn't even bothered to lock the box, knowing that no one at the convent would dream of prying into her personal possessions—much less of stealing from her.

Josselyn fell silent as they strolled along the boardwalk to Miss Hattie's cottage, trying to determine whether she should trust Durango or not. She needed him to accompany her up to the Rainbow's End, but still, she could not make up her mind about him, about his guilt or his innocence. She had been so very certain, initially, that he was the saboteur, Forbes's and her father's murderer, that she would have staked her life on it. Now, after his actions today, she was no longer so sure. Durango de Navarre was a rogue; there was no doubt of that. But he was also a puzzle, and she wanted—needed—to know more about him, for Da's sake, and maybe even her own. Besides, even if Durango *had* killed Forbes and her father, she herself was surely in no immediate danger from him. There was nothing to be gained and a great deal to be lost by either Durango or Wylie if either harmed her before he got his hands on Da's shares—her shares now—in the Rainbow's End. Only if and when she were to wed either of her father's bachelor partners in the gold mine would she have placed herself in a perilous, perhaps even fatal, position.

After a long while, she spoke again.

"Durango, I want you to do me a favor. I want you to take me up to the Rainbow's End."

"What's the matter? Did Wylie refuse to take you there?"

"Yes, he did."

"That figures. He has strong feelings about women mixing themselves in a man's business. He doesn't like it. He tolerates Victoria's interference because he . . . has no other choice, since Forbes willed her his shares in the Rainbow's End. But you . . . you are another matter entirely." Durango paused, gazing off into the distance for a moment. Then, glancing back at Josselyn, he uttered, "Well, well, well. So that's what drove you to seek me out, is it? I did wonder what brought you to the saloon. In all the excitement, I clean forgot to repeat the question."

"You will take me, won't you?"

"That depends."

"On—on what?" she queried hesitantly, imagining all sorts of wild, unspeakable answers.

"Do you ride?" he asked, to her surprise.

"Ride? You mean . . . a horse?"

"Of course, a horse." His face was bland, although his eyes now danced wickedly and his mouth twitched with amusement. "What did you think I meant?"

"Well, I don't know. I—I guess I wasn't sure. I mean . . . people ride mules and donkeys out here in Central City, too, don't they?"

"Among . . . other animals."

"What other animals?" In her mostly ignorance, Josselyn had no idea to what he was referring, although, maddeningly, it was now clear to her that he was having some sort of a private laugh at her expense. Grinning openly now, he bluntly shared the joke.

"Two-legged ones, Josselyn. However, as, frankly, I thought it quite obvious that you were unlikely ever to have ridden one of those, I felt no need to clarify my meaning initially. But if I am mistaken, pray edify me, for I confess that the idea that you have . . . past experience of which I was until now unaware interests me greatly." His hooded eyes swept over her speculatively, flaring suddenly, like stoked coals.

Josselyn's cheeks flamed as, at last, she realized what he was teasing her about. She felt as though she were on fire with shame, embarrassment, and some other disgraceful sensation that set her pulse racing, her heart pounding, her body trembling. At the convent, though such explanations had rarely, if ever, been given by the Sisters, there had always been whispered talk among the girls themselves about what happened between a man and woman; and of course, Antoine had, during their clandestine rendezvous, taught her his own swift, tantalizingly incomplete lessons. But Josselyn did not know much in elaborate detail, and so, however scandalized she was by it, she was also naturally curious, eager to learn more—and Durango was obviously a man with considerable knowledge and experience. Still, she knew their discussion was shockingly improper, and so, despite herself, she tried indignantly to end it.

"You—you ought not to speak to me so," she murmured, her voice sounding strangled. "You—you are no gentleman, Durango!"

"So you've told me previously—on several occasions. But then, I've never claimed I was, have I? In fact—unlike Wylie—I thought I had taken great pains to make it quite clear to you what I am. You still have not answered my question, Josselyn."

"No . . . that is, I—I have never ridden a horse—or—or anything else!"

"A novice, then, in more ways than one, it would appear," he noted softly, insolently. "Why, Josselyn, you're blushing. Have I said something to offend?" His tone and his eyes mocked her.

"Oh! You are a devil—and no mistake! I—I don't know why I ever thought to have anything to do with you!"

"Because the Rainbow's End is no fit place for a lady, and Wylie is too much of a *gentleman* to take you there," Durango responded coolly, infuriatingly unruffled.

"And you're not?"

"No. Isn't that what you counted on? Because even you realize there *are* certain advantages in my not being a stickler for etiquette—although I, at least, unlike Wylie, do believe in usually giving a lady what she wants. Besides, so long as I am with you, you'll come to no harm at the gold mine. The worst you'll suffer is a pair of burning ears from the salty language of the miners, and doubtless a bruised derriere from the ride."

"But I—I don't know how to ride, I told you," she reiterated as they came to a halt at last out in front of the boardinghouse, "and even if I did, I don't have a horse— apparently, Da didn't own one—nor do I have enough money to rent one. I expected . . . that is . . . I thought that you would take me in your buggy.''

''My charmingly chaste sweet, I should love nothing better, I assure you, than to take you in my buggy . . . or my bed or anywhere else, for that matter,'' he drawled impudently, his voice choked with laughter, causing her to blush scarlet with humiliation again as she realized she had inadvertently said something risqué. ''But, alas,'' he continued shamelessly, grinning, ''much as I feel confident I could, under the right circumstances, rise to the occasion, I don't really care to risk jolting my vehicle so strenuously, however well sprung it may be.'' He pushed open the gate, then stood to one side so she could enter. ''It's hard enough for a wagon to get up to the Rainbow's End. There's not much of a road, just a rough trail—with a lot of ruts and rocks.''

''Then what do you suggest, pray tell?'' Josselyn inquired stiffly, incensed and thinking suddenly, suspiciously, that for someone who had agreed to escort her up to the gold mine, he certainly was putting plenty of obstacles in her path to prevent her from going.

''Don't worry, Josselyn.'' Durango's eyes gleamed in a way that made her wonder uneasily what other demonic thoughts were chasing through his mind. ''If God won't provide, I will. Tomorrow morning, ten o'clock sharp. I'll pick you up here, shall I?''

Then, after tipping his sombrero to her, he sauntered up the street, whistling tunelessly, while she stared after him thoughtfully, reflecting on his puzzling, plaguing character —and Da's will. She was so lost in reverie that she did not notice the grimy old miner perched on a stoop halfway down the street, watching her covertly over the top of the harmonica he held to his mouth. But Durango did. Pausing in his stride, he looked intently at the man's bowed head for a moment, still not wanting to believe what he suspected, what he felt almost positive of right now. Then, tossing a quarter into the hat that sat on the ground beside the miner, he said: ''Hey, old-timer, if you know 'Irish Eyes,' play it, will you? 'Cause

I think, yes, I really do believe they are actually beginning to smile at me.''

Hearing that, it was all that Red O'Rourke could do to restrain himself from leaping up and, with his bare hands, throttling Durango then and there.

Chapter Eight

"I tell ye, Nellie, he knows!" Red ran one hand agitatedly through his hair as he paced back and forth across her parlor floor. "Somehow, Durango knows I'm alive. Why else should he have given me a quarter—and a second time, at that? I tell ye, Nellie, he looked straight at me just as cool as ye please and asked me would I play 'Irish Eyes,' 'cause he thought they were beginning to smile at him. He was trying to get at me, I'm telling ye, to make me mad, to make me reveal me true self. That's why he wants me to think he's after me daughter."

"On the other hand, maybe he really is . . . after Josselyn, I mean," Nell suggested worriedly. "After all, thanks to your dreadful will, neither he nor Wylie has proved slow to court her. Besides, even without the added inducement of your shares in the Rainbow's End, Josselyn—at least what you can see of her under that veil and habit—is a beautiful young woman, Red; and Lord knows, Durango and Wylie both have always had an eye for the ladies.''

"Aye," he reluctantly confessed, "but still, 'twasn't supposed to happen like this! I meant for the two of them to be fighting tooth and nail with each other over the Rainbow's End, so I could discover which is the bloody bastard who killed Forbes and who's been sabotaging the gold mine—not for the one rascal to be squiring me daughter all over the damned countryside and the other to be figuring how he can best lift her skirts! Whist! Me blood's boiling at just the thought! For if Durango knows I'm alive, ye can be certain 'tis not marriage he has on his mind—realizing he'll not be getting me shares in the Rainbow's End for it!''

"Even so, you can't be sure he has somehow learned you're not dead," Nell pointed out logically. "You might only be imagining it, because of your guilty conscience; and if so, why, 'tis no more than you deserve, Red, for you ought to be ashamed of yourself for using your own daughter as poor, unsuspecting bait in your wicked scheme, and that's the God's honest truth of it! Besides, I went to Wylie's mercantile this morning, and according to Wylie's clerk, Quigg, Durango and Wylie exchanged more than just harsh words at the store yesterday afternoon. In fact, Quigg told me that Wylie accused Durango straight out of murdering you and Forbes both, and that Durango said that the next time Wylie repeated that remark, he'd better be toting more than that little derringer of his, because Durango would kill him.''

"Well, now, that's more like it." Red smiled grimly with satisfaction at hearing how his rash plan had begun to work, after all.

"Red O'Rourke! Do you mean to stand there and say that you hope Wylie and Durango will *murder* each other?" Nell blurted, shocked.

"Why, no, lass. 'Twill not be coming to that, for Wylie has far too much sense to become involved in a shooting match with Durango, and Durango would never draw on a man who wasn't armed fair and square. No, whatever will be done will be done on the sly—and that's when I'll know for certain the identity of the underhanded whoreson who wants the Rainbow's End all to himself! Meanwhile, Nellie, me darling girl, 'tis counting on ye I am to give that wayward daughter of mine a few wise words of motherly advice about men—especially scoundrels like Durango and Wylie!''

"And just how do you think I'm to accomplish that?" Nell demanded tartly, glaring at him. "Thanks to you and your miserable will, the poor colleen will have naught to do with me—and I can't hardly say as I blame her. She thinks I'm a designing hussy who stole you away from her and who now intends to get my grasping hands on her inheritance. She blushes red as a strawberry every time she makes some polite excuse for declining to visit me, so I can't help but know that the lass is lying and feeling guilty as sin about it; and she has rebuffed every single overture of friendship I've tried to make in her direction. So, just what would you suggest?"

"Faith, Nellie, I've never known ye to lack wit or gumption before." Red eyed her as though astonished. " 'Tis an actress ye are, aren't ye? And a damned fine one, too, I have always thought. Pretend ye have no manners, and a thick skull, besides, me love. Invite yourself to tea, and don't take no for an answer. Then go and sit yer pretty backside down in Miss Hattie's parlor and refuse to budge until Jossie joins ye. It all seems quite simple to me."

"Men!" Nell sniffed haughtily, her eyes rolling. "May the devil take the lot of you! So I'm to be portrayed not only as conniving, but crass and clod-headed, as well, am I? Red, I'm warning you: When all this is over, you'd better fix things right between me and Josselyn, or so help me God, not only will she never forgive you, but I won't, either!"

"Now, now, Nellie, me darling—"

"No, don't you 'me darling' me, Red O'Rourke!" she exclaimed huffily. "And you keep your distance, too, for I'll not be swayed by any of your blarney or kisses. One of us has got to retain some common sense and help that dear child—before Wylie leads her up a wedding aisle or Durango lures her down a primrose path!'' Snatching up her hat, reticule, and gloves, she announced, ''That being the case, I'm off to make a social ruin of myself—which, I suppose, is at least slightly better than the fool you've made of yours!''

''*Bravo*, Nellie, me love!'' Red crowed, grinning and applauding. ''That's the spirit! I knew ye'd not let me down. Now, get out there and break a leg!''

''Oooooh! You—you . . . oh! I can't even think of anything bad enough to call you!'' she cried. Then, trailing a cloud of attar-of-roses scent in her wake, she banged the door so hard behind her that all the windows in the cottage rattled.

''She may not have red hair, but she's for damned sure got an Irish temper,'' Red remarked to himself ruefully after she'd gone. Then he jumped a mile, startled, as, without warning, the reverberation of the slammed door caused a vase jarred from its position on the mantel to topple off the edge and shatter upon the hearth.

True to her gender, Nell had got the last word, after all.

Chapter Nine

Some weeks earlier, the Reverend Mother Maire had settled back in her chair, firmly affixed her wire-rimmed spectacles to her nose, and begun to read Josselyn's letter. It was long—several heavily crossed pages, in fact—and here and there, the ink had spattered and run from what the Reverend Mother had known must be teardrops. Josselyn certainly had not been having an easy time of it, it had seemed, in Central City. Her father's unorthodox will had upset her deeply. She hardly knew his three partners, between two of which, she had explained, if she were desirous of obtaining her inheritance, she must choose to wed; and at least one of these was a shocking knave, from all appearances. There was also her original intent to become a nun to consider; and she had begged urgently for the abbess's counsel.

Sighing heavily as she had finished reading Josselyn's

words, the Reverend Mother Maire had refolded the pages and carefully tucked them back inside the envelope, which she had then tapped thoughtfully upon her desk for a moment. Then, laying the letter aside, she had removed her glasses and rubbed her eyes tiredly. It had been a long day. There had been many problems at the convent that had required her attention—not the least of which had been Sister Toiresa's report on the state of the convent's finances. The convent was poor—and getting poorer. Unhappily, there had been no avoiding that fact. The Irish Catholic families who had used to send their daughters to the convent for schooling were almost all gone now from the North End, having moved to other sections of Boston. Now, the North End was an area inhabited principally by Jewish immigrants.

The Reverend Mother had already written numerous letters to various of the Church's authorities, informing them of the changes in the neighborhood and that she had, for lack of both funds and students, been forced to close one wing of the convent. Those persons who had so far replied had sympathized, but the abbess had not been encouraged. She had understood that they could do little, if anything, to assist her. As they had pointed out—and she had already known in her heart—times were hard, and the moving of an entire convent could not be lightly, or cheaply, undertaken. There were other priorities, needs more pressing elsewhere. Even in a town like Central City, located at the heart of the "richest square mile on earth," there were, according to Josselyn's letter, widows and orphans in want. The thought of these children, particularly, had tugged at the Reverend Mother Maire's heart, for she loved youngsters. They were filled with such wonder and awe, and were always so eager to learn, that she loved teaching them. They were, after all, the promise of tomorrow.

Well, she might not be able to do anything about the convent at the moment, but she could at least advise Josselyn. Taking a pen and paper from her desk, and reaffixing her glasses on her nose, she had begun to write in her long, beautiful, flowing hand, which was the envy of every Sister at the convent and, the Reverend Mother was forced to admit to herself, her one secret vanity.

Dear Josselyn . . .

At last, completing the painful message, the abbess had posted it, hoping that it would not prove too hard a blow to the young woman already laboring under such grievous burdens in Central City.

The sun had burned away the early morning mist to reveal a gorgeous spring day and, at the gate of the boardinghouse on Roworth Street, Durango mounted upon his black stallion, Diablo, and leading, to Josselyn's mingled dismay and amusement, a small grey donkey.

"You see, Sister," he greeted her, tipping back his hat and grinning, his black eyes dancing at her obvious discomfiture, "I told you that you didn't need to worry. As you can see, God—with a bit of help from me, I confess—has provided. This is Sassafras, the sweetest, and possibly the laziest, little donkey you'll ever meet. She's quite affectionate, but I don't think she's traveled faster than a walk in years, so you don't have to fear that she'll bolt and run away with you. In fact, you'll probably need a switch just to prod her into moving at all. And since she's not very big, if you do somehow find yourself unseated, at least you won't have too far to fall."

"Is this your idea of a joke, Durango?" Josselyn was not certain whether to be grateful or indignant as she eyed the donkey askance.

"No, indeed." He pretended to look wounded. "In fact, Sassafras was so clearly heaven-sent that I thought there could be no doubt that the Lord intended her for you."

"What do you mean? How did you come by her?" She glanced at him skeptically, for she would not have put it past him to have stolen the donkey.

"I won her," Durango announced gleefully, "in a card game last night at the Mother Lode. I would not usually have accepted a donkey in a wager, you understand. But the prospector who put her up as his bet was an unfortunate fellow, down to his last few dollars and intent on returning to his home back East; and since I was drawing to a royal straight, I thought my odds of winning the hand were remote, to say the least. But as luck would have it, Providence intervened, smiling on me. I drew the queen of hearts, which was the very card I needed; and I decided then and there that since I myself have no use whatsoever for a donkey, God must have intended her for you, Josselyn. So if you'll have her, she's yours."

"Well, I—I hardly know what to say." Josselyn was somewhat ashamed, now, that she had suspected him of stealing the donkey—though she thought that winning it at gambling was only slightly better. Still, her need was such that she felt she could not look a gift horse—or donkey, as the case was—in the mouth.

"Say yes, and let's be on our way." Durango swung one long, lithe leg over his saddle and dismounted, dropping gracefully to the ground. "I had Ho-Sing pack us a lunch" —he indicated the picnic basket hanging from his saddle horn. "There's rather an odd mix of food inside, I'm afraid—Chinese, Mexican, and otherwise—but at least you won't go hungry."

Josselyn was not only surprised, but touched by his thoughtfulness, for it revealed yet another aspect of his character that she had difficulty reconciling with the image she had of him as a murderer. She had been so sure, in the beginning, of Durango's guilt. But now, more and more, she found herself reconsidering her original suspicion of him. Yet if neither Durango nor Wylie, whom she felt certain was innocent of the deeds, was the culprit responsible for blowing up the Rainbow's End, for killing Forbes and Da, who was? Victoria? That seemed unlikely—unless she had had help, of course. One of the men who worked at the gold mine?

That appeared to be the only other logical conclusion, Josselyn thought slowly. But even so, she was forced to admit she was hard put to come up with a motive for any of the miners, since on the surface, it looked as though none of them had profited from either the Rainbow's End's being effectively shut down for months or from Forbes's and Da's deaths.

Durango assisted her into the sidesaddle that was cinched onto the donkey, showing her patiently how to hold the reins and guide the animal. Then, at an easy pace, they set off toward the gold mine, Josselyn urging the poky, recalcitrant Sassafras along with a small stick Durango had cut from a tree in Miss Hattie's front yard.

On Eureka Street, they were spotted and hailed by Nell, who had been, she explained as she reached them, on her way to the boardinghouse to insist on having tea with Josselyn.

"I'm so sorry to disappoint you, Nell." Josselyn flushed at the lie. "But Durango is taking me up to the Rainbow's End today. I want very much to see the gold mine that was so much a part of Da's life and in which I am now a partner. Perhaps you and I can get together some other time."

"How about tomorrow afternoon?" Nell pressed, adamantly refusing to take no for an answer. Unable to think of yet another plausible excuse for avoiding her, Josselyn was compelled for politeness's sake to accede to Nell's request.

After stating that she would arrive at Miss Hattie's promptly at four o'clock the following day, Nell hurried off, seeming suddenly strangely eager to be gone; and Durango and Josselyn continued on their way. Soon, Central City was behind them and they had begun their ascent into the surrounding hills.

Josselyn, who had been nervous when she had first mounted the donkey, grew more confident about handling the reins as the morning passed, gradually realizing that not only was the animal not going to run away with her, but that it was actually content to trot obediently after Durango's stallion. Thus only an occasional switch was needed to keep Sassafras moving along, and Josselyn was finally able to relax and take note of her environment.

In the early years of the gold rush, the hills for miles around had been densely forested. Now, many were wholly devoid of trees, which had been cut down for timber to build the towns that sprawled along the gulches and to shore up the gold mines that dotted the countryside. On the nearest hills, only an occasional stump remained. Farther on, a few lone trees began to appear, then thin stands of woods that eventually thickened into the forests of spruces, pines, and aspens characteristic of the region. On the barren knolls, grasses and wildflowers rippled like a vast, rolling sea in the wind, while high above the tree line, the snowcapped peaks of the towering mountains glistened white as foamy waves beneath the sun. Misty cloud wisps drifted across the cobalt-blue sky. Once the smoke and soot of the towns below had been left behind, the air was filled with the sweet, green scents of spring and of the rich, fertile earth.

Josselyn, having grown more accustomed now to the high altitude, the thin atmosphere, inhaled deeply the fragrances of nature that wafted to her nostrils, mingling with the not-unpleasant aromas of the horse and the donkey, and well-oiled saddle leather. Sassafras smelled of grain and sweat and dust. Her fur was short, and rough when rubbed the wrong way, as Josselyn discovered when she bent forward to give the animal's neck a friendly pat. One of Sassafras's ears lopped to one side, giving her a sadly comical appearance that brought a smile to Josselyn's face as she surveyed the little beast. Now and then, Sassafras twitched her long tail to flick away some bothersome insect, more often than not swatting Josselyn in the process, as though to get even with her for the times when, with her small stick, she switched the donkey when it lagged behind out of sheer orneriness or to snatch a mouthful of grass from the side of the trail.

The track was indeed, as Durango had warned, little more than a couple of deep wagon ruts carved by frequent use into the rocky terrain. Here and there, stones washed down from higher ground during the spring thaws strewed the path, making the going difficult. But though the ride was jolting, Sassafras proved a surefooted animal; and Josselyn thought she need not fear that the donkey would stumble and fall or topple off the edge of the trail in those dizzying places where the earth fell away sharply and steeply into the narrow, twisting gulches and creeks below. Still, being a novice rider, she clung tightly to the saddle horn and did not release it until the Rainbow's End came into sight.

Although she had, from a distance, viewed many gold mines over the past three months, the Rainbow's End was a disappointment to her. It was in a sorry state; in fact, it appeared more dilapidated than some of what she had previously assumed must be the poorer gold mines of the region. The site was littered with piles of rock and other debris from the excavation currently in progress; and the buildings that rose before her were so crudely constructed and in such poor repair that she marveled that a strong wind had not blown them down. Boards, evidently jarred loose by the explosion from the tall shaft house and the pump house, lay scattered on ground that was muddy from both the spring rains and the water pumped up from the gold mine. As she gazed at the rubble, the ramshackle edifices, and the mire, a bitter lump of anger and anguish constricted Josselyn's throat. This was Da's dream, the Rainbow's End, what he had worked so hard for and one of the reasons he had never sent for her to join him in Central City. At the realization, she felt a desire to laugh until she cried, and it was only with difficulty that she quelled the wild sound that threatened to erupt from her throat.

"Not quite what you expected, is it?" Durango asked quietly, studying her, his eyes shuttered so she could not read his thoughts.

"No. No, it isn't," she managed to choke out, swallowing hard and looking away so he would not see the tears that brimmed without warning in her eyes.

"Yeah, well, appearances are often deceiving," he remarked enigmatically; and Josselyn received the impression that he was not referring only to the gold mine.

The notion intrigued her. Was Durango trying to tell her something about himself, as well? she wondered. Covertly, she peeked at him from beneath her lashes. She had seldom seen him when he did not have the wide, flat brim of his black sombrero pulled down low over his eyes, when he did not look as though he had been in the saddle for over a fortnight and needed both a bath and a shave, and when he did not have one of his thin black cigars hanging from his lips and that bottle of clear liquor—mescal, she had learned that it was called—in hand. Even now, as she watched, he pulled this last from his saddlebag, unstoppered it, and took a substantial draft before wiping his mouth off on his sleeve. Observing her frown of disapproval, he grinned hugely.

"Riding's thirsty work," he declared as he jammed the cork back into place and returned the bottle to his saddlebag. "Come on. I'll show you around and introduce you to the miners—that is, if you haven't changed your mind about coming up here, now that you've actually seen what a rough, run-down claim the Rainbow's End is—as Wylie told you, no fit place for a lady."

"Are you having second thoughts about my being here?" Josselyn's eyes narrowed suspiciously.

"Not at all," Durango assured her, seemingly unperturbed by her question. "I simply thought that *you* might be."

"Not at all," she insisted, echoing his own words.

"Then, in that case, let's go."

They nudged their mounts forward, and presently, they reached the Rainbow's End. There, Durango helped Josselyn to dismount, his hands sure and strong about her waist as he swung her down from the saddle. Indeed, if not for his secure hold on her, she would have fallen, for one of her feet landed on a sharp stone and her ankle bent beneath her, throwing her momentarily off-balance, so she was cast into his arms. Involuntarily, she clutched him, and his grip on her tightened as she tried to steady herself. For an instant, her breath caught in her throat as she felt the hard length of his body suddenly pressed against her own soft one, his powerful, sinewy muscles flexing beneath her slender hands. Dimly, she realized that for all his unkempt appearance, he must have bathed earlier that morning, for he smelled clean and good, the fragrances of spicy soap and bay rum mingling with those of cheroot smoke and the faintest trace of alcohol on his breath, warm against her skin. She looked up into his unshaven face; her green eyes locked with his own black ones, which glittered in a way that sent an unexpected shiver down her spine, curling her toes. Her heart began to pound loud and hard and fast at his nearness; and deep within her, something she did not want to name stirred, both frightening and exciting her, making her feel so hot and flushed that for a moment she feared she might faint. Her cheeks stained with color, and flustered, she disentangled herself and drew away from him, carefully avoiding stepping again on the stone that had pitched her into his embrace. When next she glanced at him, his eyes were hooded; his face was impassive—though she did not guess what the effort to mask his emotions cost him.

It had all seemed to happen so naturally, Durango thought, the manner in which Josselyn had so innocently stumbled into his arms. It might genuinely have been an accident, he knew. But still, doubt plagued him. It could just as easily have been the carefully calculated contrivance of a clever actress. The trouble was, he was not sure which supposition was correct. More unsettling was the fact that, unintentional or deliberate, he could not deny that the scent of her, the feel of her, had aroused him. She had smelled of lavender and springtime; her body had felt soft and supple against his, making him wish she were not clothed in her novice's habit, which so effectively concealed her figure. Durango had a sudden, wild urge to peel away . . . very slowly . . . those layers of garments that enfolded her. His fingers itched to tear away her veil, so he could see for certain what color of hair lay beneath it. He cursed the fact that he did not know whether she was truly a nun—or the deceitful witch that, in that moment, he half hoped she was.

He tied their mounts to the hitching rail in front of the cookhouse. Then, retrieving the picnic basket hanging from his saddle horn, he took Josselyn by the arm and led her toward the long, low building, pointing out the rest of the structures along the way and briefly explaining their use. Inside the cookhouse, Durango introduced her to the first of the nine men she would meet at the gold mine, a thin, wiry old-timer who went by the moniker "Old Sourdough," having been called this for so many years that even he had almost forgotten his real name.

"Red's daughter, did you say? Well, I'll be danged!" Old Sourdough shook his head with disbelief. "I didn't even know that Red had a daughter. Pleased to meet you, Sister."

"Sourdough does all the cooking at the Rainbow's End, Josselyn," Durango told her as he set the picnic basket down on the long table inside the common room. "But if you value your stomach, you won't eat a bite of any meal of his, for his beans taste like grapeshot and his biscuits are so leaden that you could use them for cannonballs. We're all convinced he stirs black powder into everything he prepares."

"Aw, git on with you, Durango!" Old Sourdough grumbled, vigorously chewing the wad of tobacco in his mouth, then spitting on the floor, as though to demonstrate just what he thought of his boss's remarks. "Anybody what sells that rotgut whiskey you do don't have no cause a-tall to complain about my cookin'!" He turned to Josselyn. "Don't you pay him any mind, Sister. He's jest joshin' you, that's what. He and the rest of the boys like to gimme a hard time, see if they can rile me. Well, what I say is this: If they don't like my cookin', then they oughta elect a new cook. Ain't gonna hurt my feelin's none, 'cause I never claimed to be able to do more than bake a right tasty loaf of sourdough bread, anyhows, 'cause I've always been smart 'nuff to keep a little bit of the dough each time as a starter fer the next batch—

which is how I come by my handle, don't you know? So, let 'em git somebody else; that's what I say. But till then, they should keep their danged mouths shut and stay outta my kitchen! I mightn't be able to whip up nothin' fancy like that danged Chinese cook of Durango's, but at least when a body sits down to my table, they know what they's a-fixin' to eat—and that's more 'n I can say fer all that mess Ho-Sing dishes up! Dog meat! I swear that's what it is!''

At this, as she thought of the lunch Ho-Sing had prepared for Durango and her, Josselyn's smile at Old Sourdough's grousing faltered. Skeptically, she glanced at the picnic basket, and then at Durango, who laughed outright at the dismayed expression on her face.

"I assure you, Josselyn," he said, still grinning, "that no matter what Sourdough may insist to the contrary, Ho-Sing does not use dog meat as a staple in his cooking. Sourdough, you ought to be ashamed of yourself for filling Josselyn's head with such nonsense. Why, I've got half a mind not to ask you for some of that bread you bragged about and that I had hoped you would contribute to our lunch."

"Well, now"—Old Sourdough beamed in spite of himself—"I reckon I can manage to rustle up a couple of slices and mebbe some butter, too, seein' as how it's fer Red's daughter and all." He turned to Josselyn. "I wouldn't want you to go hungry, Sister, and if there's anythin' a-tall worth eatin' in that picnic basket, I'll be a mule's as—er— hind end!"

At that, leaving Old Sourdough to his kitchen, Durango and Josselyn headed for the tall shaft house that harbored the main entrance and the hoistway to the gold mine. Inside was a conglomeration of what looked like very complex structures and machinery, although Durango informed Josselyn that, in principle, their operation was relatively simple. Of primary importance were the gallows frame—a wooden scaffold that was mounted over the top of the shaft and that carried the hoisting rope, a thick, braided steel cable—and the windlass, which, to her untrained eyes, appeared a tangle of variously sized wheels and gears, all creaking and grinding together as Novak, the brawny hoistman, by means of winding or unwinding the cable on a huge spool, alternately raised and lowered the primitive ore bucket, sending supplies down the shaft and hauling loads of ore and debris back up.

From far below the shaft-house floor came the dull roar of additional machinery and tools—drills, air hoses and water hoses, sinkers, sledgehammers, moils, picks, shovels, axes, blowers, and the pump—the loud clanging of ore cars, and the incessant ringing of the bell that was the only real means the men below had of communicating with the hoistman above, and vice versa. In a larger, more profitable mine, there would have been at least two or three distinct bells and a like number of separate elevator cages, each run by its own engineer; but the Rainbow's End, being underfinanced, lacked even a single such cage. The miners had to ride up and down the shaft in the same ore bucket that brought rock to the surface, and were forced to rely solely on Novak to ensure that their ascents and descents were safely completed.

It was no wonder, Josselyn thought upon learning this, that when Durango introduced her, the big, sober Slav barely spared her a glance and no word, merely nodding tersely in her direction. The very lives of the men below depended upon his keeping his attention fixed on his labors. A single error on his part could send the miners crashing to their deaths, their bodies ricocheting down the shaft to be torn to pieces by the rock walls and timber shoring until at last, far below, what remained hit the bottom and slid into the sump, a pit of boiling-hot water that was responsible for much of the steam that rose from the shaft. Such had been the ugly fate of the unfortunate Forbes Houghton. When this happened, as with Forbes, the body fragments had to be recovered by means of small grappling hooks and either wrapped up in canvas or placed in wooden candle boxes to be carried above for burial. Such falls were the most common cause of death in hard-rock mines. This was because, particularly at the end of their shifts, when the miners ascended rapidly to the cool surface from the fiery interior below, they were prone to become light-headed and thus sometimes to tumble inadvertently out of the ore bucket.

As she grasped these ghastly facts, Josselyn's stomach heaved without warning, and she began to have second thoughts about inspecting the underground workings of the Rainbow's End. The idea of climbing into the ore bucket and dropping like a lead weight through the five-foot-wide, quadrangular hole in the shaft-house floor into the gloomy darkness and the thick clouds of steam billowing up from the gold mine's unknown depths terrified her.

"There's no need to be afraid, Josselyn," Durango said quietly as he observed her ashen face. "Novak knows his job. However, if you'd rather skip going below, we can."

"No," she replied at last, shaking her head and lifting her chin resolutely. "No, if I'm going to own a gold mine—or, at least, a quarter of one—I think that it's important I fully understand every aspect of how it operates. Otherwise, you and Wylie and even Victoria will always have an advantage over me in our partnership."

"Certainly, either Wylie or I will, in any event, if you have actually decided to fulfill that foolish condition set forth in Red's will, so you can inherit his shares," Durango pointed out, a mocking smile curving his lips, his eyes gleaming speculatively. He paused briefly, allowing his words to penetrate. Then, his voice carefully noncommittal, his face now an unreadable mask, he casually inquired, "Has Wylie asked you to marry him, then?"

For a wild, wicked instant, Josselyn was tempted to answer yes to see how he would react. Then she recognized that if Durango really had murdered Forbes and her father, she would be placing herself in jeopardy with such a response. All at once, the shaft seemed too close for comfort, gaping like a yawning maw at her, its shadowy depths sinister, the puffs of rising steam it emitted like the breath of some hideous monster. If Durango were suddenly to push her into that murky hole and then claim she had stumbled and fallen into it, it was highly unlikely that Novak, so intent on his duties, would be able to testify otherwise. In that moment, she sensed that for all his nonchalant appearance, Durango was tense as she, awaiting her reply. She could almost feel how tightly coiled he was, like some predator preparing to spring upon her and rip out her throat. Was he even now planning how he would shove her into the shaft—as he perhaps had shoved Forbes? Her head reeled at the thought, and nervously, she started unobtrusively as possible to sidle away from the menacing hole in the floor. She dared not take a chance on baiting him, she realized, lest her initial suspicion that he was a saboteur and a killer be proved abruptly and horribly correct.

"No," she stated flatly. "Wylie has not yet spoken to me of marriage."

"But you think he will before the stipulated year is out, is that it?"

"I think," Josselyn began, choosing her words carefully, "that none of us—including you, Durango—wants to see Da's shares in the Rainbow's End squandered on an opera house for Nell Tierney."

"No," he agreed slowly, "I don't suppose any of us do. So, since I ain't a marrying man, I suppose we'll both just have to hope that Wylie can bring himself to go down to Pine Street, to Father Flanagan's, to learn the catechism, so that if and when he finally *does* come up to scratch, you'll be able to say yes, hmh?"

Despite her sudden previous dread of him, Josselyn found herself perversely piqued by this observation, by the knowledge that even if it cost him Da's shares in the Rainbow's End, Durango apparently had no inclination to wed her himself—not that she would say yes to *him*, the slovenly brute! Still, the idea that he actually had little or no interest in her, or in her inheritance, either, continued to puzzle her, causing her fear to recede slightly. This lack of concern simply did not fit in with the profile of a man who had blown up the gold mine and murdered two of his partners; and now, she was again forced to reconsider her suspicion of Durango.

Was he truly innocent—or playing some horrid, vicious cat-and-mouse game with her? She did not know. Her heart prompted her to trust him; a man who would give money to a beggar and a home to an orphan like Cisco was an unlikely candidate for committing sabotage and murder; but her head warned her that appearances could be deceiving, as Durango himself had said, and that to lower her guard against him might be to sign her own death warrant.

"Are you ready to go below?" he asked, startling her from her reverie as he indicated the ore bucket that Novak had cranked up to the surface of the shaft and that was now waiting to take them down into the gold mine.

"Y-y-yes, I suppose so." Despite her attempt to quell her uneasiness, Josselyn's voice quavered and her face was white with fear.

Although Durango had told her that the ore bucket could carry eight men—two inside, four on the rim, and two in the cable ring—it looked to her to be terribly small and insecure, swaying precariously, it seemed, at the end of the heavy cable from which it dangled. The shaft itself was somehow even darker and more ominous than before. The steam that eddied from its depths hissed like a serpent. To think of descending into that hellhole was frightening enough; to think of doing so with Durango at her side was suddenly petrifying.

"You don't have to do this, you know," he reminded her as his gaze took in her pale countenance and her wide eyes, her nostrils flared with apprehension and the way in which she bit her lower lip, as though to still its quivering.

"I—I know," Josselyn choked out softly, trying to get a grip on herself, on her churning emotions. "But somehow, I—I think I must."

"In you go, then," he declared. "Don't look down."

Before she had time to comprehend what he intended, he caught hold of her trembling figure, lifted her from the floor, and swung her out over the shaft. Her head spun sickeningly as, through the roiling steam, she spied the abyss that fell away horrifyingly beneath her feet. Despite his admonition, her eyes fixed morbidly upon the giddying sight. She froze. Utterly. Her heart leaped to her throat as all her surroundings appeared suddenly to whirl about her, unbalancing her. For an excruciating eternity, it seemed, she hung suspended over the seething hole, her life cradled in Durango's palms. In that instant, she truly believed she was but a heartbeat from death. At the thought, she squeezed her eyes shut and prayed; and then, to her unmitigated shock, he dropped her. Firmly. Into the ore bucket, steadying her as it knocked against one wall of the shaft from the impact of her entry. Josselyn was so relieved that she had not been sent plunging to her demise that only the secure span of his hands about her waist and her own fingers instinctively clutching the rim of the ore bucket prevented her from collapsing as her knees buckled without warning beneath her.

"For God's sake, Josselyn!" Durango hissed sharply, giving her a savage little shake. "Don't faint! You're liable to topple out of the ore bucket and be killed!" Even as he spoke these last words, he was catching hold of the weighty cable above her head, stabilizing the swinging ore bucket, and jumping in beside her. His hands clasped her arms so hard that she knew she would have bruises on them tomorrow. "Are you all right?" His voice was harsh with worry. "Josselyn, are you all right?"

"Y-y-yes," she managed to whisper, nodding, her eyes slowly fluttering open, fastening once more on the darkness writhing below, threatening to engulf her.

"Christ! Didn't you hear what I told you? I warned you not to look down— ¡Jesús! Don't do it again!" Abruptly, he jerked her into his arms, crushing her face against his broad chest so she could no longer stare into the depths of the shaft to which her gaze was drawn and that dizzied her so. "What you're feeling is called vertigo." His tone was gentler now; his right hand stroked her veiled head soothingly, as though she were a child. "It's often caused by heights. You'll be fine if you just don't look down. Will you promise not to do that anymore if I let you go now?"

''Yes.'' Her voice was muffled by the crisply starched folds of his white cambric shirt; and as she breathed in the scent of the freshly washed and pressed fabric, Josselyn wondered vaguely at its cleanness and how he always managed somehow to look so untidy, nevertheless.

Slowly, Durango released her; but he kept his hands poised above her arms, ready to grab her once more should she, despite his warning and her promise, look down again and panic. But although her wild urge to peer into the shaft—even, incredibly, imcomprehensibly, to leap into it—was nearly overwhelming, she somehow managed to keep her eyes focused on his face. Josselyn was both surprised and touched by his evident concern for her, for she was so accustomed to his treating her in an irreverent, cavalier fashion that it was sometimes difficult for her to remember he was entirely capable of better conduct when he desired.

''You're doing fine.'' Durango smiled at her encouragingly. ''Just keep watching me the way you are now. In a moment, I'm going to have Novak start lowering us into the shaft. We'll drop very rapidly, but there's nothing to be afraid of; the windlass cable is quite secure. You can brace yourself against the sides of the ore bucket if you need to, but keep your whole body well *inside* of it. Otherwise, you could lose your fingers or even a hand, an arm, or worse, because the shaft is narrow and its walls are irregular, with places where the rock juts out at dangerous angles and is sharp-edged as a knife. Do you understand?''

Weakly, Josselyn nodded, feeling sick to her stomach and sorry, now, that she had come to the Rainbow's End and had insisted on seeing the dark, underground reaches of the gold mine. She wanted desperately to climb out of the ore bucket, to feel her feet once more planted on solid ground. But every time she thought of the step she would have to take across the fathomless shaft to get from the ore bucket to the shaft-house floor, her terror rooted her where she stood, her wishful words stuck in her throat.

She knew now why, despite all her pleading and cajoling,

Wylie had adamantly refused to accompany her to the Rainbow's End. With all her heart, Josselyn wished that Durango had proved as immune to her entreaties. Silently, she cursed him for a scoundrel that he had not been. So frightened was she at this moment that she did not, as she would have done just a few short months ago, quickly beg God's forgiveness for her uncharitable condemnation of Durango. Indeed, she felt no guilt or shame at all at the unaccustomed, unladylike words that formed in her mind.

Truly, she must be utterly mad, she told herself, to have asked him to escort her here, to the Rainbow's End, knowing that in all likelihood, he had murdered Forbes and her father, and perhaps meant to kill her, too, so she could not wed Wylie, who would then own one half of the Rainbow's End. Perhaps even now, Durango was plotting how, once they were alone, below ground, he would rid himself of her—or worse. Josselyn shuddered as, without warning, she recalled what had nearly befallen her at Antoine's cruel hands, and her thoughts took a wholly unexpected but equally horrifying turn. Images of every woman's nightmare filled her mind.

What if all Durango's comments about his not being a marrying man were but a ploy meant to lull her into a false sense of security in his presence, because he knew with certainty that if he asked her outright to wed him, she would reject him as a husband? After all, hadn't she made it clear that it was Wylie—even though not of her faith—whom she preferred? What if, realizing this, Durango had determined to rape her, hoping thereby to coerce her into marriage? Josselyn would not put such a wicked deed past him. He was no gentleman, as well she knew, for had she herself not remarked upon it often enough? Although a Catholic, Durango was not, she supposed—given his swearing, his drinking, his gambling, and, almost certainly, his whoring—very devout; she could not be assured that because of his faith, he would honor and respect her veil and habit, if not herself or her virtue—especially with a gold mine at stake. How foolish she had been not to have considered all this before!

Josselyn stared up at him, stricken by her appalling speculations; Durango looked so big and strong, and she felt so small and fragile in comparison. What chance would she stand against him if, once they reached the bottom of the shaft, he suddenly decided to drag her into some secluded passage of the gold mine, fling her down upon the hard rock floor, and brutally force himself on her? None. She would be totally helpless against him; for she could have no hope of successfully fighting him off, and it was doubtful that, with all the noise that inevitably accompanied the hard-rock mining process, any of the men laboring below would even hear her terrified screams. Even now, the rhythmic thud of the nearby massive timber-and-iron pump rod was deafening. She could only imagine how its volume would increase as she and Durango were lowered down the shaft. For the first time, she was grateful that they would make their descent in an ore bucket rather than an elevator cage. Surely, he would not be so brazen and foolhardy as to attempt improper advances in the wobbly bucket!

Even as the thought crossed her mind, however, Josselyn, to her dismay, found herself pitched against Durango as, with a nauseating lurch that caught her off guard, the ore bucket started abruptly to move downward. She had been so lost in her distressing rumination that she had not seen him give the signal to Novak to begin lowering them down and so had failed to brace herself adequately.

"Steady on, Josselyn." Durango's breath was warm and electric against her ear, tickling her sensuously.

She felt a thrill of fear mingled with inexplicable excitement shoot through her as, like a steel band, his arms encircled her again, holding her close as the ore bucket whooshed at an alarming rate past the cool, wet walls of the shaft, dropping so precipitously—as he had warned her it would—that the earth itself seemed suddenly to fall away horribly from beneath her feet, leaving her suspended in his grasp. Her breath caught sharply in her throat. Her belly heaved. The pounding of her heart rivaled that of the thunderous pump rod as she clung to him. Her blood roared like a storm in her ears as the wind in the shaft whistled by her, whipping her veil and habit, and as, like a cresting sea, the darkness and the steam whirled up to engulf her and Durango, sealing them in a cocoon broken only by the water that streamed down the crooked rock walls to splash like raindrops upon them.

Pressed against his chest, Josselyn could hear the slow, steady beat of Durango's heart, in pointed contrast to the frantic thrumming of her own. She could feel the heat of him, the strength of him; and she trembled at his nearness, his maleness. Durango felt her quivering like a trapped animal in his embrace, and he wondered if it was from fear of the ore bucket's falling so swiftly—as though it were not securely attached to the gallows frame and the windlass above, but hurtling inescapably toward doom—or from fear of him. If the latter, she was truly innocent, virginal, he thought—or exceedingly skillful at portraying the role she had chosen to play. Which was the real Josselyn, the nun or the deceiver? Durango did not know, not yet; but sooner or later, he would. He would not rest until he had found out, he swore.

Her breasts, crushed against his chest, felt soft and round and full beneath her habit, their nipples hardened into twin peaks from her fright and the chilliness of the shaft—and perhaps because of his own proximity, too. This last notion gave Durango no small measure of satisfaction, for it meant that Josselyn was not so insusceptible to him as she loftily pretended. With every rapid, shallow breath she took, her breasts brushed against him, taunting him, tempting him, making his loins tighten with sudden, sharp desire. As his blood and his breath quickened, Durango wanted both to laugh and to curse that he should be attracted to her, aroused by a nun, who was forbidden him, forbidden any man.

He was arrogantly confident where his ability with women was concerned, for none had ever denied him. He knew that if not for the tiny seed of doubt Josselyn had planted in his brain—that she might, in fact, be telling the truth about her convent upbringing—he would already have bedded this woman he now held in his arms. How that would have tangled the web Red had woven by making that heterodox will of his. How it would have spoiled her for Wylie, into whose unprincipled plans Durango would maliciously thrust whatever spoke he could. Cold, callous Wylie, an honorless thief, who had taken faithless Victoria while Forbes was yet alive, and afterward—and who would take Josselyn, too, if he could.

Suddenly, Victoria's inflammatory words that day outside of Killian's office rang again in Durango's ears, and there rose in his mind a vision of Wylie and Josselyn in bed together. Both were naked, save for the veil Josselyn wore upon her head, a nun's veil, a bride's veil, and Wylie's hands were upon the breasts that, even now, Durango could feel pressed against his chest, nipples taut and teasing.

Involuntarily, his arms tightened fiercely around Josselyn, startling her, causing her to gasp, and then to cry out a little. Hearing her in the darkness, Durango thought: *So would she sound when being made love to by a man*; and he felt a sharp, unanticipated stab of jealousy and anger that Wylie should be that man. If Josselyn had truly been brought up in a convent, then she had been reared to regard marriage as being based on both love and fidelity, neither of which Wylie would offer her.

He shall not have her!

So strong was this unbidden thought that for a moment, Durango believed he had spoken the words aloud. Then, realizing he had not, he experienced a wild desire to laugh at the idea that he had, even briefly, actually considered permanently saddling himself with a nun—and for no better reason than to prevent her from falling victim to Wylie. Annoy and cause trouble for Wylie, he would; marry Josselyn, he would not. Wylie was more than welcome to *her*, Durango told himself savagely, although not to her inheritance. After all, if the truth were known, she was probably a liar, a cheat, and a harlot, anyway, a party to whatever dastardly scheme her father had dreamed up. No matter how badly, at this instant, Durango wanted to believe otherwise, she was no doubt willing to sell herself to the highest bidder—as Victoria always had been, he reflected sourly.

The one, the *only* thing that he could not like was that Red's shares in the Rainbow's End came part and parcel with Josselyn. It simply would not do at all for Wylie to get his hands on those, although, if Durango's nagging suspicion were correct and Red were still alive and not dead as everyone supposed, Red must be the gold mine's saboteur and Forbes's murderer, and planning somehow to rid Josselyn of her unwanted husband, so she and Red would wind up with one half of the Rainbow's End between them. In that case, if Wylie wed Josselyn, he would be signing his own death warrant. Nor, Durango decided grimly, could he himself, or Victoria, either, for that matter, expect to be long for this world after that; for why would Josselyn and Red, having already committed two murders, balk at committing a third, and then a fourth, when all would result in their becoming the sole owners of the gold mine? After all, blood was thicker than water, or so it was said.

Durango wished suddenly that he could see Josselyn's face clearly, but because of the darkness and the steam that enveloped them, he could not. He could only feel her, trembling against him, her body young and alive and paradoxically all the more seductive for being swathed in the layers of her bewitchingly billowing habit. It made her seem like an angel, he thought—an avenging angel. In that moment, he both wanted and damned her, wondering if she was, even now, plotting how she and her father would kill him.

Book Two

Heart of the Mine

Chapter Ten

The Rainbow's End, Colorado, 1877

Though still afraid, Josselyn was no longer cold, for the lower they descended into the shaft, the hotter and muggier it became, the churning steam now like the waves of heat that, in the dead of summer, would rise from the Boston sidewalks. Its primary source, Durango explained, was the sump, a pool of water at the bottom of the shaft. Heated by the inferno that was the earth's molten core, the sump, hissing and bubbling like a witch's caldron, could achieve temperatures of more than 150 degrees, so a miner so unfortunate as to slip and fall into one—as Forbes had—even from just a short distance above, seldom, if ever, survived. Just last month, a newspaper called the *Territorial Enterprise* had reported one such mining accident, in which the victim, a man by the name of John Exley, had plunged only up to his hips into a sump. Though he had been quickly rescued by his fellow workers, he had nevertheless lost all the skin on his legs and had soon died.

By the time the ore bucket had reached the bottom of the shaft, Josselyn's entire body was drenched with perspiration; her veil and habit were sticking to her most uncomfortably, and she was having difficulty breathing in the stifling, sultry air. After Durango assisted her from the ore bucket, she withdrew her handkerchief from the pocket of her habit to wipe away the moisture trickling down into her eyes and beading her upper lip, while he notified Long Tom Henry, the shaft man, that they were now safely below. It was Long Tom's job, Josselyn was informed, to oversee everything that went up and down the shaft, and to ring the bell that signaled Novak above, which Long Tom now did. He seemed a pleasant enough man. But still, even aside from the fact that she must practically yell to be heard above all the noise in the gold mine, Josselyn could hardly bring herself to talk to him; for with the exception of a narrow-brimmed felt hat, a pair of sturdy denim breeches, and his socks and shoes, Long Tom was naked, his tall, thin but sinewy, damp body glistening in the dim light cast by the few lanterns hanging on the walls of the tunnel that branched off from the shaft.

"What are you wearing underneath that habit, Josselyn?" Durango shouted at her over the roar of the machinery and tools, the pounding of the pump rod, the gushing of water, and the seething of the sump, all of which cacophony was deafening.

Turning, she was so mortified to see that he himself was in the process of unbuttoning and stripping off his own shirt, baring his chest, matted with a sprinkling of fine, dark hair, to her stricken gaze, that his impertinent question didn't even register. Josselyn had not, since her early childhood, observed a single man in even a partial state of undress. But although after her initial, much-shocked glance, she had somehow managed to keep her eyes averted from Long Tom's half-nude body, now, to her deep embarrassment and utter shame, she found herself irresistibly captivated by the sight of Durango's half-naked torso. Unlike Long Tom's white skin, Durango's was bronze as a statue of some pagan god. He was powerfully built but lithe as a whipcord, even so; and as, unwillingly, Josselyn thought of how, coming down in the ore bucket, he had held her against that muscular chest, she inhaled sharply, a sudden tremor running through her body, making her feel even hotter and more flushed than she already did. Noting her discomposure, Durango grinned wickedly.

"I guess I . . . er . . . forgot to mention that nobody with any sense wears much clothing down in a hard-rock mine," he declared, his black eyes dancing with deviltry.

At that, anger overcame Josselyn's embarrassment, for she knew that he was lying, that he had deliberately neglected to tell her that all the miners—and even he himself—would be in a state of partial undress in the gold mine's interior. Why? Because he had known that, learning this, she would have refused to come below, and he wanted her here for some nefarious purpose of his own? As the thought crossed her mind, all of Josselyn's earlier fear and suspicion that Durango planned to ravish her, in order to force her into wedding him instead of Wylie, returned to haunt her. How convenient that he was able to discard at least a portion of his garments beforehand! And what was it he had asked her? Even as she wondered this, trying to remember, he repeated the question, as though he had read her mind.

"What are you wearing underneath that habit, Josselyn?"

Durango's eyes roamed over her leisurely, licentiously; and for the first time, she became aware of how soaked her habit was, how it clung to her, like ivy to a wall, revealing every line and curve of her figure. Her cheeks grew scarlet, and she bit her lip uneasily, self-consciously folding her arms across her breasts, as though this might offer some protection against him.

"You are no gentleman, to ask me that," she said, her green eyes flashing.

To her indignation, however, instead of firmly putting him in his place, as she had hoped, she only succeeded in causing him to gibe, "My sweet, I thought we had already established that!" before he threw back his head and howled with laughter. Then, after a moment, he sauntered toward her—until he was standing right before her, almost but not quite touching her, close enough so only she could hear the words he spoke.

"For heaven's sake, Josselyn!" Durango's voice still shook with amusement. "Do you honestly think that if I wanted to rape you, I would do so in front of Long Tom Henry? For shame! There are better ways—and better places than the hard rock floor of a sweltering gold mine, my sweet," he drawled sarcastically, not missing how she blushed with humiliation at realizing he had guessed her secret apprehension, her derogatory opinion of him, and had deliberately, crudely, voiced it aloud. "As you may have noticed, Josselyn, it is hot as hell down here; and in all those layers of clothes, coupled with the infernal temperature, you are inevitably bound to be overcome . . . at least by heatstroke, that is. To avoid that, I was merely going to suggest that if you happen to be wearing—as, indeed, I strongly suspect you are—quite a number of extremely modest undergarments, you remove as many of them as possible to lessen the likelihood of your passing out."

"Your concern is touching, Durango." Josselyn's outraged tone gave the lie to her words. "But I believe I'll take my chances, dressed as I am."

"Please yourself," he rejoined, shrugging. Then, mockingly, he added, "I confess I find the notion that you feel safe enough in my presence to faint dead away highly flattering. I suspect that any other virtuous young woman in your position would be afraid that—rogue that I am—I would find it well nigh impossible to resist . . . taking advantage of such a situation." His gaze raked her slowly, lewdly, making his meaning plain.

"You—you wouldn't!" Her eyes widened with alarm.

"Perhaps you are right," he agreed. "But then again"—an insolent grin once more curved his mouth—"perhaps you are wrong. Shall we go?"

Much as she wished otherwise, Josselyn had little choice but to accept the hand he extended to her. It was she who had insisted on seeing the Rainbow's End, she who had insisted on coming below. Wylie had warned her over and over that the gold mine was no fit place for a lady; even Durango—cad that he was!—had said as much. But stubbornly, she had refused to listen to either of them. She had no one but herself to blame for her predicament. Oh, why was she always so willful and impetuous? All her life, she had been so, and time and again, the Reverend Mother Maire had warned her that the day would come when she would live to rue it. Well, she rued it now, Josselyn thought—deeply. She ought to have stayed in Boston, in the convent, where she belonged, instead of traipsing halfway across the country to Central City. If she were honest with herself, she must admit that it was not grief at Da's death alone that had brought her, but her curiosity about his will, her desire for vengeance against his murderer, and, most of all, her longing for adventure and excitement at least once again in her life before embarking upon a nun's placid, routine existence.

Hadn't the Reverend Mother also said that, one way or another, God always answered one's prayers? Well, He had surely answered hers, Josselyn reflected miserably. She had had enough adventure and excitement today to last her a lifetime. She didn't want or need any more—especially the kind that involved her being led by a half-naked blackguard through a maze of shadowy, unknown passages to what might ultimately prove a fate worse than death. Already, she was so faint from the heat that she regretted rejecting Durango's advice about shedding some of her undergarments. She wanted to tell him she had changed her mind, after all, about inspecting the underground workings of the gold mine, but pride and sheer perversity kept her silent. Even if the price of the knowledge were her virtue or her very life, Josselyn vowed she would discover whether Durango had killed both Forbes and her father; and despite everything, now and here seemed the ideal time and place.

Still, her resolve was once more shaken as, taking up a lantern and holding it aloft to light their way, Durango pulled her after him into the tunnel that seemed to stretch away endlessly ahead of them. At their entrance, gemlike orbs suddenly glowed bright as fool's gold in the flickering lamplight before melting away into the darkness, scattering pebbles as they went.

"What—what were those things?" Josselyn queried nervously.

"Rats," Durango announced matter-of-factly. "There are literally thousands of them down here. They're pets . . . of a sort, tame enough, at least, to come around like clockwork every day at feeding time, to sit and wait for whatever scraps the men toss away from their dinner pails. In fact, we get real anxious when the rats don't show up. They sense things we often don't, such as infinitesimal movements in the rock; so we know that when the rats are skittering around like crazy, searching for a safe hole in which to hide, it's a pretty sure bet that there's about to be a cave-in."

Hearing this, it abruptly dawned on Josselyn just how unstable the gold mine really was, hundreds of feet beneath the surface of the earth, the huge timbers that shored up the whole operation the only thing that bulwarked it against its being buried beneath a mountain of dirt and rock. With no small measure of trepidation, she glanced about, realizing that it was entirely possible that at any moment, the Rainbow's End could—and might—collapse and kill her. She shuddered at the macabre understanding, surreptitiously inching closer to Durango, as though he were capable of shielding her from disaster. If he noticed her sudden desire for his nearness, however, he mercifully decided not to remark upon it.

As they progressed into the gold mine's interior, it became evident that it was a veritable rabbit warren of secondary shafts; tunnels—drifts and crosscuts and "turned houses," passages that made sudden changes in direction—and raises, winzes, and stopes. In many places, the floor, which Josselyn had imagined would be solid rock, was instead composed of wet, miry clay that Durango wryly referred to as "gumbo," claiming that it was the bane of every miner's existence. In the actual lodes, he explained, they employed a support system developed by Philipp Deidesheimer for the famous Comstock Lode and known as the square set, in which massive, six-foot-long timbers, mortised and tenoned at the ends, were joined to form hollow, interlocking cubes. This permitted the laying of several levels of plank floors, so the miners could work more easily and securely.

"Of course, some mine owners scrimp on expenses by failing to use proper timbering," Durango elucidated, "or they don't bother checking to ensure that their superintendents are and that they're keeping the sets wedged up tight against the ore, besides. But Red never believed in cutting costs when men's lives were at stake, and he always made damned certain that the timbers were put in right."

"Yes, he would have," Josselyn confirmed softly, "because that's the kind of man he was. That's the kind of man I remember him as being."

They were both silent for a moment, thinking about the fact that this was where—if he were truly dead—Red had met his tragic and untimely end. Without warning, tears brimmed in Josselyn's eyes, spilling over to mingle with the perspiration that streamed down her face, despite her mopping at it repeatedly with her handkerchief. Surely, Durango thought, such a quiet, spontaneous display of grief could not be feigned—or could it? After all, Victoria's frequent, pitiable shedding of crocodile tears always seemed real enough, he mused acidly, if one weren't already familiar with her carefully enacted charades. After a while, he spoke again, his voice made hard by his thoughts of Victoria and his suspicion of Josselyn.

"I'd show you some of the lodes," he told her, a sneer

in his tone, "but unfortunately, every single one of them was sealed off by the explosions set by our elusive and mysterious saboteur."

"But . . . why?" Josselyn asked, confused by his abruptly derisive manner and still puzzled, although she had contemplated the matter at great length the past few months, by what the culprit responsible for the blasts had hoped ultimately to accomplish. "Why would anyone want to do such a dreadful thing?"

"To halt production of the mine, of course." Durango's dark, demonic visage, fitfully illuminated by the wavering lantern light, was closed, an unreadable mask.

"Yes, I understand that," Josselyn said, trying hard not to shiver as she suddenly realized how far they had walked from the shaft, how utterly alone they were here, in this place where they now stood. Even the constant cacophony of the gold mine was muted, sounding faint and far away, the background hum broken only by the steady dripping of water somewhere nearer and the chittering and skittering of the rats. For an instant, Durango's face seemed to blur before her eyes; with a hand that trembled, she swiped with her sodden, crumpled handkerchief at the sweat that blinded her. She felt as though she were burning up with fever. She longed intensely for a drink of cool water, another sliver of the ice Durango had given her earlier from a special chamber in the gold mine, where it was kept for the men to suck on so they would not dehydrate in the roasting atmosphere and suffer a heatstroke. "What I can't comprehend is . . . why just shut down the mine? Why not destroy it? I mean, wouldn't that have been much easier, much less dangerous, much more . . . permanent?"

"Oh, yes, indeed." His black eyes glittered at the shrewdness of her questions. "But you see, my dear Josselyn," he continued mockingly, "if your father's speculations were correct, when the first of the sabotage began, before Forbes was killed, we were within months, perhaps even weeks or days, of hitting a mother lode. In that case, to destroy the mine would also have meant destroying forever any hope of reaching—if it truly exists—the mother lode. Simply sealing the mine off, on the other hand, however difficult—and believe me, it took one hell of a dynamite man to do the job —left it in a condition to be reopened and excavated at a later date, as we are in the process of doing now.''

"Who—who knew about the possible mother lode?'' Josselyn licked her dry lips nervously, scarcely able to contain herself at the thought that, finally, she might be on the verge of uncovering something concrete that would give her a clue as to Durango's innocence or guilt in her father's murder. Her pulse raced uncontrollably as she waited with bated breath to hear his reply.

"Your father knew, naturally, and Forbes—but of course, he was dead by the time the Rainbow's End was blasted to smithereens—and Victoria and Wylie knew . . . and I,'' he said.

"That's—that's all?''

"Yes, Josselyn, we four still alive then were the only ones with any real motive to blow up the Rainbow's End, so we could buy time to do away, one by one, with the rest of our partners and have a chance—alone—at millions,'' Durango jeered, disgusted, infuriated by her probing, her obvious lack of trust in him. He wondered if she had interrogated Wylie like this, decided that she probably had not, and grew even more enraged.

"And who among you is—is . . . 'a hell of a dynamite man'? Isn't that—isn't that how you phrased it?'' Despite herself, Josselyn's gaze was irresistibly drawn to his. She felt mesmerized, as the victim of a rattlesnake is mesmerized— before the serpent strikes, fangs sinking deep and venomously into its prey.

"Yes, that's how I phrased it,'' he answered slowly, his voice low, silky, deceiving. "Your father was an expert at handling explosives; he could have set those charges. So could Wylie.''

"And—and you, Durango?''

"And I."

These last two words echoed ominously in the silence punctuated only by the distant but relentless dribbling of the water, the small noises of the rats, which Josselyn had heard earlier. Suddenly, it seemed to her that Durango grew ten times again his normal size, looming over her, tall, satanic, and menacing, intent on doing her some mortal injury. Involuntarily, her hand fluttered to her throat. Gasping, she took a startled step backward, unaware that directly in her path lay a giraffe, an incline car used for hauling supplies and ore up and down the winzes. Durango reached out to grab her, intent on averting what he perceived as an impending disaster. But to Josselyn, oblivious of what was behind her, it appeared instead that he was bent on seizing her murderously. A scream tearing from her mouth, she turned to run, stumbled over the chain by which the giraffe was pulled along the narrow track laid throughout the gold mine, and fell flat on her face in the bed of the incline car. The impetus of her fall sent the giraffe rolling forward, rapidly gathering momentum as it plummeted over the nearby edge of the opening of the drift into the relatively steep winze below.

It all happened so quickly that Durango didn't even have time to shout a warning. Not delaying long enough even to set down the lantern he carried, he instinctively raced forward to the mouth of the tunnel. Momentarily, his muscles tensed, coiled, and then he was flying through the air, a human projectile, straight down the winze, toward the incline car. Both his split-second timing and his aim were right on target, and he landed heavily atop Josselyn's prone body. But there was not a moment to spare for voicing his concern for her or for comforting her. Paying no heed to her cries of shock, fright, and pain, he jammed the lamp into one corner of the giraffe, realizing dimly, from the sound of tinkling glass, that the lantern had shattered in his hand and was even now doubtless spilling oil into the incline car, perhaps even leaving a trail of kerosene in their wake. Durango's heart pounded as he thought of the fuel's igniting, the flames spreading, perhaps setting ablaze the dangerous pockets of volatile gases the gold mine harbored here and there, causing them to explode. Unplanned, uncontrollable fire in the hole—every miner's worst nightmare. He sighed with gratitude when the lamp's wick sputtered and died; and though he and Josselyn were abruptly plunged into darkness, he caught hold of the giraffe's raised sides to brace himself against his being jerked out of the bed and began to drag his booted feet hard along the ground, in a determined effort to slow the treacherous speed of the now-runaway incline car.

Josselyn, by now hysterical, could not take in the catastrophe that was occurring. She knew only that she was so hot that she felt on fire, smothering in the flames. She couldn't breathe! She was suffocating! Mindlessly, dizzy and sick and gasping for air, she writhed and twisted beneath Durango's body, somehow managing to get herself turned faceup, after which she struck out at him blindly, beating him about the head and shoulders, scratching his face and chest, and shoving against his half-naked torso, trying vainly to push him off her.

"Goddamn it, Josselyn!" he spat through gritted teeth, unable to release his tight hold on the sides of the giraffe and so forced to duck his head as best he could in a futile attempt to dodge both her blows and her fingernails. "Stop it! Stop it! I'm trying to save your life, you little fool!"

But irrationally, she didn't believe him; and so, frantically, she kept right on pummeling him with her fists, raking him with her fingernails—until the moment when the giraffe reached the bottom of the winze and, continuing to rocket forward into the drift below, smashed with a bone-jarring clang into a string of ore cars and timber trucks lined up on the track. Having suspected that such a collision was imminent, Durango had, just before the last minute, let go of the incline car to gather Josselyn's wildly protesting figure into his arms. Crushing her against his chest, cradling her head in his hands, he had pulled her onto his lap, half turning himself beneath her, wrapping himself around her to shield her as much as possible, so his own body would absorb the impact of the crash. When it came, his right shoulder and back slammed agonizingly into the front of the giraffe, scraping his bare skin raw, and his head snapped forward roughly. He clamped his jaws together hard to keep from crying out at the pain, deliberately compelling himself to relegate it to the back of his mind, to focus all his concentration and energy on Josselyn, who moaned and stirred weakly in his protective embrace as, finally, the giraffe shuddered to a grinding halt.

"Are you hurt? Josselyn, are you hurt?" Durango's voice was sharp with anxiety, and inwardly, he cursed the darkness that enveloped them, making it impossible for him to see her clearly. "Josselyn!"

"No, I—I don't . . . think so," she responded faintly, feeling ill and dazed from the infernal temperature, the harrowing ride in the incline car, the jolting collision. "At least, I—I don't feel any pain. I just feel hot and—and . . . a little strange . . . and—and thirsty . . . so very . . . thirsty . . ." Her voice trailed away as her tongue flicked out to moisten her dry lips.

She thought dully, longingly, of a cool drink of water and, in some hazy corner of her mind, imagined intensely, as though the strength of her desire alone would somehow make it happen, the snow upon the towering peaks of the Rocky Mountains melting down slowly through the earth to the gold mine, trickling all over her. The vision was so real that she actually believed she could hear water dripping down the walls of the tunnel. Then she realized that, of course, she could; it was an inevitable part of a hard-rock mine.

"Hang on," Durango ordered grimly, not knowing if she was injured. Naturally, she was bound to be shaken up; and her thirst, he knew, was from the heat. Damn it! He had warned her about wearing all those clothes. Why hadn't she been sensible instead of modest and taken off some of her undergarments? "Josselyn, can you just hang on, while I try to light the lamp?"

"Yes. I'm—I'm fine; really, I am," she declared more strongly, trying to rise; for even if she was a trifle light-headed and badly rattled, she didn't want him to know it. There was no telling what he might do if he thought she were defenseless against him.

"Just relax," he insisted, conscious of how she had stiffened against him, her every muscle taut as a thong. "I'm not going to hurt you, I swear."

Gently, making no sudden moves to alarm her, Durango laid her down in the bed of the giraffe. As he did so, his hand brushed against what, after a moment, he realized must be her veil, somehow snatched from her hair during the course of the accident. Grabbing it up to use as a makeshift pillow, he wadded it up and placed it under her head, in the hope of making her more comfortable. Greatly relieved that he did nothing more, Josselyn rested quietly, trying to collect herself, while he fumbled around in the darkness for the broken lantern. Finding it at last, he reached into his pants pocket for the small box of matches he always carried with him. In order to avoid accidentally igniting any of the spilled oil in the bed, he carefully perched the lamp upon the right-hand corner of the incline car, where the front and one side met, then cautiously struck a match and lighted the lantern. After a moment, the wick caught and flared, and then began to burn steadily—thankfully, there was enough kerosene left in the base for that—and he turned back to Josselyn, his breath unexpectedly catching in his throat at the sight of her.

¡Sangre de Cristo! She was beautiful.

With her veil gone, Durango saw her hair for the first time, tumbled loose from its confining pins, in all its full, crowning glory, masses of it, red as her father's—as Durango had guessed it would be—cascading thickly, silkily, to her knees and looking so like shimmering waves of wildfire in the flickering lamplight that it seemed almost alive. He had never before seen such gorgeous hair. Despite himself, he experienced a sudden, nearly overwhelming desire to burrow his

fingers through it, to press his mouth to it, to bury his face
in it, to draw it across his throat, to feel it wrapped about
him, caressing his naked flesh and binding him to her. Like
a fiery halo, it framed her piquant, heart-shaped face, em-
phasizing not only her high cheekbones, thrown into sharp
relief by the play of light and shadow in the drift, but the
lines and curves of her voluptuous body, too. Her wide, sloe
eyes were open, green as aspens in the summer, set beneath
delicately oblique brows and fringed with thick, sooty lashes
that arched like crescent moons against her pale, creamy skin.
Her nose was finely chiseled, her mouth perfect as a bloodred
rose, her upper lip short and bowed, her lower full and generous.

Somehow during their perilous journey down the winze,
her habit had been torn as though an impatient lover had
ripped it from her shoulder to her waist; and now, like her
hair, for the first time, the smooth expanse of her swanlike throat and the soft swell of her ripe breasts beneath
her plain but enticingly damp, translucent white cotton camisole were revealed to him, and his eyes feasted on their
bounty. Perspiration lay like morning dew upon her skin,
glistening, trickling slowly down the deep hollow between
her breasts, which rose and fell shallowly with her every
breath, their roseate crests visible and alluring beneath her
clinging camisole. The lamplight shone upon her, illuminating her still figure, as though she were an angel cast down
to earth from some faraway, heavenly realm, while all about
her was shadow, fading, like the misty edges of a vignette,
into darkness.

She was a nun. The unwelcome thought came unbidden to
Durango's mind—and then the certain realization that if he
touched her, he would be lost . . . as would she, because
afterward, he would never permit her to go back to Boston,
the convent, to take her final vows.

His jaw set purposefully. Sternly, he told himself that he
would not lay so much as a finger on her, that, despite all
his jesting to the contrary, he was not so base as to take

advantage of her under the circumstances. But mutely, her eyes pleaded with him, for help or mercy—or something more? He did not know. He knew only that she needed him—and that he wanted her. He swore, the word falling soft as the footfall of some predatory beast into the silence, causing Josselyn to shiver with apprehension—and some other, darker, more primitive emotion she did not care to name.

He was like proud Lucifer after the fall, she thought uneasily, kneeling there beside her, his dark face shadowed but he himself unbowed, unchastened, unrepenting—and undeniably tempting, this handsome prince of this hell in which she lay, consumed not only by its infernal flames, but a fire of a different sort, a slow-burning heat she had never felt before, not even for Antoine. Durango's sombrero hung down his back, exposing to her fearful but fascinated gaze his thick black hair, soaked with sweat, gleaming like the rain-drenched wings of a raven. His black eyes glittered strangely, locked on her own green ones, holding her breathless, spellbound. She could see the muscles that tensed and rippled beneath his bronze flesh; and her body, already overwrought, tingled peculiarly at the sight, as though restless with yearning—but for what, she did not know, did not want to know, because she was afraid—even in Antoine's arms, she had always held back, had always been afraid—that to know would be to loose some devil within her own self, some devil that had always, no matter how hard she had attempted to deny its existence, lurked deep down inside of her, waiting . . . waiting to be freed.

Even now, it clamored for release, howling like a hound of hell. Try as she might, Josselyn could not seem to silence it. It was like Pandora's wicked box; it would not be shut up. Louder, it screamed, and with its cacophony came a torrent of chaotic images and desires she had known she harbored and from which she had sought escape in the convent, images and desires potent and prohibited as the forbidden fruit, filling her brain near to bursting. Desperately, she shoved them away. But there was no eluding the fact that she might have been killed had not Durango saved her, that she owed him something for that—though, still, the knowledge did not lessen her fear of what she believed he would demand from her.

She had meant to be a bride of Christ, not the whore of Lucifer; and yet when, slowly, as though she had no will of her own, she wordlessly held her arms up toward him, it was not only a gesture of self-defense, but of supplication and surrender.

She would be wasted in a convent, wasted on Wylie, Durango thought—and perhaps she was not really a nun at all. . . .

"Jossie . . ." he muttered huskily. And was lost.

There was between them a moment like the sudden flash of heat lightning, taut, highly charged, filled with the adrenaline that still surged frenziedly through them at their torturous ride, at their having come so close to death, so narrowly escaped it. They were young and alive; life was sweet, and they clung to it, clung to each other as, without warning, Durango's eyes darkened with passion, and growling low in his throat, he swept Josselyn into his arms, his hands twisting roughly in her unbound hair, his mouth closing, hard and hungry, over hers.

Whatever she had expected, it was not this, not the wild savagery that leaped high and potent between them in that instant when he claimed her lips, like electric blue fire in a mountain storm, crackling, splitting the roiling heavens asunder, unleashing a torrent. She felt as though she had been struck by lightning; her blood roared like thunder in her ears; she seemed all at once to be sucked into a churning morass of black clouds from which she felt she would never escape. Dazed, she fought him. At first, fearing him, fearing *herself*, she fought him. But she was no match for him, as she had known she would not be. He was too strong for her to battle, or even to push away. His hands, tangled in her long tresses, arched her body against his determinedly, relentlessly forcing her down as he bent over her, dominating her, exhausting her, his demanding mouth clinging to hers, devouring her, swallowing her breath, until, little by little, her struggles ceased as, at last, against her will, he compelled her to respond.

She was devastated, shattered. In her wildest imaginings, she had not dreamed that it would be like this; Antoine had never kissed her like this, violently, waking within her emotions and sensations so fierce and exquisite as to be overpowering, all-consuming. She felt weak and dizzy, as though she stood at the pinnacle of James Peak, her breath snatched away by the high altitude, the thin atmosphere. She gasped for air and found it in Durango's breath as he kissed her again, and yet again, his tongue tracing the outline of her lips before plunging between them to drink deeply, lingeringly, of the milk and honey within.

Low in her throat, Josselyn whimpered against this intimate invasion and plunder, even as her lissome young body treacherously betrayed her by welcoming it, yielding to it, reveling in it. Of their own volition, her hands crept up his bare chest to wrap around his neck, drawing him down to her. Her tongue melted, warm and sweet, against his, twisting, twining, learning eagerly the lessons he taught as, brutally, he breached the walls of her convent upbringing to show her the world beyond, in a way that Antoine never had, lips hot, urgent, insistent against hers, giving her no time to think, to consider—only to feel.

And she felt . . . the earth upheaving, falling away from beneath her feet, taking with it all she had ever known that was safe and secure, leaving in its stead what was dangerous and uncertain, both frightening and exhilarating her. His bold tongue was insidious as the serpent in the Garden of Eden, tempting her with forbidden fruit, exhorting her to taste of it, to know its nectar and ambrosia—and be damned, cast out. And so Eve's sin became her own, and she fell, as Lucifer had fallen, Lucifer's mouth moving exigently on hers, his hands roaming her body, until, with every last fiber of her being, she kissed him, craved him, and gloried in his brazen assault, her eyes fully opened to all they had been half blind to before.

In that moment, somewhere deep inside her, a dam suddenly burst, and a desperate flood of want, of need too long suppressed sluiced through her, sweeping her up ruthlessly as a maddening sea, bearing her swiftly, helplessly, toward some dark, unknown, unexplored shore—where desire and destiny waited and all that mattered was Durango. She had feared he would wrest her virtue from her—and now, as his feverish lips scorched their way across her cheek to her temple, across the strands of her damp copper hair, she no longer cared. It was her fate, she thought dimly, as though, somehow, all her life had been leading up to this moment, this crucial turning point, where she must choose between what was chaste and tame, and what was wanton and wild.

And she had chosen—or Durango had chosen for her. She was floating on the waves of sensuality, the tide of passion he was evoking inside her, and she could not halt her onrushing journey. She had no strength to do so; it was as though he had sapped it from her, as though all of her bones had dissolved inside her, leaving her fluid as quicksilver, limp, and lethargic. She had no will of her own anymore; he had taken it from her, bending her to his own stronger one as he pressed her down into the bed of the incline car, his hard body covering her own soft one, weighing her down, making her acutely aware of his maleness, his virility—and of her own womanliness and vulnerability. She felt small and fragile in his embrace, powerless against him, his to shape and mold as he pleased—and did.

Her hair was all Durango had imagined it would be as he wove his fingers through it, buried his face in it, inhaling deeply the heady scent of her lavender perfume that clung to the satin tresses, to the smooth, pearly throat laid bare for his taking and down which, groaning, he trailed a path of ardent kisses. The stubble on his unshaven face grazed Josselyn's tender skin roughly as she writhed beneath him, moaning, exciting him, making his loins quicken sharply with desire. Involuntarily, she bucked against him, honing his passion to a keen edge. Her head thrashed wildly from side to side as he fastened his mouth to the hollow at her throat, his tongue flicking out to tease the tiny pulse that throbbed frenziedly there, echoing the frantic beat of her heart.

"Sweet . . . sweet . . ." he whispered thickly against her throat.

An inconceivable thrill shot through her at his words. She was set aflame by his kisses, his caresses—and still, she longed instinctively for more, her body like fire and ice, burning and melting beneath him. Her skin felt so incredibly sensitive that his every touch was like a brand, searing her; the sizzling kisses he rained upon her were like sparks from a catherine wheel, singeing her. Savagely, his hands snarled in her hair, pulled her face up to his. His lips seized hers possessively once more, bruising them, his tongue shooting deep into her mouth, ferreting out its innermost secrets, ravaging its moist recesses.

The dark hair that matted his chest was like silk beneath her palms and, through the thin material of her camisole, against her heaving breasts and their sensitive tips. So caught up was Josselyn in the feelings he was arousing in her that she did not even realize how her habit had been torn, exposing her to him, until his lips found her throat again and his hands moved down to cup her breasts, squeezing them, molding them to fit his palms, causing her to gasp with shock and fear and delight. Her breath came quickly, raggedly, as his thumbs traced tiny circles about her flushed areolae, then brushed across her nipples, making them pucker and stiffen, strain seductively against her camisole, inflaming him. Her heart thudded erratically as ripples of unbearable rapture coursed through her. In some hidden recess of her mind, Josselyn knew that it was too much, too soon, that within minutes, he would have her and she would be lost, impotent to prevent his taking her.

Desperately, she strove against him, some primal instinct driving her to renew her struggles to escape from him. But easily, Durango captured her hands, pinioning them behind her back, forcibly compelling her body to arch beneath his, his thighs powerfully imprisoning hers. His fingers ripped impatiently at the lacings of her camisole, yanking the ribbons loose, shoving the edges of the fabric apart, freeing her breasts from their flimsy constraints. His breath was hot, inciting against her naked flesh as his tongue slowly, tantalizingly, licked away the sweat that ran down the valley between her breasts and his hand closed over one soft, swollen mound, his thumb taunting its rigid crest.

"¡Dios mío, Jossie! How I want you!" he rasped, before he lowered his mouth to her breast to lave her nipple, his tongue stabbing her with its sharp, serrated heat.

She cried out, feeling suddenly, violently, so overcome, so hot that she thought she would die of it. She was a mass of unimaginable sensation; her emotions were in a turmoil. Wicked. She was wicked and wanton. Somewhere deep down inside, she had always known that it was so. Now, as she had always secretly feared, she was burning in hell for it, an angel fallen, lying wrapped in Lucifer's infernal, soul-stealing embrace, a willing captive of his fiery, subterranean domain.

Through the blur of the perspiration that poured into her eyes, she could see his black eyes glowing like embers in the wavering lantern light. She could feel his half-naked body, sheened with sweat, pressing her down, the corded muscles in his arms bulging as he clasped her to him, his burning lips seeming to be everywhere upon her flesh, branding her forever as his. Her head swam tumultuously, as though she were about to faint. Her heart pounded as though it would burst within her breast.

"Durango . . ." she breathed, clutching him frantically as he and the drift appeared without warning to spin away before her stricken, passion-drugged gaze. "Durango . . ."

And then a merciful blackness swirled up to engulf her, and she knew nothing more.

Chapter Eleven

¡Jesús! He had nearly *raped* Josselyn! *Would* have raped her if she had not passed out, Durango thought, inhaling sharply. Then, as he stared down at her, at her luscious, tempting dishabille, his eyes narrowed. No, not raped her, for even though scared at first, she had, in the end, wanted him as badly as he had her—and she had not been entirely innocent, besides! He had not been the first man ever to kiss her; he had had enough women to know that. Yet despite the unbelievable passion he had wakened in her, she had been no skilled coquette, no seasoned trollop, either, experienced and practiced at the art of lovemaking. The understanding confused him; he realized he was no closer now to knowing whether she was an angel or a witch than he had been before. It was possible she had slipped away from that convent in

Boston to meet a lover; young women did that, sometimes
—those without any vocation, that was, Durango added to
himself grimly, thinking, now, that regardless of whatever
else she might be, for all her veil and habit, Josselyn was no
honest nun. Of that, he now felt certain. But still, no actress,
no matter how skilled, could have feigned that frightened,
uncertain naïveté coupled with that incredible, sweet passion
she had displayed when he had initially kissed her. Thus it
yet remained for him to discover just what game she was
playing—although, surely, even if she *were* hand in glove
with her father, she had this day got more than she had
bargained for!

Half ashamed of himself now, Durango groaned at the
memory of how he had flung himself upon her—as though
he were no better than a stag in rut—and brutally compelled
her to submit to his abrupt, overwhelming desire for her. He
had been savage as an animal, he thought, paying no heed
to her cries and her struggles against him, but violently forcing
her down and ruthlessly seizing possession of her lips, deliberately arching her body against his so she would have no
doubt about how much he wanted her. No wonder she had
fought him. He had behaved like a beast, a monster. She
would never forgive him; and as he gazed down at her unconscious form, her long, tangled hair; her bruised, swollen
mouth; her pale, creamy skin; and her lush, bare breasts, he
felt an unimaginable pang of regret that it should be so. He
had wanted her, wanted her still, desperately, with every last
fiber of his being; and all he had almost surely accomplished
was to drive her straight into Wylie's arms—and Wylie's
bed. As he thought of Wylie's fingers running through that
unbound red hair, Wylie's lips kissing that beautiful rosebud
mouth, Wylie's hands cupping those full, ripe breasts, Wylie
thrusting himself deeply inside her, Durango was without
warning gripped by such a murderous jealousy and rage that
if Wylie had been there in the tunnel, he would have killed
him.

"Damn you, Red!" he swore under his breath. "Damn you to hell for making that accursed will and placing Jossie in such an untenable position!"

She was much too good for a low-down skunk like Wylie—much too good for a ruffian like him, too, Durango admitted ruefully to himself, even if she were a liar and a cheat. But still, one way or another, he was suddenly fiercely determined to have her. Such was his resolve about this that he was sorely tempted to finish what he had started; and it was all he could do to make himself carefully rearrange Josselyn's garments and to lift her up and carry her from the drift.

It was the heat that had caused her to swoon, Durango knew. He had to get her out of the gold mine, into the cool, fresh air above, and replenish her dehydrated body's water as quickly as possible. Rapidly, he strode through the passages toward the main shaft, hoping fervently all the while that she would not hate him too badly for what he had abruptly made up his mind to do, how he planned to ensure beyond a shadow of a doubt that she never gave herself to Wylie—much less married him—that she would have no choice but to turn to him, Durango, instead.

At the back of his mind, Red had been uneasy ever since Nell's hurried return to the cottage on Spring Street to inform him that Durango was taking Josselyn out to the Rainbow's End. However wayward she was, Red simply could not envision his genteel, convent-reared daughter's insisting on seeing the gold mine, which surely Wylie, and possibly even Durango, had warned her was too rough and dangerous for a woman to enter. But since he *could*, however, certainly credit Durango's escorting her there, Red had immediately, in Nell's buggy, set out after the couple, determined not to let them out of his sight. The going had been difficult, as he had known that it would be; for Nell's trap was not built to travel on a track that was little more than a couple of wagon ruts. But Red had persevered, knowing that if the buggy had survived the trip once—as it had done the night he had blown the Rainbow's End to kingdom come—it could do so again, although it *had* required a new rear axle after that first furtive journey.

In time, Red had reached the place where Nell, according to their prearranged plans, had waited for him while he had set the explosions that night; and he had halted the trap and firmly tied the horse to a nearby stout bush before making his way up to the top of the steep hill from where he would be able to spy on the Rainbow's End. Fortunately, he had had the foresight to bring Nell's opera glasses along with him, and so, from his vantage point flat on the grass on the knoll, he had a nice, close view of the gold mine below.

He had become increasingly anxious as the long minutes had ticked by, wearing both on his nerves and his guilty conscience about his having involved his unwitting daughter in his wild scheme, and Josselyn and Durango, having vanished into the shaft house, had failed to reappear. Red had not approved of his daughter's going down with his partner into the dark, hazardous passages of the gold mine, perhaps into some secluded tunnel, where Durango might try to force himself on her and where no one would hear Josselyn if she screamed. In fact, when this chilling thought had occurred to him, Red had almost jumped up and raced down to the shaft house to drag Josselyn away. But then, he had told himself sternly that even Durango was not so base as to commit rape; and not wanting to expose—for what was probably nothing more than his imagination run rampant—the fact that he was still very much alive, Red had further reassured himself with the idea that Josselyn was unlikely to set foot in the ore bucket, much less go below.

But still, as the time had passed, Red had grown more and more doubtful of his earlier decision to stay put. What in the bloody hell was taking them so long? he wondered. Damn it! They ought to have been back outside by now! Finally, just when he had concluded that, unnecessary mistake or not to reveal himself, he *had* to make sure that his daughter was all right, the shaft-house door opened and Durango stepped from the shadows into the sunlight. Red's relief at the sight of his partner was short-lived, however, for as he observed Josselyn's clearly unconscious figure in Durango's arms, her veil gone, her hair wildly streaming free, her habit torn, his worst fear was realized.

"Holy Mary, miither of God!" he blurted aloud to himself, roiling with anger and rent with anguish. "The misbegotten son of a bitch bloody well *has* raped me daughter!"

At that, not caring who might see him, Red leaped to his feet, intending to run down the hill and kill Durango. But in Red's frantic rush, his foot slipped into a rocky crevice, and he fell heavily to the ground, his ankle snapping sickeningly beneath him.

"Goddamn it! Goddamn it!" he swore, his face contorted with agony as he thought of both his daughter and his ankle, the one surely ravished, the other doubtless broken.

For a moment, he breathed hard with fear and torment at his inability to rescue Josselyn, knowing with certainty that this was God's own terrible punishment on him for using her as bait. Then, groaning at the tremendous pain of it, Red crawled to his hands and knees, rocked back to a seated position, clutched his leg tight, and deliberately wrenched his ankle from the narrow fissure in which it was stuck, gritting his teeth against his crying out as his skin was scraped raw and his ankle bone brutally jarred. Unluckily, such was Red's strength at yanking himself free that he could not halt his momentum and toppled over backward to roll hell-bent for leather down the steep hill.

"Bloody heeeeell!" he bellowed as he tumbled head over heels, bumping violently, it seemed, into every protruding rock and root along the way.

At last, he came to rest at the bottom of the acclivity. For a long while, the wind knocked from him, his ankle throbbing horribly, he simply lay there, his arms outstretched, his legs

spread, resembling, attired as he was in his usual higgledy-
piggledy disguise, a scarecrow blown to the ground by a
strong wind. Then, after a time, he managed to get his breath
and to drag himself over to Nell's buggy. Catching hold of
one of the wheels to haul himself upright, Red hopped on
his good leg to the horse, untied it, then hopped back to the
trap and, moaning at the effort, sweat beading his brow,
somehow pulled himself up into the buggy's seat. By now,
his ankle pained him so dreadfully that he saw no other choice
but to drive back to town and enlist Nell's aid; for how could
he himself, in his current condition, hope to prevail against
Durango? He was, at least for the time being, compelled to
leave Josselyn in Durango's callous hands, and Red shivered
at the thought of Nell's wrath when she learned what had
happened. She would not, he quite rightly supposed, spare
any pity for him because of his broken ankle, but would
lambaste him with the full force of her Irish temper and sharp
tongue.

"Oh, Jossie, what have I done? What have I done?" he
lamented aloud, feeling as sorry for himself as he did for his
daughter, as he slapped the reins down upon the horse's back,
heading toward Central City and Nell's fury, which he felt
wretchedly that he certainly deserved.

But how was he to have known? he asked himself bitterly.
Durango and Wylie, too, had been like sons to him. He had
loved them, and he had not truly believed until now that
either one of them was the saboteur. Indeed, until Forbes had
been found dead in the sump, it had been Forbes himself
whom Red had suspected of causing the so-called accidents
at the Rainbow's End. Only afterward, when Forbes was
buried in his grave and the accidents had still continued, had
Red realized that either Durango or Wylie must be to blame
for all the sabotage, was perhaps—unimaginable as it had
seemed—guilty even of murder. But even then, Red had
rebelled against the notion, not wanting to believe it. Now,
feeling violently ill, he thought that there could be little question remaining about Durango's being the culprit; for surely,

only a man so reprehensible as to commit sabotage and murder would not have balked at raping a nun.

"Forgive me . . . oh, please . . . forgive me, me darling daughter," Red gasped, as, with a lurch that jolted his ankle excruciatingly, the trap began to roll roughly down the poor trail toward home.

Josselyn had thought to find herself in hell when she awoke, so, initially, she was conscious only of how cool she was, of how refreshing and pleasant was the breeze that wafted in through the open window, billowing the plain muslin curtains gently inward. She had had such an awful dream, she reflected drowsily, a hideous nightmare. But thank heavens, she was safe in her own room at Miss Hattie's cottage, after all. Only gradually did she remember that the curtains in her room at Miss Hattie's were blue-checked gingham, and glancing down, she grasped that she was clothed only in her undergarments.

"Nooooo," she moaned softly, one hand going to the damp cloth on her aching head as she tried weakly to rise, wondering wildly where she was, what had befallen her. The nightmare! It *hadn't* been a dream, then, she realized, shuddering as she looked up and saw Durango. "Oh, nooooo."

"Shhhhh. Hush, Jossie." His face, as he bent over her, was filled with concern. Tenderly but firmly, his hands pushed her back down upon the bed in which she lay. After that, taking up the cloth that had fallen down into her lap, he dunked it into a basin of water that sat on a nearby nightstand, wrung it out, then replaced it on her brow. "Don't try to talk or get up just yet. You've suffered a mild heatstroke. You're in a small lean-to off the cookhouse at the Rainbow's End, a room that your father used to stay in and that Wylie and I still use if for some reason we need to remain overnight at the gold mine. You'll be fine in a bit. Do you think you can manage to drink a few sips of water?"

After a moment, her eyes wide with alarm, Josselyn nodded, the wheels of her mind churning furiously as she stared at him, cringing from him, fearful of displeasing him. He had kissed her—passionately—and done other horribly intimate things to her before she had fainted in the tunnel. She understood that now; it was all suddenly coming back to her, in a terrible rush. With mortifying clarity, she recalled his mouth on hers, hard, hungry, and demanding, his body coercing her own down ruthlessly into the giraffe, his hands tangling savagely in her hair, his breath hot against her skin as he had pressed his lips to her bare breast, his tongue darting forth to taunt her nipple sensuously. . . . Oh, God.

Everything was black after that. What had happened after she had passed out? Josselyn did not know, and she was panicked by the realization. Merciful God in heaven! Had Durango *raped* her? Stricken, she searched his face intently for an answer, but there was none. His eyes were hooded; his countenance was set as a mask. She could not read his thoughts.

Surely, I would know if he had, she assured herself frantically. But she had so little knowledge of such things, so little experience that she could not be sure.

She racked her brain, trying to remember all that had been whispered by the girls in the dormitory at the Boston convent, ignorant speculations and ill-formed judgments, for the most part, Josselyn concluded now; for most of the gossip had centered on romantic acts, stories that had cast men in an appealing, heroic light—not the dark, harsh reality of a virile man's forcing himself upon one. She shivered with shame and horror at the memory, at the thought that perhaps, in the drift, Durango had finished what Antoine had only started. Had those same hands even now—despite how she shrank from them—assisting her into a sitting position, holding a glass of water to her mouth, brutally shoved up her skirts and . . . ?

Stop it! Stop it! she told herself angrily. *You don't know that he did anything!*

You don't know that he didn't, either, a voice inside her responded grimly. *Ask him. For God's sake, ask him!*

But although she desperately yearned to do just that, Josselyn found she could not bring herself to speak, to insist that Durango tell her what had happened in the tunnel, if she was now no longer chaste, but defiled. She thought of her own ignominious willingness, her wicked wantonness in his arms. Would he fling it up in her face? No, she could not confront him at this moment, when he stood so close to her, watching her as a panther its prey.

All this, Durango knew or guessed as his eyes took in her pale, scared face and the manner in which she trembled and visibly shied away from him. He had been right, then; Josselyn might not be a nun, but surely, she was no harlot, either. However infinitely desirable and unexpectedly passionate she had this day proved to be, she was, in truth, no more than a green girl, terrified of what had leaped so suddenly, so electrically, between them in the drift. He remembered the courage she had exhibited in the shaft house, how she had so bravely, in spite of her fear, stayed in the ore bucket, compelling herself to conquer her unexpected vertigo and to descend the shaft into the gold mine; and he could not help but admire her. Not many women would have had either the resolve or the mettle for that. It made him feel guilty and ashamed now at seeing her so dispirited and at not immediately putting her mind to rest about what had passed between them in the tunnel, when she had lain passive and unconscious in his arms. But every time he thought of her lying with Wylie, perhaps even somehow managing to get him to marry her, Durango's purpose hardened and his determination instead to remain silent strengthened. Josselyn would not, he suspected, go sullied to Wylie's bed. If— however mistakenly—she believed herself damaged goods, she would, Durango thought, see no alternative but to turn to him, her seducer. He would at least have succeeded in maintaining the balance of power at the Rainbow's End and might not need to jeopardize his own life by wedding her.

He did not want to believe that Red was still alive, the culprit responsible for all that had occurred at the gold mine, and quite capable of murdering him, but he could not afford to take chances.

"Come, Jossie," Durango said, holding out his hand to her. "Now that you appear to be feeling better, I'll take you home. I'm sorry about our not getting to sample the contents of our picnic basket, but I really believe that it's best if we postpone our lunch together—at least, until tomorrow, don't you? I think we've both had enough excitement for one day. Besides, you've been out like a light for quite a while, and the afternoon has grown late."

Tomorrow? How could he honestly believe that she would ever go anywhere with him again? Josselyn wondered, shocked and appalled. The man was not only a blackguard, but a lunatic! She could not trust him, and she would never forgive him for what he had done to her—or might have done to her—today. Though she had yearned fervidly for the cool drink of water he had offered her, it had been all she could do to swallow even a few sips, such was her apprehension at his proximity. A man who had raped her once—if he had—certainly would not hesitate to do so again; and she had no intention whatsoever of becoming Durango de Navarre's whore! Right now, however, she was still totally at his mercy, Josselyn recognized, and so she decided she would be wise to humor him until she was safe in her own room at the boardinghouse on Roworth Street. Even so, she was loath to take his hand. Instead, nervously clutching the bed sheet to her breasts, she spoke tremulously.

"Where—where are my veil and my—and my habit? I— I can't leave here without my clothes. Someone might see me, and then there would be . . . ugly talk."

It was as close as she could come to asking him about what had occurred in the tunnel. But to her despair, Durango did not take the hint. Instead, his reply, when it came, was both enigmatic and discouraging.

"Yeah, well, people always tend to assume the worst, and

sometimes, the worst is true," he declared, hating himself for purposely misleading her. But then he thought again of her and Wylie lying together and forced himself to smile mockingly. "But of course, a nun's behavior is above reproach, or should be. However, I daresay you would know far more about that than I. Now, if you'll excuse me, I'll just step into the kitchen to fetch your clothes. I had Old Sourdough wash and dry them—naturally, they were covered with grime from the incline car"—deliberately, he let his eyes roam over her body lewdly, meaningfully, causing her to flush scarlet with shame and embarrassment—"and I also had him try to sew the tear in your habit. I sincerely doubt that his unskillful attempt at needlework will meet your high standards. However, it should be good enough to keep you adequately covered until we get back to Miss Hattie's cottage and you can repair the damage."

True to his word, Durango retrieved Josselyn's clean, mended garments from the kitchen and, returning to the lean-to, handed them to her. Then, much to her dismay, instead of leaving her alone, he leaned casually against the window frame and, lighting a cheroot he withdrew from his shirt pocket, dragged on it deeply, waiting and watching her expectantly. Why, he actually meant to remain in the room, the scoundrel!

"Please. If you don't mind, I'd—I'd like some privacy in which to dress," she stated as coldly as possible, her heart sinking as she saw his carnal mouth curve with amusement at her words.

"Don't be tiresome, Jossie," he drawled, to her horror, and with a glance that set her heart to thrumming jerkily in her breast. "It was I who undressed you; and surely, after all that passed between us today, my sweet, you can have little regard for your modesty where *I* am concerned!"

To her deep mortification, she thought that this was probably the truth, and she bit her lip hard to keep from bursting into sudden tears. Oh, if only she weren't stuck up here at the Rainbow's End with him, she would give him a piece of her mind. But as it was, Josselyn felt she dared say or do nothing to provoke him, knowing, as she now did, full well of what he was capable—and, worse, how easily her own defenses against him could crumble beneath his onslaught. Truly, Durango was a villain of the worst sort! But at the moment, she hardly considered herself above him.

For this reason, she told herself that it didn't matter if he watched her dress. Her modest undergarments covered her quite adequately; and many perfectly respectable ladies, she had heard, in similar states of undress, admitted men to their boudoirs while completing their toilets. But still, Josselyn's cheeks stained with color as she slid from the bed to begin donning her habit. Much as she longed to do so, she was afraid to turn her back on Durango; so he was treated momentarily to an enchanting glimpse of her willowy figure beneath her camisole and petticoats before she hurriedly snatched her habit down over her head and twitched her skirts into place. With shaking hands, she tied her cestus about her waist. Then, lacking her hairpins, she braided her tresses into a single, long, thick plait, which she stuffed as best she could under her veil as she yanked it onto her head.

Through all of this, Durango spoke not a single word. Indeed, when Josselyn once more summoned her courage to look at him, he was gazing out the window, smoking his cigar and seemingly oblivious of her presence—though she did not guess what it cost him to appear so, especially when, more than anything, he itched to fling her down onto the bed and make her his. He did not understand these violent feelings she was arousing in him. She was only a woman, like any other woman. But even as the notion occurred to him, Durango knew that it was not so. She was, in truth, different from all the women he had ever known, a bewitching mixture of purity and passion, holding him at arm's length, even as she had drawn him to her in the drift, responding to him in a way he would not have believed possible. For despite everything, Josselyn *had* responded to him, he thought again, with unbridled sensuality, revealing a wealth of untapped emotion and desire beneath her vestal facade.

Now that he had tasted of its sweetness, he longed to drink deeply of what was bottled up inside her, to drain it to the dregs, be they bitter or not. He felt as drugged with lust for her as though she had slipped him some potion that had clouded his senses and placed him under her spell. Why else should he suddenly have become so fiercely determined to have her? He ran a *saloon*, for Christ's sake! He was as different from her as night from day. And yet . . . and yet, when he remembered her glorious mass of fiery hair loosed wildly about her, her beautiful head flung back, her swanlike throat laid bare for his kisses, he did not care. He wanted only to drag her down from her lofty pedestal and show her what it was to be possessed, body and soul, by a man—by *him*! And he would, Durango vowed savagely to himself. Somehow, some way, he would have her in the end—whatever the cost to them both.

Chapter Twelve

Josselyn felt so mixed up inside that she did not think she could even begin to fathom her chaotic emotions; and guilt at her reaction to Durango's kisses, his caresses, overwhelmed her. Even now, as she remembered what had passed between them at the Rainbow's End, she was stricken anew with shame and dread that she was not only unfit to take her final vows—which she had always known in her heart, anyway—but, worse, a brazen hussy who would have given herself willingly, disgracefully, to either of the two men who had ever in her young life kissed her—and both of them sinners of the lowest order!

After Durango had compelled her to dress before him, he had declared that after the mishap in the gold mine and the mild heatstroke she had suffered, she, a novice horsewoman, was in no condition to ride. Despite all Josselyn's protests, he had adamantly insisted on leaving her donkey at the Rainbow's End and carrying her home, mounted before him on his black stallion, Diablo. Even now, she shivered at the feel of his strong arms wrapped around her, holding her close all the way down the rough, rock-strewn track wending from the Rainbow's End to Central City, and thence along the winding roads to the boardinghouse. Still, if she were honest with herself, Josselyn knew she must admit that it was not only fear with which she trembled at Durango's nearness, but with the tempestuous thing that, in the gold mine, had seized her in its dark, savage grasp and filled her with such desperate hunger and need. She was so relieved to arrive home at Miss Hattie's cottage that after Durango lifted her down from his horse, she practically ran through the white picket gate, up the walk to the front porch, hoping to escape from him.

But to her despair, instead of taking the hint that his company was most unwelcome, he determinedly kept pace beside her, even striding a little ahead to open the front door for her and to ensure that he accompanied her inside. Once in the foyer, she turned on him furiously, intending to tell him to get out. But before she could speak, Zeb pushed open the swinging door to the kitchen, stuck his head out, and grinned at her shyly, reddening with pleasure as, to spite Durango, she bestowed upon Miss Hattie's grandson her sunniest smile.

Why, the young fool's half in love with her! Durango thought hotly, wondering suddenly just what in the hell was going on under Miss Hattie's roof. Maybe he had been wrong about Josselyn's having slipped away from the convent to meet a lover. Maybe it was Zeb Munroe who had been kissing her all along—right under his and Wylie's ignorant noses! This notion so incensed Durango that it was all he could do to keep from thrashing the beet-red young man gazing so worshipfully at Josselyn.

"Hey, Miss Josselyn," Zeb greeted her, bravely daring to shoot Durango a glance of envy and dislike. "I thought that'd probably be you. How was your outing? Grandma told me that you'd gone up to the Rainbow's End. If I'd have known that you wanted to see your pa's gold mine, I'd have been more 'n happy to drive you up there in our wagon. Well . . . er''—observing the muscle that began to work in Durango's set jaw at that, Zeb's courage abruptly deserted him and he stumbled over his words—''er . . . anyway, what I wanted to tell you was . . . that letter you've been waitin' for? . . . it came today, while you were gone.'' He indicated an envelope propped up on one arm of the hallstand in the foyer and addressed to Josselyn.

Seeing at a glance that it was from the Reverend Mother Maire, she cried out softly. Then, snatching it up as though it were the answer to a prayer and clutching it to her breast, she carried it quickly into the parlor to open it, distressed that, although she so plainly wished to be left alone, Durango perversely persisted in staying, flinging himself down into a chair beside her and, without asking her permission, lighting one of his cheroots. When Josselyn frowned at him censuringly, he did, however, grinning mockingly, remove his spurred boots from Miss Hattie's tea table.

''Don't mind me, Jossie,'' he told her as he blew a cloud of smoke into the air. ''Go ahead and read your letter. I can wait. From what that foolish young swain of yours said, its contents must be important to you.''

Briefly, she glowered at him.

''Zeb Munroe is *not* my swain; he's just a—just a friend, that's all!''

''How glad I am—for his sake and yours—to hear it,'' Durango drawled coolly, but Josselyn did not mistake the hard edge to his voice or the way his black eyes raked her possessively, as though she belonged to *him* and he would not countenance her looking at another man.

She shuddered at the thought, for surely, if he considered her his to command, it could only mean that he *had* taken her virginity. No!—she simply would not think that, would not believe it until she learned for certain that it was true.

Fiercely resolving to ignore him, she eagerly ripped open the envelope, unfolded the heavily crossed pages inside, and began to read. She was so stunned that she read them twice. Then, after she had finished, she simply sat there for a very long while, in shock, for she could not believe their contents. Instead of advising her to return to Boston to take her final vows, as she had thought would be the case, the Reverend Mother had urged her seriously to consider honoring the terms of her father's will and marrying either Wylie or Durango.

Of course, if neither of these two men is acceptable to you, Josselyn, the abbess had written, *then you must let God and your conscience be your guide and do what you think is best in the matter. However, I have some sad news I feel I must impart to you, because it may affect your decision, and thus ultimately your entire future. As you know, we are a poor convent, and Sister Toiresa has informed me that we are growing ever poorer. I have exhausted every resource at my disposal, seeking financial assistance, but unfortunately, there are so many in the world who are in need that there is precious little money forthcoming.*

I would not burden you with our grievous troubles on top of your own. However, things are so bad here that I am deeply afraid that the convent may be forced to close its doors before the year is out; and in that case, dear Josselyn, if you still wish to become a nun, you will need to approach Father Flanagan there in Central City for help in finding another convent, for if my worst fears are justified, it will be impossible for you to return to us here in Boston. The good Sisters and I will soon be scattered far and wide, although I do not know where any of us will go or what will become of us. Our future I entrust to the hands of God and the Church.

There was more, but what stood out indelibly in Josselyn's mind was the fact that the haven to which she could have retreated at any time, the very thought of which had comforted her in the disturbing, upside-down world she had entered, was now gone, casting her adrift. She was beset by sudden panic at the realization. She felt herself in a position precarious as that of a trapeze artist who has just discovered that the rope on one side of her bar is rapidly fraying, and then looks down to see, to her horror, that the safety net below had some time ago collapsed. God had known she had no true vocation born of His calling, and now, He had punished her for her sacrilege, her dishonoring of her faith by even daring to consider perpetrating such a sham as becoming a nun, of living such a wicked lie—and in His name. This revelation, coming hard on the heels of everything else, pitched Josselyn into the depths of despondency. Never had she felt so miserable, so low. Her whole life, once so ordered and settled, had now gone totally awry.

"Josselyn, what is it? What's wrong?" Durango queried sharply, noting her ashen face, her frozen figure. When she did not respond, he leaned forward to pluck the letter from her unresisting hands and read it himself. "Well," he said, "it is not glad tidings, I suppose, but even so, I do not know why you should be sitting there, looking like someone just smashed you over the head with a whiskey bottle! After all, you must have known that you could not both claim your inheritance and return to the convent—and do not tell me that you were serious about taking your final vows, because after today, I think we both know that you were not!" He paused for a moment. Then he added, "Or could it be that you were only looking for a few hot memories to sustain you in your nun's cold bed?"

"Shut up!" Josselyn hissed, jolted from her unhappy reverie. "Shut up, you unprincipled rogue! How dare you speak so to me? What do you know about anything—about me?"

"I know that you were not meant to be wearing that veil and that habit, my sweet—for being a man of the world, I would wager my last dollar that I was not the first man ever to kiss you! Or are you denying that that oh-so-inviting mouth of yours has done more before today than just chant off the decades of your rosary?" He laughed shortly, unpleasantly, at the blush that colored her face crimson. "No, I see that you are not. Well, hell, Josselyn! You are not the first young woman to chafe at the strictures of a convent, and I doubt that you will be the last. So, now that we both know what an unchaste fraud you are—''

"That's a lie!" she cried heatedly. "While it's true that I—that I may have intended to become a nun for—for all the wrong reasons, I am still a maid. . . ." Her voice trailed away, catching on a sob as she suddenly recalled that, after today, she no longer knew even this with any certainty.

"Ah, yes, my sweet," Durango jeered, reading her mind, his black eyes glittering with a strange, exultant light at the thought that whatever she had done before, she was yet a virgin. "While your previous lover may have proved gentleman enough to deny himself the whole of your desirable charms, do you really think that the same can be said of an 'unprincipled rogue' like me?"

The silence that fell at that was fraught with both promise and menace.

"You—you didn't?" Josselyn whispered, stricken.

His cavalier reply was like a brutal slap in her face.

"Ask me again tomorrow, and perhaps I will answer. Until then, *señorita*, I will leave you to reflect long and hard upon the hazards of deceit!" With that parting shot, Durango abruptly left her.

Oh, God, Josselyn thought, moaning softly to herself, like some small, wounded animal, after he had gone. *He's not to be trusted! No matter what he did, I must have nothing more to do with him ever again. If . . . when he calls on me tomorrow, I must show him firmly to the door, strictly forbid him ever to see me again, and give him the cut direct when I see him. . . .*

But then she remembered the grim, determined thrust of his jaw, and she knew that he would not so easily be dismissed. If she asked Miss Hattie to turn him away at the door when he arrived tomorrow, he would probably forcibly push his way inside. Had he not obliquely threatened even poor, callow Zeb? And that because he simply *thought* that the young man was courting her. Josselyn was so wrought up that she envisioned one terrible scene after another, until she was half convinced that no one at the boardinghouse, least of all her, was safe from Durango de Navarre.

But what else could she do except try to send him packing?

But if he had raped her . . . Now, for the first time, Josselyn thought to consider all the consequences to herself if he truly had. Not just the shame and degradation of the act and of her own willing participation that had urged him to commit it, but the fact that he had ruined her for any other man . . . for Wylie. How could she wed Wylie, knowing she was no longer a virgin, but sullied by Durango? If Wylie ever discovered that she had duped him into marrying her, he would, feeling as he did about Durango, surely at the very least divorce her; and then where would she be? A woman of notoriety, of scandal, cast off, scorned, destitute, totally alone in the world. Josselyn shivered at the realization, for it was too hideous to consider. Merciful God! Durango might even have got her with child!

It was imperative, she grasped suddenly, that she learn whether he really had taken her virtue; for if he had, she would have no choice, she now realized, but to hope and pray that he saw fit to make an honest woman of her—even as she quivered at the notion of placing herself irretrievably into his power, his possession, of becoming his absolutely. But if she did not, what would become of her? She did not know. He *must* wed her! Even her inheritance did not now seem too high a price to pay for that. Then she shuddered at the understanding that this was why Durango had done what he had. This was what he had wanted and meant to have all along—and at last, she knew for certain, terrified, that it must indeed have been he who had blown up the Rainbow's End and murdered her father.

Chapter Thirteen

It was but a mocking reprieve, Josselyn thought miserably, that Wylie, instead of Durango, was first to call on her late the following morning at the boardinghouse on Roworth Street. She tried to fob him off with a lame excuse, ill with anxiety that Durango, whose arrival was surely imminent, would show up to find him there with her in Miss Hattie's parlor. But Wylie, who wished to escort her to lunch and then on a leisurely drive, stubbornly refused to take no for an answer; and before Josselyn could protest further, he firmly whisked her outside and practically tossed her into his buggy.

"Not another word, Josselyn," he said, almost curtly. "I am quite hurt by the notion that you have lately been neglecting me, when I had thought us fast becoming good friends. Yet you have evidently had time, and time to spare, to waste an entire day, jaunting up to the Rainbow's End with Durango, even though I warned you repeatedly that it was no fit place for a lady; and now, I understand from Fiddler Dan and Old Sourdough, who drove into town this morning for supplies, that you not only visited the gold mine yesterday, but actually *inspected* its *interior*, during which time you suffered an accident. While I am, of course, relieved to find that you are not injured, I must tell you, Josselyn, that if you had been, it would have been no less than you deserved for disregarding my warnings and gallivanting off with Durango, who, as we both know, has so little care for any woman's sensibilities! I confess I am sorely disappointed in you—to find you so reckless about your person and so heedless of my advice. I would not have thought it of you, Josselyn.''

As he had spoken these words, Wylie's mouth had compressed into a thin, grim line, so she could not help but be aware of both his displeasure and his disapproval. Sighing heavily, she steeled herself against him as she grasped that his true purpose in taking her out today was not to entertain her, but to subject her to a severe lecture, which she felt she could not endure—particularly when she thought of all that had befallen her at the Rainbow's End, the worst of which she devoutly hoped that Wylie was ignorant. Surely, Durango had not boasted of his conquest—if such it had been—to the miners! The thought was horrifying.

"Have you no word to speak in your defense? None?'' Wylie continued implacably, his voice cold. "Well, I shall presume, then, to hope that you have learned your lesson and are now properly chastened. I, for one, cannot think what possessed you to insist upon viewing the gold mine—and in Durango's questionable company, besides—but I shall be most happy to hear your apology, and then to forget the entire, unfortunate episode!''

Recognizing from this that, amazingly, Durango had, for once, actually adhered to the code of gentlemanly conduct, that Wylie was indeed unaware of what had taken place in the drift, Josselyn's apprehension was abruptly replaced by both astonishment and anger. Why, Wylie actually expected her to say she was sorry for daring to investigate her inheritance! For a moment, she could only gape at him, incredulous. The nerve of the man! The gall! The conceit! How did he dare? She was so outraged that for a moment, she was sorely tempted to give him the sharp side of her tongue. But then she realized she could hardly, like some virago, begin shouting at him in the buggy on the main street of Central City. People would think she had gone totally berserk. Her reputation would be in shreds afterward.

"I am sorry you feel that way, Wylie." Despite her attempts to gather her composure, her slanted green eyes flashed and her voice quavered with ill-suppressed fury. "For I do not intend to apologize for visiting the Rainbow's End. As a one-quarter partner in the gold mine, I have as much right to go there as you and Durango and Victoria, and I shall certainly do so again if I think that it is necessary. However, I do regret your being so upset, for I should not like us to be on bad terms with each other."

For an instant, Wylie's whole body went so rigid with rage and his hands tightened so convulsively on the reins that Josselyn knew that it was only with the greatest of difficulty that he held himself in check. Feeling as though he were a powder keg sitting beside her on the buggy seat, she braced for his explosion, surprised when it did not come.

"Perhaps it is I who should apologize," he stated stiffly, staring straight ahead at Eureka Street, obstinately refusing to meet her gaze. "Until recently, you seemed not only quite willing, but most happy to drive out with me. I believed that you understood this to be a—a courtship and that you accepted it as such. I thought . . . that is, I hoped that, eventually, we would . . . come to an understanding." He laughed shortly, bitterly. "I had even begun to make tentative inquiries of Father Flanagan— Forgive me. I assumed too much . . . a proprietary interest where I see none is wanted or warranted. If you would rather I didn't call on you anymore—"

"Oh, no, Wylie! It's not that!" Josselyn cried, stricken,

for if he had indeed paid a visit to Father Flanagan with regard to being instructed in the catechism, then Wylie must, in fact, be serious about intending to marry her; and she would not see that chance thrown away until she learned the truth from Durango as to whether he had taken advantage of her.

"It's just that . . . I want to be an equal partner in the Rainbow's End. I want to contribute, to pull my own weight. I don't want to be dependent on you or Durango or even Victoria to tell me what to do, to make up my own mind for me when it comes to decisions affecting the gold mine. It's not that I don't trust you, but—"

"But the truth is, you don't," Wylie interrupted, his tone dry, offended. "After all, it must be obvious to you that one of us killed Forbes, blasted the Rainbow's End to smithereens, and murdered your father." The statement was as bald as his accusation against Durango that day in the mercantile.

Like a wide, peril-ridden abyss, his words stretched between them, distancing them, making each suddenly wary of the other. Wylie's anger and affront were readily visible in the steeliness of his grey eyes and the stern set of his square jaw. Was he truly indignant that she had insulted him by suspecting him of stooping to sabotage and murder—or was he cleverly erecting a false front to conceal his culpability for his crimes? Josselyn did not know. For the first time, uneasily, she seriously considered the fact that, like Durango, Wylie had possessed the necessary knowledge, motive, and opportunity to have done the deeds. She had believed him a gentleman. But now, she recognized that, even so, he could be cold, even cruel, when he chose. After a time, she spoke again.

"I wasn't going to phrase it quite that way . . . but, yes, I think that it's more than likely that either you or Durango set those explosions and killed Da; even Victoria could have hired help to do it—and nobody else had anything to gain by sealing off the gold mine and murdering two of its partners, or at least, so far as I have been able to determine."

Wylie's nostrils flared; a muscle throbbed in his cheek.

"I take it, then, that despite your permitting me to squire you around these past several weeks, I am still on your short list of suspects? My dear Josselyn, if that is how you feel, I am surprised at your consenting to drive out with me! Are you not afraid of my carrying you out to some isolated spot and doing away with you?"

"No, for as matters now stand, it would avail you nothing, and I do not think you are such a fool as that. As you well know, under the terms of Da's will, if I were unwed at the time of my death, his shares in the Rainbow's End would pass to Nell Tierney, who is not stupid and who therefore would not be apt to sell them until she had fully apprised herself of the gold mine's worth. It is also possible, perhaps even likely, that, being Da's . . . close companion and confidante, she was—and remains—well aware of his belief that he was on the verge of discovering a mother lode at the Rainbow's End, and that for that reason alone, she would not part with the shares under any circumstances."

"I . . . see. Yes, you are quite right, of course." Wylie was silent for a long moment, staring off into the distance, contemplating her words and his own course of action, for he did not want her to turn against him or side with Durango. Understanding how close he was to losing her before she was even his, Wylie continued more quietly, more evenly, his tone now earnest and sincere. "Regardless of what you may think to the contrary, Josselyn, I did not blow up the Rainbow's End. I did not kill either Forbes or your father. Each in his own way was my friend; and in addition to the gold mine, I own two other thriving businesses, the mercantile and the shipping company. If it would help to convince you that I am not in dire financial straits, that I am, in fact, innocent of that of which you would accuse me, I would be more than happy to show you my account books. I have nothing to hide. As I've told you before, it is Durango who is the saboteur and murderer."

"Have you any proof of that?" Josselyn asked, feeling sick inside; for Wylie's words bore an unmistakable ring of honesty, of truth—and they served to reinforce her own suspicion that Durango was indeed the culprit. And to think she had lain willingly in his arms, Eve to his serpent, tempted, beguiled, seduced by that wild, sweet taste of forbidden fruit. . . . As the memory swept over her, Josselyn shut her eyes tight against it, as though by doing so, she could blot out the shame and the horror of it.

"No, I have no proof as yet," Wylie reluctantly admitted, his voice breaking into her thoughts, "although, of course, I hope to obtain it, in time. Till then, I can only ask that you have faith in me, Josselyn, that you trust my word as a gentleman when I tell you that I am not guilty of these heinous crimes."

"I—I believe you, Wylie," she replied at last, thinking: *Though you shall never know how much I wish I did not. God help me if Durango raped me*. . . .

Unaware of her inner turmoil, supremely satisfied by her answer, Wylie, observing that they had reached John Best's soda fountain and pharmacy, pulled the buggy to a halt out front. As he stepped down to tie the horses to the hitching rail, he deliberately bent his head to his task so Josselyn would not see the smile that curved his lips at the thought that at least where she was concerned, he had finally succeeded in cutting Durango's knees right out from under him.

While they were eating lunch, Victoria entered the pharmacy, looking as attractive and coolly, intriguingly, remote as always in her fashionable widow's weeds. No one, not even her lover, Wylie, knew what it cost her to appear so; for beneath her poised, sophisticated facade, Victoria was a mass of apprehension and turmoil.

She had never wanted to wed Forbes. He had been forty years her senior, and she had both feared and hated the loud, vulgar, self-made man who had not scrupled to steamroller anyone who had got in his way. But in the end, Forbes had compelled her to marry him, holding over her head a fistful of ruinous IOUs of her father's and threatening to cast her and her father into the gutter if the notes were not redeemed—one way or another. So, seeing no other choice, Victoria had woodenly consented to the wedding. It had been the beginning of what, to her, had been a nightmare.

Night after night, she had borne Forbes's slobbering lips on her moist red mouth, his groping hands on her perfect, champagne-glass-sized breasts, his gross, corpulent body on her soft, curvaceous one. He had revolted her to the point where she had longed fervently to retch—and what thanks had she reaped? The fat, frigging fool had either stumbled drunk or had got himself shoved into the main shaft at the Rainbow's End, leaving her in a horridly precarious situation financially. Forbes had had money once, but over the years, he had wasted it in profligate spending, always putting on a show to impress people. He would have long ago bankrolled the Rainbow's End to high heaven, had not Red, Durango, and Wylie stoutly refused to exchange the majority of their shares in the gold mine for his unconditional backing, preferring slow and substantial rather than speedy but meager profits for themselves. So Forbes had made other investments instead, most of which, unfortunately, had not panned out; for he had always been too obstinate to listen to anyone.

As a result, as only Victoria, her attorney, and her banker knew, she was not the wealthy widow that everyone presumed her to be. In fact, the explosions that had sealed off the Rainbow's End had devastated her; she had been counting on the discovery of a mother lode to stave off her creditors. Her gowns from Worth alone cost a small fortune each season, to say nothing of her jewels and all the other expensive folderols she felt absolutely essential for any lady worthy of the title. The thought that she might be forced to sell her mansion on The Casey appalled her. Because of her father's bad judgment, she knew what it was like to be desperate, dunned for payment of debts; and she could not bear to be placed in such an untenable situation again. The prospect of that's happening gnawed at her daily, as though she were already a bone to be picked clean by buzzards. If not for Wylie's occasional and wholly unpredictable spurts of generosity, she would even now be destitute.

Now, as she gazed at Wylie's handsome reflection in the gleaming glasses that lined the shelves behind the soda fountain, Victoria thought heatedly that it just wasn't fair that Forbes had frittered away the riches on which she and her lover could have lived together so luxuriously for the rest of their lives. Now, if they wished to gain between them controlling interest of the Rainbow's End, Wylie must— inevitably—marry that dull, drab nun seated beside him and stay married at least long enough to get his hands on her inheritance.

Despite her taunting words to Durango that day outside of Killian's office, the notion filled Victoria with both anxiety and jealousy. She loved Wylie with a passion she would not have believed possible; the idea of sharing him, perhaps even losing him, was frightening to her. If she had only known years ago what she knew now, she would never have offered herself first to Durango, who, of the two young men, she had mistakenly assumed would be more likely to overlook the fact that she was Forbes's wife and to ease her loneliness and misery. If Wylie were aware of what she had done, his pride must have been deeply wounded, she knew. Doubtless, that was why he had never told her that he loved her, though she felt that in his own cold fashion, he did care for her. Still, even after Forbes had died, Wylie had not asked her to wed him. Now, perhaps he never would, and for that, she cursed Red O'Rourke with all her heart.

Such was Victoria's ability to conceal her emotions, however, that nothing of her inner tumult showed upon her face as she stepped forward smoothly to greet the couple seated at the soda-fountain counter.

"Why, Wylie," she said, latching one hand possessively to his arm, a gentle reminder as to whom she hoped he truly belonged. "And Josselyn. What a surprise. I was just out doing a little shopping and, when I spied you, thought I would stop and say hello. I didn't expect to see either of you here.''

This last was a barefaced lie; Wylie had left her bed only a few short hours before, and she had known that he was coming here with Josselyn. Normally, Victoria would not have intruded; but today, for some unknown reason, she had not been able to stay away, but must view her rival yet again. Now, she was struck not only with a faint sense of relief, but with an abrupt flash of contempt that Josselyn O'Rourke was plain as the habit she was wearing. Glancing down at her own modish attire that emphasized to perfection her slender throat and her hourglass figure, Victoria reassured herself firmly that her sleek brunet beauty cast Josselyn into the shade ten times over and that, surely, the nun could not harbor even a prayer of winning Wylie's affection away from her. Her jangled nerves somewhat soothed by the thought, Victoria preened with satisfaction at realizing how, even now, despite having made love to her earlier that morning, Wylie could not seem to take his eyes off her. She had seen that look on his face before and knew that he was remembering what they had done in bed together just hours ago—and wanting to repeat it. Surely, she had nothing to fear, she told herself again. Surely, everything would turn out the way she hoped and planned.

As Josselyn studied the two of them standing there together—for courteously, Wylie had risen at Victoria's approach—both of them so exquisitely dressed, their manner so elegant, she could not help but feel a sudden stab of envy, a forlorn sense of not belonging, of not fitting in. All at once, she wondered how she had ever dared to think that she might stand a chance at becoming Wylie's wife, at moving in the polite circles he moved in. It now seemed ludicrous even to contemplate the idea, impossible to believe that Wylie could actually be interested in her when he had someone like Victoria Stanhope Houghton practically throwing herself at his feet.

A lump rose in Josselyn's throat, choking her, so it was

all she could do to manage to swallow the last of her vanilla ice cream. Suddenly, all the brightness appeared to have gone out of the spring day. Dismayed, depressed, she wanted nothing more than to return to the boardinghouse on Roworth Street, even if Durango *were* there, waiting for her. She deserved no one better than he, anyway, she mused morosely. For what was she, after all? The daughter of an Irish miner who had known little more than how to write his name and a bad letter. How had Da and Wylie ever managed to achieve any common ground, she wondered now. How could *she* and Wylie ever hope to achieve any? At this instant, it seemed unlikely that they could. Perhaps she was, in truth, more suited to Durango, however disdainful of manners he was.

Josselyn could only be glad when, at last, after reminding them about the small, private supper she was holding at the Teller House one evening later on that week—"to welcome Red's daughter properly into our midst," as she phrased it —Victoria took her departure.

The cloying fragrance of her expensive French perfume trailed in the widow's wake, and Josselyn abruptly informed Wylie that she had developed a splitting headache and begged him to take her home.

Chapter Fourteen

The outing with Josselyn, Wylie reflected, in irritation, had not been a success. Damn Victoria! Why hadn't she stayed away? She was so beautiful and high-spirited that no doubt, poor, modest, unassuming Josselyn—so amusingly straitlaced and annoyingly righteous—had felt like a moth in the presence of a butterfly, and that was why she had suddenly wanted to go home. Wylie felt like throttling Victoria; and if he learned she had ruined his chances with Josselyn, he would be sorely tempted to do so. He smiled unwillingly at the thought, realizing he could never really hurt Victoria; she might be self-centered as a cat, but he adored the way she purred.

His ill humor was not at all improved when he and Josselyn arrived back at Miss Hattie's cottage to discover Durango's black stallion tied up to the white picket fence out front. Wylie scowled at the sight. Really! The contest between

Durango and him, born of Red's will, had been diverting at first, but enough was enough. Durango was now starting to turn into a tiresome pest. Why, it was as though he actually believed he stood a chance at cutting Wylie out of the running for Josselyn's hand—and damned well meant to. That was absurd, since Wylie could not imagine Durango's settling down with any woman, much less permanently saddling himself with a nun! Why, then, did he keep hanging around her, where he wasn't wanted, trying to thrust a spoke into Wylie's wheel? It was clearly no more than a blatant attempt to rile him, Wylie decided, to push him so hard and so far that he would have no choice but to call Durango out.

But that, Wylie would never be so foolish as to do, knowing, as he did, that Durango could shoot the pip out of a playing card at fifty feet—seventy-five, if he were sober—and that even he would not be so arrogant and lackwit as to turn up drunk at a showdown. No, Wylie thought, if Durango wanted to get rid of him, then he would have to come up with a plan as clever as the ones he had employed to murder Forbes and Red, and that would not be easy; for knowing that Durango had killed their luckless partners, Wylie intended to remain on his guard against him. Durango would not catch him unaware, as he had undoubtedly caught Forbes and Red. Nor would Durango be getting Red's shares in the Rainbow's End by marrying Red's daughter. About that, Wylie was determined.

With that thought in mind, spying Durango watching them from the front window of Miss Hattie's parlor, Wylie deliberately turned to Josselyn sitting beside him on the buggy seat and, leaning slightly toward her, casually slid his arm behind her, along the top of the backrest, so it appeared as though he were preparing to embrace her.

"I'm sorry that this day has not gone as pleasantly as either of us would have wished," he said gently, taking her hand in his. "I confess I was quite upset at your courting danger by visiting the Rainbow's End, and I'm afraid I took it out on you, which was both wrong and churlish of me. And then

Victoria! Well, I guess I ought to have been rude and made it plain that she was bothering us. But I know that it's been hard for her since Forbes died, and I just simply didn't have the heart to hurt or offend her. I hope that you can forgive me on both counts, Josselyn.''

"Oh, of course, I can, Wylie!''

Her earlier wrath at him dissipated as, now, relief and gratitude swept through her at his kindness and generosity, at the fact that their quarrel should be so easily mended, so quickly forgiven and forgotten. Perhaps their friendship *could* develop into love. How fine and decent and honorable Wylie was! How truly lucky she would be if he asked her to become his bride and she found she could go virtuous to their wedding bed. His anger at her ignoring his advice about visiting the gold mine had been due solely to his concern for her well-being; the pleasantries he had exchanged with Victoria had been prompted only by his gentleman's manner.

When he raised her hand to his lips and kissed it warmly, lingeringly, then suddenly drew her into his arms and claimed her mouth with his, Josselyn offered no resistance; indeed, she found herself wanting strangely to kiss him back, to discover if he would evoke in her the same fierce response that Durango's hard, hungry lips had demanded of her and aroused in her. Wylie's unexpected kiss, however, while expert—she knew enough to know that now, although she did not hold his past against him—was gently firm and unhurried. Somehow, it reminded her unpleasantly of Antoine's kisses—cool, almost calculating, even—nothing at all like Durango's hot, impassioned kisses, a circumstance for which Josselyn supposed she ought to feel grateful but which, to her bewilderment, left her feeling oddly unmoved and disappointed instead.

Wylie, however, sensed only her restraint, her lack of response—although, much to his provocation, she had not proved as inexperienced as he had certainly had every reason to suppose and expect that she would be. Because of this, he knew he was not the first man to kiss her, and he thought he knew, too, who had been: Durango! While he, Wylie, had refrained for weeks from pressing his attentions on her, respecting the fact that she was a nun, or almost a nun, and afraid of rushing her, of scaring her off, Durango had escorted her out to the Rainbow's End, and there, he had boldly taken what he had wanted—Wylie just knew it!

Now, for the first time, he wondered if more had occurred in the gold mine than he knew. No, surely not. He simply could not envision prim, proper Josselyn willingly submitting to Durango or Durango's having been so base as to have raped her, either. But even the idea that Durango had kissed her was enough to incense Wylie, for it was to him further proof of his partner's intent to prevail over him, to acquire both Red's daughter and Red's shares in the Rainbow's End. Well, Wylie thought grimly, he had bested Durango once, where Victoria had been concerned, and he would best him again with Josselyn.

So thinking, Wylie finally broke off the thoroughly unsatisfactory kiss—Lord, how distasteful he found the notion of being compelled to marry this passive, pious prude!—resolving that the next time he took Josselyn into his arms, he would give her something to do penance for. Nothing of this showed upon his face, however, as, remembering Durango standing at the parlor window, spying on them, Wylie smiled at her contentedly as a cat lapping up cream as he assisted her down from the buggy and opened Miss Hattie's front gate.

"I'll leave you here . . . sweet Josselyn," he announced, "for I've an appointment at the shipping company, which I have only just this minute recollected, such is your heady effect on me." His grey eyes surveyed her in a way that made her blush shyly with pleasure. "So I shall say goodbye until I see you again. Till then, dream of me, promise?"

"I—I promise," she answered softly at last; and then, after a moment, as though her feet had wings, she turned and fairly flew up the walk to Miss Hattie's front porch, completely forgetting that inside the boardinghouse, Durango was impatiently waiting.

Miss Hattie's grandson, Zeb, met Josselyn at the front door. His obvious anxiety made her abruptly recall Durango's horse's being tied up outside and the fact that Durango himself must be waiting for her in the parlor.

"Durango's been here for purt' near two hours—drinkin', I suspect, for he's in as ugly a mood as I've ever seen a man in, mad enough, I'd reckon, to spit nails clean through a barn board!" Zeb warned her. "I—I wouldn't go in the parlor if I's you. If you want me to, I'll—I'll try to send him away —though I don't know if it will do any good, seein' as how he didn't pay no attention to me before, when I tried to tell him that you'd gone off with Mr. Gresham and prob'ly wouldn't be back anytime too soon."

"No, that's all right, Zeb." Josselyn was touched by the young man's concern for her, and for his sake, she tried not to allow her sudden fear to show. "Thank you, but I think that it's probably best if I take care of Mr. de Navarre myself."

"Well, all right, Miss Josselyn, seein' as how you insist and all. I'll just finish tidyin' up the dinin' room, so's I'll be close at hand, just in case you need me."

Josselyn took a deep breath and, after slowly crossing the hall, reluctantly opened the door to the parlor. Immediately, she was assailed by a cloud of cigar smoke that almost gagged her. Striding to the window, she flung it open wide, then turned to face Durango, who was lounging in one of Miss Hattie's red velvet Queen Anne chairs, a cheroot in one hand, a bottle in the other. At the sight of her eyeing him nervously but with disapproving expectation nevertheless, he leaned forward to grind out his cigar in an ashtray and to deposit his bottle on a nearby occasional table. Then he rose and, spurs jingling, swaggered across the floor to shut with a definite click the door that Josselyn had left open. He moved toward her, his hands clenched at his sides, as though to prevent himself from doing her some violence.

"Where in the hell have you been?" His voice was low and held a threatening note that sent a shiver up her spine. "We had a date to share a picnic lunch together this afternoon, and I damned well don't like being stood up—especially for Wylie!"

"If you remember correctly, then you know I never agreed to go out with you today!" Josselyn trembled involuntarily with fright and rage. He now loomed over her menacingly, making her feel small and helpless and vulnerable before him. But still, her green eyes flashed with defiance as she confronted him. "Oh! How dare you come here—dirty and drunk!—and terrorize Miss Hattie and her grandson, Zeb, and no doubt the rest of their boarders, too? I don't know why somebody didn't send for the sheriff and have you arrested!"

"Nobody had guts enough to, that's why—and you don't, either!" Durango sneered.

"Well, we'll just see about that!"

With that, Josselyn strode toward the door, fully intending to jerk it open and instruct Zeb to fetch the sheriff. But before she was even halfway across the room, Durango halted her progress, grabbing hold of her and yanking her up hard against him, roughly pinioning her arms behind her back when she struggled to escape from him.

"There are ways . . . very pleasant ways, I might add . . . of silencing you, Jossie," he declared silkily as she opened her mouth to call for help. Just as abruptly, she closed it when, breathlessly, her heart thudding wildly, she realized that he meant to smother her cries with kisses. "I see that you understand me," he continued sardonically, his eyes appraising her boldly, in a way that made her shudder and desperately wish herself anywhere but in his steely arms, at his utter mercy. "Clever girl. I knew that you would, although

I confess I find myself deeply wounded by the fact that you would encourage Wylie's advances and spurn mine—particularly after what passed between us at the Rainbow's End yesterday. Ah, but I forgot. You fainted, did you not? And I never answered your question yesterday, did I? What a pity that you should therefore remain in ignorance of your fate at my hands.''

At that, Josselyn blanched as though he had struck her. Oh, he *had* raped her; he *had*! Surely, he would not be so cocky otherwise—the murdering bastard! Her head reeled; she felt as though she was on the verge of swooning— No! She mustn't do that! Durango had already demonstrated he had no compunctions about taking advantage of her unconscious state and would certainly not hesitate to do so again. Her head fell back against his arm, and she closed her eyes, sick and ashamed that this man should have known her so intimately.

As he stared down at her ashen face, Durango knew a moment of guilt and shame for treating her so ruthlessly. Then he remembered her kissing Wylie just minutes past, and he resolutely hardened his heart against her.

"Ask me again, Jossie, and maybe this time, I'll answer,'' he whispered huskily in her ear, his breath warm and exciting against her skin, making her tingle all over despite herself. "Ask me what we both know is on your mind, what is bound to have preyed on your mind since yesterday, when you awoke in the lean-to off the cookhouse at the Rainbow's End.''

"No, I—I don't want to know," she lied, pathetically biting her lip. "I—I don't want to talk about it. . . .'' Because if it was true, what choice did she have but to wed him?

"No?'' One demonic black brow lifted coolly; his sensual mouth twisted derisively. "Come now, my sweet. As I told you yesterday, such modesty where I am concerned is surely beyond you now. You are dying to ask me. It is only gentility and fear that keep you silent, the fact that ladies are not supposed even to *think* about such things, let alone *mention* them. But despite that, you *have* been thinking about them, Jossie, have you not? Oh, yes. Do not bother trying to deny it, for I know better. You have dwelled long and hard on those kisses we exchanged yesterday at the gold mine—and no doubt, you have done penance on your knees for them, too, rosary in hand, haven't you? Haven't you?'' Durango demanded, giving her a savage little shake.

"Yes . . . yes," she whimpered, ashamed, tears she could not hold at bay beginning to trickle from her eyes.

"Because you enjoyed those kisses, didn't you?" he went on unrelentingly.

"No, no, it's not true—"

"Damn you! Don't lie to me, Jossie! Never lie to me . . . because you *are* lying. I know that you are, and you know it, too. Shall I prove it to you? I think I shall—"

"No!" she gasped, frantic at the thought, at the highly charged atmosphere that permeated the parlor, electrifying and ominous as the distant flash of lightning, the rumble of thunder that presages a summer storm. "Nooooo . . ."— this a low moan born of her impotence against him.

"Then ask me, my sweet. Ask me if after you fainted in my arms at the Rainbow's End, I raped you. That's what you want to know, isn't it? Isn't it?" He gave her another small shake.

"Yes, damn you! Yes!" she blurted wildly, heatedly, unable to hold back any longer the words that tumbled heedlessly from her lips, and not caring that she swore at him. "Did you? For God's sake, Durango! Did you?" Blasphemy, too. Only hear to what he had driven her!

"Why, Jossie, I'm surprised at you," he drawled in a voice that dripped honey—and held the cruel, piercing sting of a bee. He smiled down at her mockingly, maddeningly. "As a lady, you of all people should know that a gentleman never kisses and tells!"

She inhaled sharply at that, something inside her snapping so suddenly, so violently, that it was as though she had without warning received a crushing crack to her skull. A red mist formed before her eyes, her head rocked, and her heart pounded so hard that she thought it would burst from her breast. Her blood roared in her ears as an incredible rage like nothing she had ever before felt welled up inside her to spew forth irrepressibly as a thunderous geyser.

In that moment, she lost all control, as though she had been seized by a frenzied demon and were no longer in command of her own mind or body. Some small part of her that was still sane wrenched itself from her being, and she had the strangest sensation that she was floating in midair, watching with shock and horror as, of a sudden, she went berserk as a rabid dog, wresting her hands from Durango's grasp and springing at him ferociously, fingers spread wide and curled like claws, poised as though to rip his jugular vein from his throat.

She knew a deep satisfaction as her nails viciously raked his cheek, leaving bloody furrows in their wake. She would wipe that supercilious smirk from his face! Then, with one hand, he caught her wrists in a pitiless, bruising grip and held them behind her back. He captured her jaw between the strong, slender fingers of his other hand and forced her face up to his.

"You may look like an angel, *querida*," he muttered, his breath coming in hard rasps, his black eyes glittering like shards in the sunlight that streamed in through the window as he stared down at her intently, "but . . . *¡por Dios!* There is a devil in you somewhere, and come hell or high water, I am going to unleash it!"

Then, abruptly, he ground his mouth down on hers—hard.

She hated him for that—passionately, vehemently, with all her heart—and hated him all the more for making her feel, as his lips possessed hers, as though, somewhere deep down inside, she did not really hate him at all. This could not be happening to her, she thought. It had to be a nightmare; it could not be real. Yet sickened, ashamed, she knew she had never felt more awake, more alive, than she did in Durango's arms. Every fiber of her being tingled, vibrated with an incredible awareness of him and all he aroused in her, emotions and sensations she had known in the drift with him and that, now, as his mouth ravaged hers, again burgeoned inside her, quick and savage and exultant, no matter how she fought them, fought *him*. The struggle was futile. Both he and she knew she had not the strength, the will, or the heart for it, all her defenses having been swept away in that moment when his lips had seized hers.

His onslaught was as wild and relentless as a roiling sea against a vulnerable shore, eroding all she had ever known or been, crumbling the walls of her innate modesty and maidenly fears, redefining the limits of her existence, the boundaries of her being. Like mist in the wind, her veil floated to the floor, dragged from her head by his rough, impatient hands even now yanking the hairpins from her long chestnut tresses, loosing the heavy mass, sending it tumbling like a waterfall down her back. His fingers plunged into the cascade, dipped and dove into the streaming ripples of her hair afire in the golden sunlight. Fiercely, he tilted her face up to his. His tongue cleaved her mouth, thrust deep into the dark, moist cavity of her, seeking . . . finding. Her lips softened, quivering tremulously as they yielded, a scarlet rosebud unfurling to surrender the nectar at its heart. His tongue fluttered and stung, a bee in her mouth, drinking deeply, gorging itself, her lips and tongue bloodred petals, enfolding him, sweet . . . sweet . . .

The heady taste and scent of her intoxicated Durango, manna and wine steeping, drugging his senses, heaven-sent. He did not deserve her; he knew he did not. For despite his suspicion of her—which would not be banished, which he could not afford to banish—he knew in his heart that she was innocence and purity and light. He was none of those things, had not been for a very long time. And yet, deep within himself, he rejoiced and marveled that such as she walked the face of the earth. In a thousand lifetimes, he had not thought to find her like. In that moment at the Rainbow's

End, when he had seen the halo of her hair spilling down about her, her angel's face pale and luminous in the lantern light, he had known she was the woman of his dreams, come down from a realm he had years ago relinquished any hope of entering. Fear of losing her made him barbarous; instinct made him bold. If he gave her time to think, all she had been taught at the convent would weigh upon her—and against him. He had aeons past fallen from grace; he had no illusions otherwise. And still, he wanted her. He was a sinner daring to aspire to a saint. He would have laughed at the irony of it had he not been so in earnest.

That Red should have spawned such a daughter astounded him. The luck of the Irish, legendary as the mythical pot of gold at a rainbow's end. How fitting that her true self should have been revealed to him at the mine, Durango thought. *Josselyn* . . . Angel-witch. Her hair was ribands of silk rippling through his fingers; he wove, he knotted, a tangled skein, binding her to him, her head drawn back, cradled in his strong hands. A low whimper escaped from her throat, inflaming him. Her melon-ripe breasts strained against him with her every quick, uneven breath. His mouth moved on hers, starving, savoring what was so temptingly offered up to him, passion fruit and pomegranate melting upon his tongue. He licked and lapped and feasted long and well— and still, he hungered for more. *Josselyn* . . . Witch-angel. Liquid gold and copper in the sunlight that slanted across her fair face, illuminating it, making of her a gilded lily, petal lips parted, slender throat laid bare, soaking up the kisses he rained upon her. Her sloe green eyes were closed, her thick, sooty lashes spread like delicate fans against her cheeks. His gaze and his mouth drank her in. His indrawn breath rasped against her soft skin; he exhaled, a sigh, a groan. Christ had enough brides. He, Durango, had need of this one.

Más vale tener que desear. Better to have than to desire.

His lips burned hers, were flame upon her flesh as he pressed his mouth hotly to her throat, bending her back, arching her against him, his corded thighs holding her prisoner, making her intensely aware of his want, his need. Josselyn felt dizzy, as though she had drunk too much wine, boneless as a rag doll, languid with the passion he wakened inside her and that rushed like an opiate through her body. What power did he possess, what magic did he wield to make her feel so? She did not know. She no longer cared. There was no use fighting it, fighting him, when she knew she could not win and feared, in some dark chasm of her brain, that she did not even want to. It was as though a madness beset her when he kissed her, touched her, so that her mind became a blank and the world turned upside down, making what she knew to be wrong, gloriously, inevitably right.

Her traitorous arms had long ago found their own way about his neck, and now, they tightened upon him, drawing him to her as his plundering lips and insidious tongue continued to work their sweet, seductive will upon her, teasing and tormenting her, setting her ablaze with desire. Josselyn moaned as his hand slipped down to cup her breast through the coarse fabric of her habit, sending a wild, rapturous surge of electrifying sensation sizzling through her body. Roughly, urgently, he squeezed the mound heavy and swollen with passion, kneaded it, molded it. Then, after a long moment, in sharp contrast to his previous motion, his hand tensed, his fingers spread wide, and his palm began to glide in slow, sensuous circles over her taut nipple. The new movement took her breath away. Crying out, she trembled in his arms, a fragile willow shivering at the beguiling caress of a wind primeval. Her mouth parted with a sigh; her tongue darted out to moisten her dry lips. She thought longingly of a still pond dappled by sunlight . . . before she ceased to think at all.

She felt hot as she had in the tunnel, blind and deaf to everything but Durango and the atavistic yearning he aroused in her. Droplets trickled from her temples into her unbound hair. As a slow-burning candle radiates its scent, so the warmth of her stoked and diffused her lavender perfume, her female fragrance. The mingled essences permeated the air, wafted to his nostrils, inciting him. Her hair was a tangle of russet ivy, ensnaring them both; her breasts were blossoms bursting against his palms, puckered centers hard as currants against her habit, responding to the butterfly flick of his thumbs. Where he and she were, lush, languorous summer unfolded its sultry garden of delights; Eden's sun bathed them in its sweltering golden glow. The bee that was his tongue stung her breasts again and again as he fed among roses and lilies, his face buried deep in the valley between the flowering mounds. Slowly . . . feverishly, he slid down the lissome length of her, trailing a path of torrid kisses in his wake as he sank to his knees in a place that, in his mind, was green, green grass and rich, dark earth, his hands gripping the smooth curve of her buttocks to pull her to him. Born of his overpowering nearness, his expert kisses and caresses, honey dripped between Josselyn's thighs; she ached deep at the heart of her with the sweetness of it, burned with the slow-melting heat of it. Of a sudden, she felt so hollow at the secret core of her, so empty, that she hurt unendurably and longed instinctively to be filled by him. As though with a life of their own, her fingers twisted convulsively in his hair. She wanted . . . she wanted . . .

Sensing her desperate need, the bee came at long last to light upon the soft, succulent swell of her womanhood, to sting—just once, lightly, quickly—through her skirts the ripe, rubicund fruit that nested at the pith of her nether lips, berry juices sweeter than wine, sweeter than nectar. At his exquisite touch, a violent tremor rocked her. She sobbed aloud, her body racked by a long, agonizing shudder, so unbearably sweet was that exigent sting that pierced her— bitter as the cruelest barb for ending so abruptly, leaving her still aching, still burning, still wanting him utterly.

In the sudden silence broken only by their harsh, rapid breathing, Durango lifted his dark head. His hooded black eyes glittered with passion as they surveyed her intently. His hands were clenched on her hips; his body was coiled tightly as that of a cougar poised to spring.

"Did Wylie's kiss make you feel like that?" His voice, raw with restrained lust, grated with his fear—now, more than ever—of losing her.

Josselyn was so dazed with desire that for a minute, dully, she did not comprehend his words. Then, all at once, terribly, she understood. Durango must have spied on her and Wylie from the parlor window; and because of what he had witnessed, he had used her. Basely. Ruthlessly. Deliberately, he had tormented her, taken her nearly to some sweet, unknown pinnacle of passion—and then had left her hanging, punishment for her rejecting him, penance for her preferring Wylie, wanting to make very sure that she understood what each man had to offer her. . . .

Blindly, Josselyn struck out at Durango, despising him, wanting to hurt him as deeply as he had managed to hurt her. How that could be when she loathed him, cared nothing for him, she did not know, did not pause to analyze, such was her shame, her wrath, her anguish. Although he knelt before her, her attack upon him was futile. Easily, he captured her wrists, coming in one swift, graceful movement to his feet, muscular thighs rippling with the effort. Now, panicking, she struggled furiously to escape from him—to no avail. Mercilessly, he jerked her body up against his, his embrace like an iron band. His hand snarled in her hair, yanking her head back, as though he would renew his assault upon her senses.

"I hate you!" she spat, trying to wrench free of him.

"I think not, my sweet." His eyes and the smile that did not quite reach them mocked her so, that she yearned fiercely to scratch again at his face. She did not know what was wrong with her to behave so wantonly, to burn to do such violence. She had once meant to dedicate her life to the Church. Now, instead, she had been seized by a devil. "Answer the question, damn you!" Durango shook her roughly, no longer smiling, a muscle tensing in his grimly set jaw. "Did Wylie's kiss make you feel like that?" Josselyn's eyes blazed, her chin lifted. Stubbornly, she refused to respond, not caring if he beat her for defiance. After a moment, shortly, jeeringly, he laughed. "You poor, misguided fool! It's not you he wants; it's your father's shares in the Rainbow's End."

"And you . . . what do you want, Durango?" Her voice was acid with contempt.

"You," he said tersely. Then, hideously, he added, "Conscious."

Her face paled at his words; a dreadful roaring sound in her ears, and she fought frantically to hold the swooning sensation at bay.

"Lies! Wicked lies!" she hissed, shaking uncontrollably in his arms. "It's *you* who want Da's shares, not Wylie! And no matter what you've implied to the contrary, I—I don't believe that you really . . . that you—"

"Raped you?"

"Yes!"

"Why not, Jossie?" Durango sneered. "You believe me capable of having murdered your father. Why, then, should you think I hesitated to commit rape?" She had no reply to that. After a moment, softly, he gibed, "Wylie does not love you, and he will not have you when he learns what I took from you—not even for your father's shares in the gold mine. He is too proud and fastidious for that." This was not the truth. Wylie had slept with his share of whores and put no value on virginity; he could never have grown so besotted with Victoria otherwise. But Durango knew that Josselyn was ignorant of all this. He counted on it.

"You're wrong," she insisted, denying her own secret dread. "You're wrong. Wylie will know that what you did to me wasn't my fault, and he'll not hold me to blame. He's not like you. He's all the things you're not, fine and decent and honorable—"

"Oh?" One satanic black brow rose sardonically; Durango's mouth turned down at the corners as, hating himself for it, despising the whip he used, he lashed her still harder. "Is that why he came to you today, straight from his mistress's bed?"

If he had hit her, Josselyn could not have been more

stricken. Her whole body went suddenly very still and rigid, frozen with shock and disbelief. Her eyes were wide pools of hurt and entreaty as she stared up at him, horrified.

"No! No, it's not true! It's not true! You're lying to me —just as you've lied to me about everything else! I won't listen! I won't listen, do you hear?"

Briefly, Durango's eyes filled with remorse as he observed how he had wounded her. But then he thought of Wylie's lips and hands and body worshiping at Victoria's altar, and then, afterward, defiling Josselyn; and he went on unflinchingly.

"How he and Victoria must be laughing up their sleeves at you—"

"Nooooo," Josselyn wailed, even as she grasped with awful certainly that in this much at least, he at last spoke the truth.

For now, in slow motion, as though in a dream—or a nightmare—she saw again, in her mind's eye, all that had occurred earlier at John Best's soda fountain and pharmacy. Beautiful Victoria, cool and poised and elegant in her widow's weeds, her long, slender hand—stark white against her black mourning ensemble—laid so possessively upon Wylie's arm, her brunet head tilted back, her dark, smoldering eyes speaking volumes, her lush vermilion mouth parting in a mysterious smile. Wylie, unable to keep his eyes off her, devouring her with a gaze warm with the remembrance of her arms, her bed. What secrets, what silent laughter indeed they must have shared between them at the ironic necessity of his taking up with a nun. Victoria must feel so secure in her knowledge that she need not fear her rival, her shrewd brown eyes having assessed Josselyn and found her wanting. At the hurtful realization, all her feelings of plainness, of gaucheness, of not measuring up, of not belonging returned to haunt Josselyn anew. *Now, you must neither of you forget the small supper I am holding at the Teller House on Friday evening—to welcome Red's daughter properly into our midst!* Victoria had said, her lips curving with a smile of amusement that had been baffling but was now suddenly so painfully clear. *Of course, we shall be there*, Wylie had said, his smile matching Victoria's at the thought of bringing a nun to his mistress's supper, of sitting her down at his mistress's table, wooing the nun—worth her weight in gold—while making love to his extravagant mistress and plotting how to pay for her with Da's shares in the Rainbow's End. Now, Josselyn perceived why Wylie's kiss had left her so cold and untouched. Like Antoine, he felt nothing for her, had nothing to give her, wanted only to take from her; she was no more to him than a means to an end. In all likelihood, if she wed him, he would divorce her just as soon as he had got his greedy, grasping hands on her inheritance. No doubt, it was *he* who was the saboteur and the murderer at the Rainbow's End!

Yes, she could believe even that of him now, though she would not have believed it before, when she had been but a blind, trusting witness to all the evidence that now fatally damned him in her eyes, filled her with loathing and disgust for him—and for herself. A "poor, misguided fool," Durango had called her, and so she was. Da's death had shattered her world as surely as though he had deliberately picked it up and smashed it; and all the evil that she had ever secretly feared lay in wait within herself and beyond the convent's high walls had come to pass. She felt so mixed up inside that she no longer seemed to know wrong from right. She no longer knew whom to trust, to whom to turn; she appeared to have misjudged everyone so badly, perhaps even Durango among them.

Tears glistened in her eyes at the mess she had made of it all. She was unfit, unworthy. God had judged her and found her wanting. For that, He had deserted her, had cast her out into the devil's keeping.

"Don't cry, *querida*." The devil spoke, misunderstanding the reason for her tears, his voice oddly kind and—could it be?—even caring. "Don't cry. Wylie isn't worth it; he never was."

"I know that now. . . . Oh, I guess I've been a fool again, such a fool!" she wept bitterly. "I don't know whom to trust anymore. I trusted *him*! I thought he was a gentleman. I was prepared to marry him, for Da's sake, to honor Da's memory, his will, and, most of all, his last wish."

"Red meant a lot to you, then, did he?" Durango asked, his body suddenly peculiarly still, tense and alert as that of a prowling timber wolf, as he waited to hear her answer.

"Of course, he did. I loved him! With all my heart." Like rain from a leaden sky, Josselyn's tears slipped from her eyes to spill down her cheeks. "He was my father, and after Mam passed away, he was all I ever had, really. Oh, Durango! I would have given anything to have seen him again before he died! Even now, after all this time, I—I still can't quite believe he's dead. I know that it sounds queer, even crazy, but sometimes, I have the most peculiar feeling that he's watching over me still, waiting to see what I'll make of his will, knowing, as I *do* know, that he always tried to do what he thought was right and best for me, what he thought would keep me safe and make me happy."

"*I* could keep you safe, *querida*. *I* could make you happy." His voice was low, husky with the first stirrings of rekindling desire that brushed aside the niggling worry that Josselyn might be little more than a liar and cheat, hand in glove with her father.

"What—what makes you so very sure of that?" she asked, trembling a little as his hand, curiously tender, slowly wiped away her tears before his hard, carnal mouth brushed her own soft, vulnerable one, bruised and swollen from his earlier, demanding kisses.

"Say that you'll be mine and I'll show you, Jossie."

"Are you—are you asking me to marry you, Durango?" Josselyn was overcome by doubt and confusion at the thought. Her cheeks flushed, her heartbeat quickened. The idea of giving herself forever into his keeping was frightening . . . and yet, despite herself, there was, too, within her that which hungered to know the infinite breadth and depth of the passion he had wakened inside her, to be a woman whole and complete, in a way that, of a sudden, she longed for with all her heart. A home. A husband. A child.

"Marriage?" Durango laughed derisively, all his earlier gentleness gone, his eyes grown hard and gleaming with his suspicion of her, uppermost now in his mind. "Yes, that's what you would want, of course. But, no, my sweet, that was not what I was proposing, for have I not told you often enough that I am not a marrying man?"

At his low, mocking words, such shock and fear and rage assailed Josselyn that she felt suddenly as though the life were being choked from her, that she could not breathe. Her eyes widened like those of some petrified animal, and her nostrils flared. Shaking from the violence of her emotions, she struggled blindly to wrest free of his embrace. When she found she could not escape, she opened her mouth to cry out in protest, in denunciation of him; but before she could get any sound out, Durango sealed her lips with his own, silencing her.

"No, don't scream," he growled against her mouth, kissing her savagely, until she was giddy and breathless, "for it will do you no good, I promise you; and if you are thinking only to tell me how deeply I have insulted you, save your breath! However I looked at it, it was a no-win situation, *querida* . . . for if I had offered you marriage, you would only have thought that it was your inheritance I truly wanted! Such is the perversity of women—and I'm of no mind to be made a fool of for that! This way, at least, you can be sure that it's you I want . . . for I *do* want you, badly; and whatever it takes, I mean to have you in the end!" He paused for a moment, allowing this to sink in. Then he uttered bitingly, "Grow up, Jossie! This is the real world! It is you and I against Wylie and Victoria—unless you have some burning desire of which I am unaware to become *his* mistress instead of mine!" Even the thought rankled, goading him, making him cruel.

"And when my year stipulated in Da's will is up and I am

yet unwed and Nell Tierney is building the largest theater in the state of Colorado, what then? What then, Durango?'' Josselyn cried, despising him, even as her treacherous body, young and alive, responded to his insistent lips, his provocative hands.

''Before then—if it pleases me, if *you* please me—I may choose to marry you, after all,'' he announced arrogantly. ''But if I do, it will be because *I* wish it and for no other reason than that! Until then, I'll not have my hand in this game forced by anyone—not even you, no matter how much I want you.'' Then his mouth was on hers again, muddling her thoughts, crushing her resistance, making her cling to him, despite herself, as though only he were solid in an unstable world that spun and heaved, dizzying her, making the earth seem to shift precariously beneath her feet. After a time, Durango raised his head, his breathing harsh, his eyes unreadable, though a smile of satisfaction played about the corners of his lips. ''Be mine, *querida*. You want me. You know that you do, and I know it, too—just as we both know that you are only postponing the inevitable by denying me.''

''No,'' she whispered, chagrined at feeling helplessly, even so, that there was more than a grain of truth in his words. ''I hate you! I hate you!''

Once more, he laughed softly, making her shiver.

''Methinks the lady doth protest too much!'' he taunted. ''My sweet, I am not a patient man. However, I am willing to give you some time to reconcile yourself to your fate. I will give you . . . a month. After that, if you are still undecided, then I warn you: I will take whatever steps I think necessary to settle this entire affair of the Rainbow's End! Do you understand? Do you?'' He gave her yet another rough little shake.

''Yes,'' she breathed, hardly knowing what she said, perceiving only that he was a threat to her, in more ways than one—and that, even so, his was the only door open to her now.

''Then get out of the habit . . .'' he began, his eyes glinting darkly with both desire and amusement as he saw her own eyes widen with sudden alarm. "No, not your clothes, Jossie, though if you are offering . . . No? What a pity for us both." His gaze swept her warmly, leaving her no doubt as to what was on his mind. "For you will know much pleasure in my arms, I promise you. However, it was the habit of kissing Wylie to which I was referring. As you may have noticed, I am a man quite careful with . . . all that belongs to me. What is mine, I keep and let no man take away. Wylie was my friend once. For that reason, I should not like to have to shoot him. I will forgive what took place this afternoon—but do not ever let it happen again. I'll share you with no man, *querida*. Is that clear?"

"Yes," she murmured, her heart beating fast; for though that wicked smile still curved his mouth, his eyes had grown hard as twin gun barrels again, his jaw was set, and there could be no doubting that he meant every word he had spoken. She shuddered at the thought.

Durango kissed her once more, lingeringly this time, his palms cupping her breasts, sliding over them sensuously, as though it were his right.

"Only think of what heaven you are missing by being so slow to make up your mind about me, Jossie," he teased when he released her.

And then, well pleased by her abruptly downcast eyes, the hot blush that colored her fair cheeks, the way in which her hands fluttered and twisted anxiously, like the wings of some small bird beating helplessly against its captor, he left.

Chapter Fifteen

For over three months, she had told herself stoutly that she despised Nell. But now, this late afternoon, as Josselyn sat in Miss Hattie's parlor, taking tea with the actress, as promised, she found herself strangely wanting to pour out her heart and soul to this woman who had been so close to Da. For somehow, despite how little she knew Nell, Josselyn felt oddly sure that the actress would not only *not* condemn her for her revelations, but, being a woman of the world, would be in a position to offer sound advice; and the Lord knew, Josselyn thought, she was very much in need of it.

Still, she said nothing; and Nell, not wishing to offend her, reluctant to reveal how much she knew of Josselyn's past, was reticent to delve too deeply beneath the surface of their polite but somewhat strained conversation.

Durango had been leaving just as the actress had arrived.

Seeing him—his tall, dark figure that fairly seethed with animal menace and magnetism—Nell had been relieved that Red was immobilized in her bed in her cottage on Spring Street. His broken ankle had been set by the doctor, but nonetheless, he continued to vow to kill Durango.

Yesterday, despite all Red's thunderous, expletive-ridden exhortations that she drive out immediately to the Rainbow's End to rescue his daughter from the heinous clutches of his bastard partner, Durango, Nell had wisely refrained. Her immediate concern was for Red himself and any damage to Josselyn had already been done. It was pointless to try to shut the barn door once the horse had been stolen and cruel to blame Red, who was already punishing himself far worse than even Nell could have. If she confronted Durango and succeeded in getting him to plead guilty to the dastardly deed, what could she do about it? And so, despite her anxiety for Josselyn's welfare, Nell had thought that prudence dictated caution, not challenge, in the matter. Besides, although she knew the gambler to be a rascal, the actress had not been able to credit Red's bitter accusations that Durango was a saboteur and a murderer, much less that he had brutally ravished Josselyn. As a result, Nell had felt she should make certain of her facts before—as Red had alternately vindictively and plaintively charged her to do—embarking on such an irreversible course of action as informing Durango that Red was not only still alive, but planned to kill him at the first opportunity. If called out, especially unjustly, Durango would defend himself, the actress knew, and his skill with a gun was far better than Red's. Red was her man; she would not see him dead, not even for his daughter's sake.

Now, as she studied Josselyn's lovely face, becomingly flushed with color, Nell was glad—particularly after having learned about the accident with the incline car—that common sense and restraint, not Red's murderous rage, had ruled her conduct. For if she were any judge at all of human character—and she felt confident she was—Durango, when she had seen him, had not worn the expression of a man sexually sated, but, rather, that of one whose appetite had only been whetted. Nor did Red's daughter appear, for all her apparent anxiety, like a woman recently compelled to surrender her virtue; for if, indeed, Durango had not hesitated yesterday to commit rape, why should he have hesitated today? Josselyn looked a trifle mussed, as though she had hurriedly pinned up her hair and put on her veil, but that was all; and surely, if Durango had forced himself on her yet again today, she would have screamed for help.

No, he kissed her, Nell deduced shrewdly. *Both yesterday and today, he kissed her—but little more than that—however much he might have wanted to do otherwise; and really, it's not as though she hadn't been kissed before, slipping away from the convent, as she did, to meet that French scoundrel. Oh, how I do so wish she could bring herself to like and to confide in me! But it would be impolitic of me to press her. She has finally thawed toward me a little, this visit. I don't want to do anything to destroy that. . . .*

Still, had Nell realized how Josselyn yearned at that moment to divulge her innermost thoughts and fears, she would have urged the younger woman to do so and would have found the words to set her mind at rest. But Nell did not know, and Josselyn held her tongue—although she did draw a great deal of solace from Nell's cheerful, friendly face and kindly ministrations, nonetheless. Thoughtfully, Nell plumped up the pillows on the sofa where Josselyn half reclined—Nell having insisted that after yesterday's harrowing ordeal in the giraffe, the younger woman lie down and rest—poured out the tea, and kept Josselyn's plate filled with the finger sandwiches and tiny sweet cakes that Miss Hattie had prepared for the occasion. The actress also maintained a flow of light, easy chatter that Josselyn found soothing. As it required very little input from her, it allowed her mind to dwell upon the last two days' unnerving events—and Durango's desire to make her his mistress.

As a result, it was some time before she grasped that the conversation had taken a more serious turn and that Nell was now addressing her earnestly.

"I want you to know, Josselyn," the actress was saying, "that I have absolutely no interest whatsoever in your father's shares in the Rainbow's End, especially now that such a marvelous opera house is already to be built here in Central City. So I do hope that you'll choose to wed either Wylie or Durango rather than to return to Boston, to your convent. Toward that end, then, I would like to give you a bit of motherly advice, if I may. Sure and your father and I are . . . that is, we *were* so close that I confess I feel myself somewhat responsible for you, in a motherly fashion. I married young, and not long afterward, my poor husband died, leaving me penniless, which is why I took to the stage, to support myself— But perhaps you know that? Later, I was always too busy with my acting, you see, to wish to marry again; and so I—I don't have any children of my own, although I have always so longed for a daughter. . . . Well"—Nell shook her head, smiling wryly at her own whimsy—"that's neither here nor there, is it?" She paused for a moment, gathering her thoughts, remembering Red's suspicion that Durango knew he was alive and that, as a result, Durango would not have marriage on his mind when it came to Josselyn. Her brow knitted in a frown, the actress continued.

"What I want to tell you is this: According to your father's will, you've a year to make up your mind, and relatively little of those twelve months has passed. So take your time getting to know Wylie and Durango; and if either of them should happen to propose, think it over very carefully before committing yourself into his keeping, for once you're wed, you shall belong to him utterly and have no rights of your own. So, please don't feel, just for the sake of your inheritance, that you must let either of them rush you into a marriage you may come to regret, or—or into anything else, for that matter. Remember that even the best of men sometimes have dishonorable intentions toward a woman; and never forget for an instant that 'tis more than likely that either Wylie or Durango is the saboteur at the Rainbow's End, perhaps even Forbes's murderer, and that neither is therefore to be trusted.

"However, a woman's heart is a foolish thing, sometimes given much against her friends' and her own head's advice, and followed just as faithfully to ruin as to riches. So if by some chance you should happen during the coming months to fall in love with either Wylie or Durango, you should also know that what occurs between a man and woman can be, *should* be, the most natural and wonderful thing in the world and that it is nothing to fear or to be ashamed of—no matter what the good Sisters, being brides of Christ rather than of men, may have led you to believe to the contrary. God made men and women not only to love one another, but to joy in one another. Only, trust your instincts, Josselyn. Be sure— be very sure—that the man you've chosen is worthy of all you would bestow upon him." Nell ended her speech in a rush, thinking that this was all she currently dared say to Josselyn about affairs of the heart, or otherwise, without alienating her completely.

"There, now, I'm done," the actress declared briskly after a moment, "save to add that although I know I could never take your own mother's place in your heart, nor would I ever wish to displace her, I do hope that, for Red's sake, if nothing more, you'll always consider me your friend, one you can turn to and count on should you ever have a need."

"Thank you, Nell," Josselyn replied, touched, and thinking how different the actress was in reality from the way in which Da's letters had portrayed her. Could it be that she, Josselyn, had, because of her own insecurities, read something into Da's words, and into his will, too, that was not there, and that she had allowed her assumptions to cloud her opinion of Nell? If so, Josselyn felt she owed the actress an apology. But still, she did not know quite how to go about delivering it. Nor did she feel entirely comfortable confiding in Nell, who, it now seemed, suspected at least something of the nature of Josselyn's woes.

What must she think of me? Josselyn wondered, dismayed, for now, she discovered that she wished for Nell's good opinion and friendship. *How can I confess to my foolishness and wantonness without her thinking the less of me?*

And so, lest their fragile new bond be broken, Josselyn kept her own counsel, telling herself, as the Reverend Mother Maire had so many times told her, that God never gave any of His children a burden too heavy for them to bear.

Chapter Sixteen

Without even opening it, Josselyn knew what was in the brown-paper-wrapped box that had arrived for her just minutes ago. She knew because of the note that had accompanied the parcel and that she continued to stare at, as though the bold black words scrawled thereon were a nest of writhing snakes, all of them spawned by that serpent of Eden. *Wear it if you dare*, the small, plain white card read; it was signed simply *Durango*.

Inside the box was the green gown from the dress-shop window, she knew in her bones. He was tempting her to discard her veil and her habit, challenging her to wear an ensemble he had bought for her as though she were already his mistress. She would not do it, she told herself fiercely. She would send the box back, unopened. But then she thought of all the Worth-frocked, jewel-bedecked women who would be at the Teller House tonight, and of Victoria, a siren in widow's weeds, hosting her small private supper "to welcome Red's daughter properly"; and Pandora's crime became Josselyn's own: She opened the box, and yards of shimmering green wickedness came spilling out. Durango had even bought a cape to match—and lacy silk undergarments so wispy and sheer that she flushed with mortification at the thought of putting them on, at knowing he had chosen them, had handled them, and had imagined her in them. She hated him—the rogue!

Some hours later, she was not so sure.

The silk felt seductive against her skin; it whispered when she walked, gossamer gold threads glistening like a fine-spun spider's web sheened with dew, bringing out gold flecks so deep in her green eyes that she had never before known they were there, making the green all the brighter, all the more startling. Was that woman staring back at her from the mirror really her own self? Josselyn could scarcely believe that it was. Surely, her eyes' faint slant was not so mysterious; their depths were not so smoldering; her mouth was not so full and provocative; her neck and shoulders and bosom were not so white—so bare, taking her breath away. She looked brazen. She looked bewitching! A Celtic goddess rising, white-foamed, from a green sea reflecting a thousand gold stars, her copper hair swept up and back, as though by a wild wind, a cascade of tumbling curls threaded with green silk ribands plaited into a love knot at the crown. At her ears dangled her mother's long, heavy gold earrings, generations old and strangely fashioned, the only jewelry, besides her own plain wooden cross, that Josselyn possessed. She needed no other. For the first time in her life, she was aware of her own beauty, of her own body; she understood now what Durango saw in her, why he wanted her—and the thought made her shiver with both fear and excitement. She was no longer herself; the nun was gone—forever, she somehow knew, with a touch of sadness and regret for the loss of innocence and youth.

In her place stood a stranger, bold and reckless, bent on ruin and revenge.

Victoria Stanhope Houghton would not smile that sleek-cat's smile at her tonight. Wylie Gresham would not make a poor dupe of her tonight. And most of all, Durango de Navarre would not win any games with her tonight. Instead, she would torment him, and he would suffer—as he had tormented her and she had suffered. He would desire her. He would not have her. She would laugh in his face for what he had so villainously done to her, for the little he had arrogantly offered her afterward. He would be sorry he had taken her virginity and given her no wedding ring in return.

Hearing a peremptory knock upon the front door, followed by voices in the foyer below, Josselyn fastened the cape's braid frog at her throat, pulled on her gauntlet gloves, and gathered up her reticule and her fan. Gazing at her reflection one final time in the mirror, she lifted her chin with determination. Her green eyes snapped sparks; her cheeks were high with color. Tonight was war, and she was armored and armed for it. She swept down the stairs, pausing halfway down, expecting to see Wylie—ignorant of what she had learned of him—standing at the bottom, waiting for her.

It was Durango. She had the sweet satisfaction of seeing his black pupils dilate and then narrow to pinpoints, of hearing his breath draw in sharply at the sight of her.

First blood, she thought, and savored it.

Witch-angel, he thought, and in that moment wanted her as he had never wanted another woman in his life.

She had dared to wear the dress. Somehow, he had known that she would. What he had not counted on was his own violent reaction to seeing her in it. For the first time in years, his heart hammered like a schoolboy's. An unexpected tremor ran through him, making him quiver like a stallion in heat. His nostrils flared. His loins tightened with desire. He yearned to fling her down and make love to her where she stood.

Swearing silently, he balled his fists, cutting himself on the thorns of the solitary white rose he held in one hand, glad of the sudden pain.

Curse you, Red, you devil, you witch's sire! May you rot in hell for loosing her on us. . . .

Now, too late, Durango realized that giving her the gown had perhaps been a mistake. The woman who stood before him was no longer a fearful nun, but an avenging angel, girded for battle. Right or wrong, he had put a weapon into her hands—and it was clear to him that she fully intended to use it. Still, despite his reservations, his interest was piqued. He loved a good challenge; and for all that he wanted her, if it still were marriage she had in mind, she would not find him an easy mark. A wedding bed or a deathbed . . . he was in no mood to lie down in either.

Revenge was a two-edged sword, Josselyn discovered as she surveyed him; it cut both ways. She had never seen Durango look so handsome. He was freshly bathed and shaved; beneath his black sombrero, his hair, still damp from his ablutions, gleamed like jet, swept back in slick waves from his swarthy, satanic face. He was garbed in an exquisitely tailored black silk suit, a black-and-white paisley waistcoat, and a fine white cambric shirt with a frothy lace jabot and cuffs. In one lapel was a white rose boutonniere. A black silk string tie was at his throat. Silver cuff links winked at his wrists. From his vest pocket hung a silver watch chain that bore a single fob and seal. Slung low at his hips was an ornate gun belt she had not seen previously; small silver spurs, clearly for dress, adorned his shining black boots. In one hand, he carried a solitary white rose, which he held out to her as he spoke.

"Wylie was unavoidably detained," he announced, his voice low, silky, making the fine hairs on her nape rise. "A wheel somehow loosened itself from his buggy." A lie—and they both knew it, knew—as, no doubt, Wylie knew also—that Durango was to blame for the mishap.

A cheap trick, she thought as she stared down at him.

Should have crippled Wylie's horse, too, he thought as he stared up at her.

"He sends his regrets for not being able to call for you," Durango continued smoothly. "He will meet us at the Teller House."

"Then let us not be late," Josselyn said coolly, coming to the bottom of the steps and taking the rose from his hand, pressing her nose to the fragrant petals.

He opened the door for her. They walked outside into a spring night whose stillness was broken by a soft, sweet wind that bore summer and the promise of rain on its wings. Overhead, the moon shone lustrous as a pearl in a midnight-blue velvet sky set with tiny diamond stars. Beneath this wide, bejeweled crown, the mountains were slumbering kings, dressed in shadowed robes of deepest purples and blues and greens, trimmed with white ermine at the throat. As though from a distant royal menagerie came the occasional piping of the night birds, the howl of a timber wolf or coyote, the scream of a mountain lion. Durango assisted her into the buggy, then climbed in and settled himself beside her, so close that she was acutely aware of him—and he of her. He clucked to the team; the vehicle rolled forward into the darkness, horses' shod hooves ringing, clip-clop, clip-clop, on the cobblestones. The night wind sang, a melody rich with the notes of a thousand alpine flowers, delicate-throated blossoms trilling, petals beating in time, like the rose that fluttered in Josselyn's hand, long stem swaying, leaves rustling. The rose was like everything else Durango had said or done to her, she decided; it had thorns. She did not think of the sweetness at its heart.

Neither she nor he spoke. There seemed little to say; it was as though they had already said enough to each other—except that she might have thanked him for the gown, but she did not. It had not been a gift, but a challenge . . . and perhaps a bribe. But she would not be bought for the price of a new dress, no matter what, she vowed. If Durango believed otherwise, he would soon learn his mistake.

Presently, they arrived at the corner of Eureka and Pine Streets, where Teller House, four stories tall, stood, lighted up and grand as a palace with its wide, arched double doors echoed in narrower, arched ground-level windows. It was not perhaps as elegant an edifice as some in Boston, but still, there was nothing to rival it between Chicago and San Francisco. The Elevator Bar, a combination taproom and billiard parlor, was the most sumptuous of its sort in town, boasting several beautiful classic frescoes painted by an Englishman who worked as a magazine illustrator, Charles St. George Stanley, who had been laboring on the murals now for the past two years. There would be a total of nine frescoes when he was finished, including one over by the stove. In addition to the fact that they were simply visually pleasing, the murals were interesting because each contained a significant distortion that one must look closely to discern. In that of Leda and her swan, for example, the swan's head faced backward. The Teller House also contained a lovely conservatory— actually a glassed-in court—filled to bursting with potted plants and a trellis of vines, which added their own perfumes to the sultry night air. The furnishings of the entire hotel were very fine, no expense having been spared in shipping the most fashionable accoutrements—twenty thousand dollars' worth —up to the Rocky Mountains.

Victoria had reserved a small, private dining room for her supper, and the maître d'hôtel led Josselyn and Durango there upon their arrival. Victoria and Wylie had already arrived. For a moment, they gazed at Josselyn blankly, not recognizing her. Then, much to her satisfaction, shock and incredulity registered upon their faces as, finally, they realized that the vision in green was she. Victoria's countenance paled, and her smile faltered, and Wylie's reaction was much the same as Durango's had been—even more gratifying, actually, because Wylie was treated to the full, potent effect of Josselyn's stunning costume as she slowly unfastened the braid frog at her throat and allowed Durango to slide her cloak from her bare shoulders, revealing the daring décolletage of her gown, the swell of her white breasts above her tightly fitted basque.

"That's not quite your usual nun's habit, is it, Josselyn?" Victoria commented, in a voice that, despite herself, held a shrill, strident note; she was frightened and furious as she viewed her rival in this new and wholly unexpected light. Suddenly, the idea of losing Wylie now loomed as a hideously real possibility; and unbidden, Durango's words about her winding up on his side of the tracks rang unpleasantly in Victoria's ears.

"No, it is not my usual nun's habit, Victoria," Josselyn answered dryly, as Durango turned to hang her cape up on a nearby brass clothes tree. "But unfortunately, I received a letter earlier this week from the abbess of my convent, informing me that the convent will soon be forced to close its doors, due to financial difficulties. As both this news and Da's will appear to preclude my taking my final vows, I thought it only seemly to lay aside my habit."

She did not mention the fact that the green gown she wore had come from Durango; she did not know that Victoria was already aware of this. The widow had been in the dress shop earlier that day, to pick up some of her last season's hats and frocks, which she had arranged to have refurbished, in the hope that no one would realize they were not new. Ashamed of this economy that she deeply resented and cursed Forbes for, she had cringed at Durango's unanticipated appearance while the dressmaker was wrapping her packages. For an instant, she had stood at the counter, panicked and thinking he would surely recognize her old apparel, despite the alterations done to it. She had feared he would make some snide remark, but even more nerve-racking had been the worry that he would begin to wonder why she was reduced to such a frugal practice and would ferret out her true circumstances, which might lead to further exposures that would prove disastrous. Her agitation had been such that she could hardly be civil to him. But since she was so seldom polite to him, he had apparently noticed nothing amiss, and indeed, to her relief, he had not remarked on her refurbished raiment. Rather, he had seemed much more interested in having the gown on display in the dress-shop window removed from its wire mannequin. At the time, Victoria had not thought to wonder for whom he intended the gown. Now, she knew—and she was more certain than ever that she did not, after all, want to share Wylie.

He and Durango both were staring so hard at Josselyn that they looked ridiculous. Like two smitten schoolboys, mouths agape, Victoria observed to herself crossly, hoping uncharitably that each would accidentally swallow a fly—and choke on it. What if Wylie actually proposed marriage to Josselyn—and then did not prove nearly so eager to divorce her as he would have before? Victoria fretted silently. Where would that leave her? With Durango, who had spurned her because she had been Forbes's wife and who would not lift one finger to help her, monetarily or otherwise. She really would be out in the cold then, with no place left to go. She simply could not let that happen. Surely, there must be some means of at least balancing the power at the Rainbow's End—for anything else at this point appeared out of the question—and ensuring that Durango still ate the crow she had sworn to dish up to him.

After the four of them were seated at the white-linen-covered table at the center of the small dining room and the waiter had taken their orders, Victoria suddenly thought of a rash plan to accomplish both her goals, and she latched on to it desperately. Excusing herself to "powder her nose," she hurried away—not toward the ladies' room, however, but to the desk in the lobby, where she scribbled a note, then folded it and sealed it in an envelope that she paid one of the bellboys to deliver to an address in Dostal Alley. Then she rented a hotel room from the desk clerk and tucked the key into her reticule, withdrawing, as she did so, the vial of laudanum she always carried with her for her headaches. This, she slid down into her bodice, between her breasts. When her opportunity arose, as it must sooner or later during the course of the evening, she must be quick to seize it and not be fumbling around in her bag for the bottle instead. After that, she was so nervous that she really did need to use the hotel's facilities and did so, grateful for modern progress, which enabled each floor of the Teller House to be supplied by an elaborate system of pipes with water from the Teller Springs in Prosser Gulch. When she was done, Victoria returned to the small dining room, just in time for the opening course of turtle soup, although she was so keyed up that she could scarcely swallow more than a few sips.

By this time, Wylie and Durango had begun their usual cutthroat banter. Mustering her wits, Victoria forced herself to join in; it would not do to have any of the other three suspect what she was about. Still, even so, more than once, she glanced surreptitiously at the ormolu clock that sat on a nearby occasional table, ticking off the interminable minutes. Previously, she had arranged this supper only to assist Wylie in winning Josselyn's favor and to goad Durango with the idea that he was going to find himself the odd man out in the gold mine. Now, Victoria just wanted the evening to end as soon as possible—and without herself becoming a casualty of it. Always, at the back of her mind was the fact that either Durango or Wylie must have murdered both Forbes and Red; and while she attributed the crimes to Durango, she was astute enough to realize that they could just as easily have been committed by Wylie.

For this reason, she shuddered at the notion of what he might do to her should he ever learn of her deed tonight, and she made certain that the waiter kept the champagne flowing freely, in the hope that no matter how well Wylie and Durango held their liquor, their senses would still be dulled. Whether this proved to be the case, she could not tell; even drunk, the two men were notorious for their poker faces. But thanks to the amount of alcohol they consumed, they were at least compelled to excuse themselves following supper, as was Josselyn; and relieved, Victoria speedily availed herself of the chance to doctor the decanter of brandy the waiter had just brought in on a silver tray and set down upon the table. Uncertain how large a dose would be required to do the trick, she dumped the entire contents of her vial of laudanum into the decanter, then shoved the tiny bottle back into her reticule and jammed the crystal stopper back into the decanter. She really would have liked to pour the brandy into the snifters and drug only that in Durango's and Josselyn's glasses, but Durango was no fool. If only he and Josselyn felt the peculiar effects of the liquor, he was bound to grow suspicious. The deed accomplished, Victoria picked up her fan and wafted it vigorously to cool her flushed face as she waited for the others to return; she hoped fervently that she had not put so much laudanum in the decanter that they would all four of them pass out at the table.

Josselyn should not have drunk so much champagne—she knew she should not have—or had the brandy on top of it. Other than the wine at Mass, she was unused to spirits; and now her head was reeling so that she could hardly walk and, actually, was forced to cling tightly to Durango just to remain upright. She felt so incredibly sleepy that she wanted nothing more than to lie down on the boardwalk and pass out. People could just step over her, she told herself—although she knew she should be mortified at staggering like a sot from the Teller House and hanging all over Durango.

He himself was not in much better shape; and after he had somehow got them both into his buggy, he just sat there on the seat for a moment, holding the reins and shaking his head vigorously once or twice, as though to clear it. He muttered a curse; and from somewhere down the street, Josselyn imagined she heard the sound of running feet before, her eyes fluttering closed, she slumped against him, dead to the world, her head lolling upon his shoulder.

Vaguely, Durango knew that something was wrong, that

he had a hard head for alcohol and that the amount he had drunk at supper was not enough to have put him under the table. Somewhere deep in his brain, he sensed he had been drugged for some nefarious purpose. Dully, he registered the thud of boots—more than one pair—drawing ever nearer to the buggy, and he somehow understood that he and Josselyn were in danger. With every ounce of his willpower, he tried to respond to the alarm bell clanging in his mind; but in the end, he was unable to fight the waves of blackness that overcame him. His last thought was that he hoped he awoke alive, before he fell back against the seat, his arms wrapped around Josselyn, as though to shield her from whatever harm was to come.

Book Three

The Mother Lode

Chapter Seventeen

Central City, Colorado, 1877

Josselyn awoke to the horrifying realization that she had no idea where she was, that Durango lay beside her in the shared, unfamiliar bed, and that they were both stark naked.

She did not become aware of this all at once. At first, she knew only that her head pounded as though it contained a booming pump rod, that her mouth tasted dry as it had in the drifts of the gold mine, and that her stomach churned as though she were about to be violently ill. When her eyes slowly flitted open, the semidark room, illuminated by a sudden flash of lightning, seemed to spin about crazily. Feeling faint at the sight, she shut her eyelids, thinking only that if she lay very still, she might not be sick. Outside, thunder echoed in the mountains and rain pelted against the windows.

Dimly, she grasped that it was storming. That was why the morning was so leaden, as though the night had not yet ended.

Then, after a long, queasy moment, as she remembered the flare of the lightning, awareness grew that she was not in her room at Miss Hattie's cottage. At that, Josselyn's eyes flew open wide and she endeavored to rise, moaning weakly at how her head swam as she lifted it from the pillow. She could not get up; a heavy weight was pressing her down. Carefully turning her aching head, she saw that the weight was Durango. For an instant, she thought dazedly that she was not truly awake, that she was suffering a ghastly nightmare. Then, gradually, shocked and appalled, she recognized that this was no dream, but real, that she and Durango, who was still asleep, lay in a strange bed together, one of his legs tossed intimately over hers, his arm encircling her body, his palm cupping her breast. Neither he nor she had on a single stitch of clothing.

Her initial impulse was to scream—long and loud. Only instinct kept her silent, warned her to think before she took any action that might prove irreversible. Did she really want someone bursting inside the room, to discover them in flagrante delicto? Her heart beating horrendously, Josselyn attempted to gather her wits. Where was she? Still at the Teller House? That seemed likely judging from the noises she heard outside in the hall, although she supposed she might be in Durango's room at the Mother Lode. But, no, there was nothing to indicate that this room was lived in. She must be at the hotel, then. What had happened last night? She could not remember anything after supper except stumbling through the lobby, clutching Durango's arm for support. Sweet Mary, mother of Jesus! She must have been *drunk* from all the champagne and the brandy. Had she come up here willingly with Durango, then? No, no, she could not believe that. He must have dragged her up to this room and taken base advantage of her—again!

Josselyn wanted to kill him. Instead, terribly conscious now of his hand upon her breast, of what he would doubtless do when he awoke to find her lying naked beside him, she began trying furtively to ease herself from beneath his weight. To her dismay, instead of freeing herself, all she succeeded in doing was waking him. Involuntarily, his arm tightened around her, causing her to cry out and, panicked, to strive wildly to escape. Immediately, Durango came wide awake, startled, swearing, and fighting instinctively to hold on to her. After a few minutes' tussle, he pinned her to the bed. Then, pushing her masses of unbound hair from her face, he saw who lay beneath him. He inhaled sharply.

"Josselyn!" For a still, taut instant, blearily, although not without comprehension, his gaze took in the hotel room, their nudity, her frightened face. At last, he grasped their situation, recollected what he had heard last night just before he had passed out, and recalled his intuitive realization that he and Josselyn were about to be set upon by thugs—or henchmen. His eyes narrowed without warning, growing hard, skeptical, murderous as he recognized that she must have feigned unconsciousness in the buggy, been fully aware of what was about to occur, waiting for it, in fact. How cleverly he had been driven into the hunter's snare! Durango thought, infuriated, his temper not improved by the dreadful hammering in his skull that was making it difficult for him to think straight. "Just what in the hell is going on here?" he growled, even though, despite the fuzziness of his brain, he felt certain of the answer.

"I—I don't know," she stammered, distraught, her voice barely a whisper, she herself afraid and cringing from him, thinking he looked unusually satanic in the dark grey half-light—as though he would like to kill her.

"Don't you?" Durango spat, beginning to get a grip now on his senses, if not his rage. When she did not reply, he cursed softly, in a way that made her skin crawl. "Lying bitch! What a devil indeed lies behind your angel face! Is this how you thought to trap me into marrying you? To place the two of us in a compromising position, publicly, so I would be compelled to do the 'honorable' thing and wed you? Is it?'' He shook Josselyn roughly. "Answer me, damn you— or so help me, I'll break your goddamned harlot's neck! *¡Jesús!* What made you think I would care if you were ruined? I don't, do you understand? So you've lost your wager, my sweet. I'm wise to your game—and it would take more to bluff me than this cheating hand you have played!'' As his ire increased, the painful drumming in his head grew louder, harder, like some primitive beat, maddening him, inciting him, driving him on. Venomously, his hateful words continued to spew forth unchecked, unreasoningly.

"*¡Sangre de Cristo!* To think I ever thought you innocent and pure . . . even after I first kissed you and knew that you were not so ignorant as one might have supposed, even after I guessed you had slipped away from the convent to meet a lover—or was it lovers?'' he hissed meanly, sarcastically, giving her another small shake, his face dark with rancor, his eyes smoldering. "*¡Dios!* I must have been a fool or mad to fall for your tart's tricks! But even I, despite all my suspicions of you, could not truly believe that you were so accomplished an actress, so skilled a slut. Well, now, I know better. You are a whore, madam,'' he sneered, "bartering yourself for gold! Too bad you picked the wrong victim. I bed trollops, *sí*—I've a whole stable of them at the Mother Lode—but I sure as hell don't wed them! As I've told you before, I am not a marrying man.''

"Please,'' Josselyn breathed, stricken and bewildered by his tirade, his insults—when it was he who had brought her up here last night. "I—I don't understand anything you are saying. Really, I don't! If this is a—is a trap, as you called it, it is you who have laid it—to force me to become your mistress! For you know that I have no one to defend me now that my father is dead!'' Tears brimmed in her eyes at the thought. "You know that! Oh, you are heartless and vicious, an unconscionable villain! No matter what you say, I *was* a virgin, and still, you raped me! *Twice* now! For despite the fact that I remember nothing of it, I do not deceive myself about what happened in this bed last night. After all, you proved in the gold mine—did you not?—that you did not care if I was awake and aware when you took me. If I have become a whore, Durango, it is because you have made one of me! But no matter what you do to me, I won't be yours, to use as you please, do you hear? I won't! I won't!"

"A very pretty speech, my sweet," he drawled derisively, staring down at her. "And those crocodile tears"—he sneered at how she flinched as his thumb swept across the mauve crescents beneath her eyes, brushing away her tears —"so convincing. Had I not known better, I might have believed you. How unfortunate for you that I *do* know better. You little fool! Did you really think I would not know that you drugged me? What did you use? Laudanum? In the brandy, perhaps? No, do not bother to deny it; you will only be wasting your breath, for I know the truth, I tell you.

"Poor Josselyn. In light of how your ill-considered ploy has failed, I really do hope that you did not have to pay your hirelings too much to haul me up here—such a waste of good money. If you wished to sleep with me, you should have just said so. It would have cost you nothing. Indeed, I would even have paid for the room. But then, I am forgetting: It wasn't only me you wanted, but a wedding ring. What a pity I should prove so disobliging. I do so hate to disappoint a . . . lady, and in more ways than one; for since neither of us can recall it, I would venture to hazard a guess that last night was not very satisfactory for either of us." The sardonic smile he gave her did not quite reach his glittering eyes, like shards, that now surveyed her boldly, appraisingly, contemptuously, sending an icy shiver of foreboding up her spine as she felt his growing hardness against her, heard the rising intensity of the storm outside, the pummeling of the rain against the windows, the clap of thunder that rattled the panes violently. His dark, demonic face, erratically illuminated by the sporadic eruptions of lightning, was sanguine, making her shrink from him.

"However, at least the failure of last night to satisfy, I can remedy, *querida*," he went on implacably, his voice low, fraught with an unnerving note of menace—and promise—which made her heart race. "You are still a desirable woman, even if you are not quite so unsullied as once I thought; and now that we both know where we stand, there is no longer any reason for us to deny ourselves what we both want so badly of each other, is there? In fact, if you please me, I might even be persuaded still to make you my mistress, despite your being a rather tarnished angel." Josselyn's strangled wail of outrage and protest was smothered by the hand Durango clamped down swiftly and roughly over her mouth.

"Please, my sweet," he mocked mercilessly, "try to restrain your spurious screams of indignation. For I warn you: This wronged-maiden routine of yours has begun to wear thin. You see, I misled you about having had you at the Rainbow's End; it was only a ruse to keep you from Wylie. Whatever else I may be, I am not really so despicable as to have raped you, or any other woman—and you more than just that, a nun, a virgin . . . or so I thought at the time, and put your believing me down to your being too naive to know the signs that would have told you different. Now, of course, I understand that you simply had no foolproof way of telling the truth, that your virtue was long gone before ever I laid a hand on you; for why else would you have been so willing to strip yourself naked and climb into this bed with me last night? It could only have been that you had nothing left to lose and everything to gain—or so you thought. Well, it may not be what you hoped to have from me, *querida*, but still, I do not think that, in the end, you will find what I choose to give you unsatisfying."

With that, as though the turbulent storm outside had loosed something barbarous and terrible inside him, Durango's lips swooped down to seize hers, and he kissed her, long and deep, shutting off her whimpered entreaties, refusing, in his overwhelming wrath and desire, to hear what she attempted to tell him. Terrified, Josselyn began to struggle desperately against him, to no avail. He had her wrists pinioned firmly above her head, his leg thrown across her body to hold her prisoner, and as a result, there was no battling or eluding him. Indeed, her frantic writhing seemed only to increase his fierce determination to punish and possess her, for ruthlessly, he leaned his weight on her until all the air was expelled from her lungs and at last, gasping, exhausted, she was forced to lie helpless beneath him, even the sounds of her pleas and demurring muted by his hard, exacting mouth that moved on hers savagely, his tongue compelling her rebellious lips to part, invading her, pillaging the sweet secrets of her mouth, leaving her weak and dizzy and breathless, filled with fear and a perverse, perfidious, perilous excitement, as though she stood at the very pinnacle of the mountains, both defiantly and vulnerably exposed to his and the storm's full, frenzied fury.

In some distant corner of her mind, she felt shock and dismay at his revelation that he had lied to her, that he had not had her at the gold mine, that she was yet a virgin; for she knew that in moments, she would, in truth, be lost to him, and that knowledge was doubly bitter in light of what he had just told her. Anger and anguish at his trick and his converting it now to truth welled up inside her, but there was no release for it save for the hot tears that scalded her eyes and seeped from beneath her thick, sooty lashes—and half of these tears were born of her deep shame that, even now, despite everything, she should still respond to him, that that wicked, wanton thing he had wakened inside of her should leap so suddenly, so recklessly, so vibrantly, to life at his touch. It was hateful to her, unbearable, yet Josselyn could no more fight the feelings Durango aroused in her than she could fight him. She did not understand why he alone of all men should have this power over her; she knew only that he did and that she was powerless against it, against him.

She prayed that he would soon be done with her, but to her despair, he was not so inclined. As though time had stopped and he had all the time in the world to kiss her and to go on kissing her, his tongue darted forth to follow the lush curves of her mouth. As though her lips were a scarlet riband, a love knot, weaving about him a spell of enchantment he sought to loose so it would unravel and ensnare them both in its silken skein, he opened her mouth and plunged his tongue deep, binding hers, making of it a magicked captive, even as he taunted it with the false possibility of escape.

Josselyn tried to turn her head away, tried again to speak, to reason with him. But goaded by the emotions that, like a whip, stung him, lashed him, Durango would permit neither, his fingers snarling in her hair to hold her head still, his lips brutally silencing hers until, finally, despite herself, she was kissing him back fervidly, yielding to him and to inevitable fate, knowing he was far stronger than she, like the wild wind that drove the fragile rain hither and yon, heedlessly scattering it, as she felt her inhibitions fecklessly strewn as though to the four corners of the earth, her ability to think swept from her mind into nothingness. The beat of her heart was more frantic than the vehement tattoo of the rain against the windows; the blood that roared in her ears was louder than the thunder that cracked the heavens asunder. She was so caught up in the feelings he was evoking in her that she felt as though the storm itself had snatched her up, buffeting her to a place that was neither heaven nor hell, but somehow both, a primeval purgatory of darkness shot through with lightning's electrifying flame.

Durango had judged her—and found her wanting. Divine retribution was in his mouth and tongue and hands, making her pay for what he perceived as her sin against him, making her moan and thrash beneath him, acutely, painfully, aware of his hard, unclothed body covering her own soft, equally bare one. Josselyn had never in her life seen a man naked or been naked herself before a man. She was shocked, tantalized; the heat of him scorched her like a mountain fever. He was bathed in sweat, as was she, as though the rain sheeted down upon them where they lay, making their bodies glisten, one dark, one pale, both slippery as he slid across her, his turgid sex a threat portentous as the swollen thunderclouds that had presaged the unbridled storm, making her tremble, like the muddied sky, in his strong, certain embrace.

Like endless layers of rich, moist copper loam, her damp hair spread across the pillow like a mound of soft earth cradling her head, fragrant with lavender perfume. He breathed the scent in deeply as his lips slashed like a biting wind across her cheek to her temple and the strands of her hair, where he buried his face, his breath and his tongue hot in her ear, his hand over her mouth to keep her silent as he boldly muttered words to her that made her tingle with both trepidation and a tempestuous thrill that was like nothing she had ever before known.

"I want you, Jossie! I've wanted you from that moment when I saw you in the gold mine, with your hair wild and loose and tumbled down around you, shimmering like a halo of fire, and you looking like an angel, a witch, your slanted green eyes and your crimson rosebud mouth haunting me, taunting me. I knew then that I would have you in the end, no matter what; and soon . . . very soon now . . . I'm going to take you, my sweet, and you will learn what it is to have me, a man, in your bed—not those boy lovers you slipped away from the convent to meet, who knew nothing of *amor*, nothing of *you*! *I* know you, Jossie! Down to your angelic bones, down to your witch's soul. In my arms, you will learn what it is to be a woman, *my* woman." His voice was low, husky, exultant. "Because despite all the lies and the suspicion between us, that's what we both want; it's what we've both wanted all along. And after I've had you, every part of you, like this . . . and like this, no man but I will ever touch you again. You will be mine, all mine, only mine . . . to do with as I please, whenever I please, however I please—and you will beg me to do it to you, *querida*, I swear!"

His demanding lips closed over hers again, sealing off whatever sounds of futile objection she might have made, whatever words of vain explanation she might have uttered, although she had ceased now to strive against him, understanding that what was to come *would* come, even that some dark, primitive part of her wanted it, wanted *him*, and had since the beginning, as he had said, regardless of how much she longed to deny it. She *was* his, knew instinctively that it was so as his hands cupped her breasts jealously, possessively, molded them to fit his palms, glided sensuously across her nipples, teasing them into taut peaks, highly charged as the storm; for where he touched her, lightning broke within her, jagged and white-hot, shattering her, searing her down to her molten bones. Free now, Josselyn strained and arched fervently against him, no longer seeking escape, but union with the man who held her and unleashed within her emotions so tumultuous, sensations so ecstatic, that she was as a blind, mad thing, captive in some dark and atavistic place whipped by wild, chaotic elements that swept away all in their frenzy.

Her long chestnut hair was a mountain thicket, blown by an unseen wind, tangling about her and Durango, irrevocably binding them together as his mouth tasted the length of her white throat, his tongue licked the salty sweat from her flesh, his teeth bit the soft spot where her nape joined her shoulder, sending bolts of erotic pain and pleasure shooting through her as the bite turned into a kiss moist and throbbing as the rain. As though they had a will of their own, her arms twined about his neck; her fingers burrowed through his glossy black hair, urgently drawing him down to her. As though she were the earth, she drank him in, soaking him up thirstily as though he were necessary to sustain her existence, as though he were draining her very essence from her body, and then pouring it back in, making her teem and burgeon with life. The muscles of his hard, lithe body quivered and rippled beneath her hands as he bent over her, crushed her to him fiercely, his lips blazing a trail down the valley between her breasts, the stubble of his unshaven face grazing her tender skin. His tongue lapped away the perspiration that trickled like a mountain creek between the mounds that, swollen and aching now with passion, he kissed and sucked and fondled. His mouth and tongue were tendrils of curling mist enveloping the twin crests, causing her to shiver and whimper and buck against him as rapture rolled through her, like the tumid clouds across the lowering sky, massing, building to some shadowy, unknown thing that scared, that exhilarated, that took the breath and the mind away.

Where they were was a place without gentleness. He was so sure that none was needed; she was too benighted to know that it could be had even from him had he not been gripped fast by the fist of torrid, mindless emotion that clutched him as tightly as she did. She felt as though if she did not hold on to him, she would be lost, whirled away by the ferocious, feral thing that had, with carnivorous teeth and ripping talons, seized them both.

Josselyn gasped as, without warning, Durango shoved her tightly closed thighs wide apart and touched her where no man ever had, a quick, light stroke of torment that was like the first hard drops of sprinkling rain, a foreshadowing of what was to follow. Suddenly panicked, she cried out and, attempting to rise, renewed her struggles against him, her hands striking out at him blindly, her fingernails raking his face and his chest, drawing blood, causing him to snarl low in his throat and curse her before he captured her wrists in a bruising clench and dragged them beneath her, making her hips arch against him, as though in an invitation he was ready to accept. Roughly, his lips swallowed her pitiful, ragged sobs of fear and shame and perverse anticipation as, undeterred, his hand found the dark, secret origin of her desire again, lingeringly caressed the mellifluous, engorged folds of her that quivered and opened to him of their own eager, needy accord, until she moaned like a wounded animal and writhed helplessly beneath him, hollow, empty, aching unendurably to be filled to overflowing. Then, very slowly, very deliberately, in an encroachment so intimate that she wanted to die, his fingers plunged full length into her well of carmine softness. Her breath caught in her throat as they were just as torturously withdrawn, only to slide into her again. His tongue was in her mouth, mimicking the sweetly agonizing movements of his hand, the flicking of his thumb against the pulsing fount of her, until her passion for him was keen as the high wind, the drubbing rain that flailed against the windows.

She strained against him urgently, knowing nothing except that she wanted, she needed . . . and was denied. She wailed long and low with affliction when what she sought so desperately did not come, when his fingers abruptly abandoned her, leaving her cruelly unassuaged. Devastated, she opened her eyes to see Durango poised above her, dark and bronze and naked in the shadowy half-light, his saturnine features making him appear like some half man, half beast of age-old legend, his bold shaft hard and heavy with desire, his black eyes rapacious and glimmering with triumph, a mocking half smile twisting his carnal lips. Josselyn shuddered as he stared down at her, understanding, now, that he had not repudiated her, after all, that this tense moment was but the lull before the summit of the storm.

"Please . . . oh . . . please . . ." she implored, an anguished sigh, a contradictory appeal for release from his arms or into climax, though she knew, as he did, that only one was forthcoming.

At that, with a rasp, a groan, a calling of her name, the storm broke upon her as he drove inexorably down into her, lightning splintering her, riving her, splitting her asunder in a moment of penetrating, white-hot pain that was ultimate invasion and quintessential possession. She gasped, then cried out at his burning entry; and when he sensed her tearing, fragile resistance, which he had not expected, was unprepared for, his eyes flew open wide with shock and sudden remorse. Knowing then that he had wronged her badly, he swore softly, "¡Nombre de Dios!" and his entire body tensing, he tried to pull back. But it was too late; he had thrust hard and deep and sure, and the damage to her was done, her ruin complete. Tears trickled down her cheeks as she felt the dull ache that spread through her loins at the abundance of him filling her, throbbing within her. Until now, she had never truly known what to expect, had never truly comprehended this absolute incursion and her total submission, this stretching and molding of oneself to receive the other. With a gentler urgency now, he kissed her tears away, his hand stroking her hair soothingly as he lay still atop her, giving her time to recognize and accept, as he did, that what was done, was done, and to grow accustomed to the feel of him inside her.

"Shhhhh, *querida*," Durango murmured in her ear, embracing her more tightly, raining tender kisses upon her hair and face. "Shhhhh. I have hurt you, I know, and that was not my intent. But the pain will pass, and then there will be only pleasure, I promise you."

A lie, Josselyn thought dimly, like all the rest, balm to lessen the sting of her unhealable wound. But it was not so. In his words this time was truth that washed over her in euphoric waves as he began to move inside her, fierce as the sudden, wild rising of the storm that now battered them both unmercifully, entwining them inseparably and forever, flogging them to frantic want and need as he surged into her savagely, again and again, faster and faster, his strong hands sweeping her up to meet each brazen, glorious thrust, his head buried against her shoulder, his harsh, uneven breath hot against her flesh. From the soaked sheets wafted the scent of their mating, sharp and sweet, as, with each sough of the wanton wind, the hellish pain she had at first experienced gradually gave way to heavenly pleasure. Willingly then, feverishly, she enwrapped him, enfolded him, clung to him, fingernails furrowing his broad back as she reached for that shadowy, unknown thing she felt she must find or die, and she rushed headlong with him down a dark, wending passage that led from rounded hills to highest mountains, where the unearthly empyrean above seethed and roiled, and then, without warning, shattered violently, breathtakingly into such splendorous brilliance that it was almost hurtful to behold, spangled flame setting them both afire, exalting them, burning them to ashes, until, finally, with a last, ragged gasp, the storm slowly dissipated and died away.

In the stillness now, Durango held her close as, reality

cruelly intruding at last, Josselyn wept bitterly in his arms. What had she done? What had she done? She had lain with him, had yielded herself to him—a man not her husband, a drunkard, a gambler, a bastard, perhaps even her father's killer. She recoiled in fright and revulsion from the realization, ill and ashamed of what Durango had wakened inside her, of how easily he had subjugated her, had taken what he had wanted from her—the virgin's blood that now stained her trembling white thighs. She shivered at the sight, suddenly cold. Silently, noting where her eyes strayed, how gooseflesh prickled her skin, he drew the coverlet up over her, then eased himself from both her and the bed, as shaken in his own way as she was. He ran his hands jerkily through his damp, unkempt hair. He needed a smoke; he needed a drink. The wheels of his mind turning furiously, he took stock of the hotel room. Their clothes lay scattered heedlessly upon the floor, as though ripped off in the heat of passion last night. But now, he knew that it had not been so. He picked the garments up, tossing them onto a nearby chair after he had searched his pockets and withdrawn a cheroot and matches. The money he habitually carried with him was gone, further evidence that the trap could not have been Josselyn's doing.

Though she was a huntress, any wound she delivered would be shot clean and fair, not brought about by a carefully concealed snare; he knew that now. For where was the witness to her dishonor? Where was Red with his shotgun in hand, angrily bewailing his daughter's fate and demanding redress of the grievous wrong done to her? He would have been here, surely, if he were still alive and spying on Josselyn, even if she had not dealt this hand that had come from a spitefully marked deck. Surely, then, he was dead. Nor would Wylie have benefited from this underhanded game. Striking a match, Durango lighted his cigar and dragged on it thoughtfully. Then, from the crystal decanter of whiskey that sat upon a silver tray on a table, he sloshed a drink into a glass, sniffing its contents suspiciously before taking an experimental sip.

After that, grabbing an ashtray, he returned to the bed and settled himself down beside Josselyn once more.

"Tell me again, *querida*, what you remember about last night," he directed quietly.

Using a corner of the sheet to dry her eyes, she told him, and as he listened, his face grew so still and ominous that she stumbled over her words and finally stopped speaking altogether.

"My sweet, your accusations against me are as erroneous as mine against you were," Durango said after a moment. "I am a lot of things—and, indeed, not all of them pleasant; I freely admit it—but I am not such a brute as you think. I reiterate that I did not rape you at the Rainbow's End; nor did I drag you up here to this hotel room and take sordid advantage of you while you were unconscious . . . or unwilling."

This last hung meaningfully in the hushed air seasoned with the scent of their mating, for they both knew how very willing, just minutes past, she had been, how much she had craved him, for all that she had, in the beginning, struggled against him. She had wanted him; she wanted him still. That, Josselyn could not in all honesty deny. Still, she tried earnestly to think that, in the end, she would have fought harder, would not have given in to him had she not half thought, half feared that she was no longer a virgin, that she had already been his twice before.

"But you told me before that you did take me . . . in the gold mine, at least—"

"Be fair, *querida*—although why in the hell you should be, I don't know, for I was hardly fair to you, was I?" He laughed shortly, harshly, at the irony, knowing how his niggling doubt that she was not truly innocent or chaste, but a fraudulent siren had led him to want her as his mistress, although not his wife—a thought that shamed him now in the face of her genuine distress. She had tried to tell him that she was not guilty of the trap that had caught them both. Why hadn't he listened? This was not how he had meant for things to happen between them—though, no matter how it had come about, he could not honestly be sorry she was his. So thinking, he continued. "Think, did I ever say straight out that I had actually had you? No. I implied it, yes, to keep you from Wylie. But in truth, you believed what you wanted to believe, Jossie: that I raped you, that I murdered your father. I did neither. You are now certain of the first; you have my word for the last."

In that instant when she lay naked and cradled against him in the bittersweet afterglow of their lovemaking, Josselyn wished with all her heart that she could be as sure that he was as innocent of murder as of rape, yet doubt lingered, insidious as a poisonous serpent. Wylie had proved himself a liar and a cheat, but still, there had been an unmistakable ring of truth to his words when he had told her that he had not killed her father; and if not Wylie, then Durango must be guilty of the deed. There was no one else to suspect. But against that reality, Josselyn closed her eyes tightly, not want-ing to see it. Somehow, Durango had got into her blood, her bones, her soul; and her own world having collapsed, she had dared to follow him into his. What now would become of her without him? She had no one else to turn to, little money and few means of acquiring more, and no sanctuary save for the Rainbow's End—and he would take that from her, too, if he could. If she wished to survive, she had no choice but to be his mistress, provided he still wanted her.

She shuddered at the notion; he was like an animal, and some dark, wild, earthy thing inside her own self responded to him on that primitive level. She had been taught to restrain her passions, not to give unbridled rein to them. Now, she had fallen from grace, the teachings of a lifetime made dust in the wind by a single, fleeting, white-hot moment of desire. She had no illusions left now about what Durango would demand of her if she became his. There would be many endlessly long days like this one and even longer nights, lying wrapped in his embrace, his body moving urgently on hers, bullying her, breaking her, beguiling her. . . .

With silent empathy, he tightened his arm around her. Setting aside his glass of whiskey and stubbing out his cheroot, he gently kissed the tears from her cheeks. Then, after a while, want and need rising like wind in his veins, he claimed her tremulous mouth again, his tongue shooting deep between her lips, his hunger for her a devouring thing and there being no reason now not to sate it.

"No," she breathed against him. "Please, no . . . you hurt me—"

"There is always pain the first time; I told you that. But afterward, you knew pleasure in my arms, *querida*, as you will again . . . countless times again," he muttered thickly, rolling her over, weighing her down, his naked body sliding determinedly to cover hers, showing her the truth of his prophetic words as, outside, once more, the rain came hard and fierce.

Chapter Eighteen

They slept again, lulled into slumber by their lovemaking, the semidarkness of the morning, and the soothing rhythm of the steady downpour. When they awoke, Durango made love to Josselyn yet a third time, slowly and gently, making her shudder and cry out once more as he carried her to the soaring heights of rapture. Afterward, as they lay together silently, their hearts still beating fast, their naked, sweating bodies still entangled, the maid knocked upon the door, wanting to know when she could clean the room. Calling out to her to come back later, Durango sent the woman away. Then, at last, reluctantly, he moved from Josselyn and the bed. Pouring tepid water from a pitcher on the washstand into its bowl, he wet a cloth and returned to sponge her off tenderly, on his dark visage both satisfaction and a scowl as he washed away the virgin's blood between her thighs. Then he kissed her and, casting aside the cloth, turned to start putting on his clothes, instructing her to do the same. But despite everything, she was still shy of him and remained beneath the sheets, flustered at the thought of dressing before him. Glancing up at her impatiently from the chair upon which he now sat, yanking on his boots, he spied her anxious face and instantly guessed the reason for her dilatoriness.

"My sweet," he drawled, shaking his head and laughing softly, "there is no part of you that I have not staked my claim on this day. What do you have left to hide?" Standing, he tossed her her garments. "Now, get into your clothes . . . or shall I help you?"

"N-n-no, I can do it," Josselyn stammered, blushing, her emotions in a turmoil as she forced herself to rise, to begin dressing, painfully cognizant of how he watched her, his eyes gleaming lazily with appreciation, though a muscle worked in his set jaw as he lighted another cigar, and then took a drink of his whiskey.

She still felt dazed, as though all that had happened were unreal; there was such a dreamlike quality to last night— when she thought of it, it was no more than a hazy memory—and to the dark grey morning, with its euphonious cadence of rain. Even now, it seemed inconceivable to her that she had lain with Durango, that she had responded to him in a way that, previously, would have been beyond her wildest imaginings. She was torn by inner conflict. Despite herself, a part of her reveled in all that had passed between them, her intimate knowledge of him as a man, her newfound awareness of herself as a woman. But the rest of her was beset by shame and apprehension, for though he had told her often enough that he wanted her, he had not mentioned again her becoming his mistress, and his silence on the subject frightened her. He did not love her, and she worried that now that he had taken her, perhaps his desire for her had palled. She knew instinctively that there had been many women before her; why should she be any different from all the others he had used and abandoned so carelessly? Josselyn's heart sank at the notion.

She had been away overnight from the boardinghouse, and she did not think it likely that her absence had gone unnoticed or that she would be able to sneak in unobserved. Miss Hattie was bound to be scandalized; doubtless, her sense of propriety would compel her to demand that Josselyn vacate the premises at once. Where could she go, what would become of her if Durango repudiated her? She did not know. The chances of Victoria's assisting her seemed remote, and the idea of telling Wylie the whole and throwing herself upon his mercy was appalling. Even if he could be persuaded to wed her, in exchange for her inheritance, given his relationship to Victoria and how he felt about Durango, Wylie would surely insist upon an immediate divorce, and then Josselyn would be no better off than she was now. She bit her lip nervously at the thought. Fearing what her future would hold in store otherwise, she had tried hard to please Durango that last time, not fighting him, kissing him, opening herself to him, and touching him as he had wished her to and had shown her. Her face flooded with color at the remembrance. Had she failed in her shyness and her inexperience to gratify him, then? She had to know. Mustering her courage, she spoke.

"Do you—do you still w-w-want me, Durango?" she asked hesitantly in the stillness that had fallen, unbroken save for the thrumming rain. "As your—your mi-mi-mistress, I mean?" She stumbled over the mortifying words, deeply humiliated that she should be reduced to offering herself to him, to begging him to take her, to dreading that he would reject her.

"No, of course not," he said tersely, to her horror, his reply like a slap in her face, stunning her, causing her to blanch and sway on her feet, as though she would swoon. She moaned low with anguish, one shaking hand fluttering to her throat, sudden tears she was unable to hold at bay spilling from her wide, stricken eyes. "¡Jesús, Jossie!" he swore hotly, striding across the room to take her into his arms. "Don't look at me like that! Don't cry! I thought you understood; I'm going to marry you, *querida*, today. I wronged you—badly—I know. Surely, you did not think that I would not put that aright. That, under the circumstances, I would have made love to you again if I did not intend to wed you. *¡Sangre de Cristo!* Don't you think I realize that there are those who are bound to know of your ruin at my hands, that Miss Hattie is likely to turn you out on the streets? *¡Dios mío!* Did you really believe me such a monster as to take advantage of that, to make you my whore when I know you to be blameless of what was done last night . . . and this morning?"

"But . . . what else *could* I think, Durango?" she cried, scarcely able to credit his words, half afraid they were but a cruel jest. "You have told me often enough that you—that you are not a—not a marrying man."

"No, I am not," he agreed grimly, his face dark. "But neither am I such a cad as to destroy your innocence and make no reparation for it—a fact that whoever set us up must have counted on! Somebody drugged us, Jossie, and brought us up here and put us in that bed together—" His eyes glittered so with rage at the thought that she cringed in his embrace. "If I ever learn the identities of those men who did it, I shall kill them! *¡Jesús!* When I think of them stripping you naked, *touching* you—" His hands tightened on her involuntarily, hurting her, scaring her; for now, in the face of his murderous threat, all her suspicions about him returned. Suddenly, the notion of giving herself into his keeping was as frightening as being forsaken by him.

"But—but who would have done such a terrible thing?" she whispered, aghast, realizing, now, that if, indeed, he were not responsible for what had taken place last night, unknown hands had undressed her, had perhaps even fondled her while she had lain unconscious—an idea far worse some-how than when she had believed that Durango himself had done as much to her.

His bark of laughter rang unpleasantly in her ears.

"Now that I can think straight, I see Victoria's malicious hand in this." His voice had a serrated edge, and his jaw was tight with anger.

"Victoria! But . . . how? Why?"

"I suppose that, in the end, I must be held somewhat to blame," he admitted reluctantly, "for buying you that accursed, bewitching gown! Until she saw you in it, she did not perceive you as a rival to be reckoned with. I can only conjecture that last night, she received an extremely rude awakening about your true worth, which caused her to fear that Wylie, if he wed you, might not prove quite so eager as he doubtless would have been previously to divorce you after he had got his hands on your father's shares in the Rainbow's End. She must have doped the brandy while we were all gone from the table, rented this room, and hired a couple of thugs to carry you and me up here, deciding that a balance of power in the gold mine was preferable to losing Wylie and being forced to cast her lot in with me. I spurned her once, you see, and Victoria has never forgotten or forgiven me for it. No doubt, she is even now laughing up her sleeve at how she has evened the score by placing me in a position where I am compelled to marry you."

"But . . . that's unconscionable!" Josselyn exclaimed, horrified. "How could she be certain that you—that you would wed me afterward, that you would not insist upon my becoming your—your mi-mi-mistress, or even that you would not desert me?"

"Because you're Red's daughter and had intended to become a nun. Because Red was like a father to me, and devout or not, I'm a Catholic. Because, believe it or not, my sweet, I do have *some* morals, and divesting young maidens of their virtue is something I don't ever do—not only for their sakes, but because I know what it means to be illegitimate and I don't want any kid of mine to have to grow up bearing that stigma." He paused for a moment. Then he uttered quietly,

"You do realize, Jossie, that I might have got you with child, don't you?"

She nodded, not trusting herself to speak, for the thought *had* occurred to her, further cause for consternation. As a result, deep down inside—whatever Durango was, whatever he had done—she could only be glad that he was not so cruel as to abandon her to her fate, as he might easily have done. For if he were right about the plot, then he was, in truth, as much a victim as she was; and if the green dress were indeed the impetus that had brought them to this pass, then, surely, she must be held as accountable as he, for she need not have worn the gown. But her pride and her vanity had got the best of her, and her desire for revenge, too—sins, all of them, which the Reverend Mother had warned her time and again she would one day rue. Well, that day had come, and now, she must pay the price for her waywardness.

Numbly, when he said, "Come, *vamos*," she allowed Durango to lead her from the Teller House, relieved that because of the rain, there were few people abroad to spy them exiting the hotel, in their evening clothes, indisputable evidence that they had spent the night there together. Mercifully, Durango's team and buggy were still at the hitching rail out front. He assisted Josselyn into the vehicle, pulling up its calash to shield them from the elements, and then drove down to Main Street, to the Mother Lode, where he took some money from his cash register. Then they traveled back up Eureka Street to Washington Hall, the clapboard courthouse, where he obtained a marriage license. After that, they went down the hill to Pine Street, to St. Patrick's church.

This was nothing more than a stone basement that had been roofed over, the original two-story frame structure that had been converted into the first church and rectory in the entire mining district having burned down during the 1874 fire that had started in Dostal Alley. Before then, the cornerstone for Central City's permanent Catholic church had already been laid by Bishop J. B. Lamy and the basement had been dug;

but after the blaze, financial difficulties had prevented work on the new church from continuing, although, next door, the rectory, commonly referred to as "the Parish House," was now completed. Meanwhile, in order to have a place in which to worship, the Catholics had simply installed a roof on the basement of the church. Thus, St. Patrick's was not currently much to look at, and the interior of the church was as dark and dreary as the depressing day. The plain altar was not at all what Josselyn had dreamed of kneeling before when she had imagined her wedding to Antoine.

When she and Durango entered, rain-drenched and still garbed in their evening clothes, Father Flanagan, his face startled and concerned, stepped forward from the chancel to greet them. Josselyn, of course, was a member of his congregation; Durango, he knew to be a lost sheep strayed from the fold.

"My children, what brings you here at such an hour and on such a day as this?" the priest asked, his kindly but shrewd eyes now taking in the fact that Josselyn was not wearing her habit, that her face was ashen, and that her eyes, downcast, appeared unable to meet his. At the realization, he was filled with dismay. Clearly, something untoward had happened.

"We want to get married, *Padre*," Durango announced coolly. "Today. Now."

"But . . . that is impossible," Father Flanagan declared, shocked and glancing anxiously, questioningly, at Josselyn. But she made no effort to refute Durango's words; and instinctively, then, the priest began to fear the worst, that she had somehow been compromised, willingly or otherwise, by the tall, dark rascal at her side. Why else would she be here now, wanting to be wed, dressed as she was and looking far too pale, her tremulous mouth bruised and swollen as though from a man's hard kisses? Since she had joined his flock, Father Flanagan had had several conversations with her, so he was not unaware of the execrable terms of her father's will and all that Durango stood to gain by marrying her. Nor was the priest unacquainted with the gambler's notorious reputation. Still, not wanting to believe what he now suspected, Father Flanagan persisted in his refusal. "Josselyn is destined to become a bride of Christ—"

"Not anymore, *Padre*." Durango's face and voice were so grim and determined, so very certain, that, at last, the priest, deeply anguished for her, felt he could only conclude that Josselyn had not only consented to wed the gambler, but that her acquiescence had been coerced by the foulest possible means. It was all he could do to prevent himself from laying violent hands upon Durango.

"Is what this man says true, Josselyn?" Father Flanagan queried sharply, hoping to jolt her from her mute acceptance of her fate. "Speak up, my daughter! Do not be afraid. No one is going to harm you here, in God's house, I assure you! Is it indeed true that you no longer wish to take the final vows that will make of you a nun, but are desirous instead of marrying this man?"

"Y-y-yes, Father," she choked out, blushing with shame at what the priest must be thinking. In a futile attempt to allay his doubts and suppositions, she rushed on. "I had a letter from—from the Reverend Mother Maire, you see, and—and the convent in Boston is—is being forced to close, for lack of money, and I never really had a true vocation, anyway, and I—I need to secure my inheritance and my future, and . . . oh, Father! I must wed Durango! I simply must!"

"I . . . see." Father Flanagan fell silent. Then, after a long, tense moment, he continued sternly. "Josselyn, even if I were convinced that you made this momentous decision of your own free will—and I must tell you quite frankly that I am not at all sure of that!—I cannot in all good conscience, and therefore will not, marry the two of you today. The Church requires that the banns be published, and you, sir" —he fixed a cold, severe eye upon the gambler—"must confess your sins—"

"We ain't waiting three weeks, *Padre*," Durango said flatly, "and you name the sin, and I've done it. That takes care of the banns and the confession. Now, unless you've got any other objections, get on with the wedding ceremony, *Padre*, because so help me, God, you're going to perform it—if I have to hold my gun to your head to force you to do it!'' His hand dropped purposefully to the walnut stock of his holstered pistol.

"I warn you, sir, that threats will avail you nothing," the priest insisted stoutly, unafraid, "and that bloodshed will but damn your soul to hell for all eternity!"

"Oh, please, Father!" Josselyn cried, frightened for him, fearful that Durango had been pushed to his limit this day and so really would draw his revolver. "Do as he says! I do want to marry him! I do! He has . . . that is . . . Father, I am no longer . . . what I mean to say is—"

"What Jossie is so maidenly trying to tell you, *Padre*," Durango interrupted smoothly to spare her further embarrassment, "and what I gather you've already grasped, anyway, is that we . . . er . . . celebrated our wedding night a trifle early—although despite what you're thinking, I am not entirely to blame for that. You see, unfortunately, someone at the Teller House last night drugged us and left us in one of the hotel's beds together—a spiteful prank that I am now earnestly attempting, before Jossie's reputation is irreparably damaged, to remedy the only way I know how, and, I might add, that you are making mighty damned difficult, *Padre*. Now, I don't really know what Miss Hattie is going to do about Jossie's not coming home last night, but I strongly suspect that no matter how she might feel about things personally, if Miss Hattie wishes to continue running a respectable boardinghouse, as I am sure she does, then, like it or not, she's going to have to turn Jossie out on the streets; and since Jossie's got no place else to go and nobody else to turn to, if you don't marry us, *Padre*, she's going to wind up living in sin with me—and that's not a threat, but a promise,'' Durango ended softly, on his face such a look that there could be no doubt that he fully meant this last and would do whatever necessary to ensure it.

"My son, forgive me, for I confess I have wronged you,"

Father Flanagan asserted, stricken. "I thought the worst of you, and for that I am sorry. I did not understand before. I realize, now, that you are but trying to make the best of a bad situation. This is terrible! Who would have played such a shameful, villainous trick on the two of you?"

"You let me worry about that, *Padre*," Durango replied sourly, a muscle flexing in his set jaw. "You just take care of seeing me and Jossie wed proper. She's a good Catholic, even if I'm not—you know she is, *Padre*—and she'll not believe herself married unless a priest instead of a judge or a justice of the peace performs the ceremony."

"Yes, of course." Father Flanagan nodded and, turning to make his way back to the chancel, motioned to them to follow. "Under the circumstances, I agree that we can dispense with the posting of the banns. I take it that you have the license?"

"Yeah, I have it," Durango confirmed.

"Good," the priest said. "Then we can proceed."

He called to the two women arranging fresh flowers on the altar and cleaning the church, in preparation for the evening Mass, and they acted as witnesses while Josselyn and Durango knelt and repeated the vows that bound them together, he twisting an antique gold band, fashioned like a garland, from his fourth finger to serve as her wedding ring. Father Flanagan wrapped his stole about their clasped hands and blessed the couple. Then Durango kissed Josselyn lingeringly and she was legally his wife. She could hardly believe it; it had all happened so quickly that it still seemed unreal, like something from a dream or a nightmare. But the deed was done—the band she now wore upon her finger was tangible proof of that—although, as she slowly began to absorb the fact that she was really married, she did not know whether to be glad or sorry for it; and her hand trembled in Durango's own as, after thanking the priest, he led her outside and helped her back into the buggy. There, he kissed her again, hungrily this time, his hands moving on her in a way that made her fully understand that she was truly and utterly his now, that he was free to take her whenever and however he pleased, as he had promised earlier he would. Josselyn shivered at the thought and tried halfheartedly to free herself from his embrace; but this, he would not permit, tightening his arms around her possessively before, at last, he chose to release her, his black eyes glimmering hotly as they surveyed her, observing with satisfaction her flushed cheeks and the pulse that beat rapidly at the hollow of her throat.

She thought then that he would take her home to Miss Hattie's cottage. But to Josselyn's dismay, he drove her to Killian's office instead. That could only mean one thing: that he intended, as her husband, to claim her father's shares in the Rainbow's End.

"My sweet, did you seriously think I would not?" Durango drawled mockingly when she dared to question him about it. "However it came about, you are my wife"—he spoke this last word with a certain amount of unexpected relish—"and as such, you are mine, as is all that you own, including your inheritance. I want those shares locked up in my safe—not only because they legally belong to me now, but as . . . insurance, if you will, for your own behavior. You see, *querida*, I have rather a strong suspicion that once the shock of this day has worn off, your doubts about me will return to haunt you and you will start to regret having wed me. As a result, it may be that you will attempt to do something foolish, such as trying to deny me my husbandly rights or even to divorce me, neither of which I will allow, I warn you. As I told you once before, what is mine, I keep. Do you understand?"

"Yes," Josselyn breathed, her eyes huge and scared in her face; for already, as he had guessed, she was besieged by inner turmoil over their marriage.

That he would, after their wedding, waste no time in bringing her here, to Killian's office, gave her considerable pause, caused her to rethink the events of last night and this morning. Perhaps it all had been a contemptible but clever ruse on Durango's part to compel her to marry him so he could get his hands on her inheritance. Earlier, she had believed him to be as much a victim of their hapless situation as she. Now, she no longer felt so certain that he had been. But still, even if he *had* vilely tricked her, there was nothing she could do about it now, Josselyn realized dully, glancing down at the gold band that encircled her finger, marking her as his possession. It was as he had said: She was his wife, and he had every right to her and all she owned. Swallowing hard, she made no further protest as he escorted her into Killian's office.

Patrick was surprised to see them and even more startled by the wedding certificate that Durango drew from his breast pocket and handed to him, requesting that he complete at once the necessary paperwork that would transfer Red's shares in the Rainbow's End to Josselyn and thus to her husband. Positioning his wire-rimmed spectacles on his nose, the attorney examined the marriage certificate carefully. Then, clearing his throat, he spoke.

"Your wedding took place just this morning? Rather . . . ahem . . . sudden, was it not?" he asked, eyeing the two of them sharply. "To the best of my knowledge, there's been no publishing of the banns."

"Yeah, well, I persuaded Father Flanagan to dispense with the posting of 'em," Durango explained coolly. "Anyway, what in the hell does that have to do with the price of tea in China, Patrick? You can see that regardless of whatever you may think of the affair, Jossie and I are married all right; and as her husband, I want Red's damned shares due her under the terms of his accursed will. Now, get 'em and hurry up about it! I ain't got all day. I've got other matters to take care of. Jossie can't live in a saloon, for Christ's sake!"

They were only pieces of paper, just pieces of paper, Josselyn thought dimly, feeling a wild, hysterical urge to laugh until she cried as she watched the lawyer slowly open his safe and remove what Da had bequeathed her. For this, her whole life had been blighted. Pieces of paper. Numbly, she signed all that Patrick, grim-faced, placed before her, not even bothering to read any of it. What was the use? It was hers only until the instant when, from the attorney's desk, Durango picked up the papers that represented her inheritance, folded them up, and tucked them firmly into his breast pocket. She had lost everything this day: her virginity, her freedom, her shares in the Rainbow's End; and all she had received in exchange was a husband who bore her no love and whom she dared not trust. It did not seem right, somehow. But still, small solace though it was at the moment, her future was at least secure. She was wedded to a smart, strong, capable man, even if he was a drunkard, a gambler, and a bastard; and it seemed from his remarks that he intended to look after her. She would not be ruined, turned out in disgrace on the streets, and reduced to supporting herself by selling herself to Wylie—or worse. She supposed she should be grateful for that. Then she remembered what Durango would demand of her in return, and she shuddered, sensing that what she had learned earlier that morning was but the first of many lessons he would teach her.

Once they had departed from Killian's office, Durango drove on to Roworth Street, to deposit Josselyn at the boardinghouse, where he instructed her to pack her belongings, saying he would come back for her just before suppertime, after he had arranged temporary living quarters for the two of them. It was indecorous, he insisted, for her to reside at the Mother Lode, and he would not have further fuel added to the fire of gossip that was bound to spread about their marriage if he were unable to succeed in hushing the unsavory details up. Then he left her.

Miss Hattie was waiting for her inside, both worried about Josselyn's welfare and shocked at her not returning home last night. Upon learning that Josselyn was wed to Durango, Miss Hattie professed herself startled but delighted. It was obvious, even so, that she was deeply troubled by what was plainly a peculiar, if not downright scandalous, marriage, the groom a notorious gambler, the bride only yesterday having laid aside her nun's habit; and Miss Hattie's profound relief when informed that Josselyn would be vacating the premises later on that day was evident. Saddened but not wishing to cause Miss Hattie further distress, Josselyn hurried upstairs to her room. Kneeling on the floor to open her leather-bound trunk, she began to pack her meager possessions.

But the more she dwelled on the expression on Durango's face when he had slipped her shares in the Rainbow's End into his jacket, the more anguished and apprehensive she grew, her imagination running rampant, until, at last, panicked, she had convinced herself that her husband had deceived her dreadfully, that he perhaps even meant to murder her now that he had got hold of her inheritance, and that she must run away from him before it was too late.

Chapter Nineteen

Nowhere in Central City was safe; Josselyn knew that. The only hotel that was decent was the Teller House, and she could not bear to go back there. Nor was she likely to find a room at another boardinghouse on such short notice, and even if she did, Durango would surely locate her before the day was ended; there were not that many places for a woman alone and practically penniless to hide in a town the size of Central City. For this reason, she did not even consider Black Hawk, which was even smaller, or any of the other surrounding towns, knowing that it would take at most two or three days for her husband to search them and discover her whereabouts. She must get out of the gulches altogether. She would go up to the Rainbow's End, Josselyn decided rashly. It would cost her nothing to live there; and perhaps, because of how crude and rough the gold mine was, how its exterior had dejected her and its interior had terrified her, Durango would not look for her there, thinking that it was the last place in the world in which she would seek refuge.

At the very least, she would buy time—time that she meant to put to good use in ferreting out the truth of all that had happened at the Rainbow's End. And she *would* find out, Josselyn vowed, resolutely squaring her shoulders. Ever since leaving the convent and arriving in Central City, she had permitted herself to become a leaf on the wind, buffeted hither and yonder. No more. She must learn to take charge of her own life; she must discover whether she had married a sab- oteur and a killer. She owed it to Da; she owed it to herself. The gold mine, the scene of the crimes, was the logical place to start searching for the answers to her questions. She had thought so before and had allowed the accident with the giraffe to discourage her from returning to the Rainbow's End. Da, who had never quailed in the face of danger, would be ashamed of her; she had disgraced his memory. She must wipe away that stain; she must prove to herself that she was her father's daughter and see that justice was done—even if it meant the hanging of her own husband.

The notion of residing with the nine hardened men who worked at the gold mine unnerved Josselyn, but even this, she would not let deter her. They did not know that she was wed, that she was no longer a novice, destined to become a nun. She still had her veil and her habit; however wrong it was of her to wear them now, they would serve to armor and protect her. Surely, God would understand her need, for Da's sake, if not her own.

She talked adoring, impressionable Zeb into helping her, for he was only too eager to assist her in escaping from Durango, who, the lovelorn young man wildly imagined, had dragged Josselyn off and forced her at gunpoint to marry him, although she told Zeb no such thing, only that she feared she had made a mistake and needed time alone to sort out her thoughts and emotions. As quietly and secretly as possible, so even Miss Hattie would not spy their furtive activities,

Zeb loaded Josselyn's trunk into his wagon, hitched up his horses, and tied Josselyn's donkey, which Durango had some days ago fetched down for her from the Rainbow's End, to the tailgate. Then, with Josselyn sitting beside him on the wagon seat, the young man clucked to the team, and the vehicle rolled slowly out of Miss Hattie's yard, the sound of the horses' hooves and the turning wheels effectively muffled by the rain that continued to fall steadily, although not so hard as it had earlier. Zeb had taken Miss Hattie's umbrella from the hallstand in the foyer, and with it, Josselyn tried to shield him and herself from the downpour.

The journey was difficult, the track awash with muck that sucked at the wagon wheels and flooded in low-lying places where water ran down like swollen creeks from the mountains, currents swift and churning. Seeing this, Josselyn grew discouraged and several times suggested that they turn back, but Zeb refused to hear of it and recklessly pressed on, climbing down from the vehicle to haul the horses forward when they balked or the wagon became mired in the muddy ruts. He was so sick with unrequited love for her, she thought uneasily, that he would rather they were swept away and drowned than that she should belong to Durango. The young man did not know that her husband had already made love to her. As though likening himself to a white knight rescuing a damsel in distress, Zeb was clearly hell-bent on sparing her from her wedding night, although she was unaware that he further harbored some ill-formed idea of persuading her into seeking an annulment and marrying him instead. Surely, she would not so casually dismiss him now, when he had saved her, he told himself repeatedly to bolster his resolve whenever the going appeared impossible.

At last, after what seemed like hours, they arrived at the Rainbow's End. There, Zeb hoisted Josselyn's trunk down from his vehicle and carried it inside the cookhouse to the lean-to, plainly loath, now that he had actually viewed it, to leave her in such an inhospitable place. But he saw no other alternative. There was no one about at the moment—he had no knowledge of how many men labored at the gold mine, although, seeing the place, he thought that it could be no more than a mere handful. Reluctantly, in the end, he was forced to believe Josselyn's assurances that her veil and her habit would shield her from any harm and that, besides, as a one-quarter partner in the Rainbow's End, she had the authority to fire any miner who treated her disrespectfully, and she would not hesitate to do so. Still, as a precaution, after depositing her trunk on the floor of the lean-to, Zeb went back outside to his wagon to fetch his shotgun, which was already loaded. Determinedly insisting that Josselyn keep it, he thrust the weapon into her hands, instructing her in its use, should she have need of it. Then, announcing, despite her startled protests against it, that he would return for her once he had figured out a plan for the two of them to be together, he exited the cookhouse. After stabling Sassafras in the ramshackle barn, he drove away, hunched beneath Miss Hattie's umbrella. Josselyn watched him until he was out of sight, shaking her head at his foolishness, hoping that he would get home safe and that once he had calmed down, he would realize the futility of trying to wrest her away from Durango.

With no difficulty at all, she soon settled into the lean-to, her unpacking quickly completed, her few possessions neatly put away. As she glanced about at her new home, Josselyn felt somehow as though she had lived there all her life, for the sparse room very much resembled her own at the convent. Her father had slept here, she thought, and Wylie and Durango. Here, a lifetime ago, it seemed, Durango had undressed her and laid her down upon the bed after she had fainted in the drift. She repressed the memory and cracked the window, as though to rid the room of her husband's lingering presence. Then, hearing noises beyond the lean-to, she made her way through the common room to the kitchen. There, muttering to himself, Old Sourdough was coming up the wooden steps from the small root cellar below, a basket of potatoes in hand.

Slightly deaf, he had not heard her arrival over the tattoo of the rain and was obviously astonished to see her.

"Gawd a'mercy, Sister!" he cried. "Don't tell me that blasted Durango were fool 'nuff to bring you up here in this miserable weather!"

"No, no, Old Sourdough. I—I . . . came of my own accord. You see, I—I . . . well, the truth of the matter is that—that I don't have enough money to—remain at the boardinghouse any longer," Josselyn faltered over the half lie, hoping he would put her blush down to embarrassment over her pecuniary situation. "I—I need work and a—a place to stay. I thought . . . that is . . . the lean-to . . . it's empty, and I—I know how you hate doing all the—the cooking around here— Well, what I'm trying to say is that—that I plan to stay on, the new cook, if you'll have me."

After a long, hard moment, during which he studied her searchingly, the grizzled old miner finally nodded shortly, clearly loath to pry into her personal affairs, however skeptical he might be of her explanation for her appearance at the Rainbow's End. In the Rocky Mountains, a person's business was his or her own, and those who broke this unwritten code against intruding into what did not concern them frequently did so to their detriment.

Taking off his apron and handing it to her, Old Sourdough said, "Stay and be welcome, Sister. 'Twill do us all a world of good, I'm thinkin', to have Red's daughter here, at the Rainbow's End."

After that, he gave her a tour of the kitchen, showing her where everything was kept and explaining about the preparation of the meals and when they were to be served. Then, telling her that he would inform the rest of the men of her coming, he left her to get on with fixing the supper he had been in the midst of making, a cheerful spring in his step that told her more eloquently than words of his gladness at becoming a proper miner once more.

Josselyn set about her new chores with the same lightness of heart that Old Sourdough had displayed upon departing from the cookhouse. She did not know how much time she had before Durango found her, for she did not delude herself that she could hide from him forever; but she did not intend to waste a single minute of her freedom. She had much to learn about the Rainbow's End; she wanted to know everything about the hard-rock mining process and, above all, Da's death. The miners would help her, she hoped. Though a motley crew, they were not really a bad sort, she reflected as she started peeling the potatoes in the basket Old Sourdough had put on the wooden slab table in the center of the kitchen.

In addition to Old Sourdough, Novak, and Long Tom Henry, there were the inevitable Cousin Jack, the gold mine's resident Cornish expert; Frenchie the Trapper, a handsome, black-eyed young man, who mucked out the rounds of ore, laid the track, and platted the sheets; Prophet, a hulking Negro, who, as the timberman, installed the square sets in the stopes and did other heavy jobs, such as assisting the miners in setting up their drilling equipment; Mateo—"Matty the Mex," everybody called him—a husky young fellow who loaded and unloaded the ore cars and, with the aid of two donkeys, trammed them back and forth from the stopes, through the tunnels and winzes, to the main shaft or the exterior dump; and Fiddler Dan and Arkansas Toothpick, both tall, strong southerners, who, along with Cousin Jack, did most of the actual drilling and blasting.

Josselyn knew little more than this about any of the miners; nor, except in rare instances in the days to come, would she discover much more; all the men were inordinately taciturn when it came to their backgrounds, as though what was past were unimportant, as though before their coming to the Rainbow's End, they had not existed. She fancied that none of their lives had been easy; she would not have been surprised to learn that more than one among them was guilty of past crimes, had fled west to Colorado, one step ahead of the hangman—Arkansas Toothpick, especially, nicknamed for the knife he always carried with him and that Josselyn suspected he was quite capable of using, if necessary.

But still, she soon got over her initial fear of the miners, for whether due to her habit or the fact that she was Red's daughter, they treated her respectfully right from the start, carefully wiping their muddy boots off outside when they spied the cookhouse's freshly mopped floor that evening and shyly doffing their hats when they saw her. Plainly, they had even washed the grime of the gold mine from themselves and changed into fresh shirts before coming to supper; and from the slovenliness of the cookhouse prior to her at least cleaning its surface, which was all she had had time for, Josselyn could not believe that this was the men's usual practice.

"Let us pray," she said, once the miners were all seated at the long trestle table in the common room, startling and shaming those already eagerly dishing up the hot, tasty meal she had prepared.

After a moment, they bowed their heads as one and she spoke the blessing. Then the men dug in with gusto, ribbing Old Sourdough about how they all had only just now realized exactly how bad his cooking had been, that it was a wonder he had not poisoned them. He gave back as good as he got. But still, the jollity and the conversation occurred in fitful spurts, dying away into strained silence as the miners remembered Josselyn in their midst and wondered uncomfortably if their inadvertent coarse language and habitual rough manners offended her, despite each man's trying hard to be on his best behavior.

As she grasped how awkward and ill at ease the miners were in her presence, Josselyn smiled inwardly with amusement, her own tension and trepidation dissolving. Whatever the men thought of her moving up to the Rainbow's End, it was not that she was no longer a lady, that she had turned overnight into one of the strumpets with whom they consorted in town. To her relief, it seemed that although the miners were not gentlemen, they intended to play the part of such in her company. She had not wanted to believe otherwise, but she had known that by coming to the gold mine, she was exposing herself to a certain amount of risk, for these were men who had little opportunity to mix with women in general, much less ladies. She could only be grateful for the miners' decorum, for the fact that she would not be put to the test of exercising her authority by being compelled to fire any of the men and, if challenged, to enforce her dictates with the shotgun that Zeb had left behind with her.

Although she doubted her ability to use it, the weapon comforted Josselyn all the same, for once night had fallen and the miners had retired to the bunkhouse for the evening, she discovered that the lean-to seemed terribly lonely and isolated, the creaks and groans of its settling unfamiliar and thus unnerving. Except for an occasional spattering of drizzle, the rain had finally stopped. But water still dripped from the branches and leaves of the trees that forested the mountainsides; the wind soughed plaintively through the narrow passes and ravines, and the cries of the night birds, the howls of wolves or coyotes, the screams of pumas, and the crashing of fleet mule deer and lumbering bears through the thickets and the woods echoed in the night. The noises made it difficult for Josselyn to sleep. The old iron bed in which she lay seemed far larger than it actually was, and for a moment, strangely, she wished that Durango shared it with her. Despite herself, she was forced to admit that it had been warm and pleasant, sleeping with him at the Teller House.

Even now, she tingled peculiarly all over as she remembered that morning and the things he had done to her before the two of them had drifted into slumber, and then afterward, when they had once more awakened. There was still a twinge of soreness between her thighs, and now, as she thought of her husband, she felt a different kind of ache there, as well. She flushed in the darkness as she recalled how he had eased her agonizing emptiness with his fingers before filling her with himself, taking the hollow, burning pain away and bringing glorious, ecstatic pleasure in its wake. Curious, almost without even thinking, knowing only that she was suddenly swept with longing, Josselyn slowly brushed her hands over her nightgown-clad body, across her breasts, and then touched herself there, upon her womanhood, where Durango had caressed her so expertly, so intimately. Instantly, what he had aroused in her that morning sprang full-blown to life, a fever in her blood, her loins. With a gasp, a moan, she snatched her hands away, mortified by what she had done, by her yearning for her husband, who did not love her, who had married her only for her father's shares in the Rainbow's End.

But still, to her anguish and bewilderment, Josselyn tossed and turned until the tangled sheets were soaked with sweat and the moon had climbed high into the night sky. Then, at long last, she cried herself to sleep, feeling inexplicably as though her heart were breaking inside her; and when she dreamed, it was of devilish Durango, kissing her, embracing her, pressing her down to possess her, body and soul, as she gave herself up to him willingly, eternally damned and defiled . . . and desired.

Chapter Twenty

Durango was half out of his mind with wrath and worry. Josselyn had run away from him, and he could find her nowhere. He had searched every hotel, cottage for rent, boardinghouse, and even all the churches in Central City and the other surrounding towns, to no avail. He had visited every business, emporium, market, and even all the saloons and bordellos, and had checked with every train depot, stagecoach station, and livery stable for miles around, and still had discovered nothing. Josselyn had apparently vanished without a trace into the thin mountain air. Where could she have gone? He racked his brain ceaselessly, trying to figure out the answer. More than once, he went to Miss Hattie's cottage to demand she tell him what she knew; but although nearly reduced to tears by his bullying, Miss Hattie continued to profess complete ignorance of the matter, saying only that

Josselyn had packed up and "gone away," leaving behind not even so much as a forwarding address. Durango also questioned Zeb repeatedly, receiving little more than sullen stares and surly grunts in response; and though he sensed that the young man might know more than he was telling, there was nothing Durango could do about it. He could hardly call Zeb out, though he vowed to himself that if ever he managed to get the young man alone somewhere, Zeb would give him some straightforward replies if he had to wallop the tar out of him. Durango even talked to the rest of the boarders, but it soon became clear to him that they knew nothing, that they were, in fact, quite surprised by Josselyn's leaving.

In some ways, this was a relief to Durango, for it made him realize that, wisely, not wishing their boardinghouse to be besmirched by scandal, Miss Hattie and Zeb had kept quiet not only about Josselyn's not coming home from the Teller House that night, but about her marriage, too. Doubtless, after reflecting upon the affair and Josselyn's subsequent running away, they had erroneously concluded that she was not really wed to him at all, that she had fobbed them off with a lie to salvage her reputation. Well, that was fine with him. He did not care what Miss Hattie and Zeb thought. Indeed, Durango would just as soon no one learned of his and Josselyn's marriage; for he knew that, now, if he were to die, she would be worth half a gold mine, a circumstance that might prove dangerous to them both and about which, after her departure, he possessed the foresight to warn both Father Flanagan and Killian, requesting their silence, also, on the subject.

The priest, knowing what had led to their wedding, was both shocked and troubled by the idea that someone might well now attempt to kill Durango and forcibly compel his widow to the altar, and was deeply disturbed, besides, by Josselyn's vanishing. If contacted by her, he promised to get in touch with Durango at once. Killian, however, once he learned of her disappearance, had the temerity to accuse Durango point-blank of murdering Josselyn; and as a result, the two men almost came to blows.

"Goddamn you, Patrick! I ought to kill you for that!" Durango swore heatedly, balling his fists to prevent himself from throttling the attorney. "Jossie was—*is*, damn it!—my *wife*, for Christ's sake! Why in the hell should I have murdered her—especially when I've already got Red's frigging shares in the Rainbow's End locked up in my bloody safe?"

"I don't know, Durango. But still, somebody sabotaged the gold mine, shoved Forbes down the main shaft into the sump, and blasted Red to smithereens; and if you ask me, there was something mighty damned peculiar about that hasty marriage of yours!" Patrick insisted obstinately, refusing to be cowed. "I've the oddest notion that Josselyn was not the happiest or the most willing of brides—which, I don't mind telling you, has made me wonder just exactly *how* you persuaded her to wed you, Durango!"

So Durango told him, after which, stunned and appalled by what had occurred at the Teller House and convinced by the ring of truth to the gambler's words as he had related the tale, the lawyer apologized.

"There's something more you should know, then, Durango," Patrick declared gravely. "Wylie's realized that Josselyn's missing, and he's begun searching for her, too. He's been here already, making discreet inquiries about her. Oh, don't worry. I told him nothing. Red was my best friend, and because of that, my first loyalty is to Josselyn. Besides, she's the only one who isn't a player, but a pawn in this deadly game, and many's the time I've cursed Red for that. But, there. However sadly awry 'tis all gone, I've no doubt that he meant that blessed will for the best when he cajoled me into drawing it up, that he was thinking only of ensuring that his daughter's future was secure."

"Well, then, don't you forget that should I somehow be removed, like Forbes and Red, from the picture, Jossie'll be a widow who owns twice as many shares in the Rainbow's

End as Victoria,'' Durango reminded the attorney grimly, ''and that out of us four original partners, only Wylie will then remain. If by some chance that should happen, I reckon he'll be guilty by default of the crimes at the gold mine; and ¡madre de Dios! Come hell or high water, I don't intend that he should get his greedy, grasping hands on my wife, Patrick!''

This was spoken with such vehemence that it gave the lawyer pause. *My wife*, Durango had said. Not *my shares*. Interesting, that his concern seemed all for Josselyn rather than the Rainbow's End. Very interesting—as was the gambler's subsequent behavior, upon which Patrick now began to keep a sharp, speculative eye.

One night during a poker game at the Mother Lode, at which the attorney was present, Durango won a mansion on The Casey; and to Patrick's surprise, instead of wagering the property away on a later hand or disposing of it for cash, as he normally would have done, he carefully locked the deed up in his safe. A couple of days afterward, he rode up to The Casey to inspect the house, which was just a few doors down from Victoria's own. Some days after his tour of the premises, Durango hired an architect and construction workers to begin remodeling the mansion to his detailed specifications, the most astounding of which, if rumor was to be believed, was the installation of a drawbridge that would lead from the second story of the house to the privy on the hillside out back, and the fact that the outhouse itself, it was said, was in the process of being fitted with a porcelain seat. Further gossip reported on the knocking out of the wall between the master's and the mistress's bedrooms to make a single large suite, and, most curiously, given the gambler's supposed bachelor status, the expanding of the nursery and the schoolroom. Nor were the grounds being neglected, but planted with trees and flowers.

Except for his own and that of the Teller House, Durango ceased his regular visits to most of the other saloons in Central

City and the surrounding area, including the infamous Shoo Fly, with its female bartenders and burlesque shows one of the rowdiest and most popular bars in town, although it was claimed that the main attraction was the drunkenness of the male patrons and their brawls over the dance-hall girls. No one saw the gambler anywhere anymore with a woman on his arm—it was noised about that he had even stopped dallying with the whores in his own stable, including all his particular favorites; and much to the astonishment of those who witnessed his wholly unexpected appearances, he actually, on at least two occasions, showed up at St. Patrick's church for Sunday morning Mass.

No one, with the exception of Killian and Father Flanagan, who viewed these proceedings with equal measures of skepticism and satisfaction, knew what to make of Durango's actions.

Victoria, especially, was unnerved by them and at the thought of his moving in practically next door. She did not know what had happened after her henchmen, at her direction, had carted Durango and Josselyn upstairs to the hotel room that night at the Teller House, stripped them naked, and left them in bed together. The widow, who, naturally, had drunk very little of the doctored brandy, had had enough trouble getting Wylie home and into her own bed before he had passed out. Fortunately, the following morning, he had suspected nothing, putting his aching head down to the fact that he had been inebriated rather than drugged.

But now, she half feared that all must not have gone as she had calculated that it would. She had counted desperately on Durango's awakening, thinking he had ruined Josselyn, and then being forced to marry her. But Victoria had heard nothing of their having wed; and although it certainly appeared that the gambler was well on his way to becoming a reformed rake, as might be expected of a man who had finally decided to settle down and take a wife, if he had already done so, where in the hell was the bride? Where was Josselyn?

What if—horrors!—Durango had not married her? He was no gentleman, after all; perhaps he had refused to do the honorable thing! In that case, what if Wylie found her first?

Daily, the widow's agitation over this daunting prospect grew. She was furious at Josselyn's running away and now, too late, cursed herself for not having been astute enough to befriend Red's daughter, who might then have come to her for advice and assistance. Victoria would have counseled her to return to Durango and could have driven her straight to his doorstep before Wylie had had a chance to make a move in her direction. Now, Victoria could do nothing but fret and fume and make her own covert inquiries into Josselyn's departure from the boardinghouse, in the hope of locating her before Wylie did.

"Jossie gone! For nearly a fortnight! What in the blazes do ye mean, Nellie?" Red O'Rourke thundered, frantic and dismayed as he strove mightily to rise from the actress's brass feather bed in the cottage on Spring Street. "Back to Boston? Back to the convent? Is that it? Is that— By God! 'Tis all that sorry son of a bitch Durango's fault! No matter what ye have said to the contrary, he raped her, I tell ye! Why else would Jossie have suddenly upped and run off? Eh? Answer me that, then, Nellie! Goddamn that reprehensible whoreson! He raped me poor, angelic daughter, and her innocent as a lamb, pure as the Madonna— Faith! Me blood's boiling at just the thought—I'll break his bloody neck, that's what! I'll cut the no-good, lily-livered bastard's black heart out and feed it to the vultures, the worms! I'll— Oh, Jesus Christ, confound this blasted ankle! Where in the hell is that frigging, worthless crutch, Nellie?"

"I took the wise precaution of removing it, Red," she announced calmly as she struggled determinedly to press him back down upon the bed, "before informing you about Josselyn's leaving the boardinghouse. I didn't tell you before, because I didn't want you to fret, and because, well, wasn't I already knowing what your reaction would be? You've the devil's own temper, Red—and you know it! What's more, the doctor stringently warned you to stay off your ankle as much as possible, and you wouldn't have been doing that if you had been up gallivanting all over the countryside, in search of your daughter—which I already was and which there's no need for you to start or me to continue any longer, in any event, because I've finally had a note from her this morning. 'Twas shoved under the door, so I don't know who delivered it, but at least, now, I know where she is and that she's all right, thank God! So you can set your mind at ease. Josselyn's come to no harm whatsoever, and she's not returned to Boston, to the convent. I doubt that she's enough money to purchase a ticket, anyway, even if she wished to do so.''

"Then where is she?" he growled, glowering at her, only slightly appeased.

"I'm trying to tell you. But, Red, darling, do make an effort to restrain yourself at the news, because I feel quite certain that these black Irish rages of yours cannot be good for your constitution. You grow so dreadfully mottled that I fear you might suffer an apoplectic fit—''

"Goddamn it, Nellie! Will ye cease yer pothering and blathering about me health, for Christ's sake! 'Tis strong as the proverbial ox I am, and I want to know where in the hell me blessed daughter is!''

"She's at the Rainbow's End—''

"What?'' he bellowed, horrified, once more endeavoring vigorously to get out of bed. "Jossie living with a bunch of hardened, drinking, whoring miners? She's gone mad, that's what! Durango's attack upon her has unhinged her mind!''

"There! What did I tell you? 'Tis red as a beet you are!'' Nell cried accusingly, scowling at him fiercely as she attempted to push him back down. ''The blood's all rushed up to your head—there's a big blue vein popped out on your brow—and I'll wager that your ankle is throbbing like the dickens, too! Oh! Don't you dare to raise your hand to me, you brute—"

"Whist, Nellie!" Red's mouth gaped with astonishment at this indignant wail; he was filled with amazement that she should think him capable of striking her. "Though sure and many's the time ye've deserved it, I've never belted ye in me life—"

"And you shan't start now, I promise you, unless you want a crack on the skull with your crutch! Which is exactly what you're going to get if you step one foot out of that bed, and I mean it!" She grabbed up the crutch, which she had concealed under the bed, and shook it at him threateningly. "As I've told you before, if Durango did more than kiss Josselyn that day at the gold mine, I should be very much surprised. I am an actress, a woman of the world, Red—I've never pretended otherwise—and as such, I pride myself on being a good judge of character, of people, at least when it comes to *affaires des coeurs*. You simply must trust my instinct in this; for if you don't, if you call Durango out, as you appear hell-bent on doing, you most likely shall not live to rue it— and that, I could not bear, my dearest!

"As I've already told you previously—several times, in fact, I might add—he explained, and she herself confirmed his account, that she accidentally stumbled into an incline car that rolled away down a winze with her. What poor female wouldn't have looked a shambles after a harrowing ride like that? Doubtless, it was due only to Durango's quick action in jumping into the giraffe to slow it down that Josselyn wasn't badly injured or even killed! Besides, if what you say is true and he took base advantage of her, she would hardly have continued to permit him to call on her afterward; she would not have gone with him to Victoria's supper at the Teller House the other night, either, would she?"

"Aye, well, I guess ye are right at that, Nellie," Red agreed grudgingly at last, acknowledging that her logic was sound. "I'll confess that had I not witnessed with me own two eyes Durango carrying me daughter in such a sad state from the shaft house at the gold mine, I would never have believed that he raped her; indeed, I should have defended him to the hilt against his denouncer! Durango may be a lot of things—and not all of them pleasant, for he has his fair share of faults, after all—but by God, till I saw him with Jossie that day at the Rainbow's End, I'd have sworn he was not such a villain as that! Mind ye: That still doesn't explain why me daughter has suddenly got such a maggot in her head as to move herself lock, stock, and barrel up to the Rainbow's End! Answer me that, Nellie, if ye can!''

''Well, I don't know.'' Nell frowned, biting her lip. ''Her note doesn't say all *that* much, except where she is and that I'm not to worry about her. . . . Oh, Red! Isn't it wonderful that she thought to consider my feelings, to notify me of her whereabouts? Now, let me see''—she sat down on the edge of the bed and unfolded the note she had clutched in one hand, once more scanning its contents. ''Well, for one thing, it seems Josselyn has as practical a turn of mind as her father when it comes to money. She feels she has stretched the limited funds Patrick gave her as far as she comfortably can and that she can no longer realistically afford to keep on renting her room at Miss Hattie's cottage. She'll have few expenses at the gold mine, where she can live in the lean-to, her room and board free. For another thing, she states that she has been saddled, in the Rainbow's End, with three partners whom she dare not trust, and that if she wishes to forgo becoming a nun and claim her inheritance, as she says she now does, then she feels she should gain as much knowledge as she can about the hard-rock mining process, to ensure that she is neither ill advised nor cheated by Durango, Wylie, and Victoria.''

''Aye, well, Jossie has a good head on her shoulders indeed, then, for that's what I'd do if I were in her shoes.'' Red's voice was filled momentarily with profound pride in his daughter. Then, his face growing dark again with uneasiness, he snapped, "But then, 'tis not a young maid I am, shacking up at an isolated gold mine with nine rapscallious men!"

"Yes, well, whether 'tis because they mistakenly believe she's already a nun or out of respect for your memory, they are all evidently behaving like gentlemen toward her," Nell reported, reading on, "and she insists that I am welcome to visit her anytime for tea, if I'd like, although she hopes that I'll understand if she doesn't serve anything fancy; but— listen to this, Red—I'm not to tell anyone where she is, because she doesn't want Durango or Wylie coming up to the gold mine and interfering with her being there. That's all. Oh, I still can't get over it—Josselyn's trusting me enough to take me into her confidence! It must mean that she—that she has developed a little liking for me, don't you think?" The actress's piquant countenance was wistful.

"Ah, me darling girl, how could she help but grow to love ye, as I have?" he asked gruffly, pulling her into his arms and kissing her deeply.

"Do you—do you forgive me, then?" she queried tremulously.

"Aye, I reckon," Red answered at last, knowing and, despite himself, touched by the fact that it was concern for his well-being that had prompted her, however wrongly, to hold her tongue about Josselyn's leaving the boardinghouse. "But mind, Nellie: Ye're not to keep any more secrets from me!"

"No, Red?" She glanced up at him hopefully, then, at his stern expression, shook her head and sighed forlornly. "Well, in that case, although I don't want to get your hopes up about there being a possible husband for Josselyn in the offing, I suppose I really *should* tell you about Durango's new mansion on The Casey!"

Chapter Twenty-one

The long spring had at last given way to summer, Josselyn realized as she stepped outside the cookhouse at the Rainbow's End, wooden bucket in hand, to make her way to the nearby well. All around her, as she gazed off into the distance, she could see that the mountains had burst into full bloom, a riot of color, a profusion of trees and flowers and grasses, their fragrant scents mingling with that of the rich, dark, damp earth beneath her feet. Almost, at this moment, if she closed her eyes and stood very still, breathing deeply, she could imagine herself back in Boston, in the convent's garden, with the morning sun streaming down through the branches of the tall, ancient elms that had stood just beyond the high red brick walls, the whispering wind rustling the green leaves of the trees. Only the smell and sound of the water was different, the essence of the mountain creeks tinged with clouds and

snow, rushing and gurgling over myriad scattered stones polished smooth by the crystal-clear waves that echoed like
laughter in the crisp, clean air—as the salty sea sweeping in
to kiss the shores of Boston had never laughed, not even in
summer.

I was right to come here, to the Rainbow's End, Josselyn
thought, feeling within herself a sense of harmony, of quiet,
peaceful pleasure she had not known since leaving Boston to
journey to Central City. Despite everything, strangely
enough, she was happy here, felt as though she belonged
here, accepted for who she was, what she was, with nothing
more asked or expected of her than that she pull her own
weight to the best of her ability, put in an honest, hard-day's
work, with her own two God-given hands. That alone was
the test of her mettle, of her worthiness. It was no wonder
that Da had loved the Rainbow's End so. In his secret heart,
he must have felt himself king of this mountain upon which
she now stood, his own small piece of paradise. Josselyn had
never felt so close to her father as she did now, here, in this
place that had meant so much to him. She only wished he
were still alive to share it with her.

Sometimes, despite herself, she longed, too, for Durango
at her side, especially whenever she forced herself to climb
into the ore bucket to descend the main shaft into the gold
mine, where, although she did little of the heavy manual
labor herself, she watched the men at work, and learned. But
although Josselyn had hoped otherwise, returning to the Rainbow's End had, unfortunately, given her further cause to
doubt her husband.

During the past month that she had been at the gold mine,
she had discovered that the day that Durango had brought her
here, he had lied to her about all the stopes' still being sealed
off by the explosions set by the saboteur. At least two of the
stopes had been excavated by then; for some unknown but
doubtless dubious reason, he had not wanted her to know
that, had not wanted her to inspect them. She could only
assume the worst, although the miners had suggested that

perhaps Durango had simply thought to spare her the vain hope that her father was still alive; for oddly, his body, or even so much as a hint of it, had yet to be found amid any of the debris being hauled from the drifts. The scraps of clothing that had led to the discovery of Forbes's corpse did not likewise point the way to Da's body. Nothing more than his hat, the initial proof of his death during the blasts, had ever turned up. That his corpse had yet to be unearthed was both a cruelty and a blessing, for despite the men's discouragements and against all her own better judgment, Josselyn was nevertheless unable to restrain the hope that her father yet lived. Because of this, she sometimes thought that perhaps she had condemned Durango wrongly, that perhaps he had indeed, in his own peculiar fashion, been kind.

Then all her suspicions would return and she would compel herself to harden her heart against him, resolutely attempting to crush down her tenderer emotions, her poignant yearnings, and the other painful hope born of Nell's having ridden up late one afternoon, in response to the letter Josselyn had sent her, to take tea.

Josselyn had on the spur of the moment one morning, when she had found out that Matty the Mex and Old Sourdough were going into town for supplies, dashed off her note to the actress and pressed it into Old Sourdough's hands, instructing him to deliver it to Nell's cottage on Spring Street. Josselyn had further impressed upon him her desire to keep secret from everyone else her presence at the Rainbow's End, so Durango and Wylie would not learn of her being there and seek to remove her from the premises. Because always, the miners' first allegiance had been to Red, who, alone of the four original partners, had diligently worked alongside them day in and day out in the tunnels, they had felt themselves honor bound to respect the wishes of his daughter and had willingly banded together in a conspiracy of silence to protect her. Besides, they had told one another, it was just as well that no one knew of her living at the Rainbow's End. She was alone, above ground, for much of the day; and the mountains were rife with rough drifters, greedy prospectors, and just plain cutthroat criminals who might be attracted to the gold mine at the thought of a solitary, vulnerable young woman in its cookhouse.

Zeb had come once to the Rainbow's End, to speak earnestly of his love for Josselyn and to try to persuade her to run away with him. Not wanting to hurt his feelings after all he had done for her, she had attempted kindly, without going into detail, to make him understand the futility of her seeking either an annulment or a divorce, declaring that she felt quite certain that Durango would never let her go. Besides, she had reminded Zeb, what would Miss Hattie, who was without any other family, do without her grandson to help her manage the boardinghouse? The young man, wounded nevertheless and angry, too, because he had sensed the truth of her words, had left in a huff, taking his shotgun away with him. The miners had given her another from the bunkhouse. Arkansas Toothpick and Frenchie the Trapper had taught her at length how to load and fire the double-barreled weapon, and their careful lessons had been much more thorough than Zeb's hasty instructions. When the unexpected rider had approached, Josselyn had held the shotgun at the ready. Then, realizing that it was Nell mounted on the nearing horse, Josselyn had laid aside the weapon and run from the cookhouse to greet her.

Josselyn would never have believed she could be so glad to see the actress. It had been good, after days of nothing but male company, to visit with another female, to hear the latest news from town. But although she had warmed to Nell's motherly interest and concern about what had prompted her move to the Rainbow's End, Josselyn had been unable to bring herself to speak of what had occurred that night at the Teller House and of her necessary marriage to Durango. Still, her heart had leaped when Nell had casually mentioned the house on The Casey that he had acquired and was putting to rights, as though he had every intention of "finally settling down." Josselyn's heart had begun to hammer hard and fast when she had further learned that Durango was become a "changed man," to the point that he had "actually twice attended Sunday morning Mass at St. Patrick's." Thank heavens, she had had the foresight to snatch off her wedding ring and shove it into the pocket of her habit at Nell's arrival! Since the gold band, being shaped like a garland, was unusual, the actress would surely have remarked upon it and perhaps remembered that it had previously adorned Durango's own left hand. She would without a doubt have added two and two and got four, and then, however politely, she would have asked questions Josselyn did not yet feel comfortable answering.

Now, as she cranked the handle on the well's windlass, playing out its rope, lowering its pail into the cold, clear water below, and then drawing it back up to fill the bucket she carried, Josselyn contemplated again all that Nell had told her. It certainly sounded as though Durango had every intention of taking their marriage seriously, she reflected uneasily, wondering if the rage he had undoubtedly felt at her running away from him had dissipated—or only intensified during the passing weeks. Perhaps when he found her, he would still be so irate that he would beat her for her disobedience; as her husband, he had that right, too, and she did not think he would balk at striking her should the occasion warrant. Even if she had unfairly judged him and he were not a saboteur and a murderer, he was still a hard, ruthless, domineering man, and her leaving him must have been a blow to his pride and his manhood.

Josselyn was so lost in reverie and her machinations at the cistern that she never heard the swift, stealthy approach of booted feet behind her; and the jingle of silver spurs, when it finally penetrated her consciousness, was a warning that came too late. As she straightened from the well's edge, she was grabbed from behind, encircled by strong arms that tightened like an iron band around her, momentarily shutting off her breath and causing her to lose her grasp on the pail she had pulled up from below. Full to the brim, it went hurtling back down into the cistern, glancing off the stone walls and making the handle of the windlass spin and thump wildly. With a resounding splash, the bucket hit the water just as a hand clamped down brutally over her mouth, stifling the scream that issued from her throat. Struggling violently to escape, her fingers curled into talons, she clawed frenziedly at the hands that had seized her, until the corded arm that gripped her waist pinned her own arms mercilessly to her sides and a low, silky, familiar voice snarled in her ear.

"Lucky for you, Jossie, my sweet, that it's your husband and not some other ruffian who's got you, isn't it?"

She should never have been pondering him; it was as though she had wished him here, had somehow led him to her, Josselyn thought crazily. Her short-lived relief that it was Durango who held her captive gave way to panic at the unmistakable note of menace in his tone, which warned her that he was indeed, as she had feared he would be, furious that she had dared to flee from him. Desperately, she renewed her attempts to elude him. But roughly, he jerked her around to face him, his hands clenching her arms, hurting her as he backed her up against the well, his legs spread, his thighs imprisoning hers, making her acutely aware of his powerful, virile body. Beneath the flat brim of his sombrero, his eyes glittered like shards as they raked her slowly. A muscle throbbed in his set jaw, and his lips twisted with anger and distaste at the sight of her veil and her habit. With a harsh growl and a sharp, unanticipated movement that made her gasp and shrink away from him, he snatched the veil from her head and threw it down viciously, as though he would like to trample it into the ground. For an awful instant, she was half afraid he meant to rip her habit off, as well, the sudden gleam in his eyes suggesting that he was considering it.

"How—how did you fi-fi-find me, Durango?" Josselyn stammered.

"Oh, I was finally smart enough to remember your corresponding with the abbess at your convent," he informed her grimly, "and so I paid a little visit to the post office this morning to see if there happened to be any mail for you. One of the clerks was kind enough to let me know that Old Sourdough had picked up a letter for you last week. Damn you, Jossie!" He gave her a small, savage shake. "How dare you deprive me of my wedding night, run away from me, and hide up here for weeks, at the Rainbow's End, with nine men and no other woman on the place? *¡Por Dios!* I ought to beat you black and blue, you deceitful witch!" She trembled in his arms at this threat, wishing, now, in the face of his temper, that she had never thought of living at the gold mine. "What do you mean by moving up here? You knew I'd be back for you! I told you as much, didn't I? Didn't I?"

"Yes, but I—I didn't want to go with you!" she confessed nervously, cringing at how his face darkened at that. Still, hoping that perhaps he would, after all, let her go, she pressed on heedlessly, the words tumbling from her lips. "Oh, you know that neither of us wanted this marriage, Durango, so why should we pretend otherwise? I don't want to be—to be dependent on you, and I—I really couldn't afford to stay at Miss Hattie's cottage any longer, even if it had been possible. I don't have much—much money, other than what Patrick sent me initially to travel from Boston to Central City on, and that's almost gone now. I hadn't planned to—to remain in Colorado, you see. But now that it—that it seems I must, I've got to conserve what little funds I have left. I won't have any income until the Rainbow's End is—is operable again, and even you told me that might take months. In the meantime, it doesn't cost me anything to live here, in the lean-to. I earn my room and board by cooking and cleaning and—"

"And sleeping with my men? Is that it?" he grated, wroth at and wounded by her words, her unceremonious rejection of him, and irrationally envisioning the worst. She had tried in the hotel room at the Teller House to tell him that she was innocent of what he had accused her, and still, he had refused to listen, had taken her virginity. Nor had she wanted to wed him, but had done so only to save herself from ruin. Was this how she now sought to gain her revenge on him, by giving herself to the miners at the Rainbow's End? "Answer me, damn it!" he spat, causing her to flinch. "Is that it?"

"No, of course not!" Her eyes flashed, and her cheeks flushed as she stared up at him, indignant. "How dare you say such a vile, villainous thing to me, Durango?"

"You know the answer to that as well as I do, Jossie." The heat of his eyes as they swept over her possessively contrasted sharply with the coldness of his tone. "You're mine! I thought that perhaps you had forgotten that."

"I have forgotten nothing!" she rejoined, resenting his arrogance, his assurance that she was his for the taking. Then, defiantly, she cried, "But I don't want to belong to you! I don't want to be your wife!"

"Too bad," he jeered tersely, his hands tightening on her arms, as though to prevent himself from striking her. "You were willing enough to marry me when your reputation was at stake, and now, as your husband, I expect you to keep your end of the bargain. And you will, my sweet—make no mistake about that—because one way or another, I intend to make damned sure that you do!" Despite herself, a fist of fear clutched Josselyn at his words. "¡Sangre de Cristo! You little fool! You did not really think I would let you go, did you? How little you know me if that is what you believed. I've told you before: What is mine, I keep, Jossie, and that includes you! You can no more fight me than a moth can resist being drawn to a flame—and I warn you: You are as likely to be burned if you continue to provoke me!" He paused for a moment, his nostrils flaring as he fought for control of his emotions. Then he went on harshly. "If you needed money, why didn't you wait for me at Miss Hattie's cottage?"

"You know why! Because our marriage is a sham, and I don't want anything from you; I don't want to be kept by you, like a—like a—"

"Whore?" Durango supplied crudely, lifting one demonic brow. "But you're not a whore, querida; you're my wife—and you're damned well gonna start acting like it!"

"No!" She paled at the notion, distraught; for if she did as he desired, how could she live with herself afterward if he turned out to be Da's killer? "I won't! I won't, do you hear? And you can't make me!"

"Oh, but I can, my sweet—and what's more, you know it!" he sneered, giving her another rough shake. His eyes smoldered like embers as he loomed over her, his swarthy face satanic in the morning sunlight, scaring her, making her think that, in her fear and rebellion, she had pushed him too hard and too far, that he was savage as a mountain lion and that she ought not to have prodded him. "I can make you do whatever I want, because like it or not, I'm your husband and, under the law, I *own* you, Jossie! What's more, I'm bigger and stronger than you, and—no matter what your Bible says—in this world, at least, might invariably rules over right. So, regardless of how hard you struggled against me, I could tie you up, gag you, carry you home, and lock you up in my room for days or weeks or even months; and all the while, you'd be at my utter mercy, powerless to escape from me or to stop me from doing whatever I damned well pleased with you, *to* you. I could beat you, starve you into submission, or just rape you until I was damned sure I had got you with child; and in the end, you'd be glad enough to play the part of my wife, I promise you! So don't tell me what I can or cannot make you do, because compared to me, you're not even a novice at this game you would have us play; and even if it *is* unfair, unsporting, when it comes to this particular game at least, I'd rather cheat and win, than lose!"

"Why, that's—that's terrible!" she breathed, her eyes huge with fright at his threats; for surely, he was, in truth, all she suspected him of being. "You're just cruel, a—a monster!"

"No, *querida*, I'm a man . . . a man who wants you very badly and who intends, as your husband, to have you. Give me some credit for being honest with you, at least—or would you rather I lied to you, as Wylie did?" he queried sharply, conveniently thrusting to the back of his mind the fact that, at one time, he *had* lied to her, or at least had misled her into believing he had taken her virtue.

"N-n-no . . . of course not."

"Then if you would not listen to lies, Jossie, you must be willing to open your ears to the truth, however unpleasant you may find it, however reluctant you may be to hear it."

"*Your* truth, Durango?"

"You're not in a convent anymore, my sweet, where truth is black and white, wrong or right. This is the real world, where truth has innumerable shades of grey and life is seldom easy. In fact, it's damned hard—especially for a half-Mexican bastard like me. If I'd been soft, I couldn't have survived— not this long, anyway—and perhaps in your eyes, that makes me cruel, the 'monster' you called me. But then, I didn't have the benefit of a sheltered upbringing, as you did. I grew up in a poor *jacal* in Mexico, where, half the time, I was lucky even to have enough to eat. Nobody ever handed me anything on a silver plate. Whatever I've got in this world, in this life, I've had to take—as I will you, Jossie, if that's what it comes down to. Believe *that*, if nothing else, because I didn't give up my freedom for you to deny me all to which I became entitled when I put that ring on your finger! And I *won't* be denied, I tell you! I won't have you running away and hiding because you don't want to face what's between us, because you'd rather try to convince yourself that it's *me* you fear—when it's really what's inside *you* that scares you to death! You want me, *querida*, just as much as I want you; and even if I were to stand here right now and tell you flat out that I murdered your father, you'd *still* want me!"

"No, no, you're wrong," Josselyn moaned, stricken and horrified at having, in that moment, the real, ugly truth she had not wished to face so brutally exposed to the light of day. That Durango should know it, that he should so callously throw it up to her, that she should be forced now to confront it appalled her. She was wicked and wanton, disloyal to Da's memory, undeserving of the love he had borne her. How could she endure that on her conscience? She could not. "You're wrong. . . ."

Durango was silent for a seemingly interminable minute. Then, softly, his voice holding a note that made her shudder, he spoke.

"I thought I told you never to lie to me, Jossie." When she did not reply, he laughed shortly, derisively. "It has a name, my sweet—many names, in fact: desire, passion; some even call it . . . love." In his eyes now was a queer, eager, searching light as he looked at her, before his lids swept down to conceal his thoughts, hurting her; for she had felt suddenly, in that breathless instant when his gaze had held hers, on the verge of some important discovery that had, at the last moment, been heartlessly snatched away. An unwitting sob caught in her throat at the idea, choking her. It haunted her, that brief, naked glance of his; it was to haunt her for many days and nights to come. She felt strangely as though Durango had slapped her when he laughed again, harshly, his face dark with some unreadable emotion, some unknown demon that drove him, making him cruel. "But *I* would not call it that . . . no, I would not call it love, this thing of many names that lies between us, this thing that is as inescapable as fate, that you cannot outrun, that you cannot hide from, Jossie, not even here, at the Rainbow's End. So do not seek to elude me again. No matter what, you're mine, and I will never let you go. Do you understand?"

"Yes," she whispered dully, knowing that he meant what he had said, that there was no escape for her, not now, not ever. Even if she ran away from him again, he would pursue her and find her, as he had found her here, at the Rainbow's End. There was no refuge for her anywhere.

"Then kiss me," he demanded huskily.

But that, Josselyn could not bring herself to do, knowing what would follow, the inevitable assault Durango would make upon her body and her senses, compelling her to respond to him. She might, in the end, be forced to surrender to him. But she would not make his taking of her easy; for though he desired her, she did not delude herself with the idea that he actually cared for her. She would be the world's worst fool to believe that, regardless of what she had thought, with a peculiar, incomprehensible wistfulness, she had seen in his eyes in that swift, poignant instant before he had hooded his gaze against her. He had mocked her by speaking of love, and then by denying it. To him, she was nothing more than an unexpected bonus that had come with her shares in the Rainbow's End, a coveted body tossed in for his physical pleasure, to gratify his animal lust, and of which he would not be deprived. He would tire of her quickly enough, she felt sure, rent by an odd pang of anguish at the thought. *I would not call it love*, he had said. No more would she, Josselyn told herself fiercely. No more would she.

Crying out against him, she determinedly renewed her attempts to wrest herself free from his steely embrace, twisting and turning like a wild thing as Durango fought to restrain her, both of them forgetting how close they stood to the well until, somehow, during their violent struggle, they lost their balance and toppled headlong into the cistern.

Chapter Twenty-two

"When I pictured you on your knees, my sweet, this was not precisely one of the images that came to mind," Durango drawled dryly, his voice holding, besides anger, a note of ribald laughter that made Josselyn long fervently to throttle him—not only for the dreadful predicament they were currently in, but because she sensed there was something terribly lewd about his comment, a double meaning known full well to him but of which she was disadvantageously ignorant.

"Oooooh, you—you *insufferable swine!*" she hissed vehemently, even so. "You'll never know how much I'd like to break your churlish neck!"

"Quite frankly, Jossie, I don't know how you can say that when you damned near already did!—break my neck, that is," he reminded her—needlessly—setting her teeth on edge as she thought again that, in truth, she had no one but herself to blame for their sad state of affairs.

If she had just kissed him instead of lashing out frenziedly at him, they would not have wound up in the well, where Durango now dangled from the thick, sturdy rope, Josselyn's arms wrapped tightly around his waist, her hands hanging on to his belt for good measure. His strong, corded thighs were locked around her hips; her face was pressed against his body in a way that caused her a great deal of mortification, and her legs were drawn up beneath her, in a futile effort to avoid sinking into the water that, even now, dragged at her sodden skirts.

Aside from an assortment of cuts and bruises, neither she nor he was badly hurt, although she herself was quite understandably shaken up. Durango, however, despite his wrath, appeared to be deriving a considerable amount of amusement from their awkward situation, something that infuriated Josselyn no end, for she herself could see nothing diverting about it.

"Oh, why did you have to come up here to the Rainbow's End?" she asked waspishly, her arms aching from the strain of clutching him, her face flushed scarlet at the unmistakable feel of his tumescent maleness against her cheek.

"Well, it sure as hell wasn't to be drowned in a well, let me tell you!" he retorted hotly. Then, his voice filled with both grim frustration and that maddening trace of laughter, he snapped, "Now, for God's sake, will you please shut up, Josselyn! For if you keep on talking down there, I warn you: We are going to have an even worse problem than we already have—or need I spell out for you in plain, vulgar English exactly what sort of effect the close proximity of your mouth to . . . a certain vital portion of my anatomy is having upon me?"

"Oooooh," she wailed, agonized with shame and embarrassment as she suddenly grasped the shocking essence of his previous risqué remark.

"Josselyn! *¡Sangre de Cristo!* Stop . . . moaning and gasping . . . against me, too! Oh, *¡Jesús!* This is . . . *not* funny," he rasped irately, his voice still quivering with rueful laughter, even so, before he groaned and then inhaled sharply. "Be still, damn you! Just be still, will you? Or I swear, I'm going to lose my hold on this rope!" Fully aware that this would send them both plummeting into the water below, Josselyn did her best to remain absolutely immobile, scarcely daring even to breathe. After a long moment, Durango spoke again. "All right. Since none of the men will be coming up from the mine until suppertime and it is extremely unlikely we shall be discovered by anyone else before then, this is what we'll have to do if we want to get out of here. You're going to have to let go of me, Jossie, and lower yourself down the rope into the water. So long as you keep hold of the rope and stand on the pail, you won't drown, I promise. I wouldn't normally ask you to do such a thing, but I can't pull myself up to the top of the well with you hanging on to me like this. You're a dead weight at the moment—to say nothing of a monumental distraction! When I get out of the well, I'll haul you up. Okay?"

"O-o-okay," she murmured, biting her lip at the thought of descending into the dark, cold water below, not fully trusting him, but aware that it was the only way.

Even so, Josselyn could not rid herself of her suspicion that despite what he had told her, he meant somehow to trick her, to take gross advantage of her dependent circumstances. He would rather cheat and win than lose the battle between them; had he himself not admitted as much to her? He surely would not be slow, she felt, to seize any further opportunity he had to get the best of her.

"All right, then," he said. "Here we go. Remove your right arm from around my waist, slowly— Don't be afraid. I've got you, Jossie; I'm not going to let you fall, I swear. Now, ease your hand . . . between my legs and—and grab hold of . . . the rope. *¡Madre de Dios!*" he cursed, drawing in his breath harshly, his loins tightening without warning as her fingers accidentally brushed against him. "Do you . . . feel it? The rope, I mean."

"Y-y-yes," she stammered, grateful for the shadowiness of the cistern, which prevented him from seeing her crimson face as she fumbled nervously between his thighs for the rope, her hand at last closing around it tightly, her breathing rapid, her pulse racing from a mixture of fear and some darker, more primitive emotion she now recognized but did not want to face.

"Hang on to it, then," he ordered, his voice sounding strangled. "Now, your other arm, carefully. . . . Got the rope? Good. Okay, I'm going to unlock my legs from around your hips now. Without my support, the strain on your arms is going to be both sudden and tremendous, Jossie, because you're not very strong and your body will be like a ton of ore, dragging you down. Try to hold on, even so, and to lower yourself down the rope, hand under hand, as best you can without sliding, or your palms will be burned by the rope, and you'll lose your grip on it and fall. Do you understand?"

"Yes," she answered, her heart pounding, her mouth dry.

"Good girl. Ready? Down you go, then."

If Durango had not warned her about the abruptness of her weight wrenching her arms, she would have fallen, Josselyn knew. As it was, she dangled precariously for an instant, not certain she could hang on to the rope. Her arms ached so badly that they trembled, and her soaked skirts were like a morass, sucking her down. But still, somehow, she held on as though her life depended on it and began slowly to lower herself down the rope, gritting her teeth to keep from crying out at the pain that shot through her arms and her shoulders. It was almost as frightening as her descent down the mine shaft; now, as then, only Durango kept her from panicking as, finally, she felt the shock of the icy water enveloping her.

"I'm down," she cried to him, her teeth chattering; for though she stood upon the bucket, she was still more than halfway submerged in the water.

"All right. You're doing fine. Just continue to hold on. I'll pull you up in a minute."

With that, he started laboriously to haul himself hand over hand up the rope, briefly blotting out what little of the bright summer sun penetrated the dark depths of the well and leaving her in total blackness. After a moment, after he had scrambled from the cistern, the faint beams of sunlight reappeared. Far above her, Josselyn could see his face peering down anxiously. She was slightly surprised by his concern, but then she told herself crossly that, of course, Durango didn't want anything to happen to her yet—before he had wearied of her.

"Jossie, I'm going to bring you up now," he called.

At that, to her relief, with a creak and a lurch, the rope and the pail began to move slowly upward as he cranked the handle of the windlass above. She need not have been afraid; he intended to keep his word, she thought. But she had set her mind at rest too soon, for when she was nearly to the top of the well, Durango suddenly ceased to turn the windlass, his eyes, staring down at her, glimmering in a way that made her shiver with more than just the cold water that had seeped through her garments, chilling her to the bone. On his face was a mocking grin.

"My poor, bedraggled sweet. You are drenched. If I didn't know better, I would think that that bucket contained a drowned ginger cat! 'Ding, dong, bell / Pussy's in the well!' We must get you out of those wet clothes and into . . . some dry ones."

"That will not be possible until you get me out of here, Durango, as you promised you would." Silently, resolutely, she vowed to get even with him as she realized there would, after all, be a price to pay for her rescue. How could she ever have believed there would not?

"And what are you willing to give me in exchange for hauling you up, Jossie?" he inquired wickedly, continuing to leer at her.

"What do you want?" she queried tartly, glowering at him.

"You already know the answer to that, *querida,* so why do you ask?"

"I'd—I'd rather drown!"

"You know, somehow, I figured that's what you'd say— and yet . . . you were so . . . bold in the darkness of the well that I dared to hope that perhaps you had changed your mind about willingly performing your conjugal duties. . . ."

"Oh! You—you blackguard! You scoundrel! How dare you insinuate that I—that I— Curse you, Durango! You know that I did not mean . . . that I could not help . . ." Humiliated, she faltered over the words, her cheeks staining with color as she recollected how her face had been pressed between his thighs, against his hard maleness, how her hand had accidentally grazed him when she had groped for the rope.

"Too bad," he declared impertinently. "You shouldn't have shoved me into the well and—however unwittingly— aroused my . . . er . . . ardor, then. I'm a man, Jossie, as I've told you before, and I can only take so much. I don't mind admitting that this past month without you in my bed has been hell. You owe me for that."

"I don't owe you anything, you rogue!"

"Perhaps you would rather I lowered you back down into the well and left you, then?" he suggested insolently.

"You—you wouldn't! Not really . . ."

"Wouldn't I?" After giving her a moment to consider the answer to this, Durango laughed softly. "Well, what's it to be, *querida*? Shall I be such 'a naughty boy as that / To try to drown poor pussycat'? Or are you going to stop fighting me and give me what I want?"

"All right. Have me, then!" Josselyn spat, fearful that, otherwise, he would indeed leave her in the cistern as he had threatened, perhaps would even actually drown her—although, surely, he would not be grinning at her so impudently if that were his intent. Still, she dared not trust him; he was a knave—doubtless, despite the early hour, he had been drinking, too—and there really was no telling what he might do. Besides, what did it matter? He had already made it clear that he meant to demand his husbandly rights of her anyway; to deny him was only to postpone the inevitable. "I vow you shall rue the day you married me, Durango de Navarre!"

"Your word on our bargain, Jossie," he insisted, maddeningly unperturbed.

"Very well," she agreed at last, reluctantly and with ill grace. "You have it—although I shall loathe and despise you for it until the day I die, I swear!"

"How the good abbess must have quaked in her slippers at the thought of your taking your final vows, my sweet," he asserted, as, so she would not spy the exultant expression on his face at her acquiescence, he bent his head to the task of once more cranking the handle on the windlass, finally pulling her from the well and into his eager embrace. "I just know that somewhere in Boston, she is even now bestowing upon me her heartfelt blessing for sparing her the intolerable burden of your becoming a nun!"

"Please have the decency to refrain from making mock of the Reverend Mother Maire." Josselyn was stiff with fright and fury in his arms, shaken by the fact that she had surrendered to him; she had not meant to. She would have served herself far better by remaining in the cistern until the men had come up from the gold mine, she thought, no matter if she had drowned before then! Still, it was too late now to reconsider; she had given her word, and she would not renege on it. "If you must know, I was, in truth, a sore trial to her, which I deeply regret now that the convent is closing."

"Is that right? Well, perhaps I should shut down the Mother Lode, then. Maybe then you'd regret being such a sore trial to *me*!" Durango remarked, before, without warning, he claimed her mouth with his, his tongue shooting deep between her lips, ravaging her with an intensity that, despite herself, left Josselyn gasping, melting like molten ore against him, inflaming him. It seemed a lifetime since he had kissed her.

He had not lied when he had told her that the past month without her had been hell. It was as though, since having her, he had become obsessed by her. No other woman would do; all were as nothing in his eyes when compared to Josselyn. He did not understand it, knew only that she had somehow become as necessary to him as the air he breathed. He wanted to fling her down where they stood and make love to her; only the thought of someone spying them deterred him. Instead, after a long moment, raising his head, his eyes dark with passion, he muttered thickly, "Come into the lean-to, *querida*. I want you out of those wet garments."

Trembling, unprotesting, for she knew that her objections would avail her naught, she allowed him to lead her inside, to the small room she had appropriated for her own. There, closing the door firmly behind them, he yanked her again into his arms and kissed her fiercely, constraining her compliance, his fingers tangled in her dripping hair, tumbled loose from its pins during her fall into the well, to keep her from turning her head away. Feverishly, his mouth moved on hers; after a time, his hands slid down her body, tearing at her clothes, impatiently ripping her habit from shoulder to waist. After that, only the thud of nearing hoofbeats prevented him from ravishing her then and there. As, gradually, the sound penetrated his awareness, Durango lifted his head from Josselyn's, his ears cocked, listening. Then, growling an imprecation, he strode to one window of the lean-to, drew back the curtain, and looked out.

"It's Wylie," he observed unpleasantly, a muscle flexing in his set jaw at the unwelcome and untimely interruption to his lovemaking. His eyes blazing with renewed anger and sudden suspicion, he rounded on Josselyn menacingly. "Did he know that you were here?"

"No, I swear it!" she replied, terrified by his murderous expression, as though he would kill her if he discovered that she had made Wylie privy to her whereabouts, had permitted him to trifle with her.

After a seemingly interminable, tension-fraught moment

in which his hard eyes pierced her to the core, her husband finally nodded, to her relief, believing her.

"Get dressed," he ordered curtly, stalking from the room.

Her hands shaking, her heart pounding, Josselyn hurried to comply with his demand, her being pervaded by dread. Durango's foul mood and Wylie's unanticipated appearance boded no good, she thought as she nervously stripped off her sodden garments and reached into her chest for clean, dry clothes. What had brought Wylie here, to the Rainbow's End, she fretted, and today of all days? So far as she knew, he rarely visited the gold mine, a circumstance that was doubtless to blame for Durango's momentary distrust of her. She shuddered at the memory of her husband's face in that instant. He would never countenance her being unfaithful to him. Thank heavens, she had had the good sense to send poor, besotted young Zeb packing when he had stubbornly insisted on pressing his attentions on her!

Cursing her unaccustomed clumsiness, Josselyn jerked on her camisole, fumbling with its lacings. The quick glance she risked out the window informed her that Wylie had arrived and was dismounting. He looked as furious as Durango had, she reflected, her uneasiness growing. What would Wylie think when he found the two of them here together this way?

"Durango," she heard him say surlily in greeting as, after tying his horse to the hitching rail outside the cookhouse, he stepped inside. To her puzzlement, Wylie did not sound in the least surprised to see Durango; indeed, it was as though he had expected him to be here, she thought. "What are you doing here—and at this hour? A trifle early for you, isn't it? It's just now past noon."

"What in the hell does it look like I'm doing, Wylie?" Durango's own tone was so sardonic that Josselyn's impression that trouble was likely brewing was powerfully strengthened. "I'm having a drink and smoking a cigar, that's what. In my opinion, it's never too early for either."

Wylie sneered, as though he had supposed nothing less.

"What else? Perhaps I should have stated my question

more plainly. Why are you doing it here rather than at the Mother Lode—where you belong?''

"Last time I looked at my shares in the Rainbow's End, they still had my name on 'em, Wylie. You ride up here to notify me any different?"

"No, I came to learn for myself whether Josselyn is here and all right. You see, after she vanished, I set a couple of the men from my warehouse to spy on you, Durango, thinking that perhaps you knew more about her disappearance than you were letting on. Imagine my reaction when one of my men came into the store this morning to report that he had followed you up here to the gold mine, where he had observed you waylaying a nun—a tale that, knowing you, I could find only too credible. So, is it true? Is Josselyn here? If so, where is she?"

"Yeah . . . it's all true, Wylie; she's here, been here for the past month," Durango answered, as though he had known all along that she was at the Rainbow's End. "She's in the lean-to . . . getting dressed," he then announced, to Josselyn's mortification. Then, deliberately raising his voice, he shouted, "Hey, Jossie, honey, Wylie's here, and he wants to see you. Are you decent yet?" She wanted to die of shame, for she recognized that Durango had intentionally misled Wylie into assuming the worst, and she didn't know whether even to respond. Perhaps if she kept silent, the two men would leave her alone. But that hope was in vain; for after a moment, her ears discerned the scrape of Durango's chair as he pushed it back across the floor from the table, and then the strangely soft tread of his footsteps as he swaggered to the lean-to door and rapped on it peremptorily. "Jossie, did you hear me?"

"Y-y-yes, I did. I'll—I'll be out in a minute."

But she was still frantically yanking on the last of her petticoats when, as though he had every right to do so— which, of course, he did—he boldly turned the knob, and then kicked the door so it slowly swung open wide on its hinges, revealing her standing there, half dressed, her damp, tousled hair cascading down about her, her eyes snapping sparks at his temerity. His gaze raked her leisurely, lewdly, before she hastily snatched up her nearby wrapper, lying on the bed, and shrugged it on, tying it tightly at her waist. Durango took a long swallow from the bottle of mescal he must have taken from the miners' stash in the cookhouse and now held in his hand.

"You look mighty damned decent to me," he drawled, grinning in a way that made her yearn violently to scratch his eyes clean out of his head. "Come on out and join us."

As she stared at him, irate, Josselyn saw, to her horror, that he was now not only minus his sombrero, but that sometime while she was dressing—it *had* to have been while Wylie was riding in—he had unbuttoned his shirt clear down to its ends and tugged them from his breeches, unbuckled his gun belt and cast it aside, and pulled off his boots and socks, so he would look the part he had so maliciously decided to play: that of a lover who had just risen from her bed. She could have strangled him, and his mocking eyes told her that he knew it and found the idea vastly entertaining. Lifting one black brow devilishly, he stepped to one side of the doorframe to permit her to pass, indicating that he did not mean to allow her to remain in the lean-to; and seeing no other choice, she strode past him into the common room, her head held high, her eyes flashing, and her cheeks scarlet with rage, shame, and embarrassment.

As he had been that night at the Teller House, Wylie was struck dumb by the sight of her; he wondered again how he had ever considered her passionless and plain. He must have been blind or out of his mind, he told himself as his stunned eyes took in her dishabille: her loose waves of chestnut hair shimmering like fire in the golden sunlight that streamed in through the windows, her green cat's eyes spitting sparks, her lush mouth bruised and swollen from a man's hard kisses, her smooth, creamy throat sloping down to meet her heaving breasts swelling above her camisole and the edges of her wrapper, her waist slender as a sapling, and her long, lithe legs and dainty bare feet. She looked like a wild gypsy, a courtesan—no nun, but a fallen angel! His loins quickened with unexpected desire. Suddenly, not only Red's shares, but Red's daughter appeared immeasurably appealing.

And Durango had had her first.

The realization hit Wylie like a punishing blow that rendered him senseless. As though the wind had been knocked from him, he inhaled raggedly.

Damn the bastard! I'll kill him! Wylie thought, his hands clenching so hard the riding crop he carried that he almost snapped it clean in two.

"I did not want to believe that you were so unmindful of your gentle breeding as to have actually moved up here, to the Rainbow's End, Josselyn." He spoke coldly, a muscle twitching in his set jaw. "However, upon learning that you were, I nevertheless rode up here to assure myself of your well-being. I see, now, that that was a mistake, that I needn't have bothered—"

"You got that right!" Durango's voice was serrated as a knife, rudely cutting off whatever else his partner might have said. "Jossie's no concern of yours, Wylie. She's made her choice—and you ain't it! So, why don't you just ride on out of here, the same way you rode in—or isn't Victoria enough for you anymore?"

Wylie's eyes narrowed sharply with sudden understanding at that.

"You son of a bitch, Durango! You told Josselyn that Victoria is my mistress!"

"Did you really think I wouldn't? *Tsk, tsk.* Wylie, I'm surprised at you, forgetting one of the major rules of life: All's fair in love and war."

"So that's the way you want to play, is it?" Wylie retorted acidly. Then, turning to Josselyn, he gibed with feigned pity, "My poor dear, is that the story this villain spun to persuade you to surrender your virtue to him? But surely, you were not so foolish as to believe the vicious lies he has apparently stooped so low as to tell?"

"Li-li-lies?" she stammered, confused. Had her judgment been mistaken, then, in this, as in all else? Her face blanched; she felt suddenly ill.

"Lies," Wylie reiterated icily, his eyes somehow both smoldering with desire and scathing as they assessed her protractedly from head to toe. His mouth twisted contemptuously. "I warned you about Durango, did I not? Saboteur, murderer, and now arrant seducer of gullible nuns, it appears. I find it infinitely regrettable, Josselyn, that instead of my wife, you have chosen to become his *whore*!"

He was so intent on his vituperation that he never saw Durango's fist coming until, with an audible crack, it smashed him square on the jaw, knocking his bowler hat from his head, splitting open his bottom lip, and staggering him so, that he fell heavily to his knees. For a long moment, he crouched upon the floor, dazed. Then he shook his head to clear it, and his grey eyes narrowed again, glittering like steel as they abruptly snapped into focus. Gingerly, he touched his hand to the corner of his mouth, his lip curling derisively when his fingers came away streaked with blood.

"So," he uttered softly to Durango, "we have come at last to this, have we?"

"We have." Durango's voice was deadly as he purposefully stripped off his shirt and cast it aside. "Get up, you bastard! Get up and fight—or don't you have what it takes anymore, Wylie? You been unmanned, maybe, by a soft bed and a hard woman?"

"You never have got over Victoria's preferring me to you, have you, Durango?" Wylie got slowly to his feet, carelessly tossing away his whip and divesting himself of his broadcloth jacket. Shortly, unpleasantly, he laughed. "My God! All this time . . . and to think I never suspected—"

"You know, you really have preened and kidded yourself far too long on that score, Wylie. Don't you think that it's about time you got through your thick skull the fact that I've never been interested in fool's gold, especially what Houghton was mining? *You* were the claim jumper, Wylie—although I'll confess that had I known how much just the thought of it would rankle with you, I might have been tempted, after all, to have a go at pounding my stake into the ground!''

"You filthy son of a bitch! I'll kill you for that!''

"You can try." Durango's jeering smile, which did not quite reach his hard eyes, was a taunt that further fueled the flames of battle. "No holds barred?''

"But of course. I expect no better of a half-breed bastard.''

"Save your breath—you're going to need it.''

Warily, now, the two men had started to circle each other, dancing lightly on the balls of their feet, lunging, feinting, tossing a jab here, a punch there, testing each other's skill and mettle; for despite their verbal sparring, it had been a long time since they had physically tangled with each other, although neither was a novice at bareknuckle brawling. Both had, over the years, been involved in numerous barroom fracases, which had left each an expert in the rough western style of settling a difference of opinion; and after a moment, they got down to the nitty-gritty. The ugly sound of the savage blows they exchanged rang in Josselyn's ears, making her cringe as she stared at them, appalled. Everything had happened so fast that it seemed unreal.

From the gibes they had exchanged, she gathered that Victoria was not only Wylie's mistress—for of that, plainly, Durango had spoken truly—but apparently a long-standing bone of contention between the two men, as Josselyn herself now was. Even so, it was inconceivable to her that they should have come to this violent conflict. She was not even certain what had begun it, except that she felt that Durango had been spoiling for a fight and that Wylie had been only too happy to oblige him, neither man caring to give her a chance to explain the scene that Durango had so deliberately twisted and Wylie had so condemningly taken at face value.

There were other things that puzzled her, too: the fact that despite the mescal he seemed to guzzle as though it were water, Durango's thought processes were still inordinately swift. He had worked out in his mind in a matter of minutes the deceitful charade he had enacted for Wylie's benefit. Nor were his lightning maneuvers and quick reflexes those of a habitual drunk. He bashed and battered Wylie unmercifully, blackening Wylie's eye and bloodying his nose, neatly side-stepping to avoid retaliation as both combatants pummeled each other without surcease. In some clouded corner of her mind, Josselyn thought she should attach some significance to Durango's being a masterful manipulator, while Wylie was an out-and-out cheat and liar, but the notion slipped away before fully formed and reflected upon, driven out of her head by the ruthless struggle that continued to rage as the two men shoved and grappled their way about the common room, all their pent-up emotions, their strain born of the last several months now unchecked, given full, vicious rein.

Their terrible, even gleeful ferocity was horrifying, yet Josselyn was morbidly enthralled by it, unable to tear her eyes away; for there was in it a macabre beauty, each man so tall and muscular, so dark and handsome that their clash seemed like a titanic duel of two young pagan gods, narcis-sistic, arrogant, each determined to reign supreme, no matter the cost. They had been building a long time toward this, she thought dimly, like twin volcanoes inwardly seething and roiling until they had finally exploded with a fury. Their contest was over more than just her; she had served only as the catalyst, the stakes in a game whose rules, even now, she hardly understood, a game she herself had never wanted to play—although, numbly, she recognized now that she was not really a player at all, but a prize. Suddenly apprehensive, she shied away from the thought of what would become of her when the dire, cutthroat game was done.

Wrenching herself from her dismaying reverie, Josselyn saw that both men's proud faces were now marred by cuts and bruises, covered with blood. Their hard, virile bodies strained with effort, sinewy arms bulging, rippling, as, toe to toe, each man stood and slugged the other, grunting and groaning, wincing with pain. Wylie was cool and elegant, poised on his feet, cunning blows concise and to the point; while Durango was like some predatory animal, alternately sleek and stalking, wild and brutal, knowing no law but that of the land. A sharp crack testified to a broken rib; Wylie grimaced, positioning one arm to shield the now-vulnerable spot. Durango's smile was chilling as he homed in, his knuckles damaging as those of a prizefighter as he hammered Wylie's face and belly before sending him sprawling headlong on the floor. Without hesitation, Durango flung himself upon his fallen opponent; Wylie's legs came up, kicking Durango square in the groin, hurling him back, making him stumble and double over. Lurching to his feet, Wylie brought his tightly laced fists up under Durango's chin, spinning around from the impetus, snapping Durango's head back, sending him reeling.

Both men were sweating, bleeding, panting for breath, their limbs aching, grown leaden from the unrelenting tussle. Yet even now, they did not desist, bodies slamming into each other, arms locking, legs kicking and hooking as each man dragged the other down, and then jerked him back up, shattering a chair, rolling across the long trestle table and knocking over one of the benches. From the table, Durango grabbed up his bottle of mescal and brought it crashing down on Wylie's head, spraying them both with splinters of glass and spurts of alcohol. Josselyn had never seen anything like the madness that appeared to have seized them. Dully, she realized that perhaps she should run to the shaft house and fetch help; but her feet seemed to be rooted to the floor. Her face was ashen; her eyes were huge; her mouth was parted in a shocked gasp. A low whimper issued from her convulsively swallowing throat.

They would kill each other, she thought, for each man's fingers were now clutching the other's throat, choking, strangling. Gurgling, trying to gulp air, Wylie mashed his splayed hand hard against Durango's face, flattening his nose, a desperate attempt to force him off; while Durango pounded Wylie's head violently against the floor, until at last, Josselyn recognized that she was watching murder done.

"Stop it! Stop it!" she screamed, abruptly jolted from her stupor. Wrapper flying, she raced to Durango's side and, bending over him, yanked at his shoulders, trying vainly to haul him off Wylie's sickeningly prone, thrashing body. "For God's sake, Durango, please! You're killing him! *You're killing him!*"

Finally, her words penetrated his consciousness, and gradually, to her relief, his suffocating grip upon Wylie's throat slackened and his hands fell lamely to his sides. Unsteadily, he rose, his breath coming in hard rasps, blood welling from his wounds as he stared down scornfully at his beaten partner, then glanced at Josselyn, his eyes like hot coals, blistering her, blazing with the heat of the murderous fray—and desire for the spoils of the victor. That much, at least, for all her convent upbringing, she understood all too clearly, her sudden, overwhelming dread instinctive, primeval, known to every woman who had ever stood before a triumphant man. *See, the conquering hero comes!* A shift of power and of possession, the map of the world altered, again and yet again, a thousand dynasties and races vanished from the face of the earth, gone down to defeat, new blood mingling with old in the wombs of women. On such as this, for hundreds upon hundreds of years, had the world turned. An age-old process and, still, earth-shattering. For land, for women, men smote their fellows—the reward a piece of paradise for progeny, so a man might live forever. Josselyn could not have put it into words, but she grasped the essence of it as surely as though she were a Sabine slave of Rome, an Anglo-Saxon captive of Normandy. For the Rainbow's End and for her, Durango would have killed Wylie, would kill him still.

In that instant, all her suspicions about her husband overwhelmed her. She shrank away, crying out in fear, in protest, as, with a hand that bruised her, he seized her wrist and dragged her to him, his eyes darkening with passion before his fingers snarled in her unbound hair and his mouth swooped down to capture hers fiercely. If there were gentleness in him somewhere, she did not know it in that moment, for this was no tender wooing, but a brutal taking, an exultant claiming of the stakes, of her. His teeth grazed the tender skin of her lower lip; she tasted blood, coppery and bittersweet, upon her tongue, blood that mingled with that from his own cut mouth as he kissed her savagely, his tongue forcing her resisting lips to part, to open, so he might ravage the sweetness within. Low in her throat, she moaned, fighting him—futilely—filled with fright and a wild, dangerous, inexplicable exhilaration that took her breath away, leaving her gasping against him. Her head spun, and her blood roared in her ears, sweeping her away as Durango crushed her to him, his mouth hot and hard on hers. Sweat and blood beaded his body; he was like an animal attacking her, the stubble of his unshaven face grazing her skin roughly, his powerful muscles quivering and rippling beneath her palms, the hunger of his bloodlust a tangible thing, arousing and exciting her in some shadowy, atavistic place deep down inside her that suddenly upheaved, and then tore open wide to spew forth a tide of wanton emotion that engulfed her utterly. She felt as though she were drowning, going down for the last time. She was weak, boneless, faint. Her knees buckled, and she would have fallen had he not held her so tightly, pressing her against the lithe, whipcord length of him, bending her back, dazing and debauching her with the demands of his desire.

After a time, a satanic smile of satisfaction curving his lips, Durango lifted his head; and Josselyn became aware that some time ago, Wylie's closed eyes had rolled open, were now glassed over with hatred and rage as he watched them from where he lay prostrate on the floor. The knowledge of his defeat tasted bitter as gall in his mouth. His mind screamed blindly for vengeance as his loss and his resulting impotence were jeeringly hammered home to him when, deliberately, Durango once more took possession of Josselyn's lips and his hands slipped invidiously beneath her wrapper. Humiliated that Wylie should be a witness to her shame, she renewed her struggles against Durango, to no avail. He was far stronger than she. Helpless, she could do nothing but submit, knowing—as both he and Wylie knew, too—that it was to grind Wylie's face into the dirt that Durango compelled her to yield to him. She wanted to weep at her degradation, even as her traitorous young body responded to his treacherous kisses and caresses, and a soft, incoherent whimper of surrender emanated from her throat. At that, raising his head again, his eyes hard and glittering like jet, Durango spoke curtly to Wylie.

"Get up! Get out!" he snarled. "Go home to Victoria, or go to hell—I don't give a damn! Jossie's mine, and now, the shares are even!" Then he swept Josselyn up into his arms and swiftly carried her into the lean-to, kicking the door shut behind them.

"You'll be sorry for this!" Wylie ranted hoarsely as he clawed his way up from the floor, hot needles of enmity and fury stabbling into his brain. "Both of you! You'll pay!"

His throat was bruised and raw from where Durango had nearly throttled him. He seethed so badly with sanguineous emotion that he actually shook as, mechanically, he bent to retrieve his riding crop, jacket, and bowler hat, his blood boiling irrationally as he observed how the derby had been squashed during the virulent scuffle. Vehemently, he punched the flattened felt crown into some semblance of its true shape, then jammed the hat onto his head. Through a heated red film, he eyed the door behind which Durango and Josselyn lay. The unmistakable squeak of bedsprings rang like mocking laughter in Wylie's ears. His hands clenched spasmodically on his whip as he imagined Durango and Josselyn together, their bodies naked and twining, and remembered how she had looked just moments past in Durango's embrace, her long copper hair like a tangle of morning-glory vines, enveloping them, her lustrous skin white as an evening primrose beneath Durango's mouth and hands . . . a devil and an angel. Wylie felt sick and incensed at the memory. In more ways than one, she had been pure gold; and he had lost her—and, worse, lost her shares in the Rainbow's End.

Abruptly turning on his heel, he stalked from the cookhouse and mounted his horse, yanking cruelly on the reins and roweling the poor beast viciously as he spurred it into a reckless gallop down the wending mountain trail that led away from the Rainbow's End.

Josselyn was not even aware of his going, so loud was the pounding of her heart, louder than the fading hoofbeats of Wylie's mount as, despite her desperate struggles, Durango ruthlessly forced her down upon the bed, his hard body boldly covering her own soft one, his lips and hands driving all reason from her mind, even as some small part of her that was still sane, still afraid, rebelled against him, sensing the menace of his dark, triumphant mood. The hot blood of a thousand undefeated kings and armies surged in his veins. He had conquered Wylie; how much more easily would he conquer her, the prize of his victory? She could not possibly hope to prevail against him. Still, striking out at him blindly, she strove frantically to rise, only to feel his hands at her shoulders, implacably coercing her back down, and then brazenly ripping off her wrapper and tearing impatiently, determinedly, at the lacings of her camisole.

"No! No! Don't! Oh, please . . . don't!" she cried out softly, twisting and turning like a feral thing beneath him, pummeling him with her fists, scratching him with her fingernails, endeavoring vainly to halt his barbarous onslaught upon her senses . . . and yet, to her deep, unmitigated shame, somehow fiercely glad when he at last pinioned her arms roughly above her head, his sinful mouth ravishing hers with a violent sensuality that left her breathless, mindless.

"You're my wife, Jossie!" His voice grated low and harsh in her ear, making her gasp and shudder both with trepidation and a terrible, thrilling tumult that was like a dark, hell-born storm maddening, churning, breaking inside her, shattering her, sweeping her up to bear her pitilessly aloft, scattering her senses to the wind. "And before this day is done, you will know it as well and as thoroughly as I do, I swear!"

Her ragged sob of objection was swallowed by his demanding lips, his insistent tongue that traced the outline of her mouth before arrogantly insinuating itself inside, piercing, plundering the moist cavern that of its own volition opened to him, yielded pliantly to his frenzied, overpowering invasion, drank him in like potent summer wine, her tongue meeting and wreathing his, tasting sweeter than figs of paradise, bursting with ripeness and juices. He taunted, he teased, lips and tongue and hands unstill, working their devilish spell upon her, insidious as curls of perditious smoke, inciting as forks of infernal flame, making her moan and writhe beneath him, despite herself. Deliriously, she craved him, every fiber of her being incredibly alive, wholly wakened and stimulated to a feverish pitch by his skillful, fateful touch. She was no longer able to think, only to feel, a mass of inconceivable emotion and sensation as his half-naked body slid across hers, inevitably dominating her, inescapably bending her to his stronger will, constraining her to let grow all the seeds of passion that had for so many years been fighting to burgeon inside her and that now, too long parched, thirstily soaked up the nurturing rain of his kisses and caresses, to blossom suddenly into full, transcendent flower.

Soft and silken as a lush, spreading vale of heaven, the reeds of her cinnamon hair enwrapped them, drawing them down into grasses awash with the fragrance of lavender. His fingers wove a tangled web of the delicate, trailing branches, and his face nested in their autumn leaves, inhaling deeply their heady perfume. Her fair, flushed skin was lovelier than the roses of Sharon, the lilies of the valley, glowing in the sunbeams that slanted in through lucent glass to bathe her with a halo of golden light. Like a drifting cloud of sundered mist, her camisole parted to reveal her bare, beautiful breasts, delectable, engorged fruit that he plucked and devoured greedily, his hands cupping and fondling nectarine softness, his mouth and tongue sucking and laving hard piths. Josselyn whimpered and trembled at the thrill of sheer ecstasy that shot through her at his erotic caresses, that made her strain and arch against him, her once-imprisoned arms now themselves helplessly imprisoning, twining a love knot about Durango's neck, her fingers a profusion of pagan ribands in his glossy black hair.

She was a flowering angel, he a thorny demon-god, come both to worship and to desecrate the temple of her being, and she rejoiced at his blasphemous arrival, gloried in his profane assault. Naked to the waist, he bent over her, sweat and blood streaking his flesh, leaving their heathen mark upon her own, branding her irrevocably as his. His bronze body was hard as horn, in sharp contrast to the velvet of the fine hair that matted his chest, where, urgently compelled by him, she fervidly pressed her face and her palms, her lips and her tongue, touching him everywhere she could reach, feeling the thick cord of his muscles, tasting the salty spice of his skin, while he buried his visage in the fire of her tresses and scorched her throat and her breasts with kisses. His breath was like sacrificial flame against her flesh, searing her, burning her, the words he muttered in her ear and against her throat sounding like some lyrical, cabalistic chant, words of love and sex, a mixture of English and Spanish that Josselyn only half understood but that scandalized and filled her with anticipation, even so.

"I want you. *Te quiero, te quiero, mi bruja blanca.* I want to know everything about you, to know every part of you. I want to kiss you and touch you all over, until you beg me to take you. I want to lose myself in you, to fill you to overflowing. *Quiero estar dentro de tú, mi ángela dulce, te chingar, enamorar a tú. ¿Comprendes? ¿No? No tiene importancia. Aprenderás.* You will learn. *Te enseñaré.* I will teach you. Many things. *Todo de amor. Todo, mi vida, mi alma . . .*"

She was drugged, intoxicated by him, as though his mouth were a jewel-set, gold-chased cup from which she had drunk some honey-sweet, mind-numbing potion that had left her stupored and floating in a primeval place of mist and smoke and shadow, so she was scarcely aware of how Durango remorsely rent the remainder of her undergarments and tossed them aside, the bed with its spill of white sheets an altar ancient and primitive, where she now lay in naked splendor, a vestal handmaiden offered up to sate the insatiable lust of the conquering demon-god.

His breath caught in his throat at the sight of her—her skin white, so very white that he jubilated in it, feeling a deep satisfaction that it should be tainted by his own dark flesh, that this pale, Celtic high-priestess should be his, only his, forever his. His black eyes gleamed as they appraised her boldly, hotly, jealously, palms closing covetously over her full, upthrusting breasts, molding them, pressing them high as his lips lowered to taste again of their sweet ambrosia, first one, and then the other, glistening like rain and mist with the mingled sweat of their bodies, the moistness of his mouth.

Time passed; Josselyn did not know how much as she lay in his arms and, as though destiny had ordained it, let him do as he wished with her. She knew nothing but the painfully exquisite, necromantic fire Durango kindled in her, bedeviling, enthralling, garlanding her with sinuous, sorcerous smoke, consuming her with magical, mystical flame. Where they were was a place far beyond ken, a place of legend, older than heaven and hell and the Trinity, from which he had first taken her, old as the dawn of time, dark and arcane, a place of oaken forests long with shadows and stalked by fantastical beasts, of granite megaliths and dolmens where bodies tattooed with blue-woad symbols danced in naked celebration and coupled with unbridled lust beneath a mist-ringed moon, of deep crystal pools and heavy silver goblets spilling silver water and rich red wine, of powdered herbs and carved-stone talismans, of gilded harps and melodious bard-song, of cardinal witchery and burnt offerings to appease the voracious demon-gods, while far away, the earth quaked with the hoofbeats of a thousand caparisoned steeds, shook with the wheels of a thousand winged chariots, and resounded with the march of a thousand armored men fashioned in the image of those who had made them and to whom they paid homage; and sweet was the taste of victory. . . .

Tormentingly, Durango's teeth grazed her budding, roseate nipples; his tongue flicked them into small, hard cherries, licked away the dewy perspiration that trickled down the sloping hollow between her breasts, and then, to Josselyn's everlasting shock and shame, moved lower still, down her taut, quivering belly, in search of the succulent, secret fruit of her, nestled in a passion flower furled tight against his intimate encroachment. His hands caught hers, relentlessly tugged them away from the soft, swollen mound of titian moss and mysterious, wine-dark folds that, startled from her drowsy languor, she now, too late, sought to conceal from him, to defend.

"Nooooo . . ." she sobbed brokenly as she realized what he intended. "No . . . please . . . no . . ."

But Durango paid no heed to her whispered entreaties, took a perverse pleasure, even, in her frail resistance as his knees roughly spread her thighs wide, opening her to his seeking lips and tongue. This, in her wildest dreams, she had never imagined, for she had not known that such a thing could be done to her—or that she would revel in it, bucking against him wildly, silently begging for more as he tasted her lingeringly before his tongue flitted over the pulsating heart of her, making her moan and whimper with exigent want, the burning ache at the hollow core of her being unbearable. His hand moved to momentarily assuage her frantic need, fingers dipping deep into her unfolding cinnabar petals molten with desire, and then withdrawing, spreading quicksilver heat, before plunging again, and yet again; and all the while, he tongued her, honing her passion to a keen, dagger edge. Her head thrashed; her hands coiled in his hair as she strained for the rapturous release he had, when first he had claimed her, brought her, a fragile, dew-laden blossom in the dark hour before daybreak, stretching toward some otherworldly rising sun. And then, without warning, the bright dawn came, erupting over the horizon in a brilliant aurora of color and light that dazzled and dazed before slowly evanescing, leaving her basking in its warmth and mellowness.

Of a sudden, the horned demon-god was a towering silhouette against the fading rainbow, looming up over her to shed his raiment, revealing his barb, heavy and swollen, eager for the long-awaited piercing. Josselyn sprawled on the sun-bathed altar beneath him, her euphoria subsiding as her sloe green eyes, somnolent with passion, slowly fluttered open and she spied him poised over her darkly, in all his naked bronze glory, wanting, demanding his vestal bride, of which he would not be cheated, not now, not ever again. His black eyes glittered with hunger and triumph as he stared down at her. She shivered as his gaze raked her, no longer innocent, but still afraid—of what had been unleashed inside her and of what was yet to come, understanding only too well, now, that what had gone before was but a sweet, tantalizing prelude to the esoteric rite. The air was fraught with perilous promise and portent; the sun motes swirled high, golden and diffuse.

Dizzy, panicking, she struggled to rise, but Durango pressed her down mercilessly as a priest the virgin offering, while she waited for the apocalyptic blade to fall, knowing somewhere deep down inside, despite all her fear and suspicions of him, that he had been right, that she wanted this, wanted him, badly, and had ever since he had kissed her in the fiery catacombs of the gold mine, a lifetime ago. There was between them an instant highly charged as a storm, and then, "Jossie . . ." he groaned, the hard, questing thorn of his manhood abruptly stabbing swift and deep and true into the mellifluous plum ripeness of her, bursting her, splitting her asunder in a breathtaking moment that made her gasp, then cry out, a low wail of surrender that he smothered savagely with his exultant mouth as, blindly, he impaled her, again and again, his hands crushing her to him fiercely, arching her hips to meet each barbarous, throbbing thrust, dark flesh melting urgently into pale, while the summer sun enshrouded them in its gossamer cocoon of shimmering flame, sealing them eternally. Fragrant rose the scent of their primal mating as, with each sharp, wickedly entrancing prick of his maleness, her pleasure heightened, until at last, lost, as he was lost—utterly—she embraced him wildly, enveloped him wantonly, taking him deep inside her as he bore her down a rushing silver river that was the ether of life, to a distant, sylvan shore that was paradise, refulgent with the light of a thousand exploding suns, sweet gilded fire blazing, charring her to cinders as, with a long, slow shudder that racked the length of his hard-muscled body, he spilled himself inside her.

Afterward, the now somehow harsh summer light of day streaming in, revealing the poor, plain lean-to for what it was, no omnipotent, occult place at all, she wept silently in his arms, ashamed to think that she had given herself to him so easily, that she had responded to him with a passion to match his own—and, worse, that he was right, that she would again, even if he had murdered her father. Oh, God, what was it about Durango that made her feel so?

"Hush, *querida*, hush," he murmured in her ear as he cradled her head against his broad shoulder, stroking her hair soothingly, raining tender kisses upon her pale face, which he gently upturned to his own dark one. "There is no reason for your tears this time. You are my wife, and I am entitled to what is mine. Besides, it is not as though I have not made love to you before—or that I will not make love to you again."

But neither that truth nor the prospect that accompanied it comforted Josselyn.

"Love? Is that what you would call it, Durango?" she sobbed quietly, anguished, her mouth vulnerable and tremulous as he brushed it with his own lips. "Once before, you said that you would not."

"Call it whatever you will, Jossie"—his voice was low; his eyes were shuttered, concealing his thoughts from her—

"or call it by no name at all; it matters not. For whatever it is that is between us, it will not be denied. I know it, and if you did not before, you do now. There is no man for you but I, and I alone—nor will there ever be." He paused for a moment, allowing this to sink in. Then, more casually, he continued. "Whatever you may feel toward me, my sweet, the fact remains that I am your husband. You must learn to make the best of that, as I intend to. Toward that end, it might interest you to hear that I have acquired for us a house on The Casey."

"I know," she said without thinking. "Nell told me."

Durango's body went unexpectedly very still and tense at that; involuntarily, his hold upon her tightened, making her flinch. She had angered him again, Josselyn realized, dismayed, taking the actress into her confidence, while keeping her whereabouts hidden from her own husband.

"Nell knows that you are here?" he asked after a long, taut minute.

"Y-y-yes," she whispered.

"I . . . see."

And he did, Durango thought, his mouth thinning, his doubts about his wife and her father, previously allayed, now unwelcomely stirring anew. For if Red were, after all, still alive, who was more likely to know it than Nell, his mistress? Was the actress perhaps even serving as the liaison between Josselyn and her father? Was that why Josselyn had remained in contact with her? Durango's face darkened at the notion; his jaw set sternly. Perhaps his original suspicion of Josselyn that morning at the Teller House had been correct, after all. Perhaps she had indeed set him up, even sacrificed her virginity to force him to wed her, plotting with Red to kill him afterward for his shares in the Rainbow's End. Strangely, he did not want to believe this of his wife; but still, even so, he could not rid himself of his sudden distrust of her. She had run away from him, yes. But now that he reflected upon the matter, Durango recognized that she had not run so very far; she must have known that sooner or later, he would find her at the gold mine. Had she intended to be discovered, then? Had she sought to lure him up here for some nefarious purpose of her own, a so-called accident that she and her father meant to arrange? He must be on his guard, Durango told himself; he must learn whether Red was, in fact, still alive and Josselyn his accomplice—and where better to get at the truth than here, at the Rainbow's End?

"Well"—Durango spoke again at last, picking up the conversation where he had left it—"if Nell has told you about the house, then you must also be aware that I am in the process of having it remodeled. So, unfortunately, it is not, as yet, habitable. For that reason, Jossie, I am inclined to permit you to stay here, at the Rainbow's End, for the time being. But do not make the mistake of thinking, because of this, that I am granting you your freedom, for I warn you that I am not. Indeed, you can look forward to my spending a great deal of my time here with you"—his tone left her no doubt as to what exactly his visits would entail—"and if ever once I come up here to discover you gone, run away from me again, I promise you that next time, when I find you—as I will; do not be so unwise as to doubt that for a minute—I will be so sorely tempted to beat you for your disobedience that I may find it impossible to restrain myself!" Durango was silent for a moment, giving her time to consider this threat. Then he went on.

"I gather from their admirable silence about your living here that you somehow managed to bamboozle the miners into keeping your secret. But know this, my sweet: However loyal they feel toward you because Red was your father, not one of them will lift a finger to help you once they learn that you are my wife, that you belong to me, as I intend to make quite clear to them. They will, all of them, know what that means, for they are not unaware of my notorious reputation with a gun; and they will not risk my wrath, not even for you, Jossie. So do not deceive yourself into believing otherwise. There is no one and nothing that will save you from me—or you from yourself; and in the end, you will be glad of that, *querida*, I swear!''

At that, his hands twining roughly in her hair, his mouth closing inescapably over hers, he rolled over to press her down upon the soft feather mattress once more, his naked body moving inexorably, urgently, to claim her own, while outside, the day's shadows lengthened and the sun began its slow, inevitable descent on the far horizon, raining fire in the sky.

Chapter Twenty-three

Years afterward, whenever Josselyn remembered the bitter-sweet, halcyon days of that summer at the Rainbow's End when Durango made her his absolutely, she was to see them as though through a glass darkly, a vignette misty and filled with diffuse color and shadowed light. She seemed to live them in a daze, as though they were a dream, an interlude out of time, moving in slow motion.

Only Durango was real.

By day and by night, he came to her, for hours on end, as though he could not get enough of her, were obsessed with her. Time and time again, he pressed her down upon the soft feather mattress of the old iron bed in the lean-to, to weave his dark, splendorous spell upon her, until she knew every plane and angle of his body as well as she knew her own. Soon, despite herself, she lived for his coming, always in some corner of her mind listening intently, ceaselessly, for the sound of his horse's hoofbeats, the jingle of his silver Mexican spurs. When he was late in arriving, she worried he had tired of her, and she was filled with an incomprehensible, inconceivable gladness when, at last, he appeared, sweeping her into his embrace, his mouth hard and hungry upon hers. Her hours were endless, spent waiting for him, passed all too quickly when he came. In his arms, she forgot everything but him, her body a gilded, taut-strung harp that he played as a passionate master, long, slow songs of melodious enchantment, short, swift notes of discordant bedevilment, making her quiver and cry out with joy at his touch.

Sometimes, Josselyn would look at her reflection in the shaving mirror of the gentleman's chest in the lean-to and she would not recognize herself, would think that that wakened, wanton woman with her loose, cascading hair, her smoldering, slanted eyes, and her lush, provocative lips could not possibly be she; and then she would see Durango standing behind her, a dark, smoky shadow in the mirror, a lazy, triumphant smile curving his mouth as his hands slid around her to cup her breasts possessively, and she would know, down to the very marrow of her bones, that the woman was not some image in a dream, but she, become both a goddess and a slave to the demon who enshrined and subjugated her, shocking and shaming her, even as he carried her to the highest peaks of ecstasy.

Saloons and bordellos had been her husband's training ground. There was nothing he did not know, had not done, did not teach her, laughing softly at her startled eyes, mocking her, amused and perversely excited by the shyness she never quite lost, no matter how often, or in how many ways, he made love to her. There were drowsy, prolonged days when he erotically teased and tormented her until, despite herself, she begged him to take her; and vibrant, feverish nights when, long after she had fallen into slumber, he came unannounced to her bed, to force himself on her urgently, savagely, without any preliminaries. Torpid with passion and lack of sleep, she lived in a perpetual haze, moving dreamlike through her chores, oblivious of all but Durango.

What the miners thought, if they knew how he came to her, what he did to her in the lean-to, she did not know or care. It was enough that their demeanor toward her did not alter, though they would have had to be blind not to observe the change in her, the unwitting allurement of her sloe green eyes, the unconscious seductiveness of her supple, voluptuous body. There was not a one of them who did not envy Durango his prize—or fear for Josselyn, whom they each in his own way had come to adore.

Their way of life was hard and grueling, and into it, she had brought her softness and sweetness, not just cooking and cleaning for them, but looking after them as though they were children, mending shirts and tending wounds, singing and reading aloud to them in the evenings, after supper, when the sun was swallowed by the maw of the mountains, the mule deer bounded through the tangled thickets, and the night birds called, dulcet and forlorn, on the whispering night wind. For the most part poor, ignorant men, they glimpsed through her eyes a world beyond most of their experience, a world of grace and faith, of spirit and beauty—for these things, she had not lost. Durango had only enhanced them, somehow. They were in her slender hands, embroidering or counting off the decades of her rosary, in the quiet throb of her voice as she read aloud from her Bible and books of poetry so lyrical that it could bring tears to the eyes, in the swanlike tilt of her head in the lamplight, and, most of all, in her face that, unbeknown to her, shone radiant and vulnerable with her awakening as a woman and all the fragile love in her heart, so lately come, so unexpected and never hoped for, so unwelcome and yet somehow so curiously precious.

She did not want to love her husband, but she was helpless against him and all he demanded of her, as though her body alone were not enough for him, as though he must possess her heart and her soul, too, as, with his skillful mouth and tongue and hands, he claimed her utterly, refusing to be denied.

"Beg me, *querida*," Durango would rasp against her throat when he had ignited in her a fever that burned deliriously for ease. "Beg me to take you. Tell me that you want me. Tell me that you love me. Say it, damn you!" he would vehemently insist, as though he thought that if she spoke the words often enough, she would come to believe them.

And Josselyn did. Deep inside, she thought that perhaps she had loved him for a long time and just had not wanted to face it; why else should she respond to him as she did, the emotions he evoked in her stronger even than her fear and suspicion of him, making her feel that if all in the world should perish on the morrow and only he remain, she should be glad beyond her wildest imaginings?

"I love you," she would breathe, trembling at the fierce exultance in his eyes before he savagely buried himself deep inside her, making her gasp and cry out her surrender.

If her love would ever be returned in kind, she did not know—though she hoped, believed when she lay wrapped in his embrace, listening to the impassioned words he spoke when he took her, that he must, in truth, care for her, a little. But the miners had never known him—devil-may-care rogue that he was—to care for anyone or anything; and so, although Durango had married her, sometimes long into the wee hours of the morning, one or another of the men would lie awake in the bunkhouse, pretending to sleep, so the others would not know that he listened as sharply as Josselyn for the sound of hoofbeats and the jingle of Mexican spurs, waiting for the night when her husband would not come and her heart would be broken.

Yet, to their surprise, night after night, he came.

He did not even try to stay away. She drew him as inevitably as a flower a bee, and the sting was agonizingly sweet. He thought that if he had taken her virginity, she had surely claimed his heart and his soul in return, cast some ancient

Celtic witchery upon him with her white-priestess skin, her Druid-pool eyes. He had never felt for another woman what he felt for her; so even when love came, he hardly recognized it, could scarcely believe what it was that stole up on him in those languid golden days, those tempestuous ebon nights when he lost himself in her completely. He knew only that he had never known her like before, would never find her like again, not in a million years. But still, Durango had never been a man to give his trust easily, less now than ever, when not only a gold mine, but his heart was at stake. His fear of learning that Josselyn had played him false was a worm eating at him; and so, every time he made love to her, it was as though to brand her irrevocably and forever as his, that she might prove true to him in the end.

Meanwhile, ever pragmatic, he periodically rifled her belongings when she was in the kitchen, cooking for the miners. To his relief, he never found anything to interest him. There was nothing to indicate that she had been in touch with her father or even that Red was still alive. But as the rubble from each of the stopes was gradually cleared away, with still no sign of Red's body surfacing, Durango's doubt and Josselyn's hope grew in equal measure—though he never thought of Red's being alive and innocent of the crimes at the Rainbow's End, and she never thought of her father's being alive and guilty.

Only in bed was their marriage untroubled, were they so overwhelmed by their mutual want and need that nothing else mattered, though, increasingly, there were other moments when it was easy to forget that all was not as it might have been between them. Durango was a gambler who won more often than he lost. Before, he had poured most of his money back into the Mother Lode and the gold mine. Now, he spent it, as well, on the mansion on The Casey and on Josselyn, choosing and buying blouses and skirts and other clothes for her, which, declaring he never wanted to see her in her veil and her habit again, he insisted she wear, his eyes glimmering lazily with appreciation as he watched her dress. Never owning such before, she could not help but delight in her new raiment, even the wispy undergarments she suspected that her husband selected with a great deal of both salaciousness and amusement, knowing how they would shock her, how he intended to remove them with sensual, excruciating slowness or rip them off with brutal impatience upon seeing her in them.

Yet, although he would brook no refusing of his husbandly rights, Durango, much to Josselyn's surprise, treated her as an equal in all else, permitting her to continue to venture down into the interior of the gold mine. He often accompanied and instructed her, demonstrating for her astute, eager mind a respect that startled and flattered her, and he never talked down to her, but spoke always as though he expected her to understand his explanations of the hard-rock mining process. Soon, there was very little she did not know about it, even to the handling of the dynamite that was used for blasting.

"Aren't you afraid I'll accidentally blow us up, Durango?" she asked him curiously one day, as he showed her how to set the charges.

"My sweet, if I thought you were a fool, I would hardly allow you down in these drifts, much less with a stick of dynamite in your hand," her husband averred. Then, grinning, he added wickedly, "But you are so good at lighting my own fuse that I trust you will do as well with these."

Despite her deep blush at his unabashed reference to their lovemaking, Josselyn was filled with pleasure at his words, at the realization that far from feeling threatened by her intelligence and abilities, he admired her for them.

"But of course I do, Jossie!" he exclaimed, gazing with astonishment at her, when she ventured to comment upon the matter. "Why on earth should I want a stupid, scatterbrained wife? Would you wish to be saddled with an idiotic husband?"

"Well, no, of course not," she replied, failing to notice how a smile of satisfaction curved his mouth at the recognition that whatever else she might think of him, she was not without regard for his own cleverness and capabilities.

"Then, why, in God's name, should you think I wanted such a wife?" he probed, amused.

"Well, I—I don't know," she admitted. "It's just that—that I have always heard it said that most men don't like smart women, that that's why women have to pretend they're silly and helpless, even if they aren't."

"I am not most men, Jossie," he asserted arrogantly. "I thought you would have understood that by now."

She did, of course; for there was nothing about their marriage that conformed to the stories the girls at the convent had exchanged. Just the way he made love to her was scandalous, Josselyn knew, for she had been led to believe that a proper husband would never dream of insolently, immodestly, stripping his wife naked, that he would do no more than raise her nightgown—and that only for the sole purpose of begetting an heir. Clearly, Durango, if he were aware of these expectations of a husband, ignored them, just as he disregarded anything else that did not suit his fancy. No other husband, surely, would have permitted his wife to live at a gold mine, with nine other men, to mix herself in a man's business by venturing down into the tunnels to learn about the hard-rock mining process, down to the last detail, even the dynamite blasting. No other husband, surely, would have esteemed her brain and her aptitude so, would actually have encouraged her to express her own thoughts and opinions, and would have spoken to her so frankly about anything and everything, including sex, as no gentleman ought, even to his own wife. She ought to be shocked by him, Josselyn thought, and she was. But still, despite herself, she could not deny that marriage to him held a certain, unexpected but inarguable appeal, a freedom and an excitement she sensed was lacking in most. However coarse and common and corrupt Durango might be, there was something indisputably wild and thrilling about him, even so. She was sometimes forced to acknowledge to herself that she was strangely happy with him until she remembered her doubts about him; and even these began slowly but surely to diminish as the summer wore on.

The more she learned about the art of hard-rock mining, the more puzzled Josselyn grew as she realized from the men's descriptions of all the sabotage that there was something peculiar about the pattern of the so-called accidents. They had started out as inconveniences so minor that, at first, no one had even thought to consider them deliberate. Only gradually, as the scope and frequency of the incidents had worsened, had sabotage begun to be suspected, and even then, it was recognized that if such were indeed the case, it was being so cunningly done by someone so well versed in the hard-rock mining process that it was exceedingly difficult to detect. Only after Forbes's death had it grown apparent that not only a saboteur, but perhaps even a murderer was at work. This assumption appeared logical, yet Josselyn continued to be perplexed by the apparent shift in the nature of the accidents after Forbes had died.

Although, previously, the incidents had been so expertly arranged that it had been impossible to prove for certain that they were not genuine, afterward, the attempts to conceal the fact that the damage done was intentional in origin had oddly lacked their former finesse. Before, for instance, gear teeth had been cleverly sawed almost all the way through, so they would appear to have sheared off accidentally during the operation of machinery. Later on, however, cogs that had been smashed to look as though they had cracked and shattered during use had, upon closer examination, revealed obvious pick and hammer marks; and interestingly, machinery that was not even functioning, but undergoing repair, had frequently had havoc wreaked upon it as well, as though whoever was committing the crimes were wholly ignorant about what was operational and what wasn't.

These latter errors were, in fact, so blatantly stupid and senseless that Josselyn had great difficulty in attributing them to her husband. It was almost as though the saboteur had

gone berserk after Forbes's death, losing all reason; and this
did not gibe with what she knew of Durango's behavior. Often
brutish and unpredictable, he might be, but he was not a dolt,
devoid of logic—and what was the point in vandalizing machinery that was already broken? There was none; but how,
then, to account for the irrefutably expert setting of the explosions that had sealed off the gold mine? Josselyn did not
know.

Still, it became even harder to go on suspecting her husband
of sabotage and murder when one fine day he rode up to the
Rainbow's End, carrying Cisco before him on his saddle, the
child so changed that Josselyn scarcely recognized him.
Plainly, Durango had taken excellent care of the boy, who
was now a bright, eager youngster with a body strong and
sturdy from good, nourishing food. He was freshly scrubbed
and simply but nicely dressed, too.

"A present for you, *querida*," her husband drawled la-
conically as he lowered the child down from the saddle. "He's
clean and he's healthy and he mostly minds his manners, but
still, he could do with some motherly care and concern, I
expect."

That was how Cisco came to live with her at the Rainbow's
End. That the three of them together were like a real family,
that Durango had intended to foster precisely this impression
by bringing the boy to the gold mine, that perhaps her husband
even hoped for a child from her, Josselyn did not allow herself
even to consider; she thought that it would be so out of
character for him, for she had never imagined him as a father.
She was all the more startled, therefore, to hear Cisco address
Durango as "Papa," and to observe, as the days passed, how
her husband doted on the boy and how Cisco adored him in
return. She was equally shocked, however, to discover that
the child knew the rules of every game of chance imaginable,
as well as the subtle differences between pulque, mescal,
tequila, and sotol.

This last, Cisco explained to her at some length one afternoon in the kitchen, where she found him sitting upon the edge of his sleeping cot, looking so innocent and nonchalant that she immediately surmised he was up to no good.

"What is that you've got behind your back, young man?" Josselyn inquired tartly.

"Nothing. Nothing, *señora*."

"No, you're not going to succeed in hiding it under your pillow, Cisco. Now, hand it over," she insisted sternly, horrified when, at last, he sheepishly dragged forth one of Durango's bottles of mescal—from which the boy had plainly been sneaking a sip—and, at her gasp of outrage and disapproval, hastily proceeded to enlighten her enthusiastically about the distillations made from the maguey plant.

"I have even eaten *el gusano rojo*—the red worm found in all the best tequila," Cisco boasted proudly, "which is the true test of *un hombre macho*. So, what does it matter if I steal a few drinks from Papa's bottle, *señora*? Eh? It is mostly water, anyway."

"Cisco, do I look like I just fell off a cabbage wagon?" she asked crossly, scowling at him, indignant at his impudence in expecting her to believe such a lie.

"No, it's true, I swear!" the child insisted earnestly. "It is one of Papa's tricks. He told me! One day, he say to me: 'Cisco, never let folks know you're smarter than they think. You see this here bottle? Well, since you asked, I'll tell you that the reason I'm filling it two thirds of the way full with water is because if I drank as much as people think I do, I'd be dead—which anybody with any common sense ought to know. But you see, Cisco, some folks . . . well, they just ain't too bright; they don't stop to reason things out for themselves. So if they *believe* you're a drunk, they tend to get mighty damned careless around you, don't take you serious until it's too late.' Then, after a moment, Papa say: 'This way, sooner or later, I'm gonna find out which of my partners in the gold mine is so dead set on dealing the rest of us a crooked hand. I'm gonna find out who caused all those so-called accidents and shoved Mr. Forbes into the sump.' You don't believe me, *señora*? Open up the bottle and see for yourself, then!'' the boy challenged.

Despite herself, a sudden, wild hope burgeoned in Josselyn's breast. There had been a ring of truth to Cisco's words, the manner in which he had parroted so faithfully all that Durango had supposedly said. In fact, it *had* sounded so exactly like something he might have told the child that Josselyn's hand shook slightly as she jerked the cork from the bottle, sniffed its clear contents suspiciously, and then took a tentative sip. To one unused to strong spirits, the fiery liquid seemed to burn all the way down her throat; she choked, her eyes stinging, incredulous at how potent the alcohol must be in its pure form, because even she, accustomed to the watered wine at Mass, could taste that the mescal was indeed watered down. She did not know what to think.

Was it really possible that what Cisco had said was, in fact, true, that Durango was indeed blameless of what she suspected, that he only pretended to be a drunkard so he could learn who had sabotaged the Rainbow's End and killed Forbes? But why only Forbes—and not her father?

''Because, my sweet, despite the way it looks on the surface, there is no real proof that Red is actually dead,'' Durango elucidated that night, when she confronted him with Cisco's words and the mescal bottle, and demanded answers to her questions, ''and because of that, I would be a fool not to at least consider the possibility that he is still alive, himself the culprit responsible for all that has happened at the Rainbow's End—and, further, that you, *querida*, are hand in glove with him, using Nell as your go-between and plotting even now how to kill me, your loving husband, so you can get your hands on my shares!''

Josselyn was so stunned by these allegations that she could only gape at him, stricken.

''How—how could you even think such things about my father? About Nell? About *me*?'' she asked quietly, her eyes so huge and filled with hurt that Durango knew without a doubt that her shock and pain were not feigned; and at long last, he was certain in his heart that she had never been anything other than what she was: convent-reared, a guileless virgin, grieving and bereft at her father's death, a helpless victim of her father's unorthodox will and her husband's own ruthless taking of her. For had Durango not, over the passing weeks, given her—and Red—every opportunity to come at him down in the gold mine, even to the point of permitting Josselyn to handle the sticks of dynamite? And nothing had happened, not even a hint of a so-called accident. What else could it mean but that even if Red were still alive and guilty as sin of the crimes at the Rainbow's End, he knew nothing of his daughter's having wed and thus now being in a position, if Durango were to die, to acquire her husband's shares in the Rainbow's End, that she was not in touch with her father, that she was not, and never had been, a part of his dire scheme, but was innocent of any involvement?

Was it any wonder, then, that she feared him, Durango, her husband? That she fought him, even though, in the end, he forced her time and again, when he lay with her in the old iron bed, to admit that she loved him? That there was still a part of her that she withheld from him, that he could not reach, because it was not his for the taking, only hers for the giving?

I am ashamed of wanting you, of loving you, she had cried out once, afterward, wounding him to the core, causing him to think that he would never truly have her heart, only her hatred because no matter what, he was capable of making her desire him, yield to him, respond to him with a passion as fierce and all-consuming as his own. After a long moment, he spoke.

"How are my suspicions of you any different from yours of me, Jossie?" His voice held a curious note; his eyes, before he hooded them against her, were filled with that strange, ardent, searching light that somehow haunted her whenever she saw it. "Hmmmh? Tell me that, then, if you can." But she could not. She understood then that, however unlikely it seemed to her, she had hurt him with her doubts and that, because of that, he must care for her in some small fashion, or she would not have had the power to injure him. She felt suddenly ashamed, for had she ever, even once, thought to consider his feelings? "You see, *querida*, it is a sword that cuts both ways," he pointed out softly, "and always has."

"But—but if you thought such terrible things about me, why—why did you marry me?"

"You know why." His voice was now low, husky, as, without warning, his eyes darkened, smoldering like embers in the lamplight, and he reached out to draw her inexorably to him. "Because no matter what, you're in my blood and my bones, Jossie, just as I'm in yours, and I can no more fight it than you can!"

Then, crushing his mouth down on hers fiercely, Durango swept her up in his strong arms and carried her to the waiting bed, where he laid her down and made her forget everything but him.

Chapter Twenty-four

They were lovers. As she stared at Josselyn and Durango in the sudden silence that had fallen, Nell knew in her bones that it was so. She had wondered, ever since she had arrived at the Rainbow's End just a short while ago, why Josselyn had seemed so hesitant to let her in, so flustered and on edge and different, somehow—though, initially, the actress had put this last down to the younger woman's being garbed, surprisingly, in a blouse and skirt rather than her habit. That alone had been enough to worry Nell. But from beneath her lashes, Josselyn had kept glancing nervously at the door of the cookhouse, too, had had little to say, and had tried politely, though desperately, the actress had thought, to get rid of her. Perplexed and concerned, receiving no real answers to her questions, however, and finally deciding that this was plainly not a good time to intrude, Nell had just risen to take her leave when there had reached her ears the sound of hoof-beats outside, followed by the jingle of spurs and Josselyn's sharply indrawn breath. For a moment, the younger woman's hands had fluttered like a bird's wings in her laps. Then the door had opened, and she had abruptly grown still.

Now, as Durango sauntered slowly into the cookhouse, the actress understood. She had seen, in that first instant, the way the two of them had looked at each other, Durango with such knowing desire and sexual possessiveness in his eyes, and Josselyn with such helpless passion and tremulous consent in hers that, stricken, Nell had known they were lovers. A man and a woman did not look at each other like that otherwise.

Her heart grieved for Red, for the discovery that the wild seeds that he had planted had borne such bitter fruit would be agonizing to him. He had been right, she thought now, with terrible despair, and she had been wrong. Although, even now, she did not want to believe it, she feared that Durango must, in truth, have taken base advantage of Josselyn that day in the gold mine and had continued afterward somehow to compel her acquiescence. But . . . how? And then, as she observed for the first time the unusual, antique gold band Josselyn wore upon her left hand, the actress knew the answer, and her heart began to beat so hard and fast that she was afraid it would burst in her breast. Somehow, some way, Durango had succeeded in forcing Josselyn to marry him—and how else but at gunpoint? What else could account for the fact that there had been no publishing of the banns? Frightened for the young woman's life, and possibly even his own, Father Flanagan would have had no choice but to perform the wedding ceremony right then and there, as Durango must have demanded, dispensing with the posting of the banns that Red had counted on—so foolishly, as was now evident—to warn him if either Durango or Wylie had succeeded in winning Josselyn's hand in marriage.

The actress always had feared that Red had not thought this scheme through properly, had not carefully considered every angle, had not made allowances for the unexpected; and now, all had gone awry in the worst possible way—with poor, innocent Josselyn the victim of her father's rash, however well intended, plan. It would kill him, Nell thought, anguished, to learn what his daughter had suffered at Durango's brutal hands, what she even now must endure as his wife.

The actress's heart ached for Red's daughter—wed to a man who would clearly stop at nothing to possess the Rainbow's End, who had committed sabotage, murder, and rape for it, and who now held her at his utter mercy! No wonder she had kept silent, had not dared to speak out against him. There was no telling what threats he had made against her, what he had done to her, what he continued to do. Plainly, he constrained her to share his bed; perhaps he even beat her and otherwise abused her. The fiend! And Red's shares! Yes, Durango would surely have those now, too—for there was no way Killian could legally have kept them from him. He had no doubt locked them up securely in his safe at the Mother Lode, while he bided his time and wickedly plotted how to acquire Wylie's and Victoria's shares, as well.

Nell felt sick, horrified. She remembered now how, after the supposed accident with the incline car, Josselyn had started to warm toward her. Clearly, the young woman had been in dire need of a friend, so had turned to her. But still, Red's daughter had not been able to confide in her, had been too scared to do so, the actress surmised. Instead, shortly afterward, undoubtedly feeling trapped and terrified, Josselyn must have tried to escape from Durango by coming up to the Rainbow's End, which had surely, with the limited funds at her disposal, been as far as she could afford to run. That was why she had wished to keep her whereabouts a secret. Durango had obviously located her in the end and must have ruthlessly insisted on pressing his husbandly claim to her.

Oh, why hadn't Josselyn told her what had happened, asked her for help? Probably because Josselyn had not only feared the consequences to herself, but to her, Nell concluded. She shivered at the notion, now, more than ever, aware of Durango's animal menace and magnetism. Not for the first time did the actress think of his remorselessly removing Red—and anybody else who dared to stand in his way, including her. Why, now that she thought about it, it was Durango who had pulled the strings that had got her a part in a new play in town! She had been glad of the work—after all, she was not an ingenue anymore—and grateful to him, as well, for his surprising kindness; but now, she grasped that his assistance had been born not out of any consideration for her, but only to ensure that she would be so busy with rehearsals every day that she would have little time to visit the Rainbow's End, to come to Josselyn's aid.

Not that there was much that Nell could have done. Even if she could somehow have managed to help Josselyn get away, Durango would only have pursued her and found her again; and because he was her husband, there was nothing anyone could do legally to keep him from her. So, much as the actress fervently wished otherwise, she knew she was powerless to assist the young woman. Further, appalling her, was the knowledge that Red, who would feel honor bound to call Durango out, would only be shot and killed for his pains, and his daughter would be no better off than before. The situation was hopeless, Nell thought, and dangerous, like a ton of dynamite, fuses ignited, blasting caps ready to explode.

Somehow, she managed to say her good-byes and make her exit, deeply relieved that Durango made no move to halt her, incognizant of the fact that he had read her like a book and wanted nothing more than for her to return home and roust Red, if he were indeed still alive, out of the woodwork, so they could get affairs at the Rainbow's End settled once and for all.

Observing the actress worriedly peering in at them through the open window as she mounted her horse, Durango deliberately cast aside his sombrero and unbuckled his gun belt, which he tossed down on the table before he hauled Josselyn into his arms, turning her back to the window, so Nell could not see his wife's face lifted eagerly for his kiss; for ever since the night when she had confronted him with the mescal bottle, she had ceased to fight him, giving him hope that she finally believed in his innocence, perhaps even truly loved him. Her hands, pressed against his chest, began slowly to creep up to twine about his neck. Quickly jerking the pins from her hair and spreading the mass to conceal how she embraced him, Durango tangled his fingers in her tumbled tresses, clutching her to him, his mouth ravishing hers— although Josselyn, had she looked, would have been quite startled to see that his eyes were wide open, surreptitiously studying the window and Nell's stricken face. What if, fearing for Red's life, she did not tell him about what she perceived as his daughter's fate? At the provoking thought, Durango let his hands slide down to either side of Josselyn's collar, which he caught hold of firmly. Then, with a single, intentional, savage yank, he ripped her blouse in half, causing her to gasp and cry out sharply at his unanticipated action. To his deep satisfaction, Nell, blanching, did not wait to see any more, but galloped away as though the hounds of hell pursued her.

Uncharitably, Durango hoped that Red got the scare of his life. It would serve him right for making that damnable will, which had placed Josselyn in such an untenable position, and which might, if circumstances had proved different, have caused her untold harm. Durango shook with fury every time he even thought about it, how she might have been misused, perhaps even killed. The notion of her lying in Wylie's bed or, worse, cold in her grave chilled him to the bone.

Initially, he had not bothered particularly to bestir himself where the Rainbow's End was concerned, figuring that sooner or later, given enough rope, the culprit responsible for the crimes at the gold mine would wind up hanging himself. But Durango had realized that his marriage to Josselyn had perhaps placed them both in peril, and although confident that he could best any opponent, he had worried for his wife's safety. As a result, that summer, he had begun his own covert but extremely thorough investigation into all that had happened at the Rainbow's End. He now had, he thought, a fairly accurate picture of what must have occurred. All that remained unanswered was the question of Red's motive in adding fuel to the flames. Whether he had acted out of guilt or innocence, he must answer for his having used his unwitting daughter as a further catalyst to heat up the fire. About that, Durango was determined—although, despite his cursing Red, Durango could not help blessing him, for had it not been for her father's foolishness, Durango would not now hold in his arms the woman who had somehow become more precious to him than gold.

Red was horrified by Nell's tale. His ankle having at last healed, he was all for rushing up to the Rainbow's End at once to murder Durango and free Josselyn from the dastard's vile clutches; but Nell fearfully pointed out what might happen if Red failed in the attempt and he, rather than Durango, wound up pushing up daisies. Josselyn would probably never escape from her husband, and worse, was likely to be punished severely in her father's stead.

" 'Twas your own harebrained scheme in the first place that brought this terrible thing to pass!'' Nell railed accusingly, as upset as Red, terrified for both him and his daughter. "Don't jump from the frying pan into the fire by going off half cocked again! Think, Red! Think! Try to be sensible for once. You're no match for Durango with a gun, and you know it. How will you be helping your poor daughter by getting yourself shot and killed? You won't, I tell you; you'll only be adding to her misery. Trying to sneak up to the Rainbow's End and steal Josselyn away from him isn't the answer, either. Regardless of whether you succeed, he will still be her husband, with the law on his side to force her to return to him; for even though we're now certain of his guilt, we don't have one single shred of evidence that we can turn over to the sheriff to get Durango arrested and compelled to stand trial for his crimes. Why, we don't even have anything to offer him in exchange for his letting Josselyn go and giving her a divorce so she'll be rid of him forever—for you cannot tell me that he does not have your shares in the gold mine securely locked up in his safe!"

"God's blood, Nellie! Do ye think I give a good goddamn about me frigging shares?" Red cried, heartsick. " 'Tis me daughter I care about—and to hell with me blasted shares! They're to blame for everything that's happened. By God, I got Jossie into this sorry mess, and come hell or high water, I mean to get her out—and to make that perfidious son of a bitch Durango pay for what he's done, if 'tis the last thing I ever do, I swear!"

"I'm with you every step of the way, Red; you know I am," Nell insisted staunchly. "But let us bide a while yet, I say, and think things through very carefully. Then, when our chance comes, we'll be swift and ready to seize it!"

But this, Red would not do, for despite all Nell's stern admonitions and the fact that his first plan had gone so hideously askew, he had suddenly thought of another inspired scheme—and this time, he felt positive that it was absolutely foolproof, that nothing whatsoever could go wrong.

The debris from the final remaining stope, which lay at the heart of the gold mine, had at long last been cleared away; and now, Durango and Josselyn were examining the stope as carefully as they had all the rest, searching for some sign of Red's body—Durango certain, however, that they would discover nothing and Josselyn hoping irrepressibly that they would not. They had almost completed their inspection when a pair of black-sleeved arms stretched without warning from the shadows and caught hold of Josselyn tightly, dragging her with difficulty from Durango's side, as, instinctively, she began to struggle wildly against her captor. At his wife's sudden, terrified scream, her husband pivoted with a rapidity that was astonishing, his hand like greased lightning as he reached for his pistol, only to be stayed from drawing it by the cold steel muzzle of a gun abruptly jamming hard into his back.

"I wouldn't, if I were you." Wylie's voice sounded low and deadly in Durango's ear, making his whole body tense and stiffen warily. "Hands up! Up, goddamn it! That's right. Now, slowly, very slowly, lower the left one. Careful! You don't want me to have to shoot you, do you? No, somehow, I didn't think so. Unbuckle your gun belt and toss it away. Do it, you bastard!"

The barrel of Wylie's derringer unpleasantly prodded Durango into reluctant action as, in the flickering lantern light, he stared at his ashen-faced wife, held prisoner by Victoria and plainly shocked and frightened by what was occurring. Victoria had Forbes's revolver in her hand; and at the sight of Wylie with his own gun trained at her husband's back, Josselyn had ceased her attempts to escape and now, clearly uncertain what to do, stood still, her labored breathing ringing harshly in the stope. Durango's mouth tightened grimly as he took in their unexpected and threatening predicament. He had thought he had everything figured out. Was it possible he had somehow miscalculated—and fatally? His pulse raced with alarm at the idea. But still, trying with his eyes to reassure Josselyn, he forced himself to remain calm, to make no sudden moves, to do as Wylie had demanded.

"Now, move over there, Durango," Wylie ordered, motioning with his derringer to a place where Durango's back would be against the wall of the stope, all his avenues of escape cut off. Not knowing what Wylie and Victoria intended and fearing for Josselyn, Durango silently did as instructed, while Wylie, after kicking away the discarded gun belt, edged around to join the two women.

"What is the meaning of this, Wylie?" Josselyn asked sharply, although she was afraid that she already knew the answer, that he and Victoria had been in cahoots all along, guilty of the crimes at the Rainbow's End and now in the grisly process of ridding themselves of their last two unwanted partners. "What do you think you are doing?"

"Exposing Durango for the saboteur and murderer he is"—Wylie's tone was gloating; on his face was a supercilious smirk of satisfaction—"which ought to please you no end, Josselyn, since raping you and compelling you to the altar also number among his offenses—and for which he shall be made to pay, as well, I promise you!"

But the sudden, uneasy tightening of Victoria's constraining arms around her told Josselyn that the true story might be different from Wylie's accusations. And it was. Although, silently, the widow stoutly assured herself that there was no need for her to feel the slightest bit culpable or unsettled, her body language revealed her need to rationalize her own actions. After all, although she had not known it at the time, Durango must have already forced himself on Josselyn days before the drugging at the Teller House. Red and Nell had evolved that scenario and reported it last night when the four of them—Red, Nell, Wylie, and Victoria—had laid their plans to unmask Durango for the villain he was and gain Josselyn's freedom—although, of course, Victoria had not mentioned her own contribution to the affair.

Wylie and Victoria had been totally flabbergasted when Red, accompanied by Nell, had appeared at the widow's mansion on The Casey. That Red was still alive had never once occurred to either of them; they had genuinely believed him dead and buried under a mountain of rubble for months. At first, both, for their own reasons, had been extremely unnerved by his "rising from the grave," but each had gradually grown more composed as, like an enraged bull, he had paced Victoria's parlor floor, ranting and raving about Durango's treachery and how they must lay a trap to catch him once and for all. Eagerly then, they had fallen in with Red's plot, all four of them, the following day, riding up to the Rainbow's End to spy upon Durango and Josselyn.

After it had been seen that the couple was venturing down into the gold mine, the four had immediately put Red's scheme into motion, hurrying down to the entrance of the tunnel through which he had gained admittance the night he had set the explosions that had sealed off the stopes, and, taking care not to be spotted by the laboring miners, furtively combing the drifts until locating Durango and Josselyn. It had previously been decided that being physically a match for the sought-after couple, Wylie and Victoria would take the initiative. All had surmised that the shock of seeing Red alive might prove so overwhelming to Josselyn that she would complicate matters by fainting, so Red and Nell must remain hidden, acting as backup—a formidable surprise for Durango should he attempt to weasel out of the snare.

Now, as the four had arranged, Wylie withdrew from the pocket of his jacket the two pieces of paper prepared last evening, and pen and ink, and flung the whole at Durango's feet.

"Pick it all up," Wylie directed coldly, his pistol leveled at Durango's chest, "and sign your name to the documents. You needn't bother wasting time reading 'em: One is your confession to the sabotage of the Rainbow's End and the murder of Forbes, and the other is a statement whereby you relinquish your shares and any and all other claims you might have in the gold mine."

Josselyn's heart leaped with terror at this; she had no doubt, now, that once Durango had done as Wylie had instructed, Wylie meant to kill him and her both. She could not let that happen! Once before, her life had been blighted by pieces of paper. She would not permit herself to become a helpless victim again. Resolutely summoning her courage, Josselyn abruptly and viciously stamped her foot down hard as she could on Victoria's own, while, at the same time, reaching out to knock the derringer from Wylie's grasp. In moments, to Red's, Nell's, and Wylie's horror, though Wylie had recovered his gun, Durango, springing quick and lithe as a mountain cat across the stope, had retrieved his own revolver from its holster; and as the two men rose to face each other murderously, it was to see Josselyn and Victoria, like two vulgar barroom drabs, grappling upon the floor, locked in mortal combat for control of Forbes's pistol.

Josselyn now realized what demon had possessed her husband and Wylie that day they had come to such unbridled conflict in the cookhouse; for she had never in her life felt such savage, uncontrollable fury as she did now, as she went tooth and nail at Victoria, with such a terrible, gleeful ferocity that even Durango was startled. It was as though every rancorous, spiteful emotion she had ever felt toward the widow had suddenly come pouring out in a torrent. She was like a madwoman, frenziedly snatching at Victoria's hair, yanking loose a fistful of brunet strands, and clawing at her face, scarcely slowed by, or even feeling, the widow's similar retaliation. Every curse word Josselyn had ever heard Durango utter hissed and spat from her lips as she vigorously boxed Victoria's ears and socked her in the eye, making the stunned widow shriek like an enraged feline having its tail pulled.

No one, not even Durango, dared to intervene as the two women scratched and bit and kicked their way across the floor, thrashing each other unmercifully. All were too afraid that they or one or both of the two women would accidentally be shot in the process, for every so often during the struggle, Forbes's revolver discharged with a roar, the bullet zinging wildly through the air to slam into a wall of the stope.

"That's three," Wylie noted almost conversationally as yet a third blast resounded from the weapon in dispute, although he did not lower the derringer he aimed at his partner.

"Three more, and then the chambers will be spent," Durango observed just as casually, keeping the barrel of his Smith & Wesson American coolly pointed at Wylie in return. "I've got a ten-dollar gold piece that says Jossie wins," he taunted provokingly.

Wylie's nostrils flared whitely at that.

"Damn you, Durango!" he snapped grimly. "I don't know

how you've managed to survive as long as you have! Somebody should have put a bullet through you a long time ago and done the whole world a favor!''

''Maybe so—but you ain't the one to do it, Wylie! That's four.''

The two women fought on with a vengeance, neither giving any quarter, although they were both fading fast, their arms flailing more slowly, less accurately, their breasts heaving from their gasps for air, their skirts flying less wildly than before. Victoria had lost her rakishly plumed hat; her hair was a rat's nest, and one sleeve of her riding habit was torn from the shoulder. Her eye had started to swell and turn black; her cheek was gouged, and she was sporting a split lip, besides. Josselyn was in better shape—just barely. Now, having finally gained the upper hand, she reared up, straddling Victoria's prone figure; the widow, hampered by a narrow-cut skirt, was unable to buck her off. Panting hard, Josselyn pounded Victoria's wrist against the solid floor until at last, after the firing of two more shots, her eyes filled with impotent ire and hate, the widow weakly dropped Forbes's gun. Grabbing the weapon, Josselyn staggered to her feet, determinedly hauling Victoria up with her, having sense enough to keep the widow positioned between her and Wylie.

''Damn it, Victoria! Don't quit now! Break loose!'' Wylie exhorted grimly. ''She doesn't have any bullets left!''

''Is . . . that . . . true?'' Josselyn asked Durango tiredly. Then, at his affirmative response and as the widow began then, with what little strength she had left, to struggle to escape, Josselyn said, ''Well, in that case, I suppose I'll . . . just have to . . . pistol-whip her.'' Remorselessly, she struck Victoria over the head with Forbes's revolver, and then dragged her dazed, unprotesting figure over to where Durango stood, his eyes gleaming with pride and admiration at his wife's victory, although he never took his gaze off Wylie. Her own strength finally ebbing, Josselyn let Victoria's body slowly slump to the ground at Durango's feet.

''Drop the derringer, Wylie,'' he commanded softly, even

as he swiftly maneuvered his wife so his body now shielded hers, "lessen you want Jossie to finish what she started."

"By God, ye bloody whoreson!" Red roared at that, loaded for bear as he leaped up from his hiding place behind a large rock, unable to restrain himself any longer, his shotgun held at the ready. "Ye'll not succeed in making me believe that ye've scrambled me poor daughter's brain so badly that she'd commit murder for ye, ye filthy blackguard!"

"D-D-Da?" Josselyn cried, stricken, so shocked that she could only stare at her father disbelievingly. "Da!"

"Well, well, well. I did wonder when you were going to show up, Red," Durango drawled dryly. "No, Jossie, my sweet, stay where you are for the time being—and try not to swoon. I've got my hands full at the moment."

"Don't listen to him, Jossie!" Red bellowed urgently, terrified by the sight of his daughter's pale face, her eyes wide and slowly filling with hurt. "Come to me, lass; he daren't take his eyes off me and Wylie."

"He's right, querida. Don't listen to me; listen to him," Durango hissed, his voice low and throbbing with anger and pain for her, "the man who put you up as the stakes in this underhanded game!"

She was glad to see her father alive, of course; but still, her joy was marred, tempered by her husband's agonizing reminder. As she thought of Da's awful will, realized that he had, in truth, used her, allowed her to believe he was dead, while, all the time, he had plotted against Durango, she numbly remained where she was, anguished and bewildered. If her father thought her husband guilty of sabotage and murder, why had he permitted her to marry Durango?

"Jossie . . ." Red whispered brokenly when she did not move or respond. "Jossie, lass . . ." His voice trailed away; his eyes grew moist as he recognized that this plan, too, had gone miserably awry. At the understanding, his wrath at Durango increased tenfold.

"Nell," Durango called sharply in the sudden silence, "I know you're here, so you may as well come out and join the reunion, such as it is. No sense in your crouching in a crevice somewhere, when you can be comfortable. Ah, there you are," he declared as she came into view, moving to stand at Red's side. "I make you my compliments. You played your part to perfection, the performance of a lifetime, because you know what? I think Jossie actually looked upon you as her friend." His eyes were hard at the thought of how Red and Nell between them had dealt Josselyn a doubly bitter blow.

The actress was both afflicted and shamed by Durango's words. Trembling with torment, she bit her lip, laying one hand upon Red's arm to steady herself.

"The devil take ye, Durango! Who are ye to stand there so righteously, hurling abuse at us?" Red growled. "Ye, who sabotaged the gold mine, murdered Forbes, and wronged Jossie far worse than any of us ever did!"

"*I* wronged her? *Sangre de Cristo*, you fool! *I* was the only one who did right by her!—and what's more, she knows it, too!"

"Ye lying bastard!" Red retorted hotly, enraged. "Ye *raped* her! Ye raped her and forced her to marry ye so ye could get yer greedy hands on me shares in the Rainbow's End!"

"Which, I might mention, are even now locked up in my safe at the Mother Lode." Durango's voice was jeering; his face was dark with fury. "Did you really think to have it all, Red? *Your* shares, *my* shares, your daughter . . . ? What was the plan? To hold a signed confession over my head so I'd agree to give Jossie a divorce in exchange for my escaping prosecution? Well, you won't get my damned signature on that ridiculous document now, so what now, Red? Huh? What now?"

"Me daughter's all that's important," Red insisted, gazing beseechingly at Josselyn, who still mutinously refused to look at him. "The Rainbow's End is nothing compared to her happiness and well-being. So, if ye'll let her go, ye can keep me shares. Hell! Ye can have it all, Wylie's and Victoria's shares, too, if ye'll not harm Victoria, either. Sure and we'll all of us give ye our interest in the gold mine, free and clear. Isn't that right, Wylie?''

Victoria, groggily regaining awareness, saw Wylie nod curtly.

"Oh, Wylie!" The widow, astonished at what his acquiescence must mean, shook her spinning head to try to clear it and endeavored vainly to rise.

"No, you're not going anywhere yet, you conniving hussy! So just lie still until this has all been sorted out to my satisfaction," Durango grated, planting his boot squarely on Victoria's recumbent form. Then he addressed Red again. "Now, let me be sure I understand this properly. If I agree to give Josselyn a divorce and turn Victoria over to you unharmed, you'll all sign your shares in the Rainbow's End over to me, making me sole owner of the gold mine. Is that it?"

"That's it." Red began to breathe a little easier, thinking that his proposition would be accepted, that, shortly, his daughter would be shed of her rapscallious husband.

"Well, now, that's a mighty damned generous offer, Red!" Durango grinned sardonically for a moment. Then his smile slowly faded, leaving his face hard. "But I don't want your frigging shares! I don't want Wylie's shares! Hell! I don't even want Victoria's shares! I never did. All I've ever wanted is what's mine—and with or without your blessing, Red, that includes Josselyn! She's my wife, and if you don't like it, that's just too damned bad—because she's going to stay that way 'until death us do part,' just as she promised!"

Behind her husband, Josselyn gasped softly, stunned, hardly daring to believe she had heard aright, her heart beginning to hammer hard and fast in her breast. Durango loved her! she thought dazedly. Oh, he must! Why else would he have turned down the whole of the Rainbow's End for her? Suddenly, she realized how taut and still he was, unable to see her face, not knowing if she understood, if she cared. He was so proud, so arrogant, and yet he had surely laid his heart bare—and before four other people who plainly believed the worst of him and who would like nothing more than to see him spurned and brought low! Her eyes flashing defiantly, Josselyn slid her arms around his waist and pressed her head against his back, her heart filled to overflowing with her love for him. At her touch, she could feel the tension drain from his body; tentatively, at first, and then as though he would never let her go, his left hand closed tightly over hers.

"Oh." Red was stupefied, starting, with a sinking feeling, to consider himself the world's biggest fool. Gruffly, awkwardly, he cleared his throat. "Like—like that, is it?"

"Yeah, like that," Durango replied quietly, fiercely. "*I'm* the Catholic, remember? If you didn't mean her for me, Red, then you ought not to have made that accursed will!"

"Yes. Ahem. Well . . . er . . . it appears as though maybe we all . . . er . . . might have misjudged ye, made . . . er . . . some kind of a . . . er . . . mistake in thinking ye the culprit—"

"Give the man a prize! You got that right, you crackbrained jackanapes! But that's *all* you got right, damn it!" Durango growled.

"Well, bloody hell, Durango! If ye didn't sabotage the gold mine and shove Forbes down the main shaft into the sump, who in the blasted blazes did?"

"What, Victoria? Leaving so soon? But the party's not over yet." Durango pushed the widow back down again with his boot. "Don't crawl away. We're just now getting to the good part. Don't you want to hear it? It's all about a mule-headed old man by the name of Forbes, who never would listen to anyone and so made a lot of bad investments and lost all his fortune—"

"What?" Red and Wylie exclaimed as one.

"Yeah, Forbes was broke, flat busted. I checked. In fact, I've been doing quite a bit of checking—into all kinds of things." A mocking smile twisted Durango's mouth. "You know, it's simply amazing what you can learn about people if you just bother to do a little digging. Forbes, now, he liked power and money, liked to impress folks; so being on the verge of bankruptcy didn't sit too well with him at all. When he learned that, finally, we might be within striking distance of a mother lode, he decided to recoup his riches by sabotaging the Rainbow's End, in an effort to create so many costly and time-consuming delays that the rest of us three, fed up and lacking the means or the inclination to keep footing the bills, would sell him our shares. Meanwhile, he discovered that Victoria here had climbed out of his bed and into Wylie's; and not liking to be made a fool of, Forbes also plotted how to get even with 'em both by murdering Wylie and making it appear as though Victoria had done the vile deed during a lovers' quarrel.''

"Forbes . . . intended to kill me?" Wylie asked, startled. "But I thought . . . that is—''

"You thought that he trusted you, that Red or I had murdered him, because when you came up to the Rainbow's End that night, in response to Forbes's note to you—you really ought to have burned that, Wylie, and not left it lying around in your desk, which can be opened with a small knife, by the way—informing you that he had learned the identity of the saboteur, you found him dead in the sump. Knowing that both Red and I were aware of your affair with Victoria, you feared to be blamed for Forbes's killing, and so you hied it back to town, where you paid one of the dance-hall girls at the Shoo Fly to give you an alibi for that night—a mistake, that. Don't ever trust those sottish Shoo Fly girls . . . man buys 'em enough drinks, they'll spill the beans about anything.

"What you didn't know, Wylie, was that Forbes, drunk, as usual, was in the process of damaging the cable on the ore bucket, undoubtedly planning to send you to hell in it, when he lost his balance and toppled down the main shaft into the sump. Novak repaired the cable the following morning; the miners needed the ore bucket to retrieve Forbes's body, and since Forbes's so-called accident hadn't involved the ore bucket, Novak didn't make the connection with the cable. But after I discovered Forbes's note in your desk, I did. Further, I dragged the sump again and turned up a pair of Victoria's earrings. Since, to my knowledge, she hasn't ever been down in the gold mine's interior, it seemed evident that Forbes had planted them to point an accusing finger at her for your murder. It was a diabolically clever scheme, you have to admit, because if it had worked, you would have been dead and Victoria would have wound up being hanged for your killing.

"But Forbes died instead, and that's when Victoria learned that far from being a wealthy widow, she would be lucky not to have her mansion on The Casey sold out from under her to pay all those debts Forbes had accumulated. To stave off her creditors, she discreetly sold off, among other things, her late—but not lamented—husband's art collection to various private buyers. And, Wylie, when your occasional generosity added to her income a bit, she managed. What agonies you must have suffered, being reduced to practicing such economies as refurbishing your own old gowns, hmmmh, Victoria? And of course, you knew all about Forbes's sabotaging the Rainbow's End. Doubtless, he let it slip when he was drunk; perhaps he even boasted about it and the mother lode he intended to acquire . . . ? Well, no matter. After his demise, you desperately decided to carry on with his bold scheme—except that, unlike Forbes, you didn't know a damned thing about hard-rock mining, and neither did those two idiots you hired to do your dirty work. No, don't bother to deny it, Victoria, my dear. I've got them tied up in my storeroom at the saloon. They were real mad about your not paying 'em for their last job, and after overhearing their stupidly loud, careless complaints, I confronted them point-blank about what type of business they conducted for you. It was their hard luck that they mistakenly believed me a lot drunker than I really was.

"At any rate, that's why the pattern of the sabotage changed so drastically after Forbes's death, why we were all so damned confused. We kept thinking there was only one culprit. And then, Red, *you* had to toss *your* frigging chips into the pot. Not knowing what was what, who to trust, but believing that we were about to unearth the mother lode, you decided to set those explosions, sealing off the stopes so no one could benefit from the gold mine until you learned the identity of the saboteur. Further, you discovered that your daughter was fixing to become a nun, and you didn't want that, so you thought you'd kill two birds with one stone by cajoling Patrick into drawing up that crazy will, forcing Jossie to live in the real world awhile before giving it up forever.

"Oh, I'm sure you figured she'd be safe enough; after all, to the scheming partner, she wasn't worth anything dead. She had to stay alive at least long enough to be wedded and bedded, and no doubt, you thought you could prevent that easily enough, because you knew that the banns would have to be posted beforehand. You further supposed that neither Wylie nor I would prove so foolish and base as to compromise her, in order to compel her into marriage. She was, after all, almost a nun; that had to weigh with me, and perhaps even with Wylie, too. In addition, we didn't know Jossie from Adam, what she was likely to do if forcibly taken advantage of. She might have been so devastated afterward that she would have relinquished any and all claims to her inheritance and returned to the convent. She might, at the altar, have blabbed about the entire sordid affair, informed the priest that her vows were being coerced; and of course, then he would have refused to perform the wedding ceremony. Hell! She might even have been so outraged that she would have set the law on us! You figured that none of those things was a risk either Wylie or I could afford to take. Besides, Red, spying in those outlandish disguises of yours, you thought you were watching over her well enough to keep her unscathed. So, what I want to know is: Where in the hell were you that night at the Teller House, when Victoria—jealous of Jossie and afraid of losing Wylie to her—drugged the brandy with laudanum and, after Jossie and I had passed out, had those two dumb thugs haul us upstairs to one of the hotel rooms and dump us in bed together for the night?"

"What?" Red and Wylie cried as one again.

"Yeah, that's right—ain't it, Victoria? Naturally, I made Jossie my wife the following morning, and of course, under the circumstances, Father Flanagan agreed to dispense with the publishing of the banns. You never allowed for something like that to happen, did you, Red? In fact, you didn't make allowance for a hell of a lot of things, like the convent's closing, so Jossie couldn't go back there, and like my guessing that you were still alive and my thinking, until lately, that *you* were the culprit. . . . And you, Victoria, my dear . . . you thought you were doing me such a bad turn, because I wasn't a marrying man; but what you really did for me was the sweetest favor of my life, and I reckon I ought to thank you for that—however despicably it came about. So . . . where were you, Red? I'll admit I fully expected to see you that morning at the Teller House; imagine my surprise when you didn't show up."

"Well, 'twas like this, Durango, me bucko: That day at the Rainbow's End, when ye and Jossie had that accident in the giraffe . . . well, I spied ye carrying her from the shaft house, and she was in such a sad state that, naturally, I . . . er . . . thought the worst. I started to run down the hill to make ye pay for what I believed ye'd done, and I stumbled into a hole and broke me bloody ankle," Red confessed ruefully, shaking his head at his folly, "something else I hadn't counted on!"

"The last piece of the puzzle, and now, it's all fitted together to create a whole that, however senseless, is at least finally comprehensible!" Durango at last slowly removed his booted foot from Victoria's prone figure and holstered his revolver.

"Jossie"—Red laid aside his shotgun and stretched out his arms in loving appeal to his daughter—"can ye ever find it in yer heart to forgive yer foolish old da?"

"Oh, Da! Of course, I can!" Tears of joy streaming down her cheeks, she ran to him then and hugged him hard, scarcely daring, even now, to believe he was alive, was real.

"Jossie. Jossie, lass." Her father's voice was choked with emotion. "How I love ye! 'Tis so sorry I am for making that blasted will and such a mess of yer life! What can I do, lass, to make it up to ye? What ever can I do?"

As she gazed over Da's shoulder at Nell, who stood back, not wanting to intrude, but whose own eyes were blurred with tears and who, despite everything, had truly tried to be her friend, Josselyn knew what to say. She wanted everyone to be as happy as herself. Bluinse, her mother, no matter how beloved, was twelve years dead and gone. Except for Red, Nell had no one; and Josselyn could not help remembering how the actress had spoken so wistfully of never having had any children of her own.

"You can make an honest woman out of Nell, Da," Josselyn declared, smiling warmly at the actress and reaching out to draw her gently but firmly into the circle of their embrace, "for sure and 'tis plain you need a keeper—permanently!"

Across the stope, Wylie tucked his derringer into his breast pocket and strode over to where Durango was standing, watching his wife's touching reunion with her father.

"I understand now what I said to make you so mad that day at the cookhouse, Durango." Wylie spoke a trifle stiffly, but still, it was a step toward the rebirth of the two young men's former good friendship. "I apologize. I insulted Josselyn; I didn't know then that she was your wife." He paused. Then he said, "I never really wanted her, you know, any more than you ever wanted Victoria." After that, impatiently, he glanced down at the woman who still lay at Durango's feet. "Get up, Victoria!" Wylie demanded. "I'm going to beat your pretty backside black and blue, and then carry you straight to the office of a justice of the peace. You have proved yourself a filly entirely too spirited for your own good and sorely in need of a rider with a curb bit and check rein to restrain you!"

"You mean—you mean you want to *marry* me?" Victoria gaped at him, astounded, even fearful that he was playing a cruel jest upon her. "But—but, Wylie, you—you never mentioned wedding me before."

"My dear, I thought you understood that as a man, I had no desire whatsoever to be kept by you and Forbes's fortune. As a result, I'm afraid I simply cannot find it in my heart to feel sorry about your being flat broke!"

"Holy Mary, miither of Jesus!" Red suddenly swore. Having finally returned Josselyn to her husband's loving arms, he had wandered over to a wall of the stope, his eye caught by a faint, dull gleam where one of the bullets from Forbes's gun had gouged a groove. "Victoria's not busted anymore, lad. None of us are, for sure and unless I miss me guess, we're rich! We're all bloody well rich! 'Tis the mother lode, I'm telling ye. 'Tis the mother lode!"

"It is, indeed," Durango murmured in agreement—but unlike the rest, he was gazing, his heart in his eyes, at Josselyn. "And from where I'm standing, I'd say that it's unmistakably pure gold."

At the
Rainbow's End

Chapter Twenty-five

The Casey, Gregory Gulch, Colorado, 1881

"There are many ways of serving God, Josselyn," the Reverend Mother Maire had told her once, and then, some months afterward, had said, "You see, child, God did, after all, have work for you to do; He, who knows all, knew that He needed you here, in Central City, not as a nun, but as the woman who would bring light into the darkness of Durango de Navarre, and who would provide a home for the homeless. These things, you did, and God has repaid you with many blessings."

Truly, it was indeed so, Josselyn thought now, as she stood on the balcony off her second-story bedroom in her mansion on The Casey, lost in reverie and staring out over the gulches below, to the place where, at the heart of Gregory Gulch, the tall red brick building that was the Sisters of St. Ursula convent and shelter for widows and orphans rose, its soaring bell tower stretching toward the heavens. Sweet and strong and clear, the echo of the joyous ringing of the solid-gold angelus reached Josselyn's ears, mingling with the sounds, from below on the veranda, of Durango's conversation with the children—Cisco; the twins, three-year-old Blas and Bluinse; Raúl, who was one and a half; and the new baby, Seamus, whose principal contribution to the dialogue consisted of delighted coos and gurgles.

Earlier, it had rained; and now, as they caught sight of the beautiful rainbow arching over the mountains, Josselyn heard the youngsters beg their father for the tale with which their grandda frequently entertained them, an old Irish legend about leprechauns and the pot of gold at the end of the rainbow. Her shoulders shook with silent laughter as she listened to Durango's version, in which the leprechauns had somehow mysteriously turned into a motley band of miners and the pot of gold into the mother lode of a hard-rock mine. Curiously, one of the men, a gambling desperado, clearly moonstruck, rode off with a flame-haired angel, forgetting all about the fortune until she gently reminded him that it would pay for the raising of a lovely convent, with a solid-gold bell in its tower, and a shelter for all those in need, to which the rogue, his prayers having been answered, quite agreed. . . .

A short while later, the jingle of silver Mexican spurs told Josselyn that Durango had come inside and upstairs to join her on the balcony. From behind, his arms slid around her waist, and then his mouth found her neck, his kisses making her shiver with delight.

"I love you," he muttered huskily in her ear. "I love you, *mi vida, mi alma. ¡Dios!* How I love you, Jossie!"

"And I love you, Durango, with all my heart—even if you did get that story you told the children a trifle mixed up."

"What was wrong with the way I told it, *querida*? Hmmmh?"

"Nothing, you *told* it just fine." She smothered a laugh as he slowly but surely turned her around to face him, beginning to kiss her eyes, her nose, her lips. "You were just a little confused about some of the details, that's all."

"Oh, I was, was I?" His hands pulled a pin from her hair, and then another, and still another, loosing the long, heavy mass, while he went on kissing her, his mouth growing steadily more insistent, more urgent, his tongue now tracing the outline of her lips before parting them hungrily and insinuating itself inside. "Such as?" he murmured after a long while.

"Well, I don't . . . know about you, but it has . . . always been my own experience," Josselyn whispered between kisses as he lifted her up and carried her inside to their bed, "that it is not gold, but a patch of heaven that lies at every rainbow's end."

Gently laying her down, Durango considered this thoughtfully for a moment. Then, sighing deeply with love and pleasure, he took her in his arms and allowed as how she was right.

Author's Note

Dear Reader:

Central City is the nation's oldest mining town that still actively mines; and as much of the city has been preserved or restored without major, disruptive changes over the years, it is an excellent example of Victorian America. From the 1859 "Pikes Peak or Bust" gold rush until half a century later (with another upsurge in the 1930s), the "richest square mile on earth" yielded a staggering $105 million, most of it in gold. For this reason, Central City was not a typical western town or even a typical mining town; in fact, it was the seat of society and culture in Colorado until Denver rose to rival and then finally surpass it.

Unfortunately, although once inhabited by 100,000 people, the hillsides and gulches that are home to Central City and

Black Hawk now have a total population of only 650. The influx of summer tourists has waned; sales tax revenues are down, and many shops have been forced to close. Recently, in an effort to revitalize Central City and Black Hawk, approval was won on a statewide ballot to legalize low-stakes gambling in the two towns. This measure also applied to Cripple Creek, and, at the time of this author's note, was set to go into effect during October, 1991. How gambling will change these historic Colorado mining towns is not known. When the practice was adopted in the South Dakota mining town of Deadwood, within twelve months, although eighty betting parlors had opened and gamblers had dropped $281 million in bets, criminal and traffic arrests had nearly doubled and skyrocketing costs had driven many long-time residents and businesses out of town. Already, born of the knowledge that gambling is on its way to Central City and Black Hawk, property values in both towns are soaring.

During my lengthy research for *Rainbow's End*, I visited Colorado, including both Central City and Black Hawk, on more than one occasion. I found the two towns quaint and charming, like picture postcards. The townspeople were warm and friendly; someone was always willing to guide me to worthwhile research materials, to help me select those best suited to my needs. I returned home from each trip loaded down with books, maps, and other purchases, all of which strewed my desk as I labored on this novel, a constant reminder of all I had seen and learned. I especially want to thank the staff of the Golden Rose hotel—where my husband, Gary D. Brock, and I stayed during one of our visits to Central City—for their graciousness and assistance.

I would also like to acknowledge Fredda Isaacson at Warner Books, both my editor and my friend now for thirteen years. A great deal of the credit for *Rainbow's End* must go to Fredda for all her patience and understanding, her wisdom and advice, which was invaluable in shaping the structure of this novel. Sometimes, her willingness simply to listen and offer words of encouragement were all that kept me going during what has been a trying time and book for me; and for that, dear Fredda, I thank you from the bottom of my heart!

Last but never least, I would like to thank you, the reader, so very much for buying and reading *Rainbow's End*. I hope that Durango and Josselyn entertained you, that you enjoyed escaping with them to the beautiful Rocky Mountains for a little while. When I am working on a novel, my characters inevitably become not just real people to me, but friends; it is always my hope and my wish that they become so for you, as well, so that when you finally close my book, it is with the same warm emotion you feel upon closing your door after an evening spent with good friends. If you would like to write to me or to receive a copy of my free, semiannual newsletter, you may send your letter or request, along with a stamped, self-addressed envelope, to me in care of Warner Books, Inc., 666 Fifth Avenue, New York, New York 10103. Over the years, thousands of you have taken the time and the trouble to write to me; I read each and every one of your letters personally. You and they are, always, my constant source of inspiration.

Rebecca Brandewyne

FALL IN LOVE...
WITH REBECCA BRANDEWYNE!